When they reached the front door Elle turned to him. "I'm not expecting this to take too long. You'll be okay here with Bonnie?" she asked.

Anders nodded. "We'll be fine. Just be safe."

She smiled at him. "Always."

She started to walk out the door, but he stopped her by grabbing her by the arm. She turned around to face him and he leaned in and captured her startled lips with his.

He hadn't expected it; he certainly hadn't planned it. But, once his mouth took hers, he remembered just how much he'd wanted to kiss her and how often in the past two days he'd fantasized about it.

His fantasies had been woefully inadequate. The real thing was so much better. Her lips were soft and warm and welcoming. It shot instant desire through his entire body. He could kiss Elle Gage forever.

OPERATION: RESCUE

NEW YORK TIMES BESTSELLING AUTHOR

CARLA CASSIDY
& LISA CHILDS

Previously published as *The Colton Cowboy*
and *Colton's Cinderella Bride*

 HARLEQUIN

ISBN-13: 978-1-335-45485-0

Operation: Rescue

Copyright © 2020 by Harlequin Books S.A.

The Colton Cowboy
First published in 2018. This edition published in 2020.
Copyright © 2018 by Harlequin Books S.A.

Colton's Cinderella Bride
First published in 2018. This edition published in 2020.
Copyright © 2018 by Harlequin Books S.A.

Special thanks and acknowledgment are given to Carla Cassidy and Lisa Childs for their contributions to The Coltons of Red Ridge miniseries.

Harlequin Enterprises ULC
22 Adelaide St. West, 40th Floor
Toronto, Ontario M5H 4E3, Canada
www.Harlequin.com

Printed in U.S.A.

Recycling programs for this product may not exist in your area.

CONTENTS

Carla Cassidy is an award-winning, *New York Times* bestselling author who has written over 150 novels for Harlequin. In 1995, she won Best Silhouette Romance from *RT Book Reviews* for *Anything for Danny*. In 1998, she won a Career Achievement Award for Best Innovative Series from *RT Book Reviews*. Carla believes the only thing better than curling up with a good book to read is sitting down at the computer with a good story to write.

Books by Carla Cassidy

Harlequin Intrigue

48 Hour Lockdown

Desperate Strangers
Desperate Intentions
Desperate Measures

Scene of the Crime

Scene of the Crime: Mystic Lake
Scene of the Crime: Black Creek
Scene of the Crime: Deadman's Bluff
Scene of the Crime: Return to Bachelor Moon
Scene of the Crime: Return to Mystic Lake
Scene of the Crime: Baton Rouge
Scene of the Crime: Killer Cove
Scene of the Crime: Who Killed Shelly Sinclair?
Scene of the Crime: Means and Motive

Visit the Author Profile page
at Harlequin.com for more titles.

THE COLTON COWBOY

Carla Cassidy

This book is dedicated to all the editors
who showed a special kind of patience with me!

Chapter 1

Anders Colton jerked awake, his heart racing and every muscle in his body tensed with fight-or-flight adrenaline. From the nearby open window a cool night breeze drifted in, and crickets and other insects clicked and whirred with their usual night songs. They were familiar sounds and wouldn't have awakened him. So what had?

He remained perfectly still, and then he heard it…a faint shuffle of feet against wood. In one quick movement he slid out of bed and grabbed the nearby rifle that rested against the bedroom wall. He stalked out of his bedroom clad only in a pair of navy boxers.

Tonight he was going to catch the culprit who had been stealing from him for the past couple of weeks. He'd dubbed the person the "Needy Thief" because of the strange things that had come up missing.

Last night it had been fruit from the bowl on the

kitchen counter and a jar of peanut butter and a loaf of bread from the pantry. A week before that it was a mattress from the bunk barn and an old baby cradle from the barn.

Anders didn't mind the loss of the food, and he'd already replaced the mattress, but one of his grandmother's quilts had also been taken and he definitely wanted that back. His heart now beat with the sweet anticipation of finally catching the culprit.

Was the person a runaway in trouble? A criminal hiding out on the property? Was it possible it was his cousin Demi, who had been on the run from the law and had a newborn baby?

Tonight he hoped to nab the thief red-handed and find out exactly who he or she was and what in the hell was going on.

The kitchen was in complete darkness except for the shaft of moonlight that danced in through the window above the sink. It was just enough illumination to see that nobody was there.

The cabin was fairly small and it took him only seconds to check in the guest bedroom and bath and realize the thief wasn't anywhere inside. Then he heard it… retreating footsteps outside. The porch!

He threw open the front door, expecting to see a person running away. Instead he nearly stumbled over a pale yellow tote bag and the stolen wicker baby cradle. He stared at the cradle in stunned surprise. Had the thief suffered a twinge of guilt and returned it? A faint noise sounded, and he leaned over the basket and then straightened up with a new shock. Nestled in a pink blanket was a sleeping baby. What the hell?

The moonlight overhead was bright. He gazed around

the area and then looked a quarter of a mile in the distance toward the main house where his parents and his kid sister, Valeria, lived. He could barely see the huge place through a thick stand of trees. There didn't appear to be any lights shining from the mansion and there was nobody lurking around his cabin. It was just him and a baby.

Why on earth would anyone leave a baby with him? He picked up the tote bag and the cradle and carried them into the living room. He placed the cradle on his sofa and then turned on the lamp on the end table.

A tuft of strawberry blonde hair topped rosy, chubby cheeks. The baby was very small and he would guess she wasn't more than a couple weeks old. He couldn't tell the baby's eye color because she was sound asleep. Then he noticed a note pinned to the pink blanket. He carefully plucked it off and opened it.

She's a Colton.

His heart stutter-stepped. If she was a Colton, then who did she belong to? Was it possible she was his? He sank down on the sofa next to the sleeping baby.

Yes, he supposed it was possible she was his child. There had been a few women in his recent past, but nothing deep or meaningful. He didn't do deep and meaningful since he'd been betrayed two years ago. What he had now were occasional hookups. Had one of those hookups created this baby?

He stared at her little rosebud lips and tiny features and then looked away. He couldn't do this again. He couldn't get emotionally involved with a baby. The last one he'd loved so desperately had been cruelly snatched away from him and his heart had never quite healed.

Still, if she really was a Colton, he also wasn't overly

eager to hand her over to social services until he knew who she was. So, what should he do with her? Should he call somebody now? In the middle of the night? Where would she be placed if he did call social services? He didn't even know if there were any foster parents in town.

Somebody had left her here with him for a reason. But he was torn. He didn't really know anything about taking care of a baby and she'd be better off with somebody who had more experience than he did.

He opened the tote bag to find formula, bottles, diapers, toys, clothing and several other items. There was everything he needed to take care of her. He could smell the sweetness of her, that baby-powder-fresh scent that was so achingly familiar.

Who would have left her here and why? Was it possible the Needy Thief was her mother? Now the theft of the food items and the cradle and quilt all made sense. But why hadn't the mother just come to him and asked for his help? Damn, he wished he would have caught whomever it had been.

Why leave the baby here? He was a bachelor, a workaholic who spent hours out working on the ranch and chose to live in a small cabin rather than in the family mansion. He'd made the old foreman's cabin his home. He'd made the decision first of all because he was the ranch foreman, and secondly because his parents drove him crazy.

Of all the places and with all the people in the entire town of Red Ridge, South Dakota, the baby could have been left with, why him?

He found it hard to believe that it had anything to do with somebody who worked for him. All his ranch hands lived in the bunk barn in small apartments. He supplied the men who lived there not only everything they needed but also some extras to keep them happy. Besides, the note said she was a Colton.

He needed to call the Red Ridge Police Department and get somebody out here. He didn't know why the baby had been left on his doorstep, but she couldn't stay indefinitely and in any case he needed to make some kind of a report.

Was it possible her mother would return later tonight? Maybe sometime tomorrow? He couldn't take the chance of waiting around for her to come back to retrieve the baby. Eventually the baby would wake up and need something and he wouldn't know what to do.

He made the call and when he finished, the baby opened her slate blue eyes and gazed at him. Her rosebud lips curled upward and she released a soft coo. He closed his eyes and steeled his heart. No matter how cute she was, he absolutely refused to care about her.

Rookie K9 Officer Elle Gage hunkered down behind the back of a pickup truck in the warehouse parking lot. Next to her was her partner, her bulldog named Merlin, who was trained in protection.

Merlin had entered her life eight months before, after going through an intense ten weeks of training at the Red Ridge K9 Training Center. He was not only her partner, but also her best friend and companion. As far as she was concerned he was the best dog in the whole entire world.

The pavement smelled of grease and oil baked under the June sun that day. Her heart beat quickly in anticipation and her blood sizzled through her veins as she stared at the warehouse in the distance.

Tonight she was hoping to finally prove herself, not only to her chief, but also to her brother and fellow officer, Carson. She also wanted to prove herself to her brother Lucas, who was a bounty hunter.

In her mind she always thought of her brothers as South Dakota's Most Overly Protective Brothers. She was more than ready for them to trust that she could take care of herself and stop watching over her so carefully.

She stared at the warehouse that belonged to the Larson twins, suspected mobsters who were involved in everything from money laundering to drugs and gunrunning. This was where the smooth, handsome men held their meetings and it was suspected that tonight the place was packed with illegal guns and drugs.

The parking lot was filled with vehicles belonging to the twins' known associates. She'd love to be part of the team who took them down, although she hated the fact that whenever she was assigned to any job, her brother Carson made sure he was assigned to the same job. She was twenty-six years old. Jeez, couldn't a girl get a break?

She wanted to be the one to cuff one of the twins, not just because they were a menace to society, but because they stole a prized German shepherd named Nico from the RRK9 Training Center and got away with it, and they were also suspected of having one of their thugs steal a puppy from the center. Evan and Noel had clearly had an immoral veterinarian remove Nico's microchip and replace it with one declaring them the dog's owner. Nico had been a day or two from being paired with a K9 handler; that's how highly trained he was. Now he was in the wrong hands. And the puppy had cost the center a small fortune. Elle knew the Larson twins were slimeball criminals, but stealing a dog? For that crime alone, the two should be jailed for the rest of their lives.

Crouching, she moved a couple of steps closer, still hugging the body of the pickup that was her cover. All she was waiting for was the official word to go in.

Tonight she would prove to everyone that she was a good cop and could hold her own under any circumstances. Tonight she would prove to her brother that she didn't need them babysitting her anymore.

Her cell phone vibrated in her pocket. She pulled it out, unsurprised to see her brother Carson's number. She punched the button to answer, but before she could say anything, Merlin released a deep, loud grunt, his trained alert for danger.

Elle whirled around in time to see a big man barreling down on her. She dropped her phone and raised her hands in a defensive posture, her heart nearly beating out of her chest.

He was about to make full-body contact with her. She had no time to think but could only react. She quickly sidestepped and when he brushed by her body, she used her elbow to chop him on the back. Obviously surprised by her quick action, he went down hard on his hands and knees.

She gave him no time to recover. She kicked his midsection as hard as she could once, twice, and a third time. He groaned and attempted to regain his footing, but before he could get to his feet, she had drawn her gun.

"Raise up slowly and turn around," she commanded. "Ignore my instructions and I'll shoot you," she warned. He turned and she quickly snapped cuffs on his wrists. It was only then that she leaned over, breathing hard, but not as hard as her prisoner who, even though he was winded, managed to gasp out some ugly language directed at her.

"Shut up," she said as she picked up her phone from the pavement. "All I have to do is say one word and my partner here will tear out your throat."

He'd obviously thought she'd be an easy takedown because she was a woman. The joke was on him for underestimating her skill and clear focus. She'd had the same training as the men and she was as good as any one of them...including her brother.

Footsteps slapped pavement, coming toward her. She held her gun tight, unsure if it was more danger approaching. She relaxed as she saw her brother and his partner running toward her.

"Elle, are you okay?" Carson asked, his eyes blazing with concern. He stopped abruptly at the sight of her prisoner.

"Elle, why didn't you yell for help? I was on the phone with you," he said angrily. "All you had to do was say that you were in trouble."

"Cool your jets, Carson. I didn't need any help from you. He attacked me and I handled the situation." A sense of pride swept through her as she watched his panic turn to grudging respect.

"Good job," he replied. "I heard the commotion on the phone and knew you were in trouble."

"Like I said, I handled it. This is one bad guy—a thug associate of the Larson twins—who will be off the streets for a while," she replied. At that moment her phone vibrated again. Carson took control of the prisoner while she answered her phone.

It was Chief Finn Colton. "I want you to get over to the foreman's cabin on the Double C Ranch. A baby has been abandoned there with Anders Colton. Your brother can handle the surveillance without you."

An abandoned baby. It was a nonthreatening job and if she didn't know better she'd swear that her brother had talked to the chief and told him to pull her off this more dangerous case.

She hated to leave the surveillance at the warehouse. She really wanted to catch one of the Larson twins red-handed and put at least one—if not both—away.

At least her sense of pride stayed with her as she and Merlin got into her car and headed for the Double C Ranch. She'd taken care of the thug all by herself, without the help of one of her Overly Protective Brothers. She hadn't even had to set Merlin into motion.

She wasn't particularly happy to be going to inter-act with any Colton other than the police chief and her fellow officers. The feud between the Coltons and the Gages was legendary. It began a century ago when the Gage family lost a good plot of land to the Coltons in a poker game. There had been cheating accusations, and the bad blood between the two families remained today.

Most recently she had a wealth of rage directed to-ward one particular Colton... Demetria "Demi" Colton, the woman she believed had murdered her brother, Bo.

On the night before his wedding he'd been found shot through the heart and with a black cummerbund stuffed in his mouth. It was supposed to be a bachelor party at the Pour House, a dive bar in a sketchy area of Red Ridge, but there had been no party, only the murder of her brother.

Bo. Bo. His name blew through her on a wind of pain and terrible regret. The last time she'd seen him they'd had a terrible fight...and then he was dead. How she wished she could take back some of the things she'd said to him. How she wished he were still alive instead of the first victim of someone the police and press were now calling the Groom Killer.

She cast all of these things out of her mind as she pulled into the entrance of the Double C Ranch. She drove slowly past the huge mansion where Judson and Joanelle lived. The lights in the house were all dark, so apparently Anders hadn't disturbed anyone there.

Anders Colton. The only thing she really knew about him was that he was a wealthy cowboy and definitely a piece of eye candy. He was a tall, muscular man with dark hair and bright blue eyes.

Elle was immune to all men right now. At twenty-six years old, her entire focus was on her work and the need to prove herself to everyone in her family and on the police force.

In any case Anders Colton would be the last man she'd have any interest in. First of all, he was a Colton and that was enough to make her keep her distance. But, secondly and more important, it was possible he was aiding and abetting his cousin Demi, who was still on the run from authorities. Had Demi killed Bo? Was she the Groom Killer? Evidence said she was. Witnesses said so, too. And the fact that she'd fled town before she could be arrested and had been on the run ever since made a lot of people, her own relatives on the force included, think she was guilty. But the FBI had caught sightings of her far from Red Ridge on the night of subsequent murders with the same MO. Some said Demi had been framed. Others said she was smart and setting it all up herself.

All Elle wanted was for the murders to stop. And justice for her brother.

Although she didn't know specifically where the foreman's cabin was on the property, she followed the dirt road that took her past a huge barn and a wooded area.

Then she spied the cozy cabin with the porch light on. Seated on the porch was Anders Colton, rocking the baby in his arms. He didn't move as she parked her car and then got out with Merlin at her heels.

As she got closer, her heart flipped just a bit at the sight of a hot, handsome cowboy holding a bundle of pink. It didn't help that he was clad in a pair of worn jeans and a blue shirt that was unbuttoned, putting on display his firmly muscled chest.

"Looks like you've got yourself a baby," she said in greeting.

He smiled. "Looks like you've got yourself an ugly, fat baby of your own." He looked pointedly at Merlin.

Oh no, he didn't, she thought with irritation. "My baby can protect me from getting killed. What can yours do?" she asked coolly.

"Touché," he replied, and stood. His arms still rocked the baby with a gentle motion. "I'm not quite sure what to do with her. She's awakened twice and started to cry, but if I rock her she goes back to sleep. Come on inside."

She followed him into a homey living room with a beautiful natural stone fireplace and casual brown leather furniture. He placed the baby into a wicker cradle. He straightened and then motioned for her to have a seat in a recliner. "Even though my sister and your brother are together and I've seen you around, we haven't ever officially introduced ourselves. I'm Anders Colton."

She sat on the edge of the chair and tried to avoid looking at his broad chest. "I'm Officer Elle Gage and this is my partner, Merlin. Now, tell me about what's going on."

She listened as he told her about the thefts that had been occurring and then stepping outside to find the baby on his porch. While he spoke he buttoned up the blue shirt that mirrored the beautiful blue of his eyes. *Thank goodness,* she thought. She didn't need to be distracted by the sight of his bare chest.

"These thefts...were they break-ins? Do you know how the person is getting inside the cabin?" she asked.

"I never lock my doors. I'm pretty far off the beaten path and I've never had a reason to lock up," he replied.

"Even after the first theft you didn't start locking your doors?" she asked in surprise.

He shook his head. "It was obvious the thief wasn't after anything valuable. I figured if somebody was stealing food then they must need it. He or she only came in at night so I intentionally left the doors unlocked hoping I'd catch them. I just want to know who it is and if they're in some kind of trouble."

"And you have no idea who left the baby here?"

"Not a clue, but she had a note pinned to the blanket." He pulled a small piece of paper out of his pocket and then walked over and handed it to her.

She's a Colton.

Elle's heart nearly stopped as her brain worked overtime. Demi Colton had been pregnant when she'd gone on the run to avoid being charged in Bo's murder.

Was it possible? She stared at the sleeping baby. Suddenly the baby's eyes opened and she began to fuss. Elle jumped to her feet and picked her up.

She held the baby close to her heart and breathed in the sweet baby scent. If this little girl was a Colton, then it was possible she was Bo's baby. Bo and Demi had been engaged to be married for a week, and then he had dumped her for Hayley Patton, a K9 trainer.

Bo's baby. For a moment she believed she felt his spirit swirling in the room, surrounding her with warmth and love. She stared down at the baby who couldn't be older than a couple of weeks. A part of Bo…a gift from heaven. She looked up at Anders, wondering if he'd put it all together in his head.

"She may be a Colton but that means she's also probably a Gage," she said. "And if I find out that you're helping Demi stay hidden on this property, I promise I'll have you arrested so fast your head will spin."

Chapter 2

Anders didn't know whether to be amused or irritated. Elle Gage was definitely a hot number in the neatly pressed uniform that hugged curves that were all in the right places.

Her honey-colored blond hair was caught in a low ponytail that shone with a richness in the artificial light. But her pretty brown eyes stared at him with more than a hint of distrust and dislike.

Still, her pronouncement about the baby possibly being a Gage had surprised him. He hadn't considered that the baby might be Demi's and that Bo was the father. But it was definitely a possibility.

He was so damned tired of people thinking he was hiding out Demi here, although he did believe in his cousin's innocence. "I don't know anything about Demi being here on the property. All I know is that I had a thief and now I have a baby."

"But if this is Demi's baby, then Demi has to be on the property someplace," Elle replied. She studied him as if he were an insect under a microscope. If she was looking for signs of deception from him she wouldn't find any. He hadn't seen Demi anywhere around his ranch.

"It's possible she was on the property about an hour ago, but who knows where she might be now," he finally conceded.

"I know she was in touch with her brother, Brayden, declaring her innocence. She texted him on a burner phone that the baby was fine and that she's working to find the real killer. If she's so innocent, then why is she on the run? Why do so many clues point to her?"

She placed the baby back in the cradle and then faced Anders once again. "Demi isn't exactly a shrinking violet. She's a bounty hunter and is known to have one heck of a temper. She thought Bo was going to be with her, but then he dropped her to marry Hayley."

Anders considered what he'd heard and read about the murder. There was no way his cousin was capable of such violence against another human being. "Despite some of the evidence to the contrary, I still believe she's innocent, but I'll leave the investigation to the authorities," he replied.

"Right now this authority is going to take her partner and do a sweep of the area. We'll be back when we're finished." She headed for the door with the sturdy brown-and-white bulldog at her heels.

Anders released a deep sigh as they went out the front door. Was it really possible the baby was Demi's?

The answer was easy. Absolutely it was possible. Everyone knew that Demi was pregnant—and very likely with Bo Gage's baby—when she went on the run six months ago, and the timing was right for her baby to have been born within the last couple of weeks. And even though Anders and Demi had never been close, she definitely would have trusted him to take care of the infant. Demi *had* been close with Anders's sister Serena, and though Serena had sworn multiple times she hadn't heard from Demi, who knew if she had or not? Serena was romantically involved with Detective Carson Gage, so it wasn't as though Demi could ask Serena to hide her or for help with the baby. But if Anders's name had come up in their conversations, Serena would have told Demi that if she needed someone to count on, Anders was the guy.

Unfortunately Elle was right about clues pointing to his cousin's culpability in Bo's murder.

The rumor mill was rife with stories that Demi had snapped in a fit of rage over being dumped by Bo. Anders didn't listen to gossip, but he'd heard that Bo had written Demi's name in his own blood at the crime scene. He shivered at the thought. Plus, a gold heart necklace with Demi's engraved initials had been found near the crime scene and a witness had put her there, as well. When a warrant had been issued for her arrest, she'd run.

It was much easier to be on the run from the law without a newborn baby in tow. A surge of unexpected protectiveness welled up inside him as he looked at her. She was so tiny, so achingly vulnerable.

And it was also a possibility that the baby could be his. He'd always tried to make sure he had protected sex; however, he also had occasionally trusted when a woman told him she was on the pill and didn't want him to wear a condom.

He would make a good target for a woman to trick. Although his uncle Fenwick Colton and his branch of the family were filthy rich, Anders's father had done all right, too, and Anders certainly didn't have to worry about money.

Yes, he'd make a good target for an unscrupulous woman to intentionally get pregnant in anticipation of some sort of a big payoff. He looked back at the baby.

He had to figure out something to call her besides "the baby." Even though he intended to give her a name and despite the protectiveness that had welled up inside him, he refused to be drawn into caring or loving the baby in any way.

For just a moment his thoughts threw him back to a place when he'd been so happy. It had been a time when he had loved with all his heart, when baby giggles had been the sweetest sound he'd ever heard.

Damn, he couldn't even think about that time without grief pooling inside him.

He sank down on the sofa, his thoughts turning to Elle Gage. He'd occasionally seen her around town but had never really noticed how attractive she was.

It had been acutely obvious that she didn't particularly like him and she definitely didn't trust him. Of course, he was a Colton and she was a Gage. Forbidden fruit, so to speak. Not that he was interested in a romantic relationship with anyone at the moment. He'd loved once and had been devastated. He certainly wasn't eager to go there again. He had a ranch to run and plenty of work to keep him occupied.

A little cry alerted him that the baby was awake once

again. He froze and waited to see if she would go back to sleep, but her cries got louder.

He picked her up in his arms and began to rock her, hoping that the motion would calm her down as it had before. It didn't. Her little face screwed up and grew more and more red as her wails filled the cabin.

He could handle a bucking bronco or an enraged bull, but the crying baby in his arms scared him half to death. Why was she crying so hard? What was wrong with her?

The door opened and Elle and her dog came back in. "I can't make her stop crying," he said with an edge of panic. "I've tried rocking her, but that isn't doing the trick."

"Has she been fed? Have you checked to see if she needs a diaper change?" Elle walked over to the sofa and opened the tote bag. She pulled out a diaper, a bottle and a can of powdered formula.

"Give her to me. I'll change her diaper while you make her a bottle." She took the wailing baby from him and handed him the formula and the bottle.

"But I don't know how to do this," he protested.

"Read the side of the can. It isn't rocket science." She turned around and placed the baby on the sofa. "And make sure you warm it."

He hurried into the kitchen where he managed to make a bottle and warm it in the microwave. He carried it back into the living room where she was seated on the sofa and rocking the still-sobbing baby.

He handed Elle the bottle and noticed the exotic, floral scent of her, a scent he found wildly attractive. The baby latched onto the bottle's nipple and drank greedily.

"Poor little thing must have been starving," she murmured.

An edge of guilt filled him. He should have thought about the baby being hungry. "I'm assuming you and your faithful companion didn't find anyone outside," he said.

He moved to stand in the doorway between the kitchen and the living room. It was easier to concentrate if he was far enough away from her that he couldn't smell her evocative fragrance.

"No, but we both know somebody was here to leave the baby."

"You know, it is possible she could be mine."

Elle's dark eyes studied him solemnly. "If that's the case then you should know who her mother is."

"Actually, it could be any one of several women."

The look she gave him made him believe he should feel some sort of shame. He was thirty-three years old and he'd be damned if he'd let some hot canine cop make him feel guilty about his past relationships or any future ones he might enjoy.

"But she could also still be Demi and Bo's baby," she replied.

"We have to stop calling her 'she.' She needs a name, at least for tonight, because I intend to keep her here through the night," he said.

She pulled a cloth diaper out of the bag and threw it over her shoulder and then raised the baby up and began to pat her back. She looked like a natural. Merlin sat at her feet like a sentry guarding both her and the baby.

"I'll stay here for tonight to help."

A rush of relief washed over him. "Thanks, I really appreciate it."

"I'm not doing it for you," she replied. "I'm doing it

for the baby and because she might be a Gage." The baby gurgled and once again she gave her the bottle.

All of her features softened as she gazed down at the baby. He'd always thought Elle was pretty, but she looked utterly gorgeous with all her features relaxed and a soft smile playing on her lips.

"Bonnie," she said suddenly. She looked up at him. "Let's call her Bonnie."

"Sounds good to me," he replied. "Does that name mean anything special to you?"

"No, it just sprang into my head when I was gazing into her beautiful blue eyes."

He didn't care what they called her. He was just grateful Elle was staying through the night to help him with the newly named Bonnie.

"I need to call the chief and let him know we're keeping her here for the night but we'll bring her into RRPD in the morning so we can decide what the next move will be where she's concerned."

The baby had fallen asleep once again, and Elle returned her to the cradle and then pulled out her cell phone and made the call to Finn. He agreed with the plan.

"It's late," Anders said when she finished with the phone call. "I'll show you to the guest room."

"Before you do that I'm going to take one final walk around outside with Merlin." She stood and Merlin did the same, his gaze focused on Elle in what appeared to be utter devotion. "We'll be right back."

When she walked out of the door it was as if she stole some of the energy from the cabin. A weariness fell heavily on his shoulders. It had been a wild and crazy night. Thank goodness the small spare bedroom was clean and ready for a guest.

She was only gone a couple of minutes and then returned with a duffel bag in hand. "I always keep a change of clothes and some toiletries in my car. Now you can show us to the guest room." She walked over and picked up the wicker cradle. "I'll keep her with me for the night. She'll want to be fed again before morning."

"I really appreciate your help," he replied. "I don't know much about babies."

"That's fairly obvious," she replied drily.

He didn't respond, but instead led her into the room that held a double bed with another of his grandmother's quilts covering it. There was also an easy chair in one corner and a dresser.

She carried the baby to the chair and set the cradle down. "She should be okay to sleep right here for the night." She tucked the blanket around Bonnie and then straightened. "Before I go to sleep, I'd like to get another bottle ready."

"I can take care of that," he replied. He didn't intend to just dump the baby in Elle's lap and not do what he could to help her. He couldn't forget that this was his problem and not hers.

He took the near-empty baby bottle from her and then went into the kitchen. He ran hot water in the plastic bottle to make sure it was all cleaned out and then measured out what was needed to refill it again. Once he was finished he placed it in the refrigerator and then went back to the guest room.

She had unpacked the tote bag and all the items were laid out on the bed. "Whoever packed this pretty much thought of everything," she said. "As you can see, there are five sets of onesies and several little knit hats. There's an extra bottle, another can of formula, diapers and toys that she won't be old enough to play with for another month or two."

She gazed at Anders, that straightforward, sober look he found more than a little bit sexy. "Whoever left her here obviously loves her. That means she must have thought you'd take good care of the baby and keep her safe."

"I will...with your help."

"I couldn't help but notice the quilt on the bed. It's beautiful."

He smiled. "One of my grandmother's. I had another one, but the thief managed to pluck it right off the bed in here and get away." His smile faded. "Uh...do you have anyone you need to call, maybe a significant other or somebody like that?"

"No, nobody. Merlin is the only significant other I have in my life," she replied.

His gaze swept down to the bulldog sitting on the floor. "Does your dog require anything special for the night?"

"Merlin. His name is Merlin and no, he doesn't need anything special. I keep dog food in my car so I'll be able to feed him in the morning."

"I didn't know bulldogs made good police dogs." He stared at the thick-bodied brown-and-white dog whose tongue was hanging out. Thank God the floor was wooden, he thought as he spied a string of drool slowly making its way down the side of the dog's mouth.

"Bulldogs make great protection dogs. They're a lot more agile than they look. Merlin can jump almost six feet in the air. This breed bonds to people and I know he would give his life for me, although I hope that never has to happen." Her affection for the dog was evident in her voice.

"Uh…does he sleep in the bed with you?" He winced at the idea of all that dog slobber on his grandmother's quilt.

"Absolutely not," she replied. "I'm the leader of Merlin's pack. I'm the master and he knows it. I sleep in the bed and he sleeps on the floor."

A small smile curved the corners of her mouth and shot a wild unexpected heat through him. "I can tell by the look on your face that you're relieved my fifty-pound drooling dog partner won't be sleeping in your bed."

"Guilty as charged," he replied. What he'd really love to see was a real, full-out smile from her.

At that moment the baby began to fuss again. "She might have a little more gas." She picked Bonnie up once again. "She didn't really give me a good burp after drinking the bottle." She began to pat Bonnie's back once again. Merlin let out a low, long grunt, as if he were the one being burped.

Elle's eyes widened and she thrust the baby toward him. "Here…take her," she exclaimed. At the same time he heard a noise coming from the living room. He whirled around and ran out of the bedroom.

Across the living room a tall, slightly burly man in a ski mask stood several feet inside the front door. He appeared to be looking around the room.

Adrenaline shot through Anders. "Hey!" he yelled. "What in the hell are you doing in here? What do you want?"

All he could think about was Elle and the baby in the

next room. The last thing he would allow was any harm to come to them.

For a long moment the two men faced each other. Anders tried to discern facial features under the mask, but all he could see were glittering dark eyes.

He rushed forward, ready to take the creep down, but he turned and ran for the front door, which was standing open.

Anders ran out the door after him, cursing as he tripped over the side of the recliner. When he finally made it outside to the porch, the man had disappeared into the night. What in the hell was that all about? He stared out into the darkness, fighting against a cold chill. Who was the man and what did he want?

Elle stood in the bedroom doorway and waited for Anders to return. She was positively livid. Her entire body trembled with her anger. Anders Colton was just like all the other men in her life. Leave the little lady holding the baby while the big, strong man took care of any impending danger.

"A baby on the doorstep and a masked man in the living room, could this night get any more strange?" he said as he came back into the house.

"What in the hell do you think you were doing?" she asked.

"What are you talking about?"

"Have you forgotten that I'm the cop here? That I'm the one with the training and a gun? You should have taken the baby from me when I told you to and let me handle the situation out here."

"I acted on instinct, and as a man my instinct was to

protect you and the baby. So shoot me," he replied with a touch of humor.

"Don't tempt me," she retorted. She drew in several deep breaths and then continued, "Contrary to the beliefs of my Overly Protective Brothers and every other man in my life, I can take care of myself and others. I'm a cop, not a piece of fluff. Now, tell me what just what happened."

"There was a man in a ski mask in the living room. When he saw me he turned and ran out the door. I couldn't get to him in time. By the time I reached the porch, I didn't even know which direction he'd run." He sat down on the sofa.

She walked across the room to the front door. "Come on, Merlin," she said, and then walked outside. The night was dark, with clouds chasing each other across the moon. She knew it was a futile search; the man was probably long gone by now.

Still, she and Merlin walked around the wooded area. There were a lot of places someone could hide, but he couldn't hide from Merlin's nose. When Merlin didn't alert, she headed back into the house. At least her burst of aggravation with Anders was over.

When she went back inside he was still seated on the sofa. She sank down in the chair facing him and released a sigh of frustration. "Whoever it was, he's gone now. Did you lock the door after I came in the last time?"

He shook his head. "It was unlocked. The man just walked in."

"So do you have any idea who he was or what he was doing here?"

He shook his head. "Not a clue."

"Do you think he was looking for the baby?" She

couldn't help but think it was odd that on the same night the baby had been left, a masked man had broken in.

"I don't know what he was doing here or what he might be looking for," he replied, the line of frustration across his forehead doing nothing to detract from his handsomeness.

"Is it possible this guy is the needy thief you told me about earlier?"

"I don't think so." His frown line deepened. "This guy didn't look like he'd be interested in stealing a quilt and a cradle, and his mask definitely didn't make him appear like somebody in need."

"I'll tell you one thing, I was ready for bed fifteen minutes ago, but now I'm not a bit tired." The appearance of the intruder had shot her full of adrenaline and given her a second wind.

"How about I make a small pot of coffee?" he suggested. "I'm definitely not ready to call it a night, either."

"Coffee sounds great." Maybe over coffee she could figure out what was going on here because there was definitely something going on. "I'm going to bring Bonnie into the living room so we can hear her if she cries." She also wanted the baby in her eyesight.

She left the room to get the baby and once the sleeping Bonnie was in her cradle on the sofa she returned to the kitchen. What was a masked man doing inside Anders's cabin? What did he want? And it was definitely strange that he had broken in on the same night that a baby had been left on the doorstep. Did the baby have something to do with him?

If he was the baby's father, then why wear a mask and break in? Why not just knock on the door and introduce himself? Maybe the father was a bad guy who didn't have custody of the baby. But then where was the mother? Or maybe the mother was trouble and the father just wanted his baby back. These were the thoughts that shot through her head as she sat at the kitchen table and waited for the coffee to brew.

And then there were the totally inappropriate thoughts that had intruded among the more important ones. Did Anders always smell so good? Like sunshine and wind and a faint woodsy cologne?

His broad chest made her wonder what it might feel like to be held tightly against it…against him. And that sexy smile of his…he was just so hot.

Jeez, what was wrong with her in entertaining any of those kinds of thoughts? She wasn't even sure she liked him and she definitely hadn't appreciated his taking over the situation when *she* was the cop. She wasn't into macho men who felt they had to protect the little lady of the house.

"Cream or sugar?" he asked.

"No thanks, black is fine," she replied.

She was grateful when he placed a red mug of coffee before her and then sat at the table across from her with his own mug. At least when he was seated she couldn't see the entire length of his sexy physique.

"So, tell me about these Overly Protective Brothers of yours," he said.

She wrapped her fingers around the warm mug. "No matter what job I'm assigned to Carson is always there shadowing me. I think he's told the chief that he wants to be on the same assignments as me and that makes me crazy. Then there is Lucas. Neither one of them trusts me to be capable to do my job or live my life and I keep telling them to back off."

"I think I heard Demi once say that Lucas was her number one competition in the bounty-hunting business," he said.

"He often told me the same thing about her. I just wish he would stop trying to talk me out of being a cop."

"I understand them wanting to keep you safe. I feel the same way about my kid sister," he replied.

"Valeria is a real sweetheart."

He nodded and a smile curved his lips. "We haven't been close in the past, but I'm working hard to build a close relationship with her now."

"How come you live out here instead of in the big house with the rest of your family?" she asked curiously.

"My parents wanted me to live in one of the wings there, but I prefer to be out here. To be honest, my parents make me more than a little crazy."

"How?"

He took a drink of the coffee and then leaned back in the chair. "I know my parents love me, but my mother has always been kind of cold and my father definitely tries to be overbearing. Growing up it always felt like they were more interested in what people thought about them and how many tacky objects they could buy for the house than parenting." He grimaced. "I shouldn't have said all that."

"I'm not a gossiper, Anders," she said in an effort to let him know his words were safe with her.

"So, tell me more about your family."

Since he had shared so much about his, she decided to open up a little about how she felt. "With two older brothers and three younger siblings, I always felt like I wasn't seen or heard much. I guess you could say I suffered from typical middle child syndrome. There were

a lot more boisterous voices than mine in the family."
She looked down into her coffee, thinking about the one
family member's voice she would never, ever hear again.

"I'm so sorry for your loss," Anders said softly.

She looked up at him sharply. "What are you, some
kind of a mind reader?"

"No, no mind reader, you just looked incredibly sad
and I took a guess that you were thinking about Bo."

"I was." She took a sip of her coffee and drew in a
deep, painful breath. "The night before his murder we
had a terrible fight." Emotion pressed tight against her
chest, but she swallowed hard in an effort to maintain
control. The last thing she wanted was to break down
and appear weak, especially in front of Anders Colton.

"We fought and then he was dead and there was no
way for me to tell him I was sorry or take back the words
I said to him that night."

"What did you fight about?"

"It was stupid really. We got into an argument about
ethics. I told him that there were times I thought he was
ethically challenged, and he told me I was an uptight,
boring straight arrow. That really made me mad. I got
heated and he got heated and it got ugly. Of course I
didn't know that would be the last time I'd talk to him
and I hate that I never got a chance to tell him I was
sorry."

"I'm sure he knew how much you loved him," Anders said softly.

She nodded, suddenly exhausted. It had to be after
two and the night had been filled with action, but it was
the emotional drain of thinking about her brother that
had her finally ready for bed.

"I think I'm going to call it a night," she said. She drank the last of her coffee from her mug and then stood.

"I'm with you," he replied, and also got up from the table. He took the mug from her and set them in the kitchen sink, and then they both walked back into the living room where Bonnie was still sleeping soundly.

"Thanks for the coffee," she said.

"No problem."

"Don't be surprised if I'm up again with the baby. I don't want you to hear me and think I'm another intruder," she said as she picked up the cradle.

"Got it. The bathroom is in the hallway. Feel free to use towels or whatever you need from the linen closet." He walked with her to the bedroom door and gestured to the bathroom across the hallway.

"Thank you," she replied.

He held her gaze for a long moment and her breath hitched in her chest. There was something soft, something sensual in his gaze. Lordy, but the man was a handsome devil. "Elle, I'm so glad you're here."

"Me, too," she replied. She broke the gaze by looking down at Bonnie. "I would definitely hate to leave this precious girl with a man who didn't even know to feed her when she cried. Good night, Anders."

"Good night, Elle."

She closed the bedroom door and then placed the cradle on the chair and stared down at the sleeping Bonnie. Right now she was a total mystery. Was she Anders's baby or was she Bo's? She desperately wanted her to be Bo's.

She didn't have the answer as to who the baby belonged to, but the appearance of the masked man in the cabin definitely made her wonder if little Bonnie might be in some kind of danger.

If she had to she would stay here with Anders for however long it took to make sure the baby remained safe. And she told herself her commitment to stay here had nothing to do with Anders's impossibly blue eyes or his sexy smile.

Chapter 3

Anders took the fried bacon out of the skillet and placed it strip by strip on a plate covered with a paper towel. He knew Elle was up because he'd heard the shower in the bathroom running a few minutes ago.

Elle Gage. He'd thought about her way too much the night before. Sleep had been elusive and she'd filled his thoughts in decidedly inappropriate ways. He'd wondered what she'd look like with her hair loose instead of tied in the ponytail. And just how sexy would she look *out* of that uniform?

She intrigued him with her serious brown eyes that had softened so beautifully when she'd gazed at Bonnie and spoken of her brother, Bo. Anders had spent far too long before going to sleep wondering what it would be like to see that soft gaze directed at him.

Then he'd remained awake and wondered when, since

he'd met Officer Elle Gage, had he lost his mind? It had been a very long time since a woman had made him curious about her, but he was definitely curious about Elle.

Then he'd thought of the baby, wondering why she had been left with him and if she was his. Or was she Demi's? There had been so many rumors about Demi's whereabouts, he didn't know what to think.

When Elle walked into the kitchen a few minutes later clad in her uniform and with the cradle in tow, it was like déjà vu from two years ago when Rosalie had appeared on his doorstep with a dark-haired, blue-eyed baby she'd told him was his. The only difference was the bulldog who walked close at Elle's feet and the fact that they had no idea who baby Bonnie's parents were.

At that time he'd not only opened his home to Rosalie and little Brooke, but he'd also opened his heart. He wasn't about to make that same mistake again with Elle and Bonnie.

"Good morning," he said.

"It's always a good morning when you wake up to the smell of bacon," she replied.

"I hope you're a breakfast eater." He pointed to the coffee machine. "Help yourself to the coffee."

"Thanks, and yes, I'm a breakfast eater as long as somebody else is cooking it," she replied. She placed the cradle in one of the chairs at the table and then scooted it in so it was secure. "Bonnie had her breakfast about an hour ago at five thirty, and right now I'm going to take Merlin out and grab his dog food and bowl."

"How do you like your eggs?" he asked.

"Any way you want to cook them is fine with me. I'll be right back." She disappeared from the room and a moment later he heard the front door open.

Despite the smell of bacon and toast, he thought he caught a whiff of her fresh perfume. He hadn't had a woman in the cabin since Rosalie. He'd forgotten how nice it was to smell a feminine fragrance, to have somebody here to share morning coffee and pleasant talk.

The baby made a noise and he turned from the stove and walked over to make sure she was okay. Her blue eyes gazed at him and she released a soft coo as her little arms waved in the air. And then she smiled at him.

It shot an arrow of warmth straight through to his heart. Did she know he was the man who had rocked her in his arms last night when she'd fussed? No, he told himself. He backed away from the table and returned to his breakfast work.

No, there was no way in hell he was going to allow her any access to his heart. Bonnie could look all cute in her little pink outfit and she could coo and smile all she wanted. He was not going to fall in love with her in any way until he found out for sure that she was really his. He was not going to get his heart ripped out again.

He was grateful when Elle returned. She carried a big dog bowl full of food and set it just inside the back door. As Merlin began his meal, Anders cracked four eggs into a bowl, added a little milk and shredded cheese, and then transferred the mixture to the awaiting skillet.

"It's a beautiful morning," Elle said as she poured herself a cup of coffee.

"Normally I would have left here an hour or so ago. I'd be on horseback and out on the ranch checking in on my men," he replied.

"It's much nicer for you to be here fixing me breakfast," she said as she sat down at the table.

"I'll make breakfast, but I definitely will demand you

pay me back and cook dinner tonight." He then shook his head. "That was silly for me to say. There's no reason for me to think that you'll still be here at dinnertime."

"We'll see what Finn has to say when we take Bonnie into the police station this morning."

He took up the eggs, divided them on two plates, added bacon and toast, and then carried the dishes to the table. "Hmm, looks good," she said. "Oh look, Bonnie found her thumb."

Sure enough, the little girl's thumb was in her mouth and she looked delightfully happy. "Should we stop her from doing that?" he asked worriedly. Didn't that cause buck teeth?

"No, although we might want to buy her a pacifier."

"How do you know so much about babies?" he asked. And how could her hair look so pretty in the sunshine, so soft and touchable despite the severe style of the low ponytail at the nape of her neck?

"When I was a senior in high school one of my close friends got pregnant. Her parents encouraged her to have an abortion, but she decided to have the baby. When the baby was born I spent a lot of afternoons and weekends with them helping her out."

"What about the father?" he asked.

"Just another deadbeat dad," she said in disgust. "He swore he loved her and then dropped her like a hot potato when she told him she was pregnant."

"Was her family supportive?" he asked.

"Financially, yes. They didn't kick her out of the house or anything like that, but they weren't real emotionally supportive. The good news is last I heard she'd married a great guy and was finally living happily-ever-after."

"That's nice," he replied.

"Anyway, I learned all kinds of things about babies when I was there with her, although she had a boy, not a girl."

As they ate breakfast the conversation was light and easy. They didn't talk about whether little Bonnie was a Colton or a Gage. They didn't speak about the intruder from the night before; instead, they spoke about the weather.

She loved the spring and he liked the fall. They both liked winter if it involved a fire in a fireplace, cozy blankets and plenty of hot cocoa.

He told her a little about his normal day on the ranch and by that time the meal was over. They worked side by side to clean up the kitchen and then it was time for them to take the baby in to the Red River Police Department.

Immediately the first problem they encountered was they had no car seat for Bonnie. "There's the discount store just before we get to the police station. If you'll stop there I'll run in and get a car seat," Elle said. "In the meantime you'll just have to drive very carefully."

"I always drive carefully," he replied. "In all my years of driving I've never had a single traffic ticket."

"Then you're either a good, law-abiding man behind the wheel or we just haven't caught you yet," she replied with a small grin.

Her humor surprised him. His initial assessment of her had been that she was a bit uptight and way too serious. But the impish grin proved him wrong.

Thirty minutes later Bonnie was secured in a new infant car seat and sleeping peacefully next to Merlin, who was probably slobbering up his back seat. Elle had also picked up a pacifier in the store and had tucked it into the tote bag for whenever Bonnie might need it.

The Red Ridge Police Department was a large one-story brick building. Anders had never been arrested nor had any run-ins with the law, although he'd been inside the building a couple of times in the past to bail out some of his men. The charges were usually the same—drunk and disorderly—and their pay was docked until they'd paid Anders back.

Of course he knew he'd been under a lot more police scrutiny in the past six months since Demi had disappeared. And now with the baby showing up, he'd probably be under even more. He didn't care. He had nothing to hide. He had no idea where his cousin might be.

He parked in the lot and then went to the back seat and got Bonnie out. She rode on his arm in the carrier that pulled out of the car seat. Elle fell into step with him, carrying the tote bag and with Merlin by her side.

"Babies require a lot of equipment," he said.

She released a small burst of musical laughter. "Trust me, this is just the beginning. There are bassinets and bouncy chairs and toys to aid in their development. Then a crib and another car seat and more clothes, diapers and toys."

"Whoa," he said with a laugh of his own. "Let's take this one step at a time."

They walked into the building where a receptionist sat behind the front desk. "Hey, Lorelei. How's it going?" Elle greeted her.

The pretty brunette with chin-length hair and silver-framed glasses smiled at Elle. "It's going. They're all waiting for you."

He followed Elle down a hallway and into a large

room, suddenly worried that little Bonnie's fate just might be out of his hands. And then worried why that bothered him.

The names of the victims of the Groom Killer were written on a large whiteboard in the front of the room. The first name was Bo Gage and Elle's heart ached as she saw his name up there. Unfortunately, his name wasn't the only one.

Michael Haydon, Joey McBurn, Jack Parkowski and Zane Godfried were all men who had been killed the night before their weddings by a gunshot wound to the heart. Cummerbunds had been shoved in their mouths, identifying them as victims of the serial killer now known as the Groom Killer.

As a result, the town of Red Ridge had become anti-wedding. Engaged couples didn't go out in public, and Elle believed some of the public breakups between couples were staged and fake to hopefully make the man in the relationship less of a target.

Businesses relating to weddings were also taking a big hit. Nobody was rushing out to buy wedding dresses or ordering wedding cakes. Printers weren't printing wedding invitations and the popular venues for a marriage ceremony remained empty. June was the month of brides, but there were no brides in the town of Red Ridge right now.

Finn Colton stood at the head of the room. Dark-haired and with piercing dark eyes, Elle knew him to be smart and serious and focused on his job.

Besides Finn there were six other officers in the room, including Elle's brother Carson. Elle and Anders greeted everyone and then sat in the folding chairs lined up in front of the whiteboard. Merlin sank down at Elle's feet.

"Give me a report, Elle," Finn said.

She filled him in on everything that had occurred the night before and when she was finished, Finn frowned. "So, do you think the intruder was looking for the baby?"

"I have no idea what he was looking for," Anders replied.

"And we don't know who the baby belongs to," Finn said.

"Demi," Carson said. "She's got to be Demi's baby. From all we know, the timing is right. That means she was on your property last night." His voice held more than a little suspicion.

"I've told you all before, I am not hiding her out anywhere on my ranch," Anders said firmly. "I'm not helping her in any way stay hidden from the authorities. I have no idea if the baby is hers. I haven't seen or talked to her since she took off, despite what some of you think. It's also possible the baby could be mine."

"Then what you need to do when you leave here is go to the lab where we can conduct a DNA test. I want to know if that baby is Demi's," Finn replied.

Of course a DNA test between Anders and Bonnie wouldn't answer if the baby belonged to Demi, but if Anders was ruled out as the father, then the odds were good Bonnie belonged to the runaway bounty hunter who'd needed to leave her infant somewhere safe.

"In the meantime, we need to figure out what to do with the baby," Finn continued.

"I'd like to take her back home with me," Anders said. "She was left on my porch with a note saying she is a Colton. She was left with me for a reason and until I know that reason, I'd like her to stay."

"It's also possible if she belongs to Demi, then Demi might return for her. I'd like to stay on this, Chief. If I stay at Anders's place, it's possible I can make an arrest and bring her in," Elle said.

"I could definitely use Elle's help," Anders added.

"I don't think that's a good idea," Carson protested. "Elle is still a rookie. Surely we have an officer with more experience who could stay at Anders's."

"I'm definitely up for this job," Elle said with a heated glare at her brother. This Overly Protective Brother stuff was definitely getting on her last nerve. "Didn't I prove to you last night that I can take care of myself during the stakeout when that thug came out of nowhere at the Larsons' warehouse?"

"Speaking of last night, we got nada," Finn said in obvious frustration. "When the team finally went in, they found no drugs and no guns. There was absolutely nothing illegal in the building."

Elle shared Finn's frustration. The Larson twins were definitely slick. "Then where are they keeping their stash?"

"Wouldn't we all like to know that," one of the other officers grumbled.

"Back to the Groom Killer case," Finn continued. "We are still investigating Hayley Patton's admirers. As you all know Noel Larson has come up with an alibi for all of the murders so far. We need to look hard at those alibis."

"He knows a lot of thugs. Isn't it possible he hired somebody to commit the murders in some twisted obsession because he wasn't going to be the groom?" Elle asked.

Hayley Patton was the woman Bo had dumped Demi for. The day after his murder was supposed to be his wedding to Hayley. She was a pretty blonde who worked as a trainer at the RRK9 Training Center. Elle liked her okay, but hadn't really gotten close to her.

"That's what we need to find out," Finn said.

"I'm still trying to find out who is sending Hayley flowers every week since Bo's death," Carson said. "It doesn't help that the florist was murdered and his record books are missing."

"I think the creep is feeling the heat of us getting closer to identifying him," Officer Brayden Colton said.

"I wish we were close enough to make an arrest today," Carson replied.

"Let's get to your assignments for the day," Finn said briskly. "Okay, Elle…you stay out at Anders's place…at least for the next couple of days. I'm sure that you and Merlin can protect the baby since we don't know for sure what's going on or what the masked intruder wanted. You update me daily or as needed, and Anders, don't forget to stop by the lab for the DNA testing," Finn said.

They left the room as Finn continued to hand out the daily assignments to the other officers. It didn't take long in the lab for swabs to be taken from Anders and Bonnie, and then they were back in his car and headed to the cabin.

"Are you okay?" she asked him.

"Why wouldn't I be okay?"

"It's not every day you get swabbed for a paternity test." She was curious how he'd felt, what had been going on in his mind when he'd gotten tested. He'd definitely appeared tense in the lab.

"First time for me," he replied.

"Have you thought about what you want the outcome to be?"

"No, and I don't intend to think about it. I'm not into speculation. I'll see how I feel when we get the results."

"So, I guess this means I'm on dinner duty," Elle said, and looked at Anders once again.

He flashed her a quick smile. "And don't think I'm going to let you off the hook."

Why did his smile make her heart do a little happy dance in her chest? He wasn't the first handsome man to smile at her. So why did his smiles somehow feel different to her?

"You might be sorry. Cooking is definitely not in my repertoire of things I do well," she replied.

"We'll figure it out," he replied. "How long do you think it will take to get back the DNA results?" he then asked.

"If we're lucky then maybe within a couple of days, but I'm sure the lab is really backlogged with all the evidence from the groom killings, so who knows."

"The sooner the better," he replied. "Do you ever think about marriage?"

She looked at him, surprised by the question that seemed to come out of nowhere. "Not really. I mean, I'd like to be married at some point in my future, but right now I'm totally focused on my career. What about you?"

"I entertained the idea for about a minute and then decided I'm definitely a confirmed bachelor. Maybe that will change if I find out Bonnie is mine, but right now marriage definitely isn't on my mind. What were you talking about when you told your brother that last night you proved you could take care of yourself?"

She blinked at the abrupt change of topic. She explained to him about the warehouse stakeout and the takedown of the man who had been about to attack her. "I handled the situation without anyone else's help. I might just be a rookie, but I'm good at what I do," she said with a little more confidence than she felt.

"I have no doubt of that," he replied.

"I'll need to leave for a little while this afternoon so I can go by my apartment and grab some additional clothes."

"Why don't I swing by there now so you don't have to go back out?"

"Okay," she said, unsure how she felt about Anders seeing her personal space. She gave him the address to her apartment and within minutes they were there. He carried the baby and Merlin followed behind as they climbed the steps to her second-floor apartment.

The door opened into a fairly large living area with an island separating the living space from the kitchen. Her furniture was simple, a black sofa with bright yellow and turquoise accent pillows. A large wooden rocking chair sat in one corner of the room. Her flat-screen television was small and in a large bookcase that also displayed a few other items, including lots of books, both fiction—mystery and crime drama—and nonfiction police procedurals.

"I'll just be a few minutes," she said as she left the living room to go into her bedroom.

"Take your time," he replied.

She grabbed a duffel bag from her closet and opened it on her bed. She then returned to the closet and began to grab T-shirts and jeans along with several more clean and neatly pressed uniforms. She added underwear and two nighties. She wasn't a girlie girl, but she did love sleeping in silk nighties that made her feel wonderfully feminine.

She grabbed some toiletries from the bathroom and then zipped up the suitcase and carried it back into the living room. Anders sat in the rocking chair with Bonnie in his arms. "She's starting to fuss a little bit," he said as he stood.

"She's probably getting hungry again." Elle set her suitcase down and then dug into the tote bag to find the pacifier she'd bought. Once she found it, she quickly took it out of the packaging and then took it to the kitchen sink and ran it under hot water. Bonnie's fussing turned into full-fledged wails.

"She definitely has a good pair of lungs on her," Anders said.

"Let's see how this works." Elle placed the pacifier in Bonnie's mouth. She immediately latched onto it and sucked happily.

"That's a magic cure," he said in obvious pleased surprise.

"It's a cure that will only last so long. We should get going back to the cabin. I'm sure she probably needs a diaper change, too."

"Here, you carry her and I'll get your duffel bag," he offered. As she took the baby from him, his inviting scent filled her head.

It continued to be with her in the car as they traveled on to his cabin. "I hope I didn't overstep by suggesting I continue to stay with you and the baby," she said when they turned into the Double C Ranch entrance.

"Not at all," he replied. "I'm grateful to have you with me, not just to help with the baby but also to help me figure out what that man last night wanted."

"You know if I see Demi, I do intend to take her down." She looked at his profile as she spoke.

"I know." He released an audible sigh. "To be honest, I almost wish she was behind bars. At least I'd know she was safe there. I worry about her being out on the run and trying to prove her innocence. What happens if she does manage to find the murderer?"

"Demi's tough and she's obviously smart and lucky. She's managed to evade arrest for the last six months," Elle said.

"Yeah, but sooner or later her luck is going to run out." Anders pulled up in front of the cabin. They had just gotten out of the car when Merlin alerted and stared at the cabin.

"Stay here," she commanded. She pulled her gun, grateful that he'd grabbed the baby and she hadn't yet gotten her duffel bag.

She approached the cabin cautiously, her heart leaping into her throat as she saw that the front door was ajar. In a defensive crouch with her gun leading the way, she swept into the living room.

Chaos greeted her. Sofa cushions were on the floor; the contents of Anders's desk were dumped out. It was obvious a search had gone on, but was the intruder still in the house?

She checked her bedroom first. Merlin was on point next to her, his quickened breathing letting her know he was alert and looking for trouble.

Her bedroom was trashed as well, but there was nobody in there. The bathroom took no more than a glance to clear and then she headed for Anders's bedroom.

Her heart beat frantically and even though Merlin gave no alert, she didn't know if somebody was in there or not. His door was closed and as she curled her hand around the doorknob. her heartbeat accelerated even more.

She twisted the doorknob and mentally counted to three and then exploded inside the room. Her breath whooshed out of her in relief as she saw there was nobody there.

But somebody had definitely been there. She had no idea what Anders's room had looked like before it had been tossed, but now the king-size mattress had been displaced and all his dresser and end table drawers had been dumped on the floor. Clothes had been pulled out of the closet in what she was fairly certain had been a search. But a search for what?

Was this the work of the man who had come in last night? Whoever had been here hadn't been looking for Bonnie. He wouldn't have found her in a desk drawer or a closet. So what had he been looking for? And was it possible Anders wasn't telling her something?

She holstered her gun and headed back outside where Anders remained standing next to the car with the baby. "Prepare yourself," she warned him. "The whole place has been ransacked."

He frowned and she followed him back inside. He paused on the threshold and looked at the shambles. He shook his head and walked on through. He came to a halt at his bedroom door. He turned back to look at Elle.

"What in the hell is going on here?" he asked, his eyes narrowed with anger and his jaw tightened.

At that moment Bonnie spit out her pacifier and wailed as if she wanted an answer, too.

Chapter 4

Elle immediately took Merlin for a walk around the property while Anders fixed a bottle and then sat on the sofa to feed Bonnie. As he gazed around his living room he was positively shell-shocked, and he hadn't even begun to process the mess in his bedroom.

There was no question somebody had been looking for something, but what? Initially he'd believed the intruder last night might have been looking for the baby, but this obviously had nothing to do with Bonnie.

So what did somebody think he had? What were they searching for with such an intensity? Hell, he was just a ranch foreman. What on earth was this about?

He glanced over to his desk where his expensive computer and printer still remained, letting him know this break-in wasn't a robbery but something else altogether.

Remembering how Elle had burped Bonnie earlier

when she'd fed her, he pulled the bottle from Bonnie's mouth and raised her up to his shoulder.

He'd only patted her three times when she not only burped but also spewed a milky mess on the shoulder of his shirt. Great, he had baby puke on his shirt, dog drool all over the place and an intruder who had turned his house upside down searching for who knew what.

He gave Bonnie the bottle once again and at that moment Elle and Merlin walked in. "Nobody," she said in disgust. "Whoever was in here is long gone from the immediate property now. I called the chief and he's assigned me to follow through on this."

She picked up the chair cushion and placed it back in the chair. She started to sit but instead straightened back up. "Are you aware..." She brushed at the right shoulder of her blouse.

"Am I aware that I have baby puke all over my shoulder? Yes, I'm quite aware of that," he said more sharply than he intended. He drew in a deep breath. "Sorry, I didn't mean to snap at you. Needless to say I'm a bit upset about the condition of my cabin right now."

She disappeared into the kitchen and returned a moment later with a handful of paper towels. She leaned over him and wiped at his shirt. "It's not baby puke, it's baby spit-up," she said, her voice a caressing warm breath on the side of his neck.

"In my world if it goes down and comes back up again, it's puke."

She smiled and he noticed not only the pretty gold flecks in her eyes, but also her beautifully long lashes. "In the baby world it's spit-up and now it's all cleaned up." She straightened and looked around. "And hopefully if we work together we can get everything back where it belongs by bedtime."

"Your job isn't to clean up this mess," he said. "I've already got you taking care of a baby, and that's not your job, either."

"What I should be doing is seeing if I can pull any fingerprints from this mess," she said as she looked around the room.

"Do you really think a guy bold enough to do something like this in broad daylight didn't think to wear gloves?" Bonnie had fallen asleep and he set the bottle on the end table and then stood to place her in the cradle.

"You're right," Elle replied. "There's no way this guy didn't wear gloves. By the way, he came in through the back door, which he jimmied. The door still locks, but it's pretty flimsy now. He must have gone out of the front door."

"I've got another lock around here someplace. I'll replace it this afternoon. Security has never been a big deal around here…until now."

"He had to have been watching the cabin. He spent quite some time in here so he must have come in shortly after we left to go to the police station," she said with a frown.

"I think we can safely say now that he isn't after the baby," he replied.

"And we can also safely say that this wasn't a robbery attempt," she said, echoing what he'd thought about earlier. "You have a lot of pricy computer equipment sitting on your desk and it's all still there. But as we get everything straightened up you need to tell me if you find something at all missing. Why don't you start in your bedroom and I'll clean up mine and then we'll work together on the living room and kitchen. Bonnie should be fine right here."

"Sounds like a plan," he replied.

"Merlin...stay," she said to the dog, who promptly sat at the foot of the sofa where Bonnie slept. *"Beschermen,"* she said.

Anders looked at her curiously. "What language is that?"

"Dutch. Most of his commands are in Dutch. I just told him to protect the baby."

"Why are his commands in Dutch?" he asked curiously.

"The obvious reason is because we don't want other people being able to direct the dogs to do anything. But the original reason for the use of Dutch language is because many police dogs are imported from Holland. Merlin wasn't and his commands like sit and stay are in English..." She trailed off. "Sorry, we don't need to talk about dogs right now. We need to get to work."

A few moments later Anders stood in the doorway of his bedroom, his knees almost weakening as he stared at the mess. Who had done this...and why?

First the intruder last night and now this shambles. He couldn't for the life of him figure out what was going on. Right now it didn't matter. All that mattered was righting the chaos that had been left behind.

It took him a little over two hours to put the room back the way it had been. As he worked he kept an eye out for anything that might have been missing. When he finally finished up he was pretty sure that nothing had been stolen from the bedroom.

He kept an envelope of cash in his dresser and it was still there, tossed to the floor with his socks and boxers.

A nice gold watch was also still there. So it was obvious the break-in hadn't been about money or items that would be easy to pawn or sell.

He walked into the kitchen to find Elle putting plates back into the cabinet. She offered him a tired smile. "At least whoever it was didn't break all the dishes."

"Thank God for small favors. Did you get your room back to order?" He felt guilty that he hadn't helped her. After all, it was his cabin, not hers.

"It's all back to normal. What about yours?"

"The same," he replied. "So far I haven't found anything that's missing. In fact, I had cash and several pieces of nice jewelry that are still there. I did find the new doorknob to replace the one in the back door."

"That's good," she replied. "I hope it's a stronger model than the last one."

"It will do for now."

For a few minutes they worked in silence. As he replaced the doorknob she continued to work putting away dishes that had been pulled out of the cabinets. There was no question that whoever had been in Anders's home appeared to have looked for something in every nook and cranny.

"I'll let you off the hook for dinner tonight," he finally said. He closed the door and locked it and then turned to look at her.

"So you're going to cook?" she asked.

"I was thinking this is a good night for nobody to cook except maybe Chef Chang, if you like Chinese food."

"I love it," she replied. "I've never had a bad dish from Chang's restaurant. Are you going to have it delivered?"

He laughed. "No, there aren't many places who will

deliver to me all the way out here in the middle of nowhere. I'll drive in and get a carryout order."

"The sooner, the better, as far as I'm concerned."

"Do you and Bonnie want to take the ride with me?"

"No, we'll stay here," she replied.

"Will you be okay here alone?" he asked worriedly. She shot him a look reminiscent of the one she'd given her brother earlier in the day. He winced. "That was a dumb question, wasn't it?"

"Definitely dumb," she agreed. "I'll take an order of sweet-and-sour chicken. While you go get the food, I'll keep working at the cleanup. Maybe by the time you get back I'll have found your living room floor beneath all the papers and things from your desk, and then you can check to see if anything is missing."

"My gut instinct is this guy won't be back again tonight," he said. "What do you think?"

"I would have thought my patrol car parked out front this morning would have kept any bad guys away, but that didn't stop this creep, so what I think is that we have to stay on our toes. We don't know if or when he might return." Her brown eyes held his in a sober gaze. "And you swear you have no idea what that man might be looking for?"

"What exactly are you asking me? Do you think I'm involved in doing something criminal?" Her question touched a sore spot from long ago, when a Colton had spent time in prison after being framed by a Gage. That Colton, Shane, was now together with Elle's sister, Danica.

"I swear I have no idea what's going on here." It hurt his feelings just a little bit that she had any doubt, but he supposed if their roles were reversed he'd have some doubts, too. "Elle, I swear on everything I hold dear that I have no idea what's going on."

"It was a simple question, Anders. You have to remember I don't really know you, but I trust your word." She gave him a reassuring smile. "Now, go get dinner. We'll be just fine here."

He hated to leave her, but they hadn't eaten lunch and it was already close to five o'clock. She had to be as hungry as he was, and he was starving. Besides, he had to remind himself that she wasn't a piece of pretty fluff, she was a police officer with a gun.

Minutes later he was in his car and headed back to Red River. As he drove a million thoughts flew through his head. Who had broken into his home and what in the hell had they been looking for? More important, had they found what they wanted? Or would they come back?

The thought of Elle and Bonnie somehow being at risk tensed all the muscles in his stomach. Oh, he knew Elle was a trained officer of the law, but that didn't mean something bad couldn't happen to her.

Once again he reminded himself that she could take care of herself and she could always depend on Merlin. After all, the dog was trained to protect her.

He turned down Rattlesnake Avenue. He passed Bea's Bridal, a couple of ritzy restaurants and several popular boutiques and then arrived at Chang's Chinese, a relatively new eating place in town.

Already he was eager to get back to the cabin. He hurried inside the popular restaurant, placed his order to go and then sat on a bench in the entrance to wait.

His thoughts instantly went back to the DNA test.

If Bonnie was his, then who was her mother? He'd dated Vanessa Richardson around the right time, but

he'd heard she had gotten married and moved someplace back east.

To be honest, he couldn't remember all the women
he'd been dating at the time. Not that there had been so
many, but because he'd had no reason to remember who
he'd been with before now.

If the baby was really his, then why hadn't the mother
simply knocked on the door and told him she was in
some kind of trouble or needed help?

He considered himself to be a good guy. He would
have done whatever was necessary to help her out. But
the mother hadn't been on the front porch. Only the baby
had been there.

It was much easier to contemplate these thoughts than
try to figure out who had broken in and why.

Thankfully by that time his order was ready and he
got back into his car with the scent of the Chinese food
wafting in the air and making his stomach rumble with
hunger pangs.

There was something else he was hungry for. More
than once during the day he'd found himself wondering
what Elle's lips might taste like. He wanted to touch the
silkiness of her hair and kiss her until her eyes darkened
with passion. He wanted her in his bed with her exotic
scent filling his senses.

These were totally inappropriate thoughts, but they
had floated around in his head nevertheless for most
of the day. He had to remind himself that she wasn't in
his cabin because she had some sort of a romantic interest in him.

She was there solely to do her job. He didn't know
what was going on. He had no idea how much danger
they might be in. He just hoped that in trying to prove

herself to her brothers and other officers, she didn't manage to get herself killed.

Elle sank down in the living room chair with a framed picture in her hand. The picture hadn't been on display before the break-in and had been mixed in with the items that had been pulled out of Anders's desk drawers.

It was of him and a beautiful dark-haired woman Elle didn't recognize. He was holding what appeared to be a two-or three-month-old baby in his arms. They all were smiling, even the baby girl, who sported a bright pink ribbon in her dark hair.

Who were this woman and the baby? It was obvious they were, or had been, important in Anders's life. If the baby was his, then where was she now? Where was the woman?

Was she responsible for Anders's confirmed bachelorhood? Had she broken his heart? Why did Elle care if Anders's heart had been broken in the past? It was really none of her business.

She placed the photo on the bottom of a stack of paperwork she'd picked up off the floor and then once again sat in the chair. She reached down and petted Merlin.

"I know it isn't part of my job, but I wish I knew him better," she said to her canine partner. All she should want to know from Anders was if he was somehow helping Demi stay hidden from the authorities or not and what was going on out here.

But the picture had stirred a new curiosity. She was stunned to realize that as a woman, she was curious about Anders the man.

At least it was easier to think about this than dwell on

the conversation she'd had with Finn since they'd been home, which she'd found depressing.

Merlin alerted and she got out of her chair. A few seconds later Anders walked through the front door. "Wow, you've been busy while I was gone," he said as he looked around the living room.

"I just made the piles on top of your desk instead of having them all over the floor," she replied. "Hmm, that smells delicious."

"Let's go eat." He carried the food into the kitchen and she carried Bonnie. Since the break-in she didn't want the little girl out of her sight.

They grabbed plates and silverware and then filled their plates out of the cartons of food. For a few minutes they ate in silence. She felt his gaze on her and looked up. "What?" she asked.

"You've seemed a little subdued throughout the afternoon," he replied.

"I have? I guess I've just been busy working the cleanup," she replied. She stabbed a piece of the chicken with her fork and released a deep sigh. "And to be honest, the chief kind of depressed me when I called him earlier about the break-in."

"Depressed you how? What did he say?"

The heat of embarrassment and a touch of humiliation warmed her cheeks. "He basically said since I was a rookie I could handle things here because everyone else was busy doing the important work of finding the Groom Killer and getting the goods on the Larson twins. He didn't use those exact words…" Of course the implication was she wasn't good enough to be working on something big.

"This *is* an important case," Anders protested.

"Maybe not on the same level as the other two, but we don't know what's going on here. Somebody broke into my house and I don't know if the person will be back or not. I have no idea if the person is dangerous, and in the midst of all of this is a baby who suddenly appeared on my doorstep."

He reached across the table and covered her hand with his. "I can't think of another officer of the law I'd rather have here with me and Bonnie right now."

She flushed with unexpected pleasure. She wasn't sure if it was because his hand was big and strong and wonderfully warm over hers or if it was his words of confidence in her that pleased her.

He pulled his hand back from hers. "Now, tell me about Merlin."

"Are you really interested or are you just passing time?" she asked. He'd scarcely looked at the dog since they'd arrived. At the mention of his name Merlin left his food bowl and came to sit at her feet.

"A little of both," he admitted.

"Okay then, you asked for it. I have always loved dogs and from the time I was young I always wanted to be a K9 officer. I was lucky that the training center is right here in Red Ridge."

She intended to keep the conversation short, but she wanted Anders to understand how great police dogs were in general. She told him about the Greeks, Persians, Babylonians and Assyrians being the first cultures to use dogs for policing.

She also explained to him how a K9 dog's sense of smell was at least 10,000 times more acute than humans, that they could search an area four times faster and with more accuracy than human beings, and that dogs identified objects first by scent, then by voice and then by silhouette.

"Oh my goodness," she finally said. "I've been going on and on. I'm so sorry."

"Don't apologize for showing your passion about the subject," he replied with a smile. "No offense, but I haven't seen Merlin do anything yet."

"He's alerted several times since I've been here."

One of Anders's eyebrows shot up. "He has? How?"

"He gives a long, deep grunt," she replied. "He did that this morning when we got back to the cabin and the intruder had been inside."

"I remember now," he replied. His eyes lit with humor. "To be honest, I just thought he had gas."

Elle laughed. "Oh, trust me, you'll know when Merlin has gas."

The conversation through the rest of the meal was light and pleasant. "Why don't you get comfortable and relax and I'll clean up here," he said when they were finished eating.

"I need to take Merlin outside and then I'd definitely love to take a quick shower." She was still clad in the uniform she'd put on first thing in the morning and she was more than ready to put on something a little more comfortable for the rest of the evening.

"Take as much time as you need." He nodded toward Bonnie, who was still sound asleep. "I've got this covered."

"Then I'll see you in a few minutes." She and Merlin went out the back door.

As Merlin did his business, she looked around the area. The cabin was located in a beautiful wooded setting. Unfortunately the trees would make it easy for somebody to hide. Beyond the trees she knew there would be miles and miles of pastureland.

The Double C Ranch was one of the most prosperous around, and she knew that spoke highly of Anders's skill as the foreman. She needed to let him know that there was no reason he couldn't go about his business as usual while she was here.

There was absolutely no reason for him to hang around the cabin when he had a business to run.

Once Merlin was finished, they went back inside and she headed to the bathroom for a shower. As the hot water pummeled her, she tried to keep her mind focused on the break-in, but it kept taking her into dangerous territory.

She'd liked the feel of his hand around hers and she enjoyed the way his eyes crinkled slightly at the corners when he smiled. His laughter was deep and melodious and she was surprised to realize she liked Anders Colton…she liked him a lot.

She could like him, but that was as far as it would go. She couldn't help the way her heart lifted and how her breath caught just a bit in the back of her throat at the sight of him. Okay, the guy was definitely hot. Any woman would have that same kind of reaction to him.

But she wasn't just any woman. She was an officer of the law and a Gage. She wasn't about to get sidetracked in her goals by a sexy Colton.

She dressed in a pair of gray sweatpants and a pink-and-gray T-shirt. She left her hair loose and it fell in soft waves to her shoulders. She always wore it pulled back when she was working, and even though she was working every minute that she was here, she liked to keep it loose in the evenings. Otherwise, if she kept it pulled into the tight ponytail for too long she wound up with a headache.

When she came back into the living room Anders was seated at his desk and sorting through all the papers, and Bonnie was in her cradle on the sofa, still sleeping.

"You look nice," he said. His gaze felt far too warm as it lingered on her.

"Thanks." There went her heart again, doing a little dance in her chest. Why did this man have such a crazy effect on her? She sank down next to Bonnie. "You know, Anders, I realize this ranch doesn't run itself, so I was thinking tomorrow you should get back to business as usual."

He frowned. "But what about you and the baby?"

"What about us? We'll be fine here."

"But what if this creep comes back?"

"Merlin will alert me if anyone comes close to the cabin and I'll be ready for him. I'd love for him to come back here so I can get him into custody and find out exactly what's going on," she said. "And get that worried look off your face."

He laughed. "I can't help it. It's a natural instinct for me to want to protect you and Bonnie."

"Well, put your alpha away. I don't need your protection...and speaking of Bonnie..." Bonnie was awake and blinking her pretty blue eyes as her fists waved in the air. "Do you have a small blanket I could place on the floor? Bonnie could use some tummy time. She's been in that cradle far too long."

"I'm sure I have something." He got up from the desk and disappeared into his bedroom. Meanwhile, Elle got Bonnie out of the cradle and set to changing her diaper.

When she was finished she picked her up and nuzzled her sweet little cheek.

Poor little thing, Elle thought. Everything had been so crazy over the past twenty-four hours that she'd forgotten that what Bonnie needed more than anything was cuddling and love.

There had obviously been little bonding time between mother and baby, so it was vital she and Anders give Bonnie as much stroking and holding and rocking as possible. A baby who didn't get that might grow up with attachment disorder, a condition that would make relationships difficult for her throughout her life.

"Here we go," Anders said as he returned to the living room carrying a small brown-and-gold quilt. He spread it out on the floor.

"That's darling," Elle said as she gazed at the blanket. It was a patchwork quilt and in each square was a cowboy with a big hat riding a horse.

"My grandmother made it for me when I was born," he replied, a touch of wistfulness in his voice.

"You and your grandmother were close?"

He nodded. "I was her firstborn grandson and she spoiled me rotten."

She frowned. "But what about Finn? He's older than you, isn't he?"

"Finn and I are actually half brothers. He belongs to my dad and his first wife. When she passed away, Dad met my mom, and she had me and my two sisters."

Elle gestured to the quilt. "Are you sure you want to use it?"

He smiled. "My grandmother made me several quilts and each time she gifted me with one she told me the same thing. She said she didn't want them wrapped up in plastic and stuffed in a closet. She didn't want them saved for a special occasion. She wanted me to use and enjoy them."

"Your grandmother sounds like a wonderful woman."

"She was. She died seven years ago. She used to tell me that when she was gone her sons would fight over her money and her daughters-in-law would fight over her china, but nobody could take away the quilts she'd made with love for me."

"That's really nice," she replied. "All right then." She knelt down and placed Bonnie in the center of the quilt on her tummy. "Just ignore us," she said to Anders, who had returned to his seat at the desk.

Elle then stretched out on her stomach at Bonnie's head while Merlin took a position right next to Bonnie. "Hey, sweet baby girl," she said softly. "I'll bet your mother misses you desperately. I wish we knew why you were here and not with her."

She continued to softly talk and occasionally reached out to stroke first one tiny arm and then the other. She watched as Bonnie struggled to raise her head to find the voice speaking to her.

"Is that good for her?" Anders asked.

"It's very good for her. See how she's working her neck muscles to try to raise her head and look at me? This is an exercise that makes her stronger."

To Elle's shock, Anders got up from the desk and then stretched out on the floor next to her. Instantly, every one of her muscles tensed. His body heat warmed her and the scent of his cologne made her half-dizzy.

"I'm constantly amazed by your knowledge of babies," he said. "I'm surprised you don't already have a baby of your own."

She laughed and fought the impulse to jump up and get some distance from him. He was far too close to her. "It isn't time yet for married life and babies," she replied. "I want to establish myself in my job before I fall in love and have a baby." She turned her head to look at him. "What about you? Why aren't you married with a couple of babies of your own? I know you said you were a confirmed bachelor, but why?"

"As far as I'm concerned love is just a way to manipulate other people's emotions. I don't believe in the fairy tale of love and that's why I'll never marry." He abruptly pulled himself up off the floor. "And I certainly don't intend to love that baby, either."

He returned to his work at the desk and she continued to play with Bonnie. Was his seeming bitterness toward the idea of love rooted in whatever had happened between him and the woman and baby in the picture? What could have gone wrong between them? They looked so happy in the picture. It didn't matter to her if he loved Bonnie or not, although she suspected if he found out she was his he'd embrace her with all of his love. Still, it certainly didn't matter to her that he didn't believe in love.

Elle had been in love once. Two years ago she'd been mad about another rancher. The handsome Frank Benson had swept her off her feet and after six months of dating she was certain he was going to ask her to marry him.

And she had desperately wanted to marry him. She wanted to have his babies and have her career. They'd even talked about how that might work out.

She remembered the night he'd sat her on his sofa and had taken her hands in his. Her heart had beaten with the quickened rhythm of excitement and she was certain she saw her future in the depths of his green eyes.

Then he told her that while he'd been dating Elle he'd also been seeing somebody else and he was in love with the other woman. He'd told her that the other woman was exciting and intriguing and everything Elle wasn't. She had been utterly blindsided and it had taken her months to get over him.

Love wasn't on her radar at all. After Frank she had made the decision that she would devote herself solely to her work. Work wouldn't betray her. Frank might have found her inadequate, but she was going to give her all to the job and nobody would find her wanting in that capacity.

She was here in the cabin to do a job, and once the job was over she'd probably never see Anders again except for in passing. Nope, it certainly didn't matter that he didn't believe in love, because the last thing she was going to do was fall in love with him.

Chapter 5

Anders mounted his horse and headed out to the pastures. The morning sun was warm on his shoulders and he was glad to be away from the cabin if only for a couple of hours.

He wasn't accustomed to the pleasant scents of floral perfume and fresh baby powder and at the moment he felt as if he were drowning in it.

In particular it was Elle's slightly exotic scent that half distracted him, that tormented him more than just a little bit. Would he find the source of it at the base of her throat? Between her well-shaped breasts?

When he'd stretched out beside her on the floor the night before what he'd really wanted to do was reach out and pull her into his arms. He'd wanted to taste her lips and stroke his hands down the length of her very shapely body.

Last night when he'd finally fallen asleep, his dreams had been of her. They had been hot and erotic and it had taken a very long, cold morning shower to finally get them fully out of his head.

He urged his horse to run a little faster, as if he could outrun his growing lust for Elle. It hadn't helped that he'd awakened in the middle of the night and had started into the kitchen for a drink of water.

He'd been about to walk into the moonlit room when he spied Elle fixing a bottle. He'd backed up and gone back to his room, but not before her vision was emblazoned in his brain.

She'd been clad in a short nightie that had showcased her long, shapely legs and hinted at a curvaceous derriere. If he would have guessed what kind of nightclothes she wore, the sexy silk would have been his last guess. Before last night he would have guessed that she wore a pair of pajamas or a cotton nightshirt to bed.

Oh yes, he was developing a real good case of lust for the rookie cop who was his temporary houseguest. He felt as if his stomach muscles had been tensed since the first full smile he'd received from her.

He consciously shoved thoughts of her and Bonnie out of his mind and instead focused on his surroundings. Everything was a beautiful spring green and pride filled him as he saw the healthy cattle herd milling in the distance. The air was fresh and clean and he drew in several long, deep breaths.

He'd worked on this place since he was ten years old, shadowing first his grandfather and then his father and learning everything he could about ranching. He'd never wanted to do anything else. He'd never wanted to be anyplace else. This land was his heart and soul and he couldn't imagine ever leaving it.

He headed toward the big house, deciding he should probably tell his family about what was going on at the cabin. Heaven help him if they only got some silly gossip off the street. It was early enough that his father would probably be the only one up, but that was fine with Anders.

Anders loved his mother, but had never really felt close to her. She was beautiful and she'd been a young mother who had employed a series of nannies to raise him.

Joanelle Colton was also more than a bit of a snob who spent far too much of her time worried about other people's opinion of her and her family. If she knew Elle Gage was staying at his cabin, she'd have a fit worrying about gossip.

He rode around to the back door of the mansion and dismounted there, where there was a hitching post. If his father was up and around he would be in the breakfast nook having coffee and reading the morning paper.

Anders tied up his horse and then went to the window and indeed, his father was at the table. He saw Anders through the glass and gestured him to the back door.

"Good morning, Mr. Colton," Angie, one of the kitchen maids, greeted him as he came inside.

"Morning, Angie. It sure smells good in here," he replied as he swept his hat from his head.

Her dark eyes twinkled merrily. "I just pulled a tray of cinnamon rolls out of the oven."

"Ah, Angie, you know how partial I am to your cinnamon rolls," Anders replied with a grin.

"Go sit and I'll bring you one with a cup of coffee," she replied.

"Sounds good." He walked into the breakfast nook.

"Son! Sit down. Angie, bring my boy some coffee," Anders's father bellowed out as though he hadn't heard a word the woman had just said.

"Coming now," Angie replied. Before Anders had even sat down she was at the table with huge cinnamon rolls for them both and a cup of coffee for Anders.

Judson Colton was a tall, strapping man who could be a bit overbearing. Anders had gotten his father's blue eyes, but where Anders's hair was dark, his father's was blond…and receding, much to his chagrin.

"I've been waiting for you to come up and tell me what's been going on at your place. Valeria told me she saw a cop car parked out front for most of the day yesterday. Thank God Valeria didn't mention it to your mom. So, what's going on?"

"The patrol car is still parked there," Anders replied. He told his father about everything that had happened since the baby had been left on his doorstep. "Officer Gage has been assigned to the job and is staying with me."

"Carson?" Judson asked.

"No, Elle," Anders replied.

"Hmm, I've seen her around town. She's a damned attractive young woman." He narrowed his eyes. "Just remember son, she's a Gage. It's bad enough your sister Serena is involved with a Gage and won't listen to reason. We don't need you falling for one, too."

"She's there to do her job, Dad. And I definitely appreciate her helping me out with the baby."

"Is the baby yours?"

"I don't know. It's either mine or Demi's."

"Got careless, did you?"

"Maybe once or twice," Anders admitted. "We did a paternity test down at the police station so we should know if she's mine in the next couple of days or so."

For the next few minutes the two talked about ranch business. Although Judson had pretty much turned over the running of the ranch to Anders, he still liked updates often.

Then the conversation turned to the Groom Killings and Demi. "I don't know what to think about that girl. She was always a bit wild, but it's hard for me to believe she's a coldhearted killer," Judson said. "Rusty certainly wasn't a great father. You can't blame the kids for that. Hell, all four of them were raised by different mothers."

Anders knew his parents were embarrassed by his uncle Rusty, who owned the Pour House bar. The place was a dive on the wrong side of town and Anders couldn't ever remember seeing his uncle without a beer in his hand. Rusty had been married and divorced from four different women and at least for now didn't seem to want to add a fifth wife to the mix.

"Your mother will have a fit if she finds out Elle Gage is staying at the cabin with you. She was so upset when Serena got engaged to Carson Gage. Now with your younger sister deciding she's madly in love with Vincent Gage, your mother is about to lose it. You know Coltons and Gages were never supposed to mix. She thinks the family is going to hell in a handbasket."

The last thing Anders wanted to do was spend any more time engaged in a conversation about how upset his mother was by current events. In any case by that time Anders had finished the cinnamon roll and coffee and was ready to get back to work. He once again assured his father that Elle was merely at his cabin to do her job.

"Thanks for the coffee," he said. He grabbed his hat from the empty chair next to him and got up from the chair.

"You'll keep me posted about what's going on?" It was posed as a question, but Anders knew it was a command.

"Of course," he replied.

Minutes later he was back on his horse and headed out to the pastures. Once again he breathed in the clean, fresh air, relaxing with each deep breath he took.

The relaxation only lasted a few minutes as he saw in the distance a few of his men working on a portion of downed fence. He urged his horse faster and then pulled up and dismounted as he reached them.

"Hey, boss." Sam Tennison, one of the ranch hands, greeted him.

"What happened here?" Anders eyed the length of downed white fencing.

"Don't know. It was down when we made first rounds this morning," Sam replied.

"Did we lose any cattle?" Anders asked.

"We don't think so," Mike Burwell, another of the men, replied. "A couple of us rode out to look but we didn't see any."

"It looks to me like it was pulled down on purpose," Sam said in obvious disgust. He cocked his hat back on his head. "I'm thinking maybe it was Seth Richardson. I've seen him lurking around the past couple of days."

"Yeah, I saw him at the Pour House the other night and he's still ticked off about getting fired," Mike added. "It wouldn't take many drinks for him to try to get a little revenge with some of the other lowlifes that hang out in the bar."

Seth Richardson. Anders wanted to kick himself in the head. Why hadn't he thought of the man before now? Damn, he needed to tell Elle about Seth.

"Don't worry, we should have all this back up in the next couple of hours," Sam said.

"I'm not worried, I know how you guys work. If you need any extra supplies just let me know," Anders replied. He remounted, suddenly eager to get back to the cabin to talk to Elle about Seth.

Thankfully he had good men working for him. They were all well-versed in what it took to keep the place running smoothly and most of them were self-starters who didn't need anyone standing over them and cracking a whip.

Sure, he'd had to bail a couple of them out of jail over the years, but he always gave them a second chance. There hadn't been too many men he'd had to fire and even though he'd given Seth more than enough opportunity to clean up his act, ultimately the man had let him down and Anders had had to fire him.

He headed toward the stables, vaguely surprised at his eagerness not only to share the new information with Elle, but also just to see her again.

He didn't like the feeling. He definitely didn't want the feeling. He'd felt that same way about Rosalie and Brooke, and he never wanted to give a woman and a child that kind of power over him again.

He arrived at the stable and unsaddled. He then stalled his horse and got into his car to drive back to the cabin.

When he reached it, he got out of the car and went to the front door. He was pleased to find it locked. He'd told her before he'd left that morning to make sure and keep the doors locked, which had earned him another dirty look.

She opened the door before he could even pull his keys out of his jeans pocket. She had her gun in her hand.

"Let me guess, Merlin let you know I was here," he said as he walked in. Merlin stood at her side and Anders could swear the dog was smiling at him.

"What are you doing back here so early? I didn't expect to see you here again until about dinnertime."

"I thought of something I should have thought about before," he said.

"What's that?" She placed her gun on the coffee table and then sank down on the sofa next to Bonnie, who was sleeping. Elle wore that serious expression that made him want to do or say something to make her smile.

He fought the impulse and sank down on the recliner. "Last week I had to fire a man named Seth Richardson and he didn't take it very well."

She leaned forward, as if he were the most fascinating man in the entire world. Unfortunately he knew she was interested only in the information he had for her.

"What do you mean, he didn't take it very well? What did he do?"

"He threw around a lot of stupid threats."

Her brown eyes narrowed slightly. "What kind of stupid threats?"

Anders shrugged. "He couldn't wait to meet me in a dark alley and show me who was really boss. He was also going to destroy my good name around town and ruin the ranch's business. Keep in mind the man was drunk as a skunk at the time."

"Is that why you fired him?"

Anders nodded. "I'd warned him half a dozen times that if he didn't clean up the drinking then I was going to have to let him go. Needless to say he didn't clean up and so I fired him. I think it's possible he pulled down some fencing in the pasture sometime last night. My men found it down this morning and it appeared to have been deliberately pulled down."

"So you think he might have been the same person who broke in here yesterday? Maybe it wasn't a search at all but instead a trashing of the place in some childish attempt at revenge?" she asked.

He frowned thoughtfully. "I don't know. I just thought you should know about him."

Elle leaned back again into the sofa, a dainty frown appearing across her forehead. "So then do you think he was the masked intruder who came into the house after the baby was left here?"

He thought about the masked man he'd seen in his living room. "No, I don't think that was Seth. That man was physically bigger than Seth."

"But it's possible this Seth might have broken in here and tossed things around," she replied. "Where does he live?"

Anders shrugged. "I don't know. Up until a week ago he lived here in the bunk barn. He did tell me to send his last check to the Pour House and he'd pick it up there."

"Are you going to be here for a while?" she asked.

"Yeah, why?"

"I need to go change my clothes. Can you keep an eye on Bonnie? She's been fed and her diaper was just changed so she should be good for a couple of hours."

"Sure," he replied. He didn't know why she thought she needed to change clothes. She wore a pair of jeans that hugged her long legs and a navy T-shirt that clung to her full breasts. She looked more than fine to him.

The minute she left the room, Bonnie awakened. She stretched her little arms out and released a soft coo that reminded him of a dove's call.

Her sweet coo turned into a little bit of fussing. He looked toward Elle's closed bedroom door, wondering how long she would be. He mentally shook his head. He couldn't depend on Elle every time Bonnie fussed.

When the fussing turned to actual crying, Anders got up and picked the baby up from the cradle.

He returned to his chair with her cradled in his arms. She was so tiny she fit perfectly in the crook of his elbow. Instantly she stopped crying and instead she looked at him steadily.

She held his gaze and in the depths of her eyes he saw such pure innocence and a trust that humbled him.

And then she smiled at him.

He found himself smiling back. "Hey, little Bonnie," he said softly. She waved her arms and cooed as if happy just to hear his voice. He had no idea if she was his or not, but at the moment it didn't matter.

"Are you trying to talk to me?" He smiled again as a bit of baby babble left her lips. "You're a pretty little girl and you're going to have a wonderful life filled with lots of love," he said softly.

"She seems very happy in your arms."

He looked up to see Elle standing in her bedroom doorway. She was clad in her neatly pressed uniform. Her beautiful hair was pulled back in the low ponytail at the nape of her neck and she wore a somber expression.

He frowned at her. "Why the official look?"

"I'm going to do some official business," she replied.

She walked over to the coffee table, picked up her gun and then put it into her holster.

"What kind of official business?" He frowned at her, not happy with this turn of events.

"I need to check out Seth Richardson and see if he has an alibi for yesterday when we had the break-in here."

"Do you really think that's necessary?"

She looked at him with a touch of surprise. "Of course. It's not only necessary, it's my job. We need to know if Seth was the one who broke in here for some sort of revenge. If he was, then one mystery is solved, but if he didn't do it then we know it was an actual search of the place."

He stood with Bonnie in his arms. "How are you going to find Seth?" He walked over to the cradle and put Bonnie there. "He could be anywhere."

"If he told you to send his final check to the Pour House, then I'm going to have a talk with Rusty. He'll probably know where Seth is staying."

He walked with Merlin and her to the front door and tried to quash his worry. She would hate knowing he was worried about her. She'd remind him that she was a trained officer of the law and this was what she did.

When they reached the front door she turned to him. "I'm not expecting this to take too long. You'll be okay here with Bonnie?" she asked.

He nodded. "We'll be fine. Just be safe."

She smiled at him. "Always."

She started to walk out the door, but he stopped her by grabbing her by the arm. She turned around to face him and he leaned in and captured her startled lips with his.

He hadn't expected it; he certainly hadn't planned it. But once his mouth took hers, he remembered just how much he'd wanted to kiss her and how often in the past two days he'd fantasized about it.

His fantasies had been woefully inadequate. The real thing was so much better. Her lips were soft and warm and welcoming. It shot an instant desire through his entire body. He could kiss Elle Gage forever.

But the kiss lasted only a couple of moments and then she stepped back from him.

"I'll see you later," she said, her eyes dark and mysterious pools. She turned on her heel and headed for her patrol car. Merlin padded along beside her.

He watched them get into the car and he continued to watch until her car drove away. It was only then he closed and locked the door and sank down on the sofa next to Bonnie.

He probably shouldn't have kissed her, because now all he could think about was hoping he'd get an opportunity to kiss her again.

That kiss. That damned kiss burned her lips as she headed into town. He shouldn't have done it, and worse than that, she shouldn't have allowed it.

But his mouth had been so hot, so demanding and hungry against hers. It had momentarily taken her breath away and made it impossible for her to think.

She'd wanted to fall into him and feel his strong arms wrap around her. She'd wanted him to carry her into his bedroom and make passionate love to her.

The moment she'd wanted him to deepen the kiss was the same moment her good senses had slammed back into her and she'd backed away from him.

The kiss didn't change anything between them. It couldn't. She just had to forget it ever happened. Besides, she had business to attend to. She needed to make a call to Finn and let him know what she was doing.

She made the call. "Hey Chief, just wanted to check in with you," she said when Finn answered.

She explained to him about the disgruntled, fired ranch hand and that she was on her way to the Pour House to see if she could find him.

"You know to watch your back in that area of town," Finn said.

"I know. I just want to know if this guy spent his morning yesterday trashing Anders's cabin or if we're dealing with something else altogether," she replied.

"Make sure you keep me in the loop," Finn said.

"Will do, Chief."

The call ended and still Anders's kiss played in her head. Why had he kissed her? What had caused his moment of temporary insanity, for that was surely what it had been?

They'd both made it clear to each other that they weren't looking for any kind of a relationship. He was a Colton and she was a Gage, further complicating things. And she still didn't know if she could fully trust him when it came to Demi, although she realized she desperately wanted to trust him.

It didn't take her long to arrive on the seedier side of town with its abandoned storefronts and tattoo shops and liquor stores. She pulled into the rear parking lot of the Pour House but remained in the car.

Bo. His name instantly leaped into her brain. It was here, in the back of this parking lot, that he'd been found, half on the asphalt and half on the grass. He'd come here to celebrate his bachelor party and instead been brutally murdered.

Her grief was still so tangled up with her wild sense of guilt. If she could just go back in time and instead of fighting with Bo, she would have hugged him. She would have told him how much she loved him.

It was an important lesson to remember. You never knew how much time you had with your loved ones, so it was vital to tell them how much they meant to you each time you left them. But it was too late for her and Bo.

She shoved aside her grief and got out of her car. It was noon so she knew the bar would be open although surely not too busy at this time of the day. All of her senses went on full alert.

This was an area where police weren't particularly wanted and she scanned every inch of her surroundings as she walked around to the front of the building. Merlin walked beside her, constantly working to keep her safe.

The bar's front door was open and all the neon beer signs were lit up and flashing. She stepped inside with Merlin at her heels.

"Officer Gage." Rusty greeted her by raising his mug of beer. He sat at the bar alone, his unruly reddish-brown hair gleaming in the artificial lights overhead. "To what do I owe a visit from one of Red Ridge's finest?"

There was only one other man in the establishment. He sat alone at a table and hadn't even bothered looking up when she'd entered. He didn't appear to be any kind of threat.

"I was wondering if you could help me out," she said, keeping her tone light and pleasant.

She'd try a little honey first to see if that would get her the answers she needed. If that didn't work, she'd come on a little harder.

"Help you out how?" Rusty asked.

"I'm looking for Seth Richardson. Can you tell me where he might be staying?"

"He's staying at the motel, but if you wait ten or fifteen minutes he should be here." Rusty paused to take a drink of his beer and then continued, "For the last few days Seth has been doing some handyman work for me around here."

"Was he here yesterday?" she asked.

Rusty nodded. "He was. I had him paint the ladies' room. It definitely needed it and ladies are way pickier about those kinds of things than men are. Got it painted a nice light blue for the women."

"What time did he get here yesterday morning?"

Rusty frowned. "It was about nine thirty or so in the morning. Why? What's he done now? He's already lost his job at the Double C Ranch."

Before Elle could reply the door opened and a short, stocky, dark-haired man walked in.

"Ah, there he is now, the man of the hour," Rusty said. "Seth, Officer Gage here has been asking about you."

Seth narrowed his dark eyes. "What's the problem?"

Rusty stood and got a second beer. "Here, sit," he said to Seth.

Seth approached the bar and slid onto a stool, his gaze never leaving Elle. "I ain't done nothing. Why are you asking about me?" Rusty set a beer in front of Seth.

"We had some issues out at the Double C Ranch yesterday and your name came up," Elle said.

"What kind of issues?" Seth's tension was evident in his tensed broad shoulders and in the white-fingered grip on his beer mug.

"The foreman's cabin was trashed yesterday morning."

Seth's eyes widened in what appeared to be genuine shock. "I had nothing to do with something like that. I was here yesterday. Go ahead, ask Rusty. I painted for him all morning."

He wasn't their guy. She'd known it before Seth had even walked into the bar. Rusty had no reason to alibi the man and they certainly hadn't had an opportunity to talk about an alibi before she walked in. Nobody had known she'd show up here today.

"What about last night?" Elle asked, remembering what Anders had told her that had brought the man to his mind in the first place.

"What about last night?" He averted his gaze from hers and instead looked down in his beer mug.

"There was some downed fencing on the property. You wouldn't know anything about that, would you?"

"Jeez, Seth, did you do something stupid last night?" Rusty asked the man.

Seth took a long drink of his beer. "I don't know anything about it," he said, but there was definitely a lack of conviction in his voice.

Elle figured it was probable that he was responsible for the fencing, but he hadn't broken into the cabin. She stepped closer to him, close enough that she could smell his sour body odor and see the pores and broken vessels across his broad nose.

"Let me give you a little bit of advice, Seth," she said. "Stay away from the Double C Ranch. You have no business anywhere near the place. You're on my radar now. If anything goes wrong there, you'll be the first person I come looking for. You got it?"

"Yeah, I got it," he replied.

Answers gotten and message delivered, Elle nodded

to Rusty and then turned and headed for the door with Merlin by her side. She stepped out into the sunshine and practically ran into her brother.

"Carson, what are you doing here?" she asked in surprise.

"The chief mentioned that you were here and I was in the area and thought you might need a little backup," Carson said.

She stared at him for a long moment, irritation quickly taking hold of her. "You have to stop." She grabbed her brother's arm and pulled him farther away from the bar's door. "Carson, this Overly Protective Brother stuff has gotten way out of hand."

"I was just checking in on a fellow officer," he protested.

"That's a lie and you know it," she replied heatedly. "It's bad enough that I'm assigned to a babysitting job instead of working on the Groom Killer case. I can't have you constantly shadowing me and you've been doing it since the day I was sworn in, and you're getting worse instead of better about it."

He looked off into the distance for a long moment and then looked back at her. "I don't want anything to happen to you, Elle," he said. "We've already lost Bo." For a moment his eyes were dark and haunted.

Carson had been the first one to stumble on Bo's body minutes after he'd been murdered and Elle could only imagine how absolutely horrifying that had been for him.

She reached out and took his hand in hers. "Yes, we lost Bo. But Carson, I knew the risks when I became a cop. Just like you, this is what I want to do and it's important to me that you believe in me and just let me do my job."

"I do believe in you," he replied.

"But every time you shadow me, each time you show up to 'help' me with my job, you undermine my confidence in myself. And you know that a cop with no confidence isn't a good cop." She squeezed his hand and then released it.

"Let me grow up, Carson, and let me be a good cop."

He gave her a nod. "Did you get what you needed here?"

"Yes and no." As they walked back to their patrol cars she told him about Seth Richardson and why she'd come here to check him out. "I am pretty sure he isn't the person who broke into Anders's cabin, which leaves us still with a mystery," she said.

"Keep your eyes open and watch your back," he replied.

"Don't worry, I've got this," she said.

Minutes later she was back in her car and headed home. No, not home, she corrected herself…rather back to Anders's cabin. Once again her thoughts filled with Anders. Not only had he stunned her with his kiss, but before that he'd surprised her with Bonnie.

He'd been so clear that he had no intention of loving the baby, but his actions spoke louder than his words. When she'd come out of the bedroom and seen him holding Bonnie and talking to her, she'd heard the love and affection in his voice. She had seen it shining from his eyes as he gazed at the baby girl.

He had vowed so adamantly that he wasn't going to love the baby and yet there he was, with a warm smile on his face and wrapped around little Bonnie's pinkie.

It had been an unexpected turn-on…the big sexy cowboy sweet-talking a tiny baby girl. Add in that very hot kiss Elle had received from him and she was feeling more than a little vulnerable.

She had to stay focused on her job and right now her head was also filled with a lot of questions. She firmly believed Seth and some of his drunken friends might have pulled down the fencing in the middle of the night.

She also believed Seth was not the man who had broken into the cabin. She was positive that had been a search and not a trashing by a disgruntled former employee.

So who had broken into Anders's cabin? And what had they been looking for? More importantly…was the person dangerous and would he be back?

Chapter 6

Two days had passed since Elle returned from the Pour House. Nobody had come forward to claim the baby and they still had no idea who the intruder had been or what he'd wanted.

Just because nothing had happened in the past forty-eight hours didn't mean they had let their guard down. Anders was just spending a couple of hours each morning away from the cabin and the rest of the time he was inside with Elle and Bonnie.

He didn't feel right leaving Elle alone to take care of Bonnie. She wasn't here to be a full-time babysitter and he didn't expect her to be, especially if little Bonnie turned out to be his.

The one thing that hadn't happened in the last two days was any mention of the kiss they had shared. It was almost as if it hadn't happened. But it had, and he'd thought about it far too often.

She was now stretched out on the floor in the living room having tummy time with Bonnie and he was in the kitchen cooking their evening meal.

Last night he'd fried up burgers for dinner. Tonight he was making chicken and rice. In the past two days they'd fallen into a comfortable routine.

He made breakfast for them each morning and then went out to ride the range and take care of chores. When he returned about noon she had lunch ready. He'd eat and then remain in the cabin. He'd pulled out an old chess game, delighted to learn that she knew how to play, and they had passed the afternoons in hot challenges. Then in the evenings, he cooked while she played with Bonnie.

It all felt so effortless and it almost scared him just how comfortable they had become together. It felt like playing house, only at night they went to separate rooms.

Her laughter now drifted into the kitchen, tightening his stomach muscles with its pretty melody. He'd love it if for just one night they wound up together in his bed.

He opened the oven door to check on the chicken; the heat wafting out had nothing on the heat of his thoughts. Why was she under his skin so much? What was it about her that had him so off-balance?

Another half an hour or so and the chicken would be ready and then they could eat. After dinner they'd sit in the living room and talk until bedtime. So far he'd enjoyed their evening talks. He felt as if he was getting to know her better and better.

Even though he was in the kitchen, he heard Merlin's alert. Instantly every muscle in his body tensed and he ran into the living room to hear a knock on the door.

Elle was already at the door, her gun in hand. She looked at Anders and then opened the door. Anders relaxed as he saw his sister Serena, holding her nine-month-old baby, Lora, in her arms. His little niece had Serena's dark hair and eyes, although at the moment her eyes were closed as she slept.

"Whoa, this is some kind of welcoming committee," she said.

Elle lowered her gun and instead offered a smile. "Sorry about that, but we're a little bit on edge." She waited for Serena to come inside and then Elle closed and locked the door behind her.

"What are you doing here?" Anders asked as he gestured her to the chair. "You usually don't drop in this time of the day."

"Carson is still at work, so I thought it was about time I had a look at the mystery baby," she replied.

"We've named her Bonnie for the time being," Elle said. She set her gun down and then leaned over and picked up Bonnie in her arms and stepped closer to Serena.

Serena gazed at Bonnie and then looked at him and shook her head. "I know everyone is wondering if she's Demi and Bo's baby, but she doesn't look much like either of them. Of course I guess the strawberry-blond hair and blue eyes might change over time."

"Have a seat, Serena," Anders urged his sister. "Surely you can stay and visit for a few minutes."

"Just a couple of minutes and then I need to go." She sank down in the chair and smiled at Elle, who had placed Bonnie back in her cradle. "I'll bet Anders is glad to have you here."

"You've got that right," he replied. "I don't know how I'd handle all the baby stuff without her."

"I wasn't really thinking about that," Serena replied.

"I was talking about the fact that she's a police officer and is here to watch your back. Father told me about the break-ins that have happened here."

"There is that, too," Anders agreed. He looked at Elle, who had a warmth in her eyes and a smile curving her lips. He wondered if it was because Serena had seen her as a cop first and a baby helper second.

"And you don't have any idea what's going on?" Serena asked him.

"I don't have a clue," he replied.

"Have you heard if there's anything new in the Groom Killer case?" Elle asked. "I'm kind of out of the loop right now."

Serena shook her head. "Unfortunately, the answer is no. They're still trying to find out who keeps sending Hayley Patton flowers each week and they're still on the lookout for Demi. You know there are a lot of people who think she's someplace on this property, especially since the baby was left here." She shook her head again.

Anders remembered how Elle's brother, Detective Carson Gage, had been sure Serena was hiding Demi months ago, when Demi first fled town. They had become close, but as she'd said before, there was no way Demi could have risked leaving the baby with his sister, now that Serena was seriously involved with a cop.

"If she's on this property I haven't seen any sign of her and I wouldn't have a clue where, exactly, she could be," he replied.

"That goes double for me," Serena said. "I do hope Demi's okay out there on her own."

For the next few minutes they talked about town gossip and then Serena stood. "I need to head home. Elle, please take good care of my brother."

"Always," she replied.

He walked his sister to the door and dropped a soft kiss on little Lora's forehead. "Take good care of my niece," he said.

Serena's brown eyes twinkled. "You know we will," she replied. Then with goodbyes said, she left.

It was over dinner that Elle asked about baby Lora. "Is the father not in the picture at all? Carson has never told me and I haven't felt comfortable enough to ask."

"No, he isn't. My sister had an uncharacteristic one-night stand with a man she met at a horse auction. She didn't know his last name or really anything about him. The next morning when she woke up he was long gone, along with her cash and credit cards. He managed to rack up thousands of dollars of debt before she even knew he was gone."

"Oh my gosh, that really stinks," Elle said.

"It does. Anyway, fast-forward a couple of months and she realized she was pregnant. Despite my parents' having a fit about the whole thing, Serena chose to have the baby."

"She's obviously one strong lady. I'm so glad she and Carson found each other. She's good for him and he absolutely adores her and the baby."

"And as you know, she's more than a little crazy over him." He took a bite of the tender chicken.

"This is really good," she said.

"Thanks, it's got a little white wine in it."

"Do you cook like this a lot?"

"Yeah, actually I do," he replied. "I like to eat more than just the typical bachelor food of pizza and anything cooked in the microwave. I started experimenting with cooking when I moved out here by myself and discovered I really enjoy it."

"That makes one of us," she said with a laugh.

"I know you haven't fought me over dinner duty. Do you really not like to cook?" He loved the sound of her rich, musical laughter.

"It's something I've never had an interest in doing. Maybe it's because it's just me. It's always been easy to pick up fast food on the way home from work. I much prefer cleaning up the dishes after a good meal that somebody else has cooked than actually cooking one," she replied.

He grinned at her. "Then we make a good pair."

She held his gaze for a long moment and then looked back down at her plate. "For now," she replied.

For now? What did she mean by that? Did she expect them not to be a good pair as time went on? Or was she referring to the fact that she was only here temporarily?

She looked so pretty with her hair loose and clad in a coral-colored T-shirt that complemented her honey-blond hair and beautiful brown eyes.

"What are your feelings about one-night stands?" Oh God, had that question really just left his lips? What was he thinking? He couldn't believe he'd just asked that.

Her gaze shot back to him in obvious surprise and her cheeks were dusted with a pretty pink hue. "I really haven't thought about it much." She carefully set down the fork that had been poised between her plate and her mouth.

"I've never had one, but I guess I wouldn't be completely against it as long as both people were on the same page," she said.

"And what page is that?" he asked. His breath was

trapped in his chest and a wild anticipation gripped him as he waited for her response.

"I guess I'd want the understanding that it wouldn't mean anything, to be clear." She looked down at her plate again. "It would just be an expression of a physical attraction and nothing more than that."

Lordy, he could so be on that same page if it meant a night in bed with her. Did she find him physically attractive? Did she share even a modicum of the desire for him that he felt for her? He was sure that a single one-night stand with her would effectively get her out of his system.

Thankfully he didn't blurt out those questions. But he was aware that he'd made her uncomfortable and so he turned the conversation to a topic he knew she loved... Merlin.

Her eyes lit up as she told him how the breed was very sociable and loved people and especially children. She told him that Merlin loved to fetch a red ball she carried with her. And that there were times that, despite his large size, he acted like a lap dog.

When they were finished eating she cleaned up the kitchen while he rocked Bonnie and talked to her. The little girl seemed to change just a little bit each day. She was awake more and appeared more alert to her surroundings than she'd been only a few days ago.

As he heard Elle in the kitchen, he wondered if this would be what it was like if they were married and had a baby. He immediately mentally berated himself for the direction of his thoughts.

What was he thinking? Elle had made it clear she wasn't interested in any romantic relationship and he certainly wasn't ready to trust another woman in his life. He definitely wasn't looking for marriage.

So why did it feel so right to have her here? Why did he look forward to waking up in the morning and knowing her face would be the first one he'd see? Why did he spend his time out in the pasture wishing he was back in the cabin with her and Bonnie?

He needed to stop these crazy thoughts. More than anything he definitely needed to stop wanting Elle. He just had to figure out how to do it.

"I don't think I'll be in this afternoon for lunch," Anders said the next morning as they finished up breakfast.

"Okay." She looked at him with a bit of surprise. He'd been in a strange mood over the meal, unusually quiet and distant. "Problems on the ranch?" she asked as she walked with Bonnie in her arms to the back door.

"Something like that," he replied. He leaned over and gave Bonnie a kiss on the forehead and then straightened and grabbed his hat from the hook on the wall. "I'll be home in time to cook for dinner." He didn't wait for a response but rather turned on his boot heel and headed outside.

If she didn't know better she'd swear he was mad at her, but for the life of her she couldn't figure out why. She hadn't said or done anything out of line.

Not that she cared if he was mad at her. In fact, it would probably make things a little easier on her if he showed a bit of a hateful bad side.

As things were he was way too attractive to her. He was so much more than a sexy piece of eye candy. He was also intelligent and funny. He had a softness inside him that he tried to hide, but it came out in his tenderness with Bonnie. And it was that particular characteristic of his that shot such warmth straight through her heart.

Things had definitely gotten a bit too cozy between them over the past couple of days. She felt a breathless anticipation around him and she wasn't sure what exactly she was anticipating.

She shoved thoughts of Anders out of her mind and instead focused on Bonnie, who was awake and waiting for a bottle. Once Elle had it ready she sank down on the sofa to feed her.

"This wasn't what I thought police work was going to involve," she said to Merlin, who was always a rapt audience for her. "I don't know how much longer I'll be assigned here. Finn can't keep me here strictly as a babysitter and if the danger is over, then there's really no reason for me to stay on."

She looked down at Bonnie and any desire she had to be anywhere else melted away. If this baby belonged to Bo and Demi, then she wondered what Bonnie's future held.

Bo was dead and Demi was on the run. If Demi was caught, she'd be arrested on any number of charges, leaving the baby to be raised by whom?

When she was finished eating, Bonnie fell asleep and Elle placed her back into the cradle. Elle sat on the floor and gestured for Merlin. He came into her arms and tried to sit on her lap, making her laugh.

"You're my big baby boy, aren't you?" She ran her hands over the soft fur of his back, scratching him the way he liked. With Bonnie in the house, she'd neglected giving Merlin the attention she knew he loved.

He raised his big head and closed his eyes as she continued to scratch his back, then he flopped over to bare his belly for more scratching.

This dog was who she could depend on, who would never let her down or tell her she wasn't good enough. He offered her unconditional love every single day. Merlin would protect her with his life and love her until one of them died.

It was a beautiful morning and she decided to take Merlin out for a game of fetch. She went into the bedroom and put her holster on. She then grabbed the little yellow knit hat for Bonnie. Then with her gun at her side she carried Bonnie outside.

She went first to her car trunk where she grabbed the red ball. Merlin spied it and began to dance with excitement around her feet.

He chased her back to the porch where she set Bonnie's cradle down. The morning air was a bit cool, but Bonnie was warmly nestled in her pink blanket with the hat covering her head and ears.

Besides, with the sun rising higher in the beautiful blue sky it wouldn't take long for the temperature to warm up. "Merlin." He sat at her feet and stared at the ball in her hand. "Fetch," she said and then threw the ball.

He took off like a rocket, running as fast as his short legs could carry him. He grabbed the ball and then brought it back to her and set it at her feet. Even though he was having some playtime, Elle knew that if anyone came near he would still alert and would choose her safety over his ball.

As she continued to play fetch with him, she couldn't help but admire the beautiful setting and the peace and quiet. She would love living in a place like this with the beauty of nature surrounding her. Not that she wanted to live here, she told herself, just a place like here.

She couldn't count the number of times her neighbors at her apartment building woke her with loud music or raised voices. Or somebody set off a car alarm in the parking lot.

She and Merlin played fetch for about a half an hour. Finally she called a halt to the fun. The three of them returned to the house, where she pulled the hat off the still-sleeping baby and took off her holster.

It was just after ten when Merlin alerted. Elle grabbed her gun from the coffee table, her heartbeat accelerating.

A knock fell on the door. She opened it quickly, her gun level in front of her.

"Oh…my," the young woman on the porch exclaimed.

Elle smiled at Valeria, Anders's younger sister, and the woman her brother Vincent had been dating and vowed to marry. "Sorry," Elle said, and lowered her gun.

"I guess Anders isn't here?"

"No, he's out doing his cowboy work. Why don't you come on in?"

"I just thought I'd come by and…" Her gaze fell on the sleeping Bonnie on the sofa. "Oh, she's so beautiful." She walked closer to the baby.

"She's also a really good baby," Elle said. "She only cries if she's hungry or needs a diaper change. We've been calling her Bonnie while she's been here."

"I heard that it's possible she might be Demi's baby," Valeria said.

"And Bo's," Elle replied.

"Of course," Valeria said quickly.

"Please…sit." Elle gestured to the recliner and she sat on the sofa next to Bonnie.

"I also heard there was some trouble out here. Do you think my brother is in any danger?" Valeria's dark eyes filled with concern.

Elle hesitated for a moment. "I don't know, but I don't think so. We aren't really sure what's going on, but that's why I'm here."

"And I'm so glad you're here for him," Valeria replied. "Anders and I have gotten so much closer over the last couple of months and I would hate to see anything bad happen to him."

"I promise I'm going to make sure he's safe," Elle assured her, and then hoped it was a promise she could keep.

"Is your dog friendly?"

"Ridiculously friendly," Elle replied. "Merlin, go make friends."

Merlin approached Valeria with his back end wagging to and fro with happiness. Valeria held her hand out to let him sniff it, then she stroked down his back. "He's beautiful. What's his superpower?"

"Protection. So you see, I'm not the only one protecting Anders from harm. Merlin is on the job as well."

"That's good to know." She straightened in the chair and Merlin padded back to Elle. Valeria's gaze returned to Bonnie and then slid to Elle. "If she's Bo and Demi's child, then Vincent and I would love to raise her."

"You two are just barely out of high school," Elle said.

"That doesn't matter. You know we're mature for our ages and we are going to be married soon. I already spoke to Vincent and he agrees that Bonnie would be a wonderful addition to our family. Then she'd be raised by a Colton and a Gage."

"Valeria, I don't really have any say in where Bonnie is going to end up. And remember, it's still possible the baby might be your brother's."

"If that's the case, then she's one lucky baby," Valeria replied. "I know Anders, and when he loves, he loves hard."

Those words played in Elle's head, but she quickly shoved them away as the conversation continued.

The two chatted for the next twenty minutes or so. Bonnie awoke and Elle let Valeria give her a bottle. "She really is so sweet," Valeria said when Bonnie had finished the last drop and had been burped. "I meant what I said about Vincent and me raising her."

"I know you meant it. We'll just have to see how things turn out. Anders took a paternity test and we should have the results any time now."

Valeria stood with obvious reluctance. "I'd love to stay here all day with her, but I need to get going. I'm headed into town to run some errands."

Elle walked with her to the door and the two women hugged. "Anders will be sorry he missed you," Elle said.

"Tell him I'll see him soon."

"And tell my baby brother I said hello," Elle added.

Valeria's face lit with love at the mention of Vincent. "I will," she replied.

Minutes later Elle was once again alone in the cabin and thinking about the conversation she'd just had. Vincent and Valeria might be madly in love, but Elle didn't believe they were anywhere near ready to take in and care for a baby.

They were only nineteen years old. Not only did Elle believe her brother was too young to become a husband, but she definitely believed he wasn't ready to become an instant father to an infant.

There was no question the two were crazy in love with each other, but Elle hoped they didn't plan a wedding until the Groom Killer was caught. The last thing she wanted to do was lose another brother to the murderer.

I know Anders, and when he loves, he loves hard.

Valeria's words echoed inside Elle's head. Somehow she believed that about him. She wondered if he'd loved hard the woman and the child in the picture she'd found.

She thought the answer was yes. That woman had hurt him badly and now he had one-night stands that assured his heart wouldn't ever get involved again. It all made sense.

She remembered the shocking question he'd asked her about one-night stands. Why did he want to know what her opinion was of them?

Did he want to have a one-night stand with her? Her heart stuttered at the thought. Just his kiss had rocked her world; what would it be like to actually make love with him?

She jumped up off the sofa, refusing to entertain such ridiculous thoughts any further. She'd barely made it into the kitchen when Merlin gave his low grunt alert again. She grabbed her gun and opened the door to see her sister, Danica, standing on the porch.

Before Danica could reply, Merlin jumped at her, as if aiming for her arms. Danica laughed and fell to her knees to love on the dog.

Danica had been Merlin's trainer at the Red Ridge K9 Training Center. Her red-blond hair gleamed in the morning sunshine and her green eyes sparkled as she looked up at Elle.

"Hi, sis," she said, still remaining on her knees.

"Hi, yourself," Elle replied. "Are you going to get up and come inside like a normal person?"

Danica laughed again and rose to her feet. "Actually, I'm not going to come in. I was on my way to work and just decided to stop by to see how this guy is getting along." She scratched Merlin behind one ear.

"He's doing great, as you can see," Elle replied.

"This is the first time he's staying with you someplace other than your apartment. Any signs of trauma?"

"None at all. He's an amazing dog."

"How are you holding up? I've heard about the trouble out here."

"I'm doing fine. What about you?"

"Staying busy. I'm working with a new dog out at the training center."

"What kind?" Elle asked curiously.

"Another bulldog." She pulled her phone out of her pocket and checked the time. "And I really need to get going so I'm not late to work."

The two sisters hugged and then Danica left.

For the rest of the afternoon Elle kept herself busy. It had been nice to see both Valeria and Danica, even if just briefly.

It was just after four when Merlin alerted and she heard the back door in the kitchen open and close. She stepped into the kitchen in time to see Anders hang his black cowboy hat on a hook by the door.

He turned and for just a moment his features registered an open pleasure at the sight of her, but then all expression of any emotion left his face.

"How was your day?" she asked. She walked over to the counter where a flick of a button set the coffee to brew. She knew he liked a cup of coffee about this time in the afternoons.

"It was fine. What about yours?" he asked.

"Fairly quiet except both Valeria and Danica stopped by for brief visits."

He walked over to the sink and began to wash his hands. "I'm sorry I missed them. Anything new with Valeria?"

"Not really, but she told me she and Vincent would step in to raise Bonnie." Elle sat at the table.

"That's the most ridiculous thing I've heard today," he replied. He grabbed the hand towel and dried off. "They're just a couple of kids."

"I know that and you know that, but I'm not sure how you get through to a pair of starry-eyed, madly-in-love teenagers."

"I've been trying to talk some sense into Valeria for months." He walked to the cabinet and pulled out two coffee mugs. "I don't have anything against Vincent, but those two shouldn't be planning a wedding right now."

"Nobody in this entire town should be planning a wedding right now," Elle said. "Until we catch the Groom Killer all weddings in this town should be illegal."

He poured the coffee and then brought the mugs to the table. She murmured a thanks, still trying to get a read on his mood.

"Any new news on the case?" he asked.

"Not that I've heard."

There was a tension in the air between them and it emanated from him. His shoulders were bunched and a knot pulsed in his strong jawline.

"Has something happened on the ranch?" she asked.

"No, why?"

"You appeared a bit distracted this morning and you look a little tense now," she replied.

He rolled his magnificent shoulders and drew in a deep breath. "I've just been working through a few things in my head."

"Have I done something to upset you?" she asked.

"No, it has nothing to do with you." His gaze didn't quite meet hers. "Don't worry about it."

But it was difficult not to worry about it as the evening unfolded. They warmed up leftovers from the night before and ate in relative silence.

If she were a really good cop she'd be able to figure out what was bothering him, she thought as she cleared the dishes after dinner.

Whatever it was, it didn't seem to affect the way he interacted with Bonnie. His deep voice now drifted into the kitchen, not quite loud enough that she could hear the actual words he was saying. However, the tone was light and at one point his deep laughter rang out.

He sat in the recliner with Bonnie in his arms. He looked up as Elle entered the room and laughter still lit his eyes. "She just blew a big spit bubble and then smiled," he said.

"Oh, I hate it that I missed her first spit bubble," Elle replied with a laugh. She sank down on the sofa and sobered. "I really hate it that no matter how this turns out I'm going to miss a lot of firsts with her. She's definitely wormed her way into my heart."

"If she's mine, her home will be here and I'll fight for the right to raise her here with me," he replied with a touch of determination.

"If she's yours then I have to confess I'm surprised her mother hasn't shown up yet," Elle replied.

He frowned. "That makes two of us. I can't imagine why any woman I've seen in the past would just leave her baby on the porch. If she was in trouble, I'd help her. I've been expecting somebody to call about Bonnie or return for her each day."

She wanted to ask him about the photo she'd seen, about the beautiful dark-haired woman and the cute baby. But it was really none of her business. She reminded herself she didn't have the right to ask him those kinds of personal questions.

"At least she's sleeping a little bit longer through the nights," she finally said, aware that the tension was back in the room.

It remained, making conversation slightly awkward throughout the rest of the night. She was almost grateful when she gave Bonnie her final bottle of the evening and then tucked her into the cradle for bedtime.

She was about to pick up the cradle and carry it into her bedroom when Anders stopped her. "I'll get that," he said, and hurried to the sofa.

But instead of picking up the cradle he turned back to face her. "Do you really want to know what's been bothering me?" he asked. His eyes glowed bright as he held her gaze.

"Of course," she replied.

He stepped closer to her, so close he invaded her personal space, so close his body heat warmed her. "You," he said, his voice deeper than usual. "You've been bothering me with your sexy smell and wonderful smiles. I'm losing sleep thinking about you and when I dream,

I dream about having you in my bed and making love to you."

Her mouth had gone dry and an inside tremor took possession of her body at his words. "So, wha-what are we going to do about it?" she finally managed to say.

"Let's start with this." He pulled her into his arms, intimately tight against his body, and then his mouth crashed down on hers.

Chapter 7

What are your feelings about one-night stands?

Anders's question played through her head at the same time his lips on hers electrified her.

In the back of her mind she knew she should stop things right now, before they got out of control. But it was so difficult to hang on to that thought with his mouth plying hers with such heat, with his wonderfully muscled body so close against her.

As his tongue sought entry, she opened her mouth to allow him to deepen the kiss. She'd told him she thought a one-night stand would be okay as long as both people were on the same page.

Why stop this feeling? This intense desire she had to be with him? She was pretty certain they were both on the exact same page. Neither of them was looking for a relationship. Still, there was no question that there was a crazy physical attraction going on between them.

As his hands caressed up and down her back, she gave herself permission to stop thinking and just be in the moment, and in the moment she desperately wanted Anders.

She fell into a sensual haze as the kiss continued. Everything else faded away and there was just Anders, driving her crazy with his mouth, with his touch.

His lips slid from hers and trekked down her jaw and to her neck. He nuzzled just behind her ear, and her knees threatened to weaken with the sweet sensations that swept through her.

He finally released her and took a step backward. He then held out his hand to her, his eyes blazing with his desire.

She could stop this right now. If she didn't take his hand, then it would all be over right here and right now with nothing else happening between them. That would the best thing…the smart thing to do.

She leaned over and looked at the still-sleeping Bonnie and then she reached out and placed her hand in his. For the first time in her life she didn't want to do the smart thing. She desperately wanted Anders.

He led her into his bedroom and kissed her once again as they stood at the foot of his bed. The man definitely knew how to kiss. His lips demanded a response from her and she couldn't deny him. Their tongues swirled together in a dance of hot desire.

His hands caressed down her back and he gently grabbed her buttocks and pulled her more intimately against him. He was aroused and the fact that she could get that kind of response from him heightened her pleasure. When he released her again she was half-breathless.

"I want you so much, Elle," he said. "It's all I've been able to think about since the night you came here."

His naked hunger for her stirred her like nothing else ever had in her life. On unsteady legs she walked to the head of the bed, where she set her gun on the nightstand. She then pulled her T-shirt over her head not only to let him know, but to confirm to herself that she was ready to make love with him, that this was really going to happen.

He immediately pulled his T-shirt off, exposing his magnificently muscled and bronzed chest. And then they were on the bed, kissing with an intensity that spun her senses.

His hands went around her back, where he unfastened her bra. It fell away from her and then his mouth left hers and instead he licked one of her erect nipples.

She gripped his shoulders as he continued to love first one nipple and then the other. The sensations shot a flame straight through the center of her, leaving her gasping with pleasure.

But the pleasure didn't stop there. He pulled her sweatpants off and then took off his jeans, leaving her in a pair of silk panties and him in a pair of black boxers.

The faint light drifting in from the living room seemed to love each muscle and every angle on his body. He was truly a beautiful man.

When he pulled her back into his arms, she savored the skin-on-skin contact. His was so warm and smelled of his woodsy cologne. As they kissed once again their legs tangled together, hers sleek and slender and his long and strong.

He rolled her over on her back and as his hand caressed down her belly she tensed. His fingers slowly slid across the silk of her panties. Instantly the cool of the silk warmed with his intimate touch.

"You are so beautiful, Elle," he whispered into her ear.

She was about to reply, but then his fingers found the very center of her and she moaned. Oh yes, she wanted him there. She suddenly needed the kind of release she believed only he could give to her.

She arched her hips and he whisked away her panties. And when he touched her again it took only seconds before the waves of pleasure washed over her, leaving her gasping and half crying with her climax.

He rolled away from her and reached into the top drawer of the nightstand. When he turned back to her he was fully erect and wearing a condom.

Despite the thin latex covering, she stroked him, loving his sharp intake of breath at her touch. He gasped with obvious pleasure as she continued to caress him.

She kissed his neck and then down his taut stomach, loving the taste of him.

"Elle." Her name fell from his lips on a half-strangled groan.

She looked up at him. All his features were taut and his eyes glowed like a wild animal in the dark.

He shoved her hand away from him and instead moved between her thighs. He hovered there for a long moment, his gaze locked with hers.

Her entire body quivered with anticipation as he slowly eased into her. She closed her eyes, filled with him in every way. His scent invaded her head, and the sound of him whispering her name over and over again was like sweet music.

He moved his hips against hers, slowly at first and then faster and more frantic. She dug her fingers into his shoulders as the pleasure became so intense she could scarcely catch her breath.

Then the waves of a second climax crashed through her and at the same time he stiffened against her and moaned deep in his throat.

They remained locked together for several long moments. She could feel his heartbeat against hers, racing and then slowing to a more normal rhythm.

He finally rolled off her and to his back. When his breathing had evened out, he propped himself up on his elbow facing her.

He stroked a strand of her hair away from her face and then took her lips in a gentle, tender kiss that moved her far more than what they'd just experienced together.

When the kiss ended she sat up and reached down for her T-shirt on the floor. Now that it was over the need to escape him was strong.

"Don't go," he protested softly as she pulled the T-shirt over her head. "Elle, stay here with me. Sleep with me."

"No, I need to take Bonnie and go back to my room," she replied without looking at him. She was afraid that if she saw a soft appeal on his face she might relent and stay. She moved her feet to the floor and grabbed her sweatpants.

"Bonnie can sleep in here with us." He sat up and reached over to the bedside lamp. He turned it on, creating a small, intimate glow in the room.

"But I can't." She pulled her sweatpants on and stood. "I'll just see you in the morning." She picked up the rest of her clothing and her gun.

Oh, she wanted to stay. She desperately wanted to snuggle down in his sheets and cuddle against him as they fell asleep. She would love waking up in his arms in the morning. She would love to stay with him and that frightened her, and that's why she wouldn't…that's why she couldn't.

Merlin lay on the threshold of the room. It was as if he was keeping one eye on her and his other eye on the baby in the living room.

He got up as she approached and together they padded into the living room, where she picked up the cradle and then went into her bedroom.

She kept her mind blissfully blank as she took a quick shower. She needed to wash off the pleasant smell of him and the memory of his touch.

It was only when she was in bed that she allowed herself to think about the lovemaking they'd just shared. It had been more than wonderful and so intense that he'd taken her breath away over and over again.

But she couldn't let it mean anything. It was a one-night stand and nothing more. And she seriously doubted that it meant anything to him. He was accustomed to this kind of thing. He was used to making love with a woman and then walking away from her without any emotional ties.

Had he found her wanting? A bit boring like Frank Benson had apparently found her? This thought sent a wave of depression over her. Why could she never be enough?

Tomorrow she'd contact Finn and see how much longer she would be on this duty. Things had been quiet and there was no guarantee any real danger was imminent. She couldn't stay here forever playing house with Anders and Bonnie.

She was surprised that this thought sent another wave

of depression through her. She moved to the edge of the bed and dangled her arm over the side. Her hand was met with Merlin's warm fur and he snorted his pleasure as she worked her fingers across his back.

At least she was always enough for Merlin. He loved her unconditionally, and right now in her life that was all she needed or wanted.

She must have fallen asleep, for she awakened to Merlin's alert. She was instantly filled with adrenaline as she grabbed her gun and jumped out of bed.

Merlin led the way out of her doorway and into the darkened living room. He sat at the front door and alerted once again. Somebody was outside. It was the middle of the night. There was no reason for anyone to be lurking outside in the darkness of the night.

She gripped her gun firmly in her hand as her heart beat a wild rhythm of uncertainty. With the other hand she unlocked the door and then gripped the doorknob.

Drawing a deep breath, she flung open the door, thankful that her eyes were already adjusted to the darkness. She quickly scanned the area and tensed as she spied a figure standing beneath a nearby tree.

"Who's there?" she called out.

The figure remained nearly hidden in the dark shadows.

"This is Officer Gage of the Red Ridge K9 unit. Step forward and identify yourself." She waited a minute but the figure still didn't move. "You'd better step forward and identify yourself right now or I'll set my dog on you."

Merlin was next to her, his sturdy body poised for action. "What's going on?" Anders voice spoke softly from just behind her.

"I'm giving you to the count of three," she yelled out, ignoring Anders's question. It was the question of a man roused from sleep and the answer was self-evident.

"One…" she said.

"No, don't. I don't want your dog to come after me," the man said. He took a step forward but was still shrouded in darkness too great for a visual identification. His words were followed by an incoherent noise that sounded like crying.

What in the heck, she thought. The noise got louder as he took another couple of steps forward.

"Seth Richardson, is that you?" she asked. What on earth was the man doing out here in the middle of the night?

"Don't let your dog bite me. I just wanted to talk to Anders," he said. His voice was slurred and it was obvious he was drunk and blubbering. "I want my job back. I need to get my job back, Anders. Please," the man cried. Elle lowered her gun with a sigh of disgust.

"Go home, Seth," Anders called out. "It's the middle of the night and you're drunk."

"I had a few drinks, I won't lie. I… I needed some liquid courage to come out here and beg you for my job." The words were half-garbled and said between deep, wrenching sobs. "Please man, I'm begging you. I need my job back."

"Go home, Seth," Anders repeated with a firm tone. "You don't belong on this property anymore."

"What about my job?" Seth asked, and then blubbered some more.

The sigh Anders released warmed Elle's back. "Okay, meet me at the barn tomorrow about ten and we'll talk. Come sober or there will be no discussion."

"Thank you, man," Seth replied. "Thank you so much. I'll be there. I swear I'll be there."

"Don't thank me yet," Anders warned. "Now get out of here. You've disturbed our sleep."

"I'm sorry," he replied. "I'll leave you be and talk to you tomorrow."

Elle remained on the front porch until Seth disappeared from sight. It was only when she sensed Merlin relaxing that she did the same.

"Nothing like being disturbed in the middle of the night by a man who is drunk as a skunk," Anders said as she closed and locked the front door.

"What time is it?" she asked.

"Just after two."

"Bonnie should be waking up any time for a bottle. I think I'll go ahead and get one ready for her."

Anders followed her into the kitchen and sat down at the table. She felt his steady gaze on her as she fixed the bottle. "You knew he was out there because Merlin alerted?" he asked.

She nodded and put the bottle in the microwave to warm it.

"Good boy, Merlin," he said. Merlin walked over to him and eyed him expectantly. Anders laughed and scratched the dog first behind one ear and then behind the other.

This middle-of-the-night scene was far too intimate, far too familial for her. Him in his boxers and petting her dog while she was in her nightie and making a baby bottle, the whole thing made her want to run and hide.

Because she liked it. She liked it way too much. It was a glimpse into a fantasy that until now she hadn't realized she'd entertained. It was definitely a fantasy that had no basis in reality.

She grabbed the bottle from the microwave. "Come on, Merlin. The excitement is over for the night." She looked at Anders. "And I'll just say good night once again."

She didn't wait for a reply as she quickly exited. Her timing was perfect, for at that moment Bonnie began to cry.

Anders sat in his office in the barn waiting for Seth to arrive, but his head was filled with thoughts of Elle. She was like no other woman he'd ever known before.

She hadn't wanted to cuddle after making love and that morning she hadn't said anything about what they shared the night before.

Most of the women he'd been with in the past had clung to him both after sex and again the next morning. They'd wanted him to tell them how awesome he thought they were, how great the sex had been between them.

Elle had wanted none of that and it confused him. She had been an amazing partner and her silence about the whole thing made him wonder if she hadn't found him so amazing.

During breakfast she'd acted like nothing had changed between them. It was as if she'd already forgotten about their lovemaking.

But things had changed. He now knew where to touch her to make her moan with pleasure. He now knew that nuzzling her just behind her ear drove her half-crazy. Yes, no matter how much she wanted to pretend nothing was different between them, she was wrong.

What surprised him more than anything was the tenderness he felt toward her, a strange tenderness that had no place in a one-night stand and had lingered through a quiet and slightly uncomfortable breakfast.

What was happening to him? He'd thought that all he'd felt for Elle was a good dose of lust and once he had her, it would be over. But it wasn't over. He still wanted her.

He, the confirmed bachelor who always had his relationships his way, was suddenly off-balance because of a woman who delighted him, enchanted him and intrigued him more than any woman ever had.

What was even worse was that he didn't just want her again in bed. He wanted her all day long, in and out of the sheets. She had not only gotten into his bed…she was slowly worming her way into the very center of his heart. And somehow he had to stop it.

He closed his eyes for a moment and thought about how she'd looked the night before standing on the front porch clad only in a midnight-blue silky nightgown and holding a gun. She'd looked so sexy and strong and he found it ridiculously charming that the sober-eyed police officer slept in silk. He opened his eyes with a sigh.

Any further thoughts he might have entertained were interrupted by Seth appearing in his office doorway. The man held his battered cowboy hat in his hands and looked down at the floor in what appeared to be genuine contrition.

"Seth, come in and take a seat." Anders gestured him to the folding chair in front of his desk.

"First off, I gotta say that I'm sorry about all the bother last night," Seth said, still not meeting Anders's gaze. "I should have never shown up at your place in the middle of the night. I know you've given me a lot of chances and I've screwed up each time, but I'm begging you to please give me one more chance."

He finally looked up and in his eyes was a quiet desperation. When Seth was sober he was one of the best workers Anders had. Unfortunately, he wasn't sober as often as he was drunk.

"I've been working here for a long time. I don't want to work at another place," he said. "I liked working for you. You're a fair boss."

"You have a problem, Seth, and I can't have somebody working for me who is drinking on the job. That not only makes you a danger to yourself, but also a danger to all my other men."

"I know, but I swear I'm going to get help. When I woke up this morning the first thing I did was call Lester Banks. You know he runs those meetings in the basement of the Baptist church. I'm going to start attending them and he's agreed to sponsor me."

Anders reared back in his chair and studied Seth. He'd always believed in giving people a do-over, but Seth had had more than his share already. But the difference this time was the man had actually reached out for help on his own.

"You're a good, hard worker when you're sober and present," Anders said.

"Then give me another chance, boss. I swear I won't mess up again." Once again the desperation was in Seth's eyes.

"And you're really going to go to the meetings and clean yourself up? It can't just be about the job. You've really got to want it, Seth."

"I do want it. To tell you the truth I'm tired of drinking. I'm sick and tired of waking up with little or no memory of what happened the night before. I'm sick and tired of being sick and tired all the time. I'm fifty-two years old and I have nothing to show for my time on earth except a bunch of empty beer bottles."

There was a real passion behind his words. "I got stupid drunk last night and that's the truth," he continued, "but losing my job here was rock bottom for me. I want to get sober once and for all."

"I believe you can do it, Seth." Anders released a deep sigh. "Okay, I'll give you one more chance. You can move back into your room in the bunk barn, but if I catch you drinking on the job or if one of the men tells me you are, then you're out of here for good."

Seth jumped out of his chair as if eager to leave before Anders could change his mind. "I can't thank you enough," he said.

"You don't have to thank me. Just get sober."

Minutes later Anders remained at his desk, thinking about the decision he'd just made. He truly hoped Seth would succeed, that he'd fight whatever inner demons he might possess. But Anders couldn't do it for him. Seth had to believe in himself and recognize that he deserved better in his life.

His thoughts once again filled with Elle. She couldn't stay at his place forever. Nothing had happened for almost a week and he was sure Finn could better use her on the Groom Killer case instead of basically babysitting for him.

Of course he supposed it was possible Finn wanted to keep her at the cabin on the off chance that Demi would show up. If the baby was hers, then it was reasonable that she might return for the little girl.

He had no idea who had broken into his cabin and

searched it. He also had no idea what they'd wanted and if they'd gotten what they'd been looking for. But everything had been quiet since the break-in and there was really no reason to believe the person would be back or that he or Bonnie might be in any danger.

When Elle left he wasn't sure what would happen with Bonnie. Anders couldn't run a ranch and take care of her at the same time. But with the possibility of her being his, he wasn't just going to hand her over to social services. He'd hire a nanny or do whatever necessary to keep her with him.

When Elle left…the words thundered in his brain. He was surprised to realize just how much he'd hate to see her go. She'd brightened the cabin with her smiles. Hell, she brightened him with her smiles.

She not only was beautiful, but she challenged him with her intelligence. She and Bonnie smoothed out the rough edges inside him and brought laughter to his lips. Hell, he even liked Elle's dog.

Happy. He was also surprised to realize he was happy with them in his space. He hadn't thought about happiness in a long time, not since Rosalie and Brooke had ripped his heart out. This all felt like history was repeating itself.

He got up from his desk. He refused to allow that to happen. He refused to put his heart on a platter for another woman to slice into pieces.

What he needed right now was to climb on the back of his horse and take a long ride. He wanted the wind to blow out any longing he had for the woman and any affection he had for the baby; they were really nothing more than temporary houseguests.

He rode for almost two hours, stopping occasionally

to talk to his men when he came upon them. The downed fencing was once again up and in place and the herd of cattle all looked healthy.

He then returned to his barn office once again where he sat at the desk and did the payroll and ordered supplies. It was after three when he finally headed back to the cabin.

Before he even opened the back door he heard Elle's laughter. It instantly warmed his heart.

"What's going on in here?" he asked as he stepped inside. Bonnie was in her cradle in the middle of the table. Elle looked at him with her laughter still warming her beautiful brown eyes.

"Watch…" she said. She leaned over the table so she had Bonnie's full attention. "Hi, Bonnie baby," she said in a slightly higher-pitched voice. "Hi, sweet baby."

Bonnie's lips curled up into a smile and she waved her arms up and down as if in great excitement. Elle paused and Bonnie's smile faded.

"Hi, Bonnie," Elle said again in the same slightly exaggerated voice. And once again Bonnie grinned and her arms pumped. Anders found himself smiling.

"Let me try," he said. As Elle stepped back from the table Bonnie's smile once again disappeared. Anders leaned over and made eye contact with the little girl.

"Hi, Bonnie," he said. No smile curved her rosebud lips. Instead she continued to eye him soberly, a tiny frown in the center of her forehead. "Hi, baby girl." Still no smile.

"You're doing man talk," Elle said. "You have to do baby talk."

"Baby talk?"

"Act excited and raise the tone of your voice," Elle instructed.

"Hi, Bonnie," he tried again, doing what Elle had said. "I feel totally silly talking to you this way." Bonnie smiled and waved her arms and he and Elle laughed together in delight.

He looked at Elle and white-hot desire shot through his heart, through his very soul. It wasn't just the desire to kiss her or make love to her again. It was far more complicated than that and it was at that moment he knew that despite his wish to hang on to his heart, it was already too late. He was in love with Officer Elle Gage.

Chapter 8

Thunder rolled and rain pelted the windows. Elle studied the chessboard in concentration. It had been raining all day, keeping Anders inside. After breakfast he'd pulled out the chessboard and at the moment they were in a hot competition. He'd won the first game and she'd won the second. This was the playoff to determine the house chess champion.

"Who taught you how to play?" he asked her.

"Bo taught me some and then in high school I joined the chess club," she replied.

"I'll bet you were cute in high school," he said. "I can just see you strutting the halls with your backpack in a short skirt and your chess club sweater."

She gave him a baleful look. "I didn't have a chess club sweater and stop trying to distract me. It's not going to work. I intend to beat your butt."

He laughed and then leaned back in his chair. "Do you intend to make your next move anytime soon?"

"Great moves take time," she replied. The truth of the matter was even if he didn't talk to her she found him ridiculously distracting.

His scent wafted in the air and she wasn't oblivious to the way his gaze lingered on her a little too long. Thunder once again boomed overhead and she finally made her move.

"Ha, not such a great move," he said as his bishop took her queen.

"A truly great move," she replied. She moved her castle. "I believe that's checkmate."

He stared at the board in obvious astonishment. "Well, I'll be damned," he exclaimed.

"I believe that makes me the chess champion of the cabin," she said. "And I also believe that puts you on diaper duty for the rest of the day." She leaned back in her chair and grinned at him.

He chuckled once again and stood. "But you're still on lunch duty and I'm starving."

She got up from the table and began to pull cold cuts out of the refrigerator while he put the chessboard and pieces away.

Minutes later they sat at the table with ham-and-cheese sandwiches and chips. "If it stops raining later this afternoon, what do you think about the three of us going into town for dinner?" he asked.

The idea of getting dressed up and going out for a nice meal was appealing. Too appealing. It would feel like a date. It would feel like a family having a night out. And she wasn't dating Anders, nor was she part of his family. She was here working on a case.

"I really don't think that's a good idea," she replied. "I don't want to leave the cabin. We don't know if whoever was in here before might not come back."

He looked disappointed. "I guess you're right. I just thought it would be nice to get out of these four walls for a little while. Oh well, I'll just have to make a really special dinner here tonight."

"Anything is fine for dinner," she replied. "You don't have to go to any trouble on my account." She looked out the window and sighed. "I really hate rainy days."

"Why?"

"I just do." She wasn't about to confess to him that it had been raining on the day Frank had told her he didn't love her. She remembered running out of his house, so broken, and it was as if the skies wept with her. Since then rain always reminded her of sadness.

"The rain is a good thing when you're working on a ranch. It makes everything grow and get green. It's life. We could always go out dancing in the rain," he said with a twinkle in his eyes.

She laughed. "No way, not with all that lightning out there. It isn't safe for man or beast."

"Do you play poker?" he asked.

"I know the game." She got up from the table to carry her empty dish to the sink. "Why?"

"I thought maybe we could play some cards to pass a rainy afternoon."

"Ha, you're just looking for something you can beat me at," she teased.

Merlin jumped to his feet and alerted. Elle grabbed her gun off the counter and turned toward the back door where a man in a rain slicker and a cowboy hat pulled low on his forehead stood just outside.

"I got it," Anders said. He opened the door and motioned the man inside. "Sam, what's going on?"

"That big old tree in the east pasture got hit by lightning. We lost about ten head of cattle to the strike. The rain has let up so the tree is going to continue to burn and the lightning strikes are still pretty intense. We thought you'd want us to move the cattle into the north pasture where there are fewer trees."

"Go ahead and get started and I'll be out there to help as soon as possible." Anders closed the door and headed for the coat closet, where he pulled out a long rain slicker and put it on.

"I hate the idea of you being out in this," Elle said as he strode back to the door and pulled his hat from the hook. She looked at him worriedly.

"This is what I do, Elle." He shoved his hat low on his brow and then he was gone.

The thunder continued to shake the cabin and the lightning slashed the darkened skies. At one particularly loud boom Bonnie awakened, crying.

Elle quickly picked her up in her arms and murmured soothing words. For the next hour Elle was on pins and needles as she drifted from window to window, hoping to see Anders's return.

She hated to think of him on horseback, a target for an errant lightning strike. *This is what I do, Elle.* His words played and replayed in her mind.

A rancher's life wasn't all riding the range under sunny skies. He had to face all of nature's elements and unpredictable animals, and a ton of other difficult situations. But he loved what he did. Just as she loved what she did, a job that could be dangerous at times.

She sat down with Bonnie in her arms and Merlin at her feet and turned on the television to catch a weather update. Thankfully there was no tornado warning splashed across the screen. She then put Bonnie on the blanket in the middle of the living room floor.

She didn't relax until Anders walked back in the house two hours later. The brunt of the storm had moved away, leaving behind a gentle rain that was forecast to fall for another hour or so.

His features were drawn and he looked completely exhausted. She helped him off with his rain slicker and then ordered him to the bathroom for a hot shower.

Minutes later he walked back into the kitchen, smelling like minty soap and with his hair still damp. "Did you get the cattle all moved?" she asked.

"We did, and the men are taking care of the dead." He released a weary sigh.

"Go sit in your recliner and I'll bring you a cup of coffee," she said. "And I've got dinner duty tonight."

He cast her a weary smile. "Should I be afraid?"

"Maybe a little. Now go and relax," she replied. As he left for the living room she hurried to the refrigerator to see what kind of meat he'd pulled out of the freezer that morning for dinner. Chicken breasts. Surely she could handle that.

She moved over to make the coffee and when it was finished she poured him a cup and then carried it into the living room. She took two steps into the room and then stopped, her heart expanding in her chest.

Anders was reared back in the recliner and sound asleep. Bonnie slept on his chest, her little body rising and falling with each breath he took. She wished she had her cell phone in hand so that she could take a picture of them, but she knew no simple phone photo could capture the utter beauty of man and child.

She silently backed out of the room. She sat at the kitchen table and drank the coffee she'd poured for him. She couldn't get the vision out of her head.

If Bonnie was his, then Elle had no concerns about the kind of parent Anders would be. Bonnie would never have a minute of feeling unloved.

Would some woman he'd had a relationship with in the past suddenly show up on the doorstep? Would she thank him for watching Bonnie for a few days and then take the baby and leave?

She had a feeling Anders had no idea how all in he was in loving Bonnie, and she feared his heartbreak if she was taken away from him.

Anders didn't know how long he slept, but he awakened to the scent of chicken in the air and Bonnie beginning to fuss in his lap.

He righted his position in the chair and as her fussing got louder Elle appeared with a bottle in hand. "Oh, I was hoping to get her before she woke you."

"It's fine. How long have I been asleep?"

"About an hour." She sat on the sofa and fed Bonnie the bottle.

"Is that dinner I smell?"

"It is," she said with a proud look on her face. "It's a spicy chicken breast with spicy rice on the side."

"Hmm, sounds good. Is there anything I need to do to help?"

"No, I've got this." She gazed at him with her sober expression. "Sorry about your cows."

"Yeah, me, too. But it is what it is. We always lose

some cattle. Coyotes or wolves get them or they get sick. It's part of ranch life."

"I was thinking the other day that someday I wouldn't mind living in a place like this. It's so nice and peaceful and no matter where you look that landscape is beautiful."

"That's why I wanted to live out here instead of a wing at the house. I'm a simple man and I live a fairly simple life here."

"Don't you ever get lonely?" she asked.

He thought about the question before answering. It was impossible to think of loneliness when Elle and Bonnie filled the cabin with such life. "I guess there were times I'd get a little lonely, but all I have to do is drive up the way and visit with my parents or Valeria." He eyed her curiously. "What about you? Do you ever get lonely?"

She took the bottle from Bonnie's mouth and lifted her up to her shoulder. "Maybe occasionally." She gave the bottle back to Bonnie. "But that doesn't mean I want somebody in my life right now. With the Groom Killer still out there somewhere and the Larson twins running their illegal rackets, all I'm focused on is working."

He wasn't sure why, but her words depressed him just a little bit. "How long until dinner?" he asked.

"Probably another twenty minutes or so."

"I'm going to do a little work until then." He moved out of the recliner and into the chair at his desk. The dreariness of the rain had cast the cabin in an unusual darkness for this time of the year. He turned on his desk lamp and punched on his computer.

He needed to make notes about the storm and the loss of the cattle, but it was hard to concentrate with Elle sweet-talking Bonnie and with Elle's evocative scent eddying in the air.

He was almost grateful when she took Bonnie and went back into the kitchen. Fifteen minutes later she appeared in the doorway. "Dinner is ready," she announced.

"Good, I'm starving." He got up from the desk and entered the kitchen where the table was set. A red chicken breast sat on his plate, along with red rice and corn.

He sat and she did as well. "It looks...interesting," he said.

"I just hope it tastes okay." She didn't pick up her fork to begin eating but rather watched him intently.

He cut into the chicken breast, pleased that it appeared to be cooked perfectly, although it looked like she had gone overboard with the paprika.

He took a bite and instantly his mouth filled with the fires of hell. Cayenne pepper...not paprika. He chewed despite the fact that his eyes threatened to water and his throat was tightening with the need to cough. As he swallowed he reached for his water glass and chased the bite with a large swig.

"How is it?" she asked. She held his gaze steadily.

"It's definitely spicy."

She frowned and cut herself a bite. She popped it into her mouth. Her eyes widened and her cheeks reddened. She reached for her water glass. "Holy hell," she exclaimed after she'd taken a drink. "I didn't know that pepper would be hot."

"It's not that bad," he protested.

"It's awful," she said miserably. "I just wanted to make the chicken tasty, but it's not edible." Her eyes grew glassy and she jumped up out of the chair and carried her plate to the counter. She stood for a moment with her back to him.

"Elle," he said softly. "It's just dinner."

She turned around and marched over to him and grabbed his plate. "You can't eat this." She carried it to the sink and once again remained standing with her back to him.

He got up from his chair and walked over to her. "Elle, it's not a big deal. Don't be upset."

She turned around slowly and her eyes held the sheen of unshed tears. "I hate cooking."

He laughed and pulled her into his arms. "I don't care if you ever cook again."

"But what are you going to eat for dinner?" she asked, and to his dismay quickly stepped back from his embrace.

"I've got a frozen pizza in the freezer that will be ready in about twenty minutes. I don't want you to fret about this. If you'll smile for me I'll give you an A for effort."

The corner of her lips moved upward.

"You can do better than that," he teased. "Come on, give me one of those Elle smiles that light up a whole room."

"You're silly," she said.

"I'll show you silly." He reached out and grabbed her by the arm. "I'm going to tickle you until you're silly." He tickled her ribs and was delighted when she squealed with laughter.

She ran into the living room to escape him, but he chased after her. He grabbed her and wrestled her to the ground where he sat on top of her and continued to tickle her.

"Stop," she protested breathlessly. "Please…you have to stop."

She looked so beautiful with her cheeks pink and her eyes sparkling with laughter. He so wanted to kiss her. He stared down at her and her smile slid away. "Anders, go put the pizza in the oven," she said.

Reluctantly he got off her and helped her up from the floor. "At least I now know one of your weaknesses," he said. "You are wonderfully ticklish."

"And if you tell another soul, I'll have to shoot you," she replied with humor still lighting her eyes. "Now, you put the pizza in and I'll clean up the chicken mess."

A half an hour later they sat at the table sharing the pizza and talking about inconsequential things. He discovered her favorite color was purple and she hated horror movies. She loved cold pizza in the morning and going barefoot.

He felt as if he could have a hundred…a thousand more dinners with her and not know everything there was to know about Elle Gage.

After dinner they turned on a movie and she entertained Bonnie while he played a game of tug-of-war with Merlin and a length of rope with a small ball on either end.

Before he knew it the day was over and it was time to go to bed. For the first time in a very long time he was reluctant to end the day.

Despite the lightning strike, the dead cattle and the red chicken, it had been a good day. Every day with Elle and Bonnie in the cabin was a good day.

And sooner or later it was all going to come to an end.

Chapter 9

The next evening Elle and Anders sat at the table eating the meat loaf, mashed potatoes and corn he'd prepared while catching up on each other's days. He'd worked later today than usual and had immediately gotten busy cooking so they'd scarcely had time to talk before now.

"Seth has gotten through the last two days working hard without a hint of alcohol," he said.

"He should be so grateful to you. It was darned good of you to give him another chance," she said. It had oddly touched her heart when he'd come home after the morning meeting with Seth and told her he'd rehired the man.

"I just hope he can toe the line and build something healthy and good in his life," Anders replied.

"That would be nice. On another note, I got some news about Demi today," she replied, and pushed her now-empty plate aside. "When I called this morning to check in with Finn he told me Demi had texted her brother Brayden from a burner phone."

Anders looked at her with interest. "I hope she said she left her baby with me."

"Unfortunately, no. She didn't mention the baby at all. She told Brayden to get Lucas off her back. I guess Lucas is trying to track her, and if anyone can, it's her biggest local rival in the bounty hunter business. She again said that she was innocent and getting closer to unmasking the real killer."

"Well, that worries me," Anders replied. "I hate to think of her being anywhere close to such a vicious killer."

"If she thinks her text is going to get Lucas off her back, then she doesn't know my brother very well," she said ruefully. "That will only light a new fire in Lucas to find her and bring her in."

"What a mess. It feels like this killer is keeping the whole town hostage." He got up and carried their plates to the sink.

"We'll get the killer. It's just a matter of time before it happens," she said with confidence.

"Hopefully it's before any more men are murdered." He returned to the table.

"It would have been nice if Demi had mentioned the baby—given an idea whether or not Bonnie is hers. I did ask Carson to ask Brayden to text her back and ask for a photo of her baby. If she has one and texts it to us, then we can see if it's Bonnie or not."

"I have to confess, I've gotten a little attached to her," he admitted.

"I know." Elle smiled at him.

He looked at her in surprise. "How do you know?"

"I see the way you look at her and the way you talk to her. I know you told me that you didn't intend to care about her. Does that have something to do with another woman and baby?" She held her breath, knowing she was pushing into personal territory, but too curious not to ask.

"What are you talking about?" He asked the question slowly...cautiously.

"When I was picking up the living room floor the night of the break-in, I saw a photograph of you and a woman and a baby."

"Oh, that." His eyes appeared to darken and he leaned back in his chair.

"You don't have to talk about it if you don't want to," she said quickly.

"No, it's fine. It was a long time ago." He stood abruptly. "Let's go sit in the living room where we'll be more comfortable."

She followed him into the room where instead of sinking down in the recliner, he sat on the sofa next to Bonnie. She sat in the recliner, wondering what can of worms her question might have opened.

"The woman in the photo is a woman I dated for a while. Her name is Rosalie. We dated for about six months and then she broke it off." Once again he didn't make eye contact with Elle, but rather looked down at Bonnie.

"Were you in love with her?" Elle asked softly.

He cocked his head and stared just over her shoulder as if in deep thought. "I think maybe I could have been in love with her if there had been more time, although she could be impulsive and insanely jealous. She also liked to play mind games, and when it comes to relationships, I'm not a game player. We were working on things, but then she broke it off. In any case, one night a little over a year later she showed up on my doorstep with a baby she told me was mine."

He released a sigh. "She told me she wanted to try to make it work between us for the baby's sake. So she moved in. And that's when I really fell in love." He finally looked at Elle once again. "Not with Rosalie, but with Brooke, the baby."

He shook his head and his lips curved up in a smile. "Brooke was a couple months old and not only entertaining, but also a little charmer." His smile faded. "I never knew I could love that way…so incredibly deeply."

"What happened?" He looked so vulnerable at the moment. Oh God, had they been killed in a car accident? Had some tragedy happened that had taken them away from him? Her heart ached with the pain that glimmered in the very depths of his eyes.

"They'd been here about three weeks when Rosalie confessed to me that she wasn't here to try to make things work between us. She'd just needed a place to stay because she and her boyfriend had had a big fight and she wanted some time away from him. And that's when she also told me she'd lied about Brooke, that she wasn't mine. The boyfriend was Brooke's father. She walked out that day two years ago and I haven't seen or heard from her since."

"Oh Anders, what a horrible, wicked thing for her to do. I'm so sorry." She wanted to run to him, to hold him and somehow take away his pain. Her heart broke for him and what he'd been through.

He shrugged. "It's over and done, but going through something like that changes who you are at your very core." He gazed down at Bonnie. "It's why I can't give this little one my heart. If she isn't mine she's just going to be snatched away from me like Brooke."

There was a very real possibility that Bonnie wasn't his, that she did belong to Demi and Bo. There was also a wild, crazy possibility that she didn't belong to Anders or Demi, but then who else's would she be? She was so torn. On the one hand she hoped Bonnie was Anders's daughter, but on the other hand she wanted the baby to be Bo's, a part of him that would continue after his death.

"So you will never love anyone again? Is that really the answer?" she finally asked him.

He looked back at her. "I don't know what the answer is. All I really know is that I never want to hurt like that again." He cleared his throat. "So now you know the skeleton in my closet. Do you have any in yours?"

She was about to tell him no, but he'd shared a piece of his painful past with her; wasn't it only fair that she open up to him?

"My skeleton is a lot more common than yours," she began. She tried to ignore the tight press of emotions that suddenly filled her chest. It was grief, combined with an anger she'd never allowed herself to feel before.

"I was dating a man named Frank. We dated for about seven months or so and I thought everything was going wonderfully well." She cast her gaze to the wall just over Anders's head as memories cascaded through her mind.

She'd been so happy, so sure of Frank's love for her. She'd given everything she had to the relationship and his betrayal had changed her forever. She'd never be that young, naive woman again.

"And things weren't going wonderfully well?"

Anders's deep voice jerked her out of her memories and into the present.

"He sat me down one night and I was certain he was about to propose to me." The emotion once again filled her chest. "I was ready to be his wife and to have his children. But instead of a proposal, he told me he'd been cheating on me the whole time with another woman and he was in love with her."

She stared at Anders for a long moment and then to her horror she burst into tears.

"Hey, hey," Anders said. He jumped up off the sofa and walked over to her. He took her hand and pulled her off the chair and into his arms.

She was mortified that she was crying in front of Anders…that she was showing any kind of a weakness in front of a Colton. But she was unable to control the deep sobs that choked out of her.

"It's all right," he said as his hands caressed up and down her back. "Let it all out."

She buried her face in the front of his shirt and wept the tears she hadn't released at the time her heartache had happened.

The funny thing was she wasn't crying over the loss of Frank. Rather she cried over the loss of herself. Somehow she had allowed him to steal away all of her self-confidence. He'd taken pieces of her that she could never get back…her innocence and her belief in herself.

"I'm so sorry," she gasped as the tears began to abate. She tried to step back from him, but he held her tight.

"Don't apologize," he said. He kissed her tenderly on the cheek. "He obviously hurt you badly."

The tears finally stopped but she remained in his arms. His heart beat strong and steady against hers, calming her after the unexpected storm of emotions that had gripped her. All that was left inside her was embarrassment and humiliation.

"Are you still in love with him?" His soft question jerked her back from him and she couldn't help a bubble of laughter that escaped her lips.

"Goodness, no," she replied. "I stopped loving that jerk the night I discovered he was nothing but a two-timing cheat who played with my emotions."

"Then why all the tears?" he asked curiously.

She hesitated a moment, wondering if she could make him understand. "I was crying because it reminded me that I'm never enough. I wasn't enough to get attention from my parents when I was younger, and I wasn't enough for Frank. I'm not enough for my brothers to trust that I can do my job competently. Let me tell you, all of this definitely chips away at a girl's self-confidence."

Tears began falling once again and she angrily swiped at them, but apparently she wasn't finished with them yet as they chased faster and faster down her cheeks.

Once again Anders pulled her back into his arms. "I don't know why I can't stop crying," she said into his chest. "I feel like such a fool. I don't ever cry."

"It's all right. Just let it all out." Once again his hands caressed her back in slow, soothing strokes. "I just want to let you know that you're more than enough for Bonnie and you're more than enough for me."

His words did nothing to help. Bonnie was just a baby and anyone with a bottle and clean diapers would be enough for her. And in the case of Anders, she was just a woman helping care take for Bonnie. It was easy to be enough if you were only a one-night stand.

Slowly the tears dried up and she became aware of the clean scent of his T-shirt, the smell of fabric softener combined with a hint of his cologne.

His strokes up and down her back became more languid and instead of comforting her, they stoked a flame deep inside her. She finally looked up at him and he captured her lips with his.

The kiss was soft and tender, but tasted of his hungry desire. It moved her in a way that was frightening, but that wasn't enough for her to stop it.

As the tip of his tongue sought entry, she opened her mouth to him and the kiss deepened. His hands moved beneath her T-shirt, warming her back each place he touched.

His lips left hers to trail a blaze down her neck. *Don't be a fool*, a little voice whispered inside her brain where there was still a modicum of rational thought left. *Don't go there again.* She pushed against him, grateful that he immediately dropped his arms from around her.

"Elle, I want you again." His deep voice washed over her and increased the fire that wanted to be set free inside her.

"We can't, Anders." It would be so easy to go into his bedroom and let passion sweep away all remnants of her temporary breakdown.

"Why not?" His dark eyes held his hunger for her.

"Because it isn't right. I'm here in an official capacity and we shouldn't go there again. We shouldn't have gone there to begin with. It wasn't the right thing to do." She was babbling and she knew it, but she couldn't stop herself. "It will only complicate things between us. Besides, you're a Colton and I'm a Gage."

"That's the most ridiculous excuse I've ever heard,"

Anders scoffed. "We are people and so much more than our last names. Maybe Vincent and Valeria have it right. It's way past time we all get over a century-old feud that has nothing to do with any of us now."

"I'll admit, I'd never let a name stop me from loving somebody, but I can't be with you again, Anders. We had our one-night stand and now it's done."

He sighed and raked a hand through his hair. "For what it's worth, Frank was a stupid man to give you up."

"It was the best thing he could have done for me." She released her own deep sigh. "If you ever tell anyone about me breaking down, I'll have to shoot you."

He smiled at her. "Your secret is safe with me." His smile slowly faded. "Elle, you don't get your self-confidence from the people around you. You get it from within yourself. You have to believe that you're enough. You're beautiful and intelligent. You're great at your job, but unless you believe it you'll always have doubts about yourself."

"Thank you, Doctor, I'll be sure to put a check in the mail for this therapy session," she replied.

"No need to get snippy," he replied, and then grinned at her once again. "Are we having our first spat?"

"No, I'm too tired to spat, and sorry that I got snippy. It's been a long day and I'm completely exhausted." In truth she'd been tired for the past couple of days.

"Why don't I take Bonnie into my room for the night? That way you can get a good night's sleep without any interruptions and I can take care of her middle-of-the-night feeding."

She hesitated for a moment. "Are you sure?" There was no question that the night feedings were beginning to take a toll on her. She had been functioning on far less sleep than she was used to.

"I'm positive. We should have been taking turns with her from the very beginning," he replied. "And don't worry about the dinner cleanup. I'll take care of that, too."

She looked at the baby and then back at him. "Okay, and thanks. I know it's really early, but I think I'm going to go on to bed right now."

"Sleep well," he replied.

"I'll do my best." She went into her bedroom and as she undressed she thought about everything that had transpired. It had been an evening of high emotion and secrets told, and she was utterly exhausted.

As she crawled into bed, Merlin flopped down on the floor next to her. Hopefully the night would bring no further drama and she really would sleep well and deep.

She had a feeling she wouldn't have blubbered so hard if she hadn't been so tired. But even so, the release of the tears had made her feel better than she had in years.

She felt amazingly clearheaded and she knew Anders had been right. Only when she really believed in herself would she know that she was enough for anyone.

The one thing that was certain was that making love again with Anders would have been a big mistake. The forced intimacy of their situation had made a physical relationship almost inevitable. She was certain that within a week or so, if nothing else happened here, she'd be pulled out and assigned to something else.

Making love again with Anders would also be a big mistake because at some point during her crying jag, she'd realized she was in love with him.

And she desperately didn't want to be.

* * *

Anders sat on horseback and stared out over the huge herd of cattle, but his mind was on Elle. It seemed his thoughts were always filled with her.

It had bothered him that she hadn't wanted to make love with him last night. It bothered him that he had no idea what her feelings were toward him.

With each day that passed he grew more and more crazy about her. As odd as it sounded, he'd been touched that she'd cried in front of him the night before. It had spoken of the deep level of trust she had with him. He seriously doubted that she ever showed such vulnerability with anyone else.

It had felt ridiculously good to talk about Rosalie and Brooke. It had been like lancing a wound he'd carried around with him for far too long. The relief had been instant.

He'd told her that the experience had made him unwilling to give his heart away again, but he'd been wrong. This morning he'd awakened to the epiphany that the answer to heartache was not to close yourself off, but rather to love deep and hard. No matter what the consequences, in the end love was worth it.

He'd had the happiness of believing he was Brooke's father for almost three wonderful weeks, and it was forever in his memory bank, but the following heartache shouldn't break him forever.

He wanted love in his life. He wanted a special woman to stand beside him through happiness and tears. And he believed he'd found that woman in Elle.

But at the moment he intended to keep his love for her to himself. She'd talked about two people being on the same page and he wasn't sure if the two of them were there yet.

Hopefully with another week or two, she'd fall in love with him. He intended to use that time to court her, to make her see that she was more than enough for him and that they belonged together forever.

It was almost time for him to return to the cabin and with this thought in mind, he rode to the edge of one of the pastures where he knew the South Dakota state flower bloomed wild at this time of year.

Sure enough when he arrived there, the ground was covered with the light blue, golden-centered pasque flowers. He dismounted and began to pick a bouquet to take back to the cabin.

He could have easily just driven into town and gone to the floral shop, but he wasn't sure it was open. The owner was dead and he knew the police were trying to figure out who had been sending Hayley flowers since Bo's murder.

Besides, he somehow believed that Elle would prefer the beautiful wildflowers he'd picked to any flowers he could just go into a store and buy.

Breakfast that morning had been a little awkward. She'd been a bit quiet and he suspected she was still embarrassed by her display of emotions the night before.

But she'd told him she'd slept wonderfully well and he'd felt bad that he'd put the entire nighttime duty of Bonnie on her the whole time she'd been here.

With a large handful of the pretty flowers, he got back on his horse and headed for home. The cabin had never felt like home as much as it did now with Elle in it.

He shook his head ruefully. He was turning into a lovesick fool and the strange thing was he didn't mind.

He wanted his woman and he'd do whatever it took to gain her love.

Once again before he entered the back door he heard Elle's laughter. A glance through the window showed him that it wasn't Bonnie who was making her laugh. The baby was sleeping in her cradle on top of the kitchen table. Whoever she was on the phone with had evoked the laughter from her.

As he came in the door she turned to look at him and the flowers in his hand. "Oh, I have to go. Anders just got home. Okay, I'll talk to you soon."

She hung up and smiled at him. "Oh, they're lovely," she said.

"I thought you might enjoy them." He hung his hat up on the hook and then reached out to give her the flowers.

"Wait, I need to find some kind of a vase."

"There should be one under the sink," he replied.

She bent over and looked. "Got it," she exclaimed in triumph and pulled out the tall glass vase. She filled it with water, set it in the center of the table and then took the flowers from him.

She looked lovely as usual. Clad in a pair of jeans that clung to her long legs and a pink T-shirt that hugged her breasts, she looked more like a model than a police officer.

He refused to believe that he'd never again kiss her with passion or feel those long legs wrapped with his. He refused to believe that he'd never make love with her again.

"Who was making you laugh on the phone?" he asked as she began to arrange the flowers. He wouldn't be surprised if she told him none of his business, because he knew he really had no right to ask her.

"Juliette Walsh," she replied. "She's a good friend of mine. Do you know her?"

He frowned thoughtfully. "The name sounds vaguely familiar."

"It should. She's a K9 cop who once dated your cousin Blake."

"That must have been before the time Blake left town," he replied.

"Yes, it was." She finished fussing with the flowers and stepped back to admire her own work.

"I'm not close to Blake, but I can tell you that I already like your friend Juliette."

She looked at him in confusion. "How can you tell me you like her when you don't even know her?"

"I like her because she made you laugh, and I definitely think you should do more of that."

She smiled. "I've done more laughing here with you and Bonnie than I've probably ever done in my life."

"Why is that?" he asked curiously.

Her eyes twinkled with a teasing light. "Probably because you're such a goofball."

He laughed in surprised delight. "I'll have you know that nobody in my entire life has ever had the audacity to call me a goofball."

"I call them like I see them, buster. I've caught you making those silly faces to get Bonnie to smile."

She was absolutely right. When Bonnie was awake and he had a moment alone with her, he became an utter fool. He baby-talked her and made all kinds of expressions to see if he could get her to smile…to laugh.

He looked at Bonnie now. "Ah, the princess is awake. It's time to make funny faces for her."

The smile fell from Elle's face and her dark eyes held

his gaze soberly. "I know you want her to be yours, but I'm still desperately hoping she belongs to Demi and my brother." Sadness filled her eyes and it didn't take a rocket scientist to know she was thinking about her dead brother. "One of us is going to be bitterly disappointed."

"Then we just support each other no matter what happens," he said softly.

"I'm going to give Bonnie her tummy time," she said briskly, and picked up the cradle. It was obvious she wasn't going to let her emotions get the best of her today.

"And I'm going to take a quick shower and then fix dinner. How does a steak and baked potato sound?"

"That sounds perfect."

A half an hour later he was in the kitchen preparing the evening meal. Elle's voice drifted in from the living room, a soft, lovely melody that shot waves of enjoyment through him.

There was no question he'd gotten attached to Bonnie, but there was a part of him that wanted the baby to be Bo's so that Elle had a piece of her brother to hang on to. Only the DNA test would give them some answers and he hoped it came in sooner rather than later. It was definitely taking longer than he thought it would to get the results.

Forty-five minutes later they sat at the table enjoying the meal and a discussion about television shows. He was unsurprised to discover that she loved all the crime dramas while he preferred all the old Western movies and an occasional sitcom.

They were almost finished eating when her cell phone rang. "Excuse me a minute," she said as she grabbed the phone and got up from the table.

"Yes, Chief," she said as she left the kitchen and

walked into the living room. Merlin trailed after her, her ever-present partner and companion.

Maybe she'd come back with some useful information. It was possible the DNA results had come in. Or maybe they caught the Groom Killer. That would be great news for the entire town.

"Everything all right?" he asked as she returned to the kitchen.

"Fine." She sat back down at the table. "That was Finn calling to tell me that if nothing else out of the ordinary happens out here within the next five days, then after that time I'm to leave this assignment."

Five days. He only had five more days of her staying with him. It was a woefully inadequate length of time. He wasn't near ready to tell her goodbye, but he also wasn't quite self-confident enough to ask her to stay.

Still, he knew with certainty that at some point during the next five days he was going to put his heart on the line and pray that she didn't slice it in two by walking away from him.

Chapter 10

Five more days. The words thundered through Elle's head with an unwelcome rhythm as she went about her morning routine. She should be grateful to leave this babysitting assignment and work on something where she could really make a difference. But she wasn't.

Five more days. The words rang in her head like a death knell. She was supposed to be here as a police officer, but somehow in spending time in the cabin with Bonnie and Anders, she'd reclaimed herself as a woman.

She'd spent so much time trying to be tough, but here she'd rediscovered her softer side, her laughter, and she'd realized those things didn't make her weak at all.

Yes, she hated to leave here. This little cabin in the woods had felt like home. Having breakfast and dinner with Anders had felt so right. But she had to get all of that out of her head.

Her home was her apartment and it was time she got back to her real life. These days in the cabin had felt like a dream, but the dream was about to be over and it was time to get back to reality, and that meant life without Anders and Bonnie.

She stared at the flowers on the counter. He definitely didn't seem like the kind of man who would randomly pick flowers for his home. He'd picked those flowers for her. She wasn't sure why he had done such a thing, but she couldn't let it matter to her. She couldn't let *him* matter to her.

As if in protest of Elle's thoughts, Bonnie began to fuss. It was a little early for another feeding, so Elle gave her the pacifier and she immediately fell back asleep.

Elle got up from the sofa and wandered into the kitchen, deciding that it wasn't too early for her to eat lunch. She'd just finished a ham-and-cheese sandwich when Merlin alerted. She grabbed her gun and opened the door to see Carson.

"Elle, I swear I'm not here checking up on you," he said quickly.

She lowered her gun. "Then why are you here?"

"I thought I'd come by to see this baby who might belong to Bo and Demi."

"Well, if that's the case then you can come in." She gestured him inside.

"Hey, Merlin." He leaned over to greet the dog with a fast scrub of his fingers across Merlin's back. "Anders out on the ranch?"

"Yes, although I never know for sure when he'll get home." He followed her into the kitchen where Bonnie was in the cradle in the middle of the table.

Carson bent over and inspected her like he was looking at a curious crime scene. He straightened up and looked at Elle. "I don't know, to me she doesn't look like anyone. She just looks like a baby."

"But Demi has all that flaming red hair and Bonnie does have a bit of light red in her hair," Elle replied. She touched Bonnie's cheek. "It would be nice if she was Bo's." Grief pressed against her chest.

"I guess." Carson reached out for her hand. "Elle, I know you and Bo had words before his death, but I also know Bo wasn't the type of a guy to hold a grudge. You do know he loved you and he never doubted how much you loved him."

She sighed. "Intellectually I know that, but emotionally I'm just so sorry we had words at all."

Carson pulled her into a tight, big-brother hug. "You know he's up in heaven right now looking down and smiling at us. Hell, knowing Bo he's probably laughing at us all."

A small burst of laughter escaped her and she stepped out of his embrace. "You're probably right about that."

"I've got to get going, but I was interested to see the baby who might be a possible link to Demi. I've been hounding the lab for the DNA results on Bonnie and Anders. They're way behind but have promised to get them to us any day now."

Together they walked back to the front door. "Anything new on the case?" she asked.

His eyes darkened. "Nothing at all. I heard your duty here is just about over."

"Yeah, I've got five days left here. Since the big break-in nothing else has happened, so there's really no reason for me to stay on." She ignored the knot that wound tight in her chest at the thought of leaving.

"And you still don't have any idea what somebody was searching for?"

"Not a clue. According to Anders nothing was taken," she replied.

"You know there are many at the PD who still believe Anders might be hiding Demi someplace out here. They've given up on thinking Serena might be helping out Demi because of our relationship. I know Serena would never keep that kind of secret from me."

"And they should have the same respect for me—and therefore Anders. He's told everyone dozens of times that he isn't."

Carson's gaze held hers for a long moment. "Do you trust him?"

"I trust him with all my heart," she replied. "He wants Demi to be brought in as badly as the rest of us do. He's afraid for her."

"Lucas is damned and determined to bring her in." Carson opened the door.

She laughed, imagining their bounty hunter brother out there in the wilderness, tracking Demi, his biggest rival. "Lucas is always damned and determined when he's after somebody."

"I guess the next time I see you will be in the squad room." He stepped outside into the bright June sunshine.

"Five days and I'll be back in the action," she replied.

Minutes later she watched his car disappear from view and then she turned and went back into the house. Bonnie was ready for her bottle and as she fed the hungry baby, her thoughts returned to her conversation with Carson.

Did she trust Anders? She certainly hadn't when she'd first started staying here. But now she trusted him 100 percent. She wasn't sure when it had happened that all her doubts about him potentially hiding Demi had gone away, but they were gone. She also believed he knew nothing about the break-in or what somebody might have been looking for.

She'd just finished feeding Bonnie when Anders came home.

"You're home early," she said as he came through the back door. Dang, but the man seemed to get more handsome every time she saw him. His white T-shirt stretched tight over his broad shoulders and his worn jeans looked like they had been tailor-made for his long legs and slim hips.

"I got a hankering for chocolate cupcakes and decided to come in early and bake a batch for dessert tonight."

She stared at him wordlessly. One night when they'd been talking about food that they liked, she'd told him her favorite dessert was plain old chocolate cupcakes with chocolate frosting.

"What are you doing, Anders?" she asked uneasily. She put Bonnie back in her cradle.

He looked at her innocently. "What are you talking about?"

"What's with the flowers and the cupcakes?" Her heart beat an unsteady rhythm.

He shrugged. "I just want these last five days with you to be nice."

"The last five days that I'm here will be just fine without you going to any extra trouble," she replied. "You don't have to bake for me."

"Dammit, woman, let me make you cupcakes. Let me bring you flowers. You've been so good about taking care of Bonnie all this time. Let me do some nice things for you."

He swept his hat off his head and hung it up and then turned to look at her once again. "Now, if you don't mind, I have chef work to do."

"Then I'll just take Bonnie and get out of the chef's way," she replied. She carried the baby into the living room and spread down the quilt for some tummy time.

Gratitude. That explained the flowers. He was grateful to her for caring for Bonnie. Thank goodness she hadn't given him any indication of her depth of feeling for him. Thank goodness she hadn't told him she was in love with him.

She certainly didn't want to be. It wasn't time for her to fall in love, especially with a man like Anders. He was a wealthy rancher who was bigger than life. Smart and so handsome, he deserved a better woman than her.

Even though she'd regained a lot of her self-confidence since being here with Anders, the debacle with Frank still haunted her. Even her brother Bo had told her she was too boring and a stick-in-the-mud. Of course, she had said some awful things to Bo during their fight.

Besides, she was focused on her job. It wasn't time for her to have it all…a husband…a family…and her work. She didn't even know why she was thinking about it. It wasn't like he'd told her he was in love with her.

He was just grateful.

When was the right time to tell a woman you loved her? Should he tell her when the scent of rich chocolate filled the cabin? Or should he wait until she was delving into one of the cupcakes?

Was tonight the right time or would tomorrow be better? As he waited for the treats to bake, he seasoned a couple of pork chops to go into the oven as soon as the cupcakes were finished.

He was suddenly nervous. He couldn't remember the last time he'd been so filled with anxiety. He wanted to tell her he was in love with her. He needed to speak the words out loud to her. But he was terrified of what her reaction would be.

What if he told her he loved her and she laughed at him? He instantly dismissed the idea. Elle would never laugh at him; that simply wasn't in her character. But she could look at him with that sober stare and tell him she wasn't in love with him.

Then they would have four more days in the cabin together. Things would be horribly awkward between them, but he was almost willing to accept that in order to speak his words of love to her tonight.

He knew the best time to tell her would be when she had one foot out the door. That way if she told him she wasn't interested, then she would leave and he wouldn't have to look at her, want her and love her for four more torturous days.

Be patient, he told himself as he pulled the cupcakes out of the oven. Wait until she's leaving and then tell her you want her to stay with you for the rest of your life. He had to be smart about this, and that seemed like the smartest choice he could make. Decision made, he began to relax. Tonight he just wanted them to have a good meal and enjoy each other's company. He might even point out how comfortable he was with her and how much he'd miss her when she was gone.

Once the cupcakes had cooled, he frosted them and

placed them on a platter in the center of the table, and by that time the pork chops were ready.

He was particularly pleased with dinner. The pork chops were seasoned with an apple-flavored rub, the mashed potatoes had come out perfectly, and a salad rounded out the meal.

He went to the living room door and was about to tell her that dinner was ready, but the sight that greeted him stopped him. Elle was stretched out on her back on the floor. Bonnie was on her chest and both of them were sound asleep. Merlin was snuggled against Elle's side and his loud and even snores filled the room.

In that moment, a desire struck him so hard in the chest he couldn't breathe. God, he wanted this. He wanted Bonnie to be his daughter and he wanted Elle to be his wife. He even wanted the drooling dog to live with him forever.

He leaned against the doorjamb and continued to gaze at the sleeping trio, his heart huge in his chest. Bonnie was limp against Elle's chest as if she belonged there. Elle had one arm around the baby to keep her in place, but it was Elle's face he stared at.

Her features were all so relaxed and her lips curved slightly upward as if her dreams were pleasant. He hoped her dreams were always good. More than anything he wanted to keep the three who slept on his grandmother's quilt safe from harm and here in his cabin forever.

Not making a sound, he returned to the kitchen and sank down at the table. Dinner would be late, but he didn't care. Elle obviously needed some extra sleep and he wasn't about to disturb her for a pork chop.

It was a little over an hour later when she and Merlin appeared in the doorway. "Oh my gosh, why didn't you wake me up?"

He smiled. "I figured you probably needed the extra sleep."

"I can't believe I did that," she replied. "I'm really not a nap kind of person."

"You weren't the only one who caught a nap." He looked pointedly at Merlin. "He was snoring so loud the neighbors called to complain."

"Ha ha, you're such a funny man," she replied drily.

"I assume Bonnie is still sleeping."

She nodded. "Something smells wonderful in here."

"That would be dinner. Are you hungry?"

"Starving," she replied.

"Then belly up to the bar and I'll serve the meal."

As she sat, he filled their plates and then carried them to the table. "It's going to be hard to eat the meal with those yummy-looking cupcakes staring me in the face, but the pork chop looks delicious, too."

The meal wasn't so delicious. The pork chops had been warmed for so long they'd become dry. The potatoes were too stiff and the salad was a bit limp.

"I'm sorry everything isn't better," he said when they'd been eating for a couple of minutes.

"Don't you dare apologize for a great meal. You couldn't know that I was going to fall asleep. Besides, I have a feeling on your worst day in the kitchen your food would still be great."

"I definitely had some pretty bad days in the kitchen when I first started cooking. When I lived in the big house all the meals were prepared for us by a variety of hired cooks. I never had to lift a finger to eat."

"That's the way I grew up, too," she replied. "But

when I got out on my own I didn't teach myself to cook. Instead I taught myself what were the best frozen dinners I could zap in the microwave and eat."

She paused to take a drink of water and then continued, "Of course my hours working as an officer aren't always regular, especially now with the Groom Killer case. Everyone has been working a lot of overtime since the last murder."

"We are not going to talk about murder this evening," he said firmly. "Tonight we just focus on pleasant things."

"Sounds good to me," she replied with the smile that warmed his belly better than any expensive whiskey. "You know, if Bonnie is going to stay here it won't be too long before she's going to need a crib. She's growing like a weed and that cradle will only hold her for so long."

For the next few minutes they talked about Bonnie's growing needs. What they didn't discuss was how he would deal with a baby in the house if he was a single father. He didn't intend to be single.

"I'll bet you're going to be an overly protective father," she said with amusement sparking in her eyes. "I can just imagine Bonnie going out on her first date and you trailing behind them, hiding behind trees and darting into doorways so they don't see you."

"Nah, it isn't going to be like that," he replied. "I'm just going to make sure she doesn't date until she's thirty."

Elle laughed. "Good luck with that. What I'm now wondering about is, how long after dinner do I have to wait before having one of those scrumptious-looking cupcakes?"

He grinned at her. "Go for it." He picked up their

empty dinner plates and carried them to the sink. He turned in time to see her with her eyes closed and a bit of cupcake in her mouth. Dark chocolate frosting clung to her upper lip, and his love for her buoyed up inside him.

"I'm in love with you, Elle." He blurted the words.

Her eyelids snapped open and she stared at him in obvious surprise. She slowly lowered the rest of the cupcake to the table and then picked up her napkin and wiped her mouth.

His heart beat unsteadily as he waited for her to say something…to say anything. There was no happy joy shining from her eyes, but a wild hope still filled him.

"I'm in love with you, Elle, and I want you here with me forever."

"Stop, Anders," she finally said.

"I can't stop," he replied. "I can't hold it in any longer."

"I still have four days left here and you're complicating things for both of us." She stared down at the table and her body had tensed as if she wanted nothing more than to run away from him.

"I'm not trying to complicate things," he protested. "I'm trying to make things wonderful. I'm in love with you, Elle."

"Stop saying that," she said, her voice verging on anger. "I was just supposed to be a one-night stand." She tossed the napkin on the table and then stood. "I don't want to talk about this right now."

"Then when would be a good time?" The hope that he'd entertained slowly began to fizzle away. Surely if she felt the same way about him she would have jumped up and run into his arms. She would have told him she loved him, too. Instead she was trying to escape him.

"I would prefer we not discuss this again." She said

the words firmly, but as her hand reached up to shove her hair away from her face, he noticed that her fingers trembled.

He took a couple of steps toward her. "Elle, I love you and I believe that you're in love with me."

She stared at him for a long moment and in the very depths of her beautiful brown eyes he believed he saw love. It was there only a moment and then gone as she broke eye contact with him.

"Elle, tell me that you love me, too. Tell me that you want a life with me," he said as he took another step toward her.

"I can't." Her voice held pain and still she stared down at the floor.

"Why can't you?"

She finally looked up at him and this time a touch of anger burned in her gaze. "I told you I wasn't looking for a relationship. I explained to you that right now I'm focusing on my career. Dammit, I made it clear what page I was on. Right now it's not time for love."

It was his turn to stare at her in surprise. "Elle, love doesn't know a timeline. You can't control who or when you love. It just happens. Besides, I would encourage you to continue to focus on your work. I know how important it is to you."

A mist of tears shone in her eyes. He didn't know what had caused them, but his first instinct was to draw her into his arms. No matter what was happening right now, he never wanted to see her cry. And the last thing he wanted to do was cause her any pain. He reached out for her, but she stepped back.

"Don't touch me, Anders. Please don't touch me."

She wrapped her arms around herself. He dropped his hands back to his sides.

She sighed. "Anders, the truth is I'm just not in love with you."

The words seemed to echo in the cabin as the last of his hope blew away. Pain replaced the hope, a sharp, stabbing pain in his heart and through his very soul. "Well, then I guess that settles things," he said flatly.

"I'm so sorry, Anders," she said softly.

"Don't be. You can't help what your heart feels." He backed away from her and to the sink. "Why don't you finish your cupcake and I'll get the dinner dishes cleaned up."

"I'm really not hungry right now. If you don't mind, I'm just going to go into the living room and see to Bonnie."

He nodded. When she was gone he sank down at the table, his emotions too tightly wound in his chest for him to do anything at the moment.

How could he have been so wrong about her...about them? He'd been sure that she felt the same about him. He'd been so damned certain that she was in love with him.

He'd seen the joy that lit her eyes when he came home after working on the ranch. He wondered if she was even aware of how often she touched him...simple touches like a hand to his forearm, a brush across his shoulders. She'd acted like a woman in love...so what had happened?

And then he knew. She'd lied. When she'd told him she wasn't in love with him, it had been nothing more than a lie. Was she afraid to love him? Afraid that he would just be another Frank in her life? That he would somehow betray her? Surely she knew him better than that.

He thought of the tears she had shed, tears because she felt like she'd never been enough for anyone. Was it possible that was what was holding her back?

If that was the case then he had four days to convince her that she was more than enough for him. With this thought in mind he got up from the table and began to tackle the dishes, eager to get back into the living room with her.

Chapter 11

Elle got into bed and released an exhausted sigh. It had been the longest evening of her life. She'd played with Bonnie and made small talk with Anders.

Anders. Her heart cried out his name. The most difficult thing she'd ever done in her life was face him and declare that she didn't love him.

But she was doing what was best for both of them. She wasn't ready to have it all. She was terrified that she couldn't handle it.

She closed her eyes and tried to imagine what it would be like to have it all. Would he grow tired of her job? If they had children, would they suffer from a lack of a stay-at-home mother? It had to be possible to raise well-adjusted, well-loved children who had working parents. She knew women who had it all. But the real question was, could *she* do it?

No, it was better to walk away now than walk away months from now knowing that she'd failed.

Still, when he'd reached out for her, she'd known that if he touched her, if he drew her into an embrace, she would crumble. She had to remain strong enough to walk away.

However, as she once again closed her eyes, she thought about that moment when he'd first confessed his love for her. His eyes had been so blue and so filled with hope.

It had looked like love…but was it really? Whatever he felt toward her had to be tangled up with a large dose of gratitude. She'd been here day and night to take care of the baby he thought might be his. She couldn't help but think it was possible that his feelings for her might be confused.

There was no question they had been playing house and it had felt comfortable and good. He'd probably gotten caught up in a fairy tale of a family in his cabin in the woods.

But how could she dismiss his feelings of love when she shared them? Was she, too, caught up in the fairy tale? She knew she was in love with him, so why did she doubt that he really loved her?

She finally fell asleep and dreamed that the two of them were at sea. He was on a huge ocean ship and she was on a tiny raft that tossed and turned in windy, turbulent conditions. She clung tight to the bright orange raft, crying out as it nearly capsized.

"I'm coming," Anders yelled from on top of the ship. "Hang on, Elle."

She tried to shout back to him but the minute she

opened her mouth a wave crashed over her and she coughed and choked on the salt water.

The ship horn blew, a loud forlorn sound that shot fear through her. Was the ship pulling away? Was Anders leaving her behind to the sharks and the sea?

The horn sounded again and suddenly she was awake. It took her a moment to realize the ship horn was actually Merlin's alert.

She fumbled for her gun on the nightstand, frantically wondering how long Merlin had been alerting. The sound of a commotion came from the living room. Adrenaline fired through her.

She flung open her bedroom door and stepped into the living room. In an instant her brain processed the scene. The overhead light was on and a big man in a ski mask stood next to the desk with a knife in his hand.

At his feet Anders was on the floor, bleeding from a head wound. Fear for him spiked inside her. Oh God, how badly was he hurt? Next to her she sensed all the muscles in Merlin bunching up for action.

"Where is it?" the man asked, his voice a low, rough growl. "Where is the bag?"

"What bag?" she asked in confusion as she kept her gun pointed directly at him. If he even inched toward Anders with the knife, she'd fire and ask questions later. Anders hadn't said a word, nor had he tried to get to his feet. That scared the hell out of her.

What also scared the hell out of her was that the man crouched so close to Anders she was afraid to shoot, fearing that she might harm Anders.

"The bag…the damned baby bag," he replied.

The baby bag? Why would he want that? She didn't stop to consider the answer. "Merlin…*aanval*," she said, using the word for attack. *"Aanval!"* As much as she hated putting Merlin at risk against a man with a knife, this situation was exactly what Merlin was trained for.

With a deep, menacing growl, the dog launched himself across the room toward the man. The intruder instantly turned and ran toward the door. He managed to get outside and slammed the door behind him before Merlin could take a bite out of him. Merlin growled and scratched at the door, eager to carry out her command to attack, despite the obstacle in front of him.

She told the dog to relax and then rushed to Anders's side. He sat up with a hand to the side of his head. "I'm all right," he said, and winced.

"You are not all right, you're bleeding," she replied worriedly. Fear tasted bitter in her mouth. "Did he stab you? Do you have any other wounds?" Oh God, how hurt was he?

"No, and no." He slowly got to his feet. "I heard him in here and when I confronted him he slammed me in the head with my desk lamp."

"Let's get that blood cleaned up," she said. "I'm calling for backup to check the area." She made the call and then with several commands she put Merlin on guard duty at the front door. She grabbed Anders's arm and led him into the bathroom.

He leaned against the sink as she got a washcloth out of the linen closet and held it beneath the running water. "Do you feel dizzy? Are you sick to your stomach?" she asked.

"No, nothing like that. My head hurts and I'm ticked off that he got the drop on me." He stood still as she began to gently clean off the wound.

It didn't appear to be too deep and it had already

stopped bleeding. Thank God. She would have never forgiven herself if he had been seriously wounded or killed while she was on duty. Damn the dream that had made it difficult for her to recognize Merlin when he alerted the first time.

It didn't take long for her to clean it up and it was only then she became aware of Bonnie wailing in the bedroom.

"The baby bag. What would he want from a bag left on my porch filled with stuff to take care of a baby?" he asked.

"We're about to find out." She set the cloth on the sink and then together they left the bathroom and went into the bedroom where the yellow tote bag was on the floor next to the chair.

"You get her," she said. "All the commotion has her upset."

He picked up Bonnie and she grabbed the tote bag and emptied it out on the bed. The first thing she did was check the tote itself. She carefully felt for anything that might be hidden in the lining.

"Nothing," she said and set it aside. She eyed everything that was on the bed. Bonnie had quieted in Anders's arms and Elle focused solely on the items that had been in the bag when Bonnie was left on the doorstep.

She scanned the items…onesies and diapers, an unopened can of formula, the knit hats and baby powder. She stopped at the container.

Was it possible the baby powder was really cocaine? A sense of horror filled her. How many times had she sprinkled a little bit on Bonnie? She breathed a sigh of relief as she tasted it. Thank goodness it wasn't cocaine, but rather just plain old baby powder.

"I can't imagine what's going on," Anders said.

"Me, neither. But that man badly wanted this tote bag."

"He has to be the person who broke in and searched the place. I'm pretty sure he's the same man who was in the living room on the night that Bonnie was left here. Although he had on a ski mask both times, the body shape and size were the same."

"I agree," she replied. She picked up each little outfit and checked it, then set it aside. Something was here… but what? She picked up a plastic rattle and shook it. Was it possible something was inside it that shouldn't be?

She set it on the floor and smashed it with her foot. She had to hit it three times before it split in half, revealing several little bird-shaped pieces of plastic inside, but nothing more.

Bonnie had fallen back asleep and Anders put her in the cradle and joined Elle by the side of the bed. He grabbed one of the onesies and checked the material.

"It would be helpful if we knew exactly what we were looking for," he said.

"I know, but there has to be something here for that man to go to so much trouble to get it. Maybe he is the Groom Killer and Demi left clues to his identity somewhere in here."

She was frustrated that she'd let the man get away. She should have run to the front door and let Merlin loose, but she'd been so worried about Anders's condition. She'd wanted to check on Anders immediately.

In her mind a clock was ticking. Tick. Tick. Tick. There was no question that the man could return at any time and he'd probably have more than a knife in his hand.

He'd broken in the front door. The next time he could

come through the back door or a window. Now that he knew about Merlin, with a single gunshot he could take that threat out of the equation.

Her heart squeezed tight at the very thought of losing Merlin. Her fingers worked faster, desperate to find whatever the man had wanted, the thing that she was certain he'd return for.

There were three little knit hats. Elle had put the yellow one on Bonnie when they'd gone outside, but she hadn't touched the pink or white one since Bonnie had been left with them. She picked up the pink one first and as her fingers ran around the edge she felt something that wasn't soft yarn but instead hard.

"Bingo," she said softly.

"Did you find something?" Anders asked.

"I think so." The hat had a hemmed brim and she ripped out the stitching to get to the small, hard object. When it finally came free she looked at Anders in stunned surprise.

"What in the hell?" He gazed at the thumb drive she held in her fingers.

"We need to get this to the police station as soon as possible."

"Before we do that, we both need to get dressed," he replied.

For the first time since Merlin had alerted and she'd stepped out of her bedroom, she realized she was still in her silk nightie and Anders was clad only in a pair of black boxers.

"Meet me in the living room as soon as possible," she said. "We need to get out of here before that man comes back, and I have no doubt that he'll be back. Here, take this." She shoved several diapers into the tote bag and handed it to him. "You might want to take a bottle with us."

As he left the room, she grabbed a clean uniform out of the closet and dressed as quickly as she could. The internal clock inside her continued to tick a menacing rhythm. The guy could burst into the house at any moment. They had to get out of here before that happened.

The thumb drive went into her pocket. A glance at the clock on the nightstand indicated that it was just after one. Finn wouldn't be at the station, but she wouldn't hand off the thumb drive to anyone but him.

She called him and updated him again on what was going on. "We're leaving Anders's place now to bring in the thumb drive."

"I'll meet you at the station," he replied. "I've got a couple of men on the way there to check out the area."

"Good. We're leaving now."

With the call completed, she picked up Bonnie and then walked into the living room where Anders awaited her. "You take her," she said, and held the baby out to him.

"We'll take my car," he replied. "The baby seat is already in it and that will save us some time."

"Don't step out of that door until I tell you to." She pulled her gun and motioned for him to stand just behind her. It was possible the man was just waiting for them to step out of the cabin. She didn't want them to be ambushed. She threw open the door and in a crouched position she stepped out on the porch.

She narrowed her eyes and scanned the darkness, looking for danger lurking in the shadows. She saw nothing and Merlin didn't alert, but she remained in the crouch as she motioned for Anders to step outside.

She didn't relax until Bonnie was buckled into her car seat and Anders was in the driver seat. She finally slid into the passenger seat. "Go…go," she said.

Anders took off and as they gained a little distance from the cabin, she released a sigh of relief. "I was afraid before we could get out of there he'd come back and he might possibly bring friends with him."

"I thought the same thing," Anders replied. "I wonder what's on that thumb drive."

"I can't imagine. If the baby is Demi's then maybe it has clues as to who the real Groom Killer is. It's possible the Groom Killer was standing in your living room." She frowned thoughtfully. "I should have shot him. Instead of telling Merlin to attack him, I should have just shot the man, but he was so close to you. I was afraid of somehow shooting you."

"Don't beat yourself up over it. We have the thumb drive and hopefully before too long we'll know what's on it," he replied. "We'll be at the police station in fifteen minutes."

He pulled out of the Double C Ranch property and onto the two-lane road that would take them into town. Thankfully Bonnie was once again asleep with Merlin next to her in the back seat.

Fifteen minutes and it would all be over. She held the answer to the break-ins in her pocket. There would be no more reason to remain at the cabin. There would be no more reason to stay with Anders and Bonnie.

Two patrol cars passed them, heading onto the Double C property. "If that creep is still hanging around, they'll find him and hopefully get him under arrest," she said.

"And that would be a good thing," he replied. They drove in a tense silence for several minutes.

"Uh-oh, it looks like we have company," Anders said as he looked in the rearview mirror.

She turned around in her seat to see a vehicle approaching fast. "Maybe it has nothing to do with us." Even as she said the words, she doubted them.

She watched as the vehicle drew closer and closer. She could now see that it was a pickup truck. She hoped it was just going to pass them. She hoped that up until the time the truck slammed into the back of their car.

Chapter 12

"Dammit," Anders exclaimed as he stepped on the gas. He tightened his grip on the steering wheel. A glance in the rearview mirror let him know that despite his increase in speed he wasn't gaining any distance from the truck.

"Brace yourself, he's going to hit us again." He barely got the words out of his mouth when the impact occurred. Even though he thought he was prepared for it, the steering wheel spun and the car veered first to the right and then to the left before he managed to regain control.

Bonnie began to wail, a torturous sound in the nightmare situation. Despite the coolness of the night a trickle of sweat worked down his back. The truck obviously had more horsepower than his car and the road was dark and narrow, making it even more dangerous to go too fast.

He glanced over at Elle. Lit by the dashboard illumination, her face was pale and her features were taut. She had to be afraid and he hated that.

He was supposed to protect those he loved and it didn't matter that Elle didn't love him back. It didn't matter whether Bonnie was his or not. Nothing mattered more than getting them to the police station where they would be safe.

The truck hit him again, this time spinning the car around by forty-five degrees. Elle screamed as he tried to correct. If he lost complete control they would wind up in a ditch or hitting one of the many trees that lined the street.

He took his foot off the gas and fought to gain control, his heart crashing against his ribs. He finally got the car straightened out and he once again stepped on the gas.

Elle rolled down her window and stuck her head out. "Come on, you bastard," she yelled as she pointed her gun behind them.

The truck came closer as if to meet her challenge. She fired her gun at the truck. Once…twice and then a third time.

"Dammit, if I can just hit his windshield or blow out one of his tires then that might slow him down." She yelled to be heard over Bonnie's wails.

"We're only a mile or two from town. Surely he'll back off then," he replied.

But he didn't back off and the defensive driving Anders was doing made it near impossible for Elle to get off a shot that might count.

They reached the town proper and Anders ignored the speed limit. He ran red lights with the truck hot on their tail. It was only when Anders screeched to a halt in front of the police station that the truck sped on and quickly disappeared around a corner and out of sight.

"Do you really think he's gone?" Anders asked.

"He could have just turned the corner and gotten out of his truck. We can't be sure he doesn't have a gun. Just sit tight." She got out of the car and quickly came around to Anders's door, her gun leading the way.

He rolled down his window. "Get out and get Bonnie," she instructed. She moved aside so he could open his door. She didn't look at him, but rather kept her narrowed gaze shooting around the landscape.

It was at that moment he realized he trusted her completely, not just as the woman he loved, but also as a competent officer of the law. When he opened the back door Merlin jumped out and stood at Elle's side, a second sentry on duty.

He reached in and unfastened Bonnie from the car seat. "Shhh, it's all right," he said as he straightened with her and the tote bag in his arms.

"Get into the building as quickly as you can," Elle said.

He complied. He raced for the building with Elle just behind him. They flew through the front door where Finn was waiting for them.

"Problems?" he asked.

"You might say that," Elle replied and holstered her gun. "A truck chased us all the way here and slammed into our car over and over again. He was obviously trying to stop us from getting here."

Finn frowned. "I'll get some men to watch the street in front." He stepped away from them and got on his phone.

"Here it is," Elle said when he was finished. She reached into her pocket and withdrew the thumb drive.

Thankfully Bonnie had stopped crying, although she was awake and wide-eyed in Anders's arms.

"I called in Katie in case we need her," Finn said.

"Who is Katie?" Anders asked.

"Katie Parsons, tech whiz extraordinaire," Elle replied.

"She's waiting for us in her office," Finn replied. He turned and started down the hallway and Anders, Elle and Merlin followed.

They entered an office that had television screens and computer monitors on the wall. Behind the large desk sat an attractive young woman with shoulder-length dark hair sporting bright pink streaks.

"Hey, Katie," Elle greeted her. "Love the pink. Wasn't it blue last week?"

Katie grinned. "And next week who knows what it will be. Now, what do you have for me?" She looked at them eagerly.

Finn handed her the thumb drive. They all watched as she put it into her computer and the screen lit up with what looked like gobbledygook.

A fierce disappointment roared through Anders. Had they just nearly been killed for a thumb drive that was corrupted and of no use to anyone?

"It's encrypted?" Finn asked.

"Yes, but have no fear, Katie is here," she replied confidently. "And this encryption is an easy one to break. Just give me a couple of minutes."

While she worked, they told Finn about the evening's drama. "If Elle hadn't been there, I believe the intruder would have killed me to get to the baby bag," Anders said. "Elle saved my life." He looked at her with all his admiration.

Her cheeks dusted with color. "You would have managed to take care of things all by yourself. Besides, it wasn't me who made the bad guy turn and run, it was Merlin." She reached down to pat the dog's head.

"I'm just glad you all got here safely with whatever is on that thumb drive," Finn said.

"Dates," Katie said, drawing all their attention back to her computer screen. "It looks like it's dates of weapon shipments with the price next to each one."

"It's got to be about the Larson twins," Elle said, her features lit up with excitement.

"But we checked their warehouse on the night of the surveillance detail and there was nothing inside," Finn said.

"So that was a night a shipment didn't come in. I still believe it has something to do with those twins and their criminal activities," Elle replied.

"There's a name here, too," Katie said. "Donald Blakeman. The fool actually put his name on the file."

Anders frowned. "That name sounds really familiar to me. I think he might have worked for me for a couple of weeks late last year."

"Katie, pull up everything you can about the man. We'll be in my office. Bring whatever you find to me," Finn said. He motioned for the others to follow him.

Once inside Finn's office, he motioned them to the chairs that sat in front of his desk. "I didn't get a chance to let you know that the DNA results came in late this afternoon." He picked up an envelope from the desk and held it out to Anders.

For a long moment Anders merely stared at the envelope, afraid to look at it and afraid not to. He finally took the envelope from Finn, his heart suddenly pounding with an anxious rhythm. Inside was the answer as to whether Bonnie was his or not.

The warmth of her little body in his arms, the powder-sweet scent that wafted from her, shot an arrow straight to his heart. He wanted her to be his. Oh God, he wanted it so badly. Despite his desire to the contrary, the little girl had his heart.

Elle placed a hand on his arm as if she knew the tumultuous emotions that raced through him and wanted to support him no matter what.

Still he paused. He was scared to open it, yet excited at the same time. He didn't care who Bonnie's mother was, but he so desperately wanted to be her father.

The envelope burned in his fingers and he was acutely aware of both Finn and Elle waiting for him to open it.

He didn't look at either of them as he slowly slid a finger to unseal the envelope. Once again Elle reached out and lightly touched his arm.

He gave her a grateful smile and then opened the envelope.

His fingers trembled so hard for a moment it was difficult to read the contents. He scanned down the sheet to get to the probability issue. His heart crashed to the floor. Anders Colton had zero percent probability of being infant Bonnie's father.

Zero percent. There could be no mistake with zero percent. "She isn't mine," he managed to say despite the tight grief that pressed against his chest. He looked down into her sleeping face and his eyes misted.

"Oh Anders, I'm so sorry," Elle said, and squeezed his arm tightly. He looked at her and saw his pain reflected in the depths of her eyes. How could she profess not to love him when she gazed at him that way?

He tightened his arms around Bonnie. Now both the females who had been in his cabin, in the depths of his heart, would be gone. "So, what happens to her now?" he asked Finn, his voice tight with the grief that still swept through him.

"The odds just got better that she belongs to Demi," Finn said.

"And Bo." Anders looked at Elle. "I really hope she's Bo's baby." He meant it. He knew Elle would love to have a piece of her murdered brother in her life. Now that he knew for sure Bonnie wasn't his, he wanted her to be Demi and Bo's, for Elle's sake.

"What I'd like is to keep her at your place for a little while longer," Finn said. "And Elle, I'd like you to remain at Anders's place, too. I can't help but believe that if the baby is Demi's, Demi will be back. We ran an additional DNA test on the baby and DNA extracted from a toothbrush that belonged to Demi. We're still waiting for those results to come back."

"I can't imagine who else she would belong to," Anders said. "The note that was pinned to her said she was a Colton."

"What I can't figure out is how Demi got hold of that thumb drive that I'm sure relates to the Larson twins," Elle said.

Before she could say anything more, Katie appeared in the doorway, a sheath of papers in her hand. "Donald Blakeman is forty-two years old and lives at 1201 East Twelfth Street. He bought the house four months ago with cash and lists his job as an entrepreneur."

She handed them each a picture of him. "I also printed out a layout of his house."

Anders stared at the photo. Donald Blakeman looked like the unpleasant man he was. There was a cold flatness to his dark eyes and his mouth looked like it had never known a smile. "I don't know what he's doing now, but last year around Christmas time he worked for me and lived in the bunk barn."

"He doesn't look like an entrepreneur to me. He looks like a thug," Elle said. "I hope somebody can identify him as one of the Larson boys' thugs."

"He definitely fits the build of the man who hit me over the head," Anders said. He looked at Elle, who nodded in agreement.

Before anyone could say anything else Carson and an officer Anders didn't know flew into the room. "Sorry if we're late, Chief," Carson said.

"Actually, your timing is perfect," Finn replied.

"Why didn't you contact me?" Carson said to Elle. "Why didn't you call me the minute you were in trouble? I heard about your dangerous race to get here. Jeez, Elle, you could have been killed."

"I handled it," Elle replied with a hint of coolness in her voice.

"Carson, she handled it," Finn echoed firmly. Elle looked at Finn gratefully. He handed Carson the photo of Blakeman. "We need to get this man under arrest as soon as possible. He probably guesses we now have the evidence he was willing to kill for and that makes him a flight risk."

"Let me go with them," Elle said.

Although Anders wanted to protest, he kept his mouth shut. This was what Elle did. She had gotten him and

Bonnie safely out of the cabin and to the police station and he knew she could handle whatever she needed to. Besides, it was bad enough that Carson had undermined her with his comments.

Finn looked at Elle thoughtfully. "I think your brother and Officer Jones can handle it."

"It wouldn't hurt to have me there, too." Elle held Finn's gaze and leaned forward in the chair. "Come on, Chief. I really want this. I've earned this."

Carson visibly stiffened, obviously not wanting Elle along, but not willing to say anything more.

"Okay, go," Finn replied. "All of you get out of here. Katie will fill you in on anything else you need to know."

"Elle, be safe," he said.

"Always," she replied with one of her smiles that warmed his heart. And then she was gone.

Anders stood, unsure what he was supposed to do. "Elle's patrol car is still at my cabin. Would it be a problem if I just hung around here until they get back?" he asked Finn.

"Not a problem at all," Finn replied, and also stood. "In fact, I'd prefer you stay here until Elle can go back to the cabin with you. Until Blakeman is in custody I don't know whether or not you might be in danger. We have no idea how crazy he is, and he might go after you for some sort of twisted revenge."

He motioned Anders out of his office. "You can relax in the break room. Do you have everything you need for the baby?"

"Yeah, thank goodness we grabbed a bottle and a few diapers before we left," Anders replied.

"It was decided to leave Merlin here. Do you mind if he joins you? He's obviously comfortable with you and he'll just be sad if nobody is around him." Finn led him to a small room with a round table, a vending machine, a sink and microwave, and two cots.

"I'd love to have Merlin here with us," he replied.

Finn disappeared for a moment and then returned with the dog at his heels. Merlin walked over to Anders's side and sat.

"You should be fine here," Finn said.

"We will be, thanks," Anders replied, but it was a lie. He hated that Elle was without her partner, and he wouldn't be fine until she was back safe and sound.

Elle sat in the back seat of her brother's patrol car, adrenaline pumping through her. She wanted Blakeman under arrest so badly she could taste it.

Not only had he chased them through the night, but he'd also whacked Anders over the head. Anders could have been killed. They all could have been killed on the race to get to the station.

The bigger picture was that Blakeman could be the key to taking down the Larson twins' empire. If they could get him to roll over on them, then they could potentially have what they needed to put the two behind bars where they belonged.

Finn had managed to get them a search warrant and now Officer Roger Jones sat in the passenger seat using his utility flashlight to look at Blakeman's house plans.

"It's a typical ranch house with a front door and a back door," Roger said.

"He didn't display a firearm to us, but I imagine he has them in his house," Elle said. "And even though it's the middle of the night we know he's awake, because I'm certain he's the man who chased us to the station."

"Let's just hope he hasn't managed to get out of town yet," Carson replied.

"I'm sure he overestimated the time it would take us to read the thumb drive," Elle replied. "He didn't know for sure that we found it and just how smart our Katie is."

"There's no way we can go in quiet and slow on this," Roger said. "I think we need to go in hard and fast."

"I've got some flash-bangs in my trunk," Carson replied.

The flash-bang grenades blinded a person for about five seconds. The loud noise disturbed the fluid in the ears, keeping the person unable to hear and with a loss of balance.

"I know where I'd like to lodge a flash-bang," Elle said drily. "I wouldn't mind if Blackman lit up from the inside out."

Carson bit back a small laugh. "I didn't know my sister could think such things." His laughter halted as they parked down the street from Blakeman's address.

"Okay, so here's the plan. Roger and I will breach the front door and throw in a flash-bang. After it's delivered, we'll rush inside. If he manages to get to his garage, we'll hear the door go up and can stop him there. Elle, I want you at the back door to make sure he doesn't escape that way."

She wanted to protest her brother's plan. She wanted to go in the front door, she wanted to prove herself once and for all, but she kept her mouth shut. She knew she was only here because of Finn's capitulation and was to play a supportive role for the other two more experienced officers. Part of being a good cop was being a team player.

They got out of the car and Carson opened his trunk

to retrieve not only the flash-bangs, but also the tools they would need to breach the door. Finally he handed them each a set of ear protection that would protect them from the noise of the flash-bangs.

"Keep in mind, if he's home, it's possible he won't be alone," Elle warned them. "If he has anything to do with the Larson twins, then he probably has a lot of thug friends."

Carson nodded, a nearby streetlamp shining on his taut, serious features. "Okay, so we go in silent. We breach the front door and I throw in a flash-bang. Elle, when you see the flash, you'll know we're inside. Watch that back door closely because if there's a possibility for his escape, that's where he'll go." He looked at Elle and then at Roger. "Are we ready?"

They both nodded and then they were off, moving like silent shadows in the night. All the other houses on the street were shrouded in darkness, but when they grew closer to Blakeman's place, lights blazed out of his windows.

Her blood ran cold as she saw the pickup truck in the driveway…a pickup truck displaying a lot of front-end damage. It was definitely the truck that had rammed into them several times. So the bastard was home. He probably thought he had plenty of time to pack and get out of town before they could find what he'd wanted in that baby bag and decipher the code on the thumb drive.

When they reached the side of his house, Elle went around to the back door and got into position. If Blakeman came out this door, she would do everything in her power to stop him.

In an instant the thought of Anders filled her head. His voice had cracked when he'd read the paternity results and her heart had nearly broken with his pain. It was surprising for her to realize that if given a real choice, she would have preferred that Bonnie be his rather than Bo's. That made two little girls he'd been cheated out of.

I know Anders, and when he loves, he loves hard. Valeria's words echoed in her mind. And Elle had walked away from his love.

She shook her head. She had no time for such thoughts. She had to stay solely focused on the task at hand. She couldn't allow herself to get distracted by Anders's profession of love for her.

She heard a *bang* and the splintering of wood, indicating Carson and Roger had successfully broken down the front door.

She turned her face from the window as a bright white light bathed the backyard. The *boom* that followed seemed to shake the very ground beneath her feet. Elle yanked off her ear protection.

"Red Ridge Police. Halt," Carson shouted from someplace inside the house.

Elle tensed. She stood right in front of the back door, her gun steady in her hand. This time she wouldn't hesitate to shoot first and ask questions later. She should have done that after he'd attacked Anders.

"Blakeman, stop," Roger's voice rang out.

At that moment the back door flew open. Donald Blakeman stood before her, his eyes blazing with an angry desperation, a gun in his hand. "Stop or I'll shoot," she said.

In an instant his gaze shot around, as if looking for Merlin, and then he exploded out the door. Elle wanted to shoot him straight through his black heart, but she was aware that he was just a piece to a bigger puzzle. She didn't want him dead; dead men couldn't rat out their cohorts. When he turned, his gun pointed in her direction, she aimed at his leg and squeezed off a shot.

He howled and fell to the ground, the gun skittering beside him. Elle didn't hesitate; she ran toward him and kicked the weapon out of his reach before he could grab it.

Immediately Carson and Roger were at the back door. "Elle," Carson said in relief as Roger ran to Blakeman's side.

"Good work, sis." Carson threw an arm around her shoulder. "I'd take you as my backup partner anytime."

Those words warmed her heart as Blakeman was loaded up into the back of an ambulance. Carson rode with him. She was called back into the station and Roger remained at the house, where he would be joined with other officers to process the scene.

When she reached the station Finn was waiting for her. He took her into his office, where she gave him a verbal report of what had occurred.

"This was your first time shooting a suspect. How do you feel?" Finn asked.

"I feel fine," she replied. "I did what I had to do. I just did my job."

Finn looked at her for a long moment and then nodded. "If you have any problems with it, you let me know. Now, get out of here and get back to Anders's cabin. Anders and the baby and Merlin are all in the break room waiting for you. I'm hoping we're on a little bit of a roll here and when Demi comes back for that baby you'll be able to arrest her."

She left his office and walked down the hallway to the

break room door, which was closed. She opened it quietly and her heart expanded at the sight that greeted her.

Anders was asleep on one of the cots with Bonnie in his arms. Merlin lay on the floor next to them and his tail began to wag at the sight of her.

How was she supposed to continue living at the cabin with Anders after all that had happened between them? She supposed she could have argued with Finn and told him there was absolutely no danger posed to anyone and it was time for her to quit the assignment.

But Bonnie and Demi were the wild cards and Finn was right. There was still a possibility Demi would return for her baby. Elle was just going to have to suck it up and do her job.

For several long moments she remained just inside the door, staring at the sleeping man who had stolen her traitorous heart. She loved his strong jawline and the sensual lips that kissed her with such passion. Her fingers itched to caress his features, to memorize them for the time she had to really say goodbye to him.

She suddenly realized his eyes were open and he stared back at her. "I'm back," she said.

Anders sat up carefully so as not to disturb Bonnie. "Did you get him?"

"We did. He's going away for a very long time after he gets out of the hospital."

Anders raised an eyebrow. "The hospital?"

"Yeah, I had to shoot the bastard in the leg."

He grinned at her, that slow, sexy smile that always shot straight through her to the center of her heart. "Are you ready to go home?" she asked a bit curtly.

"We're all more than ready to get home."

As he drove them back to the cabin she told him

about what had transpired at Blakeman's house. Dawn's light peeked over the horizon as they arrived back at the cabin.

"I'm glad you shot him," Anders said ten minutes later when they were in the living room. "This was my favorite desk lamp." He picked up the mangled light from the floor. "He needed to be shot for ruining it."

"Just thank goodness he didn't hit you any harder than he did," she replied.

Only now could she fully process the horror of that moment when she'd walked out of the bedroom and seen him covered in blood with a man wielding a knife standing over him.

What she wanted to do more than anything now was to stand in his arms, feel the warmth of his embrace and assure herself that he was really okay. He'd not only suffered a blow to the head, but also a blow to his heart in finding out Bonnie wasn't his. She'd seen the aching sadness that had radiated from his eyes when he'd read the DNA results.

"I need to get some sleep," she said. What she really needed was some distance from him right now. She'd be strong again after she got some rest, but at the moment she was tired and felt incredibly vulnerable.

"I'll keep Bonnie with me," he said. He smiled. "You worked all night and I didn't."

She didn't argue with him. Now that the drama was finally over, she was completely exhausted. "I'll see you in a couple of hours," she said, and then without waiting for a reply she went into her bedroom with Merlin following close behind.

Minutes later she was in bed with tears pressing close against her eyelids. Why did she feel like crying now?

She'd performed in her job well and one big mystery had been solved. She should be celebrating.

But celebrating wasn't any fun all alone. At the end of a long day it was always great to come home to somebody who could share in both the celebrations and the disappointments.

Anders could be that man. This cabin could be her home. So why was she so afraid to reach out for that happiness? It was a question that haunted her until she fell asleep.

Chapter 13

It was just after noon when Elle came out of the bedroom. She was clad in her uniform and her face was utterly devoid of expression. "I got a call from Finn. There's a woman at the station claiming to be Bonnie's mother."

Anders pulled himself up from the floor where he had been playing with the little girl. "Who is it?"

"Finn didn't give me any further details, but I think it's safe to say it isn't Demi. I guess we need to pack up the tote bag."

A surge of unexpected grief shot through him. A shaky laugh escaped him. "Even knowing she isn't mine, the idea of giving her up to anyone still breaks my heart."

Elle's features softened. "I know, I feel the same way about her."

"I feel like there's about to be a death in the family

and there's no way I can stop it." God, he couldn't believe how emotional he was being. The big, strong ranch foreman felt like crying over a little girl.

To his surprise Elle walked over to him and pulled him into a hug. He wrapped his arms around her and clung to her with a desperation he'd never known before. He wasn't just losing Bonnie, but with the baby gone he would also lose Elle. There would be no more time to convince her they belonged together.

He breathed in Elle's scent in an attempt to staunch the cold wind of despair that blew through him. His home had been filled with joy with Bonnie and Elle in it, and now they would be gone and he didn't know if he would ever know such happiness again.

He released her and stepped back, because holding her another minute was just too painful. "I'll go get the tote bag," he said. He went into his bedroom where he drew several deep breaths to get his emotions under control.

As he picked up the tote bag from the chair, questions roared through his head. Did he know Bonnie's mother? If he did, then why hadn't she knocked on the door and asked for his help? If he didn't know her then why had she chosen to leave her baby on his doorstep? What about the note that proclaimed her a Colton?

And how long would it take him to forget how much he loved Bonnie? How long before he forgot how much he loved Elle? He didn't have the answers and in any case he needed to pull himself together for the trip to the police station.

When he went back into the living room Bonnie was in her cradle and all the items that had come with her were neatly piled on the sofa.

He didn't look at Elle as he packed the things into the tote bag. "At least we'll finally have some answers," he said. For a long moment he gazed at Bonnie and she released a string of babble and then smiled. He looked away.

"We'll take my car," Elle said. "We can move the baby seat when we get outside."

"Are you afraid to drive with me after last night?" It was a feeble attempt at humor.

She smiled. "I can't think of anyone I'd rather have been at the wheel last night than you. You stayed calm and in control and that's the only thing that kept us on the road." Her smile faded. "We should get going."

She picked Bonnie up in her arms and it was at that moment he realized what this new twist meant for her. "Elle…if this woman at the police station is really her mother then that means…"

"That Bo isn't her father," she said.

"I'm so sorry. I really wanted that for you."

"It's all right. It just means this baby isn't Bo's, but someplace out there is Demi's baby and we know Bo is that baby's father. If fate puts that baby in my life somehow, someway, it would be wonderful. If fate isn't so kind, then I just have to be okay with that."

The inner strength that shone from her eyes awed him. He only hoped he could be as strong when it came time to hand Bonnie over to somebody else.

Minutes later they were in her patrol car and headed into town. "I'm sorry about your car," she said. "The back end of it is pretty smashed up."

"Thank God for insurance," he replied. "And thank goodness it was just my ranch car and not the fancy pickup truck I keep in the shed."

"At least it's beautiful day," she said.

A beautiful day for heartache, he thought. "I just can't imagine who the mother might be. The note said she was a Colton, but if she isn't mine and she isn't Demi's, then how can she be a Colton?"

"Do you have any cousins who were pregnant?"

"Not that I'm aware of, and in any case why would they leave her with me?"

"I guess we'll have some answers in a few minutes."

"I'm not handing her over to just anyone," he said. "What if the woman is some kind of kook who heard about Bonnie and just decided to claim her?"

"I'm sure Finn won't let that happen."

They fell silent for the rest of the ride. Anders stared out the passenger window and wondered when exactly he'd fallen in love with Bonnie. Was it the first time she'd smiled at him, or was it on that very first night when she'd cried and then had found comfort in his rocking arms?

It really didn't matter when it had happened. He just had to steel himself for her absence in his life. When they arrived at the police station and Elle had parked the car, he had her hold the little girl while he removed the car seat.

"We won't be needing this anymore and maybe the mother will be able to use it," he said.

They went straight to Finn's office where he was waiting for them. He rose from the desk as they entered. "I have the mother in the break room. Her name is Annie King."

Anders frowned. "That name sounds vaguely familiar."

"She was Donald Blakeman's girlfriend."

Memories clicked into place in Anders's head. She

had lived with Donald in the bunk barn for the short period of time Donald had worked for him. Anders remembered her as a small, timid woman.

"I know you have a lot of questions for her and we're running a DNA test as we speak. I leaned on the lab and called in a few favors so I'm hoping to get the results within the next hour or so," Finn said.

"Then I guess it's time to talk to Annie," Elle said.

They all walked to the break room and the minute Elle walked in with the baby, the woman seated on the cot jumped up and began to cry.

"My baby, my sweet baby Angelina." She held out her arms to Elle. "Please, can I hold her?"

Elle hesitated a moment and then handed Bonnie to Annie. The petite strawberry blonde woman sat back on the cot. She smelled Bonnie's head and then stroked trembling fingers down Bonnie's cheek.

Elle and Anders sat at the small table and Finn excused himself and left the room. "Is it true?" Annie looked at Elle. "Is it true that you shot Donald?"

Elle nodded and her eyes turned wary. "It's true. I shot him in his leg."

"Thank you," Annie said fervently. "Is it also true that he's going to prison for a long time?"

"He's facing a lot of charges that will keep him locked up for a very long time," Elle replied.

"Good. He was an evil man. He beat me. He hurt me a lot, but I could never get the strength or the courage to leave him. Not until Angelina was born." She looked down at the baby who was asleep in her arms. "She gave me the strength I needed to get away."

"How and why did you end up at my place?" Anders asked.

"I don't have family in this area and Donald didn't let me have any friends. The day before he was going to pick me up at the hospital, I left. A kind nurse gave me some money to get a taxi and I had him drop us off at the Double C Ranch. I just needed time to figure out how I could get to my family in Montana. The hospital gave me extra diapers and formula and so I holed up in the old shed down by the stables."

She released a deep sigh and then continued, "I stayed well-hidden each time any police came to do a sweep of the area or any of the ranch hands were around, but it was difficult."

Once again she looked down at the baby and then back at Anders. "I tried to keep her with me and I'm ashamed to say I stole food from you, but after keeping her with me in the shed for ten days, I realized I needed help. She needed more than I could do for her. I realized I couldn't keep her with me any longer." Tears once again filled her eyes. "And that's when I left her on your doorstep. When I was at the ranch everyone spoke of how kind you were and I left that note on her hoping that would assure you'd take good care of her until I could come back for her."

Anders didn't need a DNA test to tell him she was Bonnie's mother. It all made sense now. His "Needy Thief" had been an abused mother trying to survive all on her own. Besides, her love for the baby was evident in the way she touched Bonnie, in the way she looked at her.

"What about my grandmother's quilt? Did you take that?" he asked.

She nodded her head. "It's in the shed. I didn't ruin it or anything like that. I just used it to cover us up at night when it was cold. I'm so sorry, Mr. Colton. I'm so very sorry."

"There's no reason to apologize for doing what you needed to do for your baby," he replied. Finn quietly reentered the room and stood silently next to the door.

"So, what are your plans now?" Elle asked.

"Since Donald is in jail now I can get a job and earn the money to get me to my sister's home." Once again tears glistened in her pale blue eyes. "I need to be with my family. We'll have love and support there."

"You aren't going to work a job here in Red Ridge," Anders said. "I'll personally see to it that you get to your sister's home as soon as possible."

"Oh, Mr. Colton, I can't let you do that for me," Annie replied.

"I'm not doing it for you," he replied, the tight press of emotions back in his chest. "I'm doing it for Bon... Angelina. I'm crazy about that baby and I don't want you struggling to work a job and handing her off to babysitters. I'll pay for the transportation to a place where both of you will have support and love." Annie began to quietly weep.

"The test result is back," Finn said. "This woman is the baby's mother."

"Then we're done here," Anders said. He looked at Finn. "Could you see to her travel arrangements and let me know what the cost is?"

"Of course," Finn replied.

Anders and Elle stood. Anders walked over to Annie. "Could I hold her one last time?"

Annie stood and placed Bonnie in his awaiting arms. He knew he was torturing himself, but he wanted to smell her baby sweetness one last time. He needed to see her pretty little face once more and hold her against his chest.

She had brought such happiness, such joy into his life, but more than that she had given him a new wisdom about love. She had taught him about leaving old pains behind to keep the heart open to loving again.

He turned to Elle, to see if she wanted to say a personal goodbye, but she shook her head. "No, I'm good." But he saw the pain in her dark eyes and knew she was grieving the loss of Bonnie as well. In spite of their wishes to the contrary, Bonnie had gotten deep into their hearts.

He kissed Bonnie's little cheek and then handed her back to Annie. Suddenly his emotions were too big for this little room. He walked out into the hallway and fought against tears.

Jeez, he was a rough and tough cowboy. He could wrestle steers and ride broncos, but losing one itty-bitty little girl had brought him to his knees.

Elle came out of the room and placed a hand on his arm. She didn't say anything, but it was an offer of support that calmed the screaming grief inside him.

And now he had to prepare himself for saying goodbye to Elle, and that was going to be the most painful blow of all.

"I can't believe you didn't want to hold her one last time," Anders said to Elle when they were on their way back to the cabin.

"It would have been too painful," she replied. "It's best when you're saying goodbye to somebody to just turn and leave without prolonging the agony."

And that's exactly what she intended to do with Anders. Before they had left the station Finn told her the case had been solved and he expected her at work the next morning for her usual shift.

She wanted to go inside the cabin, pack her bags and leave without any crazy emotions getting in the way. It was bad enough some of those crazy emotions were already working inside her.

"You know, I thought I loved my job because of the adrenaline rush of potential danger," she said thoughtfully. "I thought it was just about getting bad guys off the streets, but it's so much more than that. Last night we put away a bad guy, but more importantly we made it possible for an abused woman to live a better life. That's the real payoff. And what you did for Annie in paying her way to go to her sister's house was wonderfully generous."

She glanced over at him. He'd never looked as handsome as he did now just minutes before she told him goodbye. He'd never know how much he'd touched her heart when he told Annie he'd get her to her sister's home…to safety and security.

"I've got more money than I know what to do with. Hopefully with Annie going to her sister's place she can heal from whatever wounds Donald left behind and Bonnie—Angelina, I mean—will get the future she deserves."

"Even so, it was a really nice thing to do." She pulled up next to his car and they got out. Merlin bounded up to the front door as if he belonged inside.

"How about I put on a pot of coffee while you pack," Anders said as they entered the cabin. "Surely you have time to enjoy a cup of coffee before you take off."

"Okay," she agreed. This was going to be more difficult that she'd thought. She'd had it in her mind that she would pack quickly and leave before her brain could really process it.

She'd hoped not to feel anything when she left here. Her heart was already bruised by having to say goodbye to Bonnie and if she really thought about saying goodbye to Anders, she feared she'd completely break down.

She hurried into her bedroom and began shoving clothes into the duffel bag. He was just a one-night stand, nothing more. That's what she told herself as she folded up the sweatpants she'd worn on the night they'd made love.

He was a Colton and she was a Gage. For that reason alone they shouldn't be together. But hadn't two of her brothers and her sister shot that notion to high heaven? Carson, Vincent and Danica had fallen madly in love with Coltons. She smiled. Coltons and Gages weren't supposed to mix, but the new generation hadn't gotten the memo.

The scent of fresh-brewed coffee filled the air. She thought of all the mornings she'd awakened to that scent, all the mornings when she'd shared breakfast with him. And all those afternoons when she so looked forward to him returning to the cabin.

She steeled her heart and went into the bathroom to retrieve her toiletries. With everything packed up, she carried her duffel bag out of the bedroom and dropped it by the front door.

Anders was waiting for her in the kitchen. He sat at the table with Merlin at his feet. He stood as she entered the room. "Merlin and I were just having a nice conversation," he said. He gestured her to sit while he turned to the cabinet to pour the coffee.

She didn't sit. "Anders, I can't," she said as he turned back to face her with the two coffee cups in his hands.

He set the cups on the table. "You can't what?"

"I can't just sit here and have a goodbye cup of coffee with you. It would be like holding Bonnie one last time. It's just too painful."

He took a step toward her, his expression as serious as she'd ever seen it. "Why is it too painful?"

"It just is." She couldn't meet his gaze.

He took another step toward her. "I need to know why it's painful for you, Elle. If you don't have any feelings for me, then enjoying a last cup of coffee before you leave shouldn't be that difficult."

"But I do have feelings for you," she protested. "I care about you, Anders. I think you're a wonderful man."

"But you don't love me." His blue eyes held her gaze intently. "Tell me again that you don't love me, Elle."

It was as if he were sucking all the oxygen out of the room. Crazy, wild emotions pressed tight against her chest, making it difficult for her to draw a breath.

He took two more steps, bringing him so close to her she could smell the scent of him and see the bright blue irises of his eyes. She knew she needed to back away from him, but her legs refused to obey her faint mental command.

Before she saw it coming, he wrapped her in his arms and his lips crashed down on hers. The kiss tasted of something wild and wonderful, and she found herself responding with a desperate need of her own.

When the kiss ended, he dropped his arms to his sides, but didn't step away from her. "Tell me now, Elle. Tell me that you don't love me." His voice was low and filled with emotion.

It was finally she who stepped away. "Goodbye, Anders," she said, and then turned around and headed for the front door.

"You're a fool, Elle. Why can't you see we belong together?" he called after her, a touch of anger in his tone. "I would love you like no other man could ever love you. Why would you run away from that?"

She picked up her duffel bag and opened the door. "Let's go, Merlin." She needed to escape. Too much pain roared through her.

She loaded Merlin in the back seat and then got into the car. Thankfully, Anders hadn't chased her outside. She started the car but instead of putting it into gear and driving away, she remained there as tears blurred her vision.

What she'd had with Frank couldn't begin to compete with what she had with Anders. And the aching, stabbing pain that possessed her now was a pain she'd never, ever felt before.

She'd thought she could have a one-night stand with him and just walk away without her emotions involved. She'd been so wrong. She swiped at the tears with the back of her hand.

Merlin released a sad moan. He never liked it when she cried. She knew if she were on the floor he'd crawl right up in her lap and try to cheer her up.

She calmed down a bit and stared at the cabin. A pain still hitched in her chest and with a sudden clarity she realized it was a self-inflicted wound.

Why was she leaving a man who had told her he'd love her like no other man ever would? Why was she running away from a man who had brought her such happiness?

She couldn't even blame it on his being a Colton and her being a Gage. Her own siblings had taken care of that. Anyway, she'd never care what his name was; she only cared what kind of a man he was.

He was handsome and a hard worker. He was kind and had a soft heart. He was also intelligent and funny and everything else she would ever want in a man.

So why was she running?

Was she enough for him? That was the question that kept her in the car, poised to drive away. She now knew she was good enough as a police officer.

And dammit, she was good enough to be the woman in Anders's life. She was good enough to be his wife and a cop. She could have it all…a husband, a career and children. So why on earth was she running away from love instead of toward it?

Because she was a stupid fool. She'd be a fool to run away from happiness. And her mama didn't raise no fool.

A burden suddenly lifted from her heart. The pain fell away and she was left with only her love for Anders filling her heart, her very soul.

She shut off the car engine. "Merlin, I'm going to go get my man." Merlin barked as if in agreement.

She got out of the car and let Merlin out of the back seat. He beat her to the front door. She followed him through the living room and into the kitchen, where Anders sat at the kitchen table.

"Forget something?" he asked. His eyes looked so sad.

"Yes, I forgot to tell you that I'll love you like no other woman will ever love you," she replied.

Her body nearly vibrated from the emotions that

raced through her. "Anders, I don't want to leave. I want to stay here with you forever."

His eyes filled with a love so great it washed over her like a warm summer breeze. He got to his feet. "Are you sure, Elle?" he asked softly.

"I've never been so sure of anything in my entire life, and if you don't come around that table and take me in your arms, I'm going to have to shoot you."

He laughed, that rich, deep laughter she loved to hear. He hurried toward her and when he reached her, he pulled her into an embrace that nearly stole her breath away.

"I love you, Elle. I'll spend the rest of my life making you happy." His gaze bored into hers.

"And I love you, Anders, and I'll spend the rest of my life making you happy," she replied.

His lips took hers in a kiss that tasted of love and commitment, of tenderness and desire. When the kiss ended she placed her hands on either side of his face.

"I know that with your love and support I can have it all. I can have my life here with you, and my career, and eventually I can give you a baby girl that nobody will be able to take away from you."

He covered her hands with his and smiled. "A little boy might be nice, too."

"Yes, a little boy might be nice," she said with a laugh. "But we already have a little boy." She looked down at Merlin, who was dancing around their feet. She gazed back up at the man who held her heart. "We're going to be so happy, Anders."

"As long as you're in my life, I'm a happy man." He gazed at her for a long moment. "What made you decide to come back inside?"

She dropped her hands to her sides and his went to her waist. "I realized I loved you more than I feared my own inadequacies." She raised her chin. "I am enough. I deserve you and love and happiness."

"You deserve all the happiness in the world." He lowered his lips to hers once again and this time his lips tasted of not just love, but also of future and forever.

Epilogue

Elle walked down the hall toward the locker rooms with a spring in her step and Merlin at her side. The Groom Killer was still a mystery, Demi Colton continued to be on the run, and the Larson twins persisted with their suspected illegal activity. But none of that could stop the happiness that soared through her knowing that within a half an hour or so she'd be home with Anders.

It had been five days since she'd gone back into that cabin to claim her man, and those days and nights had been more than wonderful. She was certain she was where she was supposed to be, in that cabin and with Anders Colton.

She entered the locker room to find Juliette Walsh there as well. "Hey, I was looking for you earlier," she said to her friend and fellow officer.

"I've been wanting to catch up with you, too. I've

heard the craziest rumors about you…like you've fallen in love with Anders Colton and you're moving in with him."

"Not a rumor," Elle replied with a smile. "It's all true."

Juliette grinned. "You go, girl." She sat on the bench in front of the lockers. "I also heard about your harrowing ride here with a thumb drive that might bring down the Larson twins."

"One can only hope. Did you also hear that I'm going to start cross-training Merlin in the art of tactical detection? If he'd had that training then he would have been able to sniff out the thumb drive sooner than all the time it took for us to discover it."

"Merlin will do great at the new training," Juliette replied. "He's such a smart dog, aren't you, boy?" Merlin ran to her and Elle laughed as he presented his backside to Juliette, obviously looking for a good back rub.

Juliette leaned over and stroked down Merlin's back while Elle opened her locker to retrieve the lunch box that was inside. "So, why were you looking for me?" she asked.

"I heard a rumor, too." Elle closed her locker door and turned to face Juliette.

"What kind of a rumor?" Juliette straightened.

"There are whispers that Blake Colton is coming back to town."

All the color left Juliette's face. "How many whispers?" she asked in a faint voice.

"Enough to believe it's probably true. I just wanted to give you a heads-up." Elle looked at her sympathetically. She knew the secret of Juliette's child, but nobody else did. "What are you going to do?"

"I don't know, but thanks for the heads-up." Juliette stood. "I need to get home."

"I'll see you tomorrow," Elle said.

Minutes later Elle and Merlin were in her car and headed home. Home…to a cozy cabin in the woods. Home…to the man who owned her heart.

When she finally pulled up in front of the cabin, Anders sat on the front porch waiting for her. His black cowboy hat sat at a cocky angle but his smile wasn't as bright as usual.

Was something wrong? Had he changed his mind about her? About them? She and Merlin got out of the car. Merlin raced ahead of her and sat, his butt wiggling as he waited for Anders's hello.

"Hey, boy." Anders scratched the happy dog behind his ears and then stood. "And how was your day?" he asked Elle.

"It was good. What about yours?"

"It was all right." He opened the door and they all went inside. "I've got a big glass of iced tea ready for you in the kitchen."

"Sounds great." She followed him in and sat down at the table, still disturbed by the way he was acting. He hadn't really looked at her and he hadn't kissed her hello like usual.

He remained standing. "Do you want a little snack before dinner? I can get out some crackers and cheese."

"No, I'm good. Anders, is something wrong?" Had he decided he didn't want her anymore? Was he trying to find the words to let her down easy?

"Yes, something is wrong," he said, and frowned. Her stomach clenched. "I've racked my brain all day to figure out a clever way to say what I need to ask you."

Her mouth dried. "Wha-what do you need to ask me?"

He walked closer to her and pulled a small velvet box

from his pocket. He then dropped to one knee and held her gaze with his. "Elle, will you marry me?" He opened the box to reveal a beautiful diamond ring. It wasn't the shine of the ring that held her attention, rather it was the shine of love that flowed from his eyes.

She jumped up out of her chair, her heart exploding with joy. "Yes...oh yes, I'll marry you, Anders."

He got to his feet and then slid the ring onto her trembling finger. "I know you can't wear this in public until the Groom Killer is caught since that'll put me on the hit list. But *we* know we're engaged. And I can't wait to pair this ring with a wedding band. I promise to love you forever, Elle."

"And you know what happens if you break that promise?" she asked.

He laughed. "I believe I do know what will happen. You'll shoot me."

She smiled at him. "I can't wait for you to kiss me," she replied.

His eyes sparkled. "My pleasure," he said, and then covered her mouth with his.

The cowboy and the cop, she thought as his lips plied hers with heat. A Colton and a Gage. Name and position didn't matter; together they had magic, and she knew with certainty that the magic would continue throughout the rest of their lives.

* * * * *

Ever since **Lisa Childs** read her first romance novel (a Harlequin story, of course) at age eleven, all she wanted was to be a romance writer. With over forty novels published with Harlequin, Lisa is living her dream. She is an award-winning, bestselling romance author. Lisa loves to hear from readers, who can contact her on Facebook, through her website, lisachilds.com, or her snail mail address, PO Box 139, Marne, MI 49435.

Books by Lisa Childs

Harlequin Romantic Suspense

Bachelor Bodyguards

Beauty and the Bodyguard
Nanny Bodyguard
Single Mom's Bodyguard
In the Bodyguard's Arms
Soldier Bodyguard
Guarding His Witness
Evidence of Attraction
Bodyguard Boyfriend

Colton 911

Colton 911: Baby's Bodyguard

The Coltons of Red Ridge

Colton's Cinderella Bride

Visit the Author Profile page
at Harlequin.com for more titles.

COLTON'S
CINDERELLA BRIDE

Lisa Childs

With great appreciation for my amazing family—
my immediate family and to all my aunts, uncles
and cousins who support me, too!
I am so fortunate to have you all in my life!

Chapter 1

Everything happens for a reason...

Mama had told Juliette that so many times over the years and so often during the long months of her terminal illness. Not wanting to argue with or upset an invalid, Juliette had just nodded as if she'd agreed with her. But she hadn't really. She had seen no reason for Mama getting sick and dying, no reason to work two jobs to pay off Mama's medical bills and her own community college tuition.

But as she stared up at the little blond-haired angel sitting atop the playground slide, her heart swelled with love, and she knew Mama had been right. Everything happens for a reason, and Pandora was that reason.

Her daughter was Juliette's reason for everything that had happened in the past and for everything that she did in the present.

"Is it too high?" she called up to the little girl who'd convinced Juliette that since turning four, she was old enough to go down the big kid slide. She was small for her age, though, and looked so tiny sitting up so high that a twinge of panic struck Juliette's heart.

Maybe she was just uneasy because it looked as though it might start storming at any moment. The afternoon sky had turned dark, making it look more like dusk than five thirty. Since July in Red Ridge, South Dakota, was usually hot and dry, rain would be a welcome relief—as long as it came without lightning and thunder, which always scared Pandora.

Juliette probably shouldn't have stopped at the park that apparently everyone else had deserted for fear of the impending storm. But when she'd finished her shift as a Red Ridge K9 officer, and had picked up her daughter from day care, the little girl had been so excited to try the slide that she hadn't been able to refuse.

"Come on, honey," she encouraged Pandora as she pushed back a strand of her own blond hair that had slipped free of her ponytail. "I'm right here. I'll catch you when you reach the bottom." She wouldn't let her fall onto the wood chips at the foot of the slide.

"I'm not scared, Mommy," Pandora assured her. "It's supercool up here. I can see all around…" She trailed off as she stared into the distance. Maybe she could see the storm moving in on them.

As if she sensed it, too, Sasha—Juliette's K9 partner—leaped up from the grass on which she'd been snoozing. Her nose in the air, the beagle strained against her leash that Juliette had tethered around a light pole. Sniffing the air, she emitted a low growl.

Despite the heat, a chill passed through Juliette. Sasha

had been trained for narcotics detection. But what was she detecting and from where? Nobody else was in the park right now. Maybe the scent of drugs had carried on the wind from someplace else, someplace nearby.

"Mommy!" Pandora called out, drawing Juliette's attention back to where she was now half standing, precariously, at the top of the slide.

"Honey, sit down," Juliette said, her heart thumping hard with fear.

Pandora ignored her as she pointed across the park. "Why did that man shoot that lady with the purple hair?"

Juliette gasped. "What?"

Pandora pointed again, and her tiny hand shook. "Over there, Mommy. The lady fell down in the parking lot and she's not getting back up."

Like her daughter, Juliette was quite small, so she couldn't see beyond the trees and playground equipment to where her daughter gestured. She hurried toward the slide and vaulted up the steps to the top. Then she looked in the direction Pandora was staring, and she sucked in a sharp breath. About two hundred feet away, in the parking lot behind the playground area, a woman lay on the ground, a red stain spreading across her white shirt while something red pooled on the asphalt beneath her.

"Oh, no..." Juliette murmured. She needed to get to the woman, needed to get her help...but before she could reach for her cell to call for it, a car door slammed and an engine revved. That car headed over the grass, coming across the playground.

The shooter must have noticed Pandora watching him and figured she'd witnessed him shooting—maybe killing—someone.

Juliette's heart pounded as fear overwhelmed her. She

wrapped her arms around Pandora and propelled them both down the slide. Ordinarily her daughter would have squealed in glee, but now she trembled with the same fear that gripped Juliette.

The car's engine revved again as it jumped the curb and careened toward them. Juliette drew her gun from her holster as she gently pushed Pandora into the tunnel beneath the slide. The side of the thick plastic tunnel faced the car, which had braked to an abrupt stop. A door creaked open.

Juliette raised her finger to her lips, gesturing at Pandora to stay quiet. The little girl stared up at her, her green eyes wide with fear. But she nodded.

Sasha was not quiet. She barked and growled, straining against her leash. Instinctively she knew Juliette and Pandora were in danger. But with the man between them now, Juliette could not release her partner to help. And maybe that was a good thing. She had no doubt that Sasha would put her life in danger for Juliette's and especially for Pandora's.

Juliette would put herself in danger for Pandora, too.

Crouched on the other side of the tunnel so he wouldn't see her, Juliette studied the man who'd stepped out of the sedan. He'd pulled the hood of his light jacket up over his head, and despite the overcast sky, he wore sunglasses. He was trying hard to disguise himself. But was it already too late? Had Pandora seen him without the hood and the glasses?

Who was he?

A killer.

She had no doubt that the young woman he'd shot was bleeding out in the parking lot. Frustration and guilt churned inside her, but she couldn't call for help now and alert him to where she'd hidden her daughter. If not for Pandora, the cop part of Juliette would have been trying to take him down—even without backup. But because Pandora was in danger, the mother part of her overruled the cop.

Especially since he was heading straight toward the slide. But Pandora was no longer perched atop it. So he looked around, and he tensed as he noticed the tunnel beneath it. He raised his gun, pointing the long barrel toward that tunnel.

Toward Juliette's daughter...

Her heart pounding so hard it felt as if it might burst out of her chest, she raised her gun and shouted, "Police. Drop your weapon! You're under arrest!"

Instead he swung the gun toward her, and his glasses slid down his nose, revealing eyes so dark and so cold that a shiver passed through Juliette.

He shook his head and yelled, "Give me the damn kid!"

And she knew—Pandora had seen him without the hat, without the glasses. Then the wind kicked up again and blew his hood back, and Juliette saw his dark curly hair. And something pinged in her mind. He looked familiar to her, but she wasn't sure where she'd seen him before.

"Put down the gun!" she yelled back at him.

But he moved his finger toward his trigger, so she squeezed hers. When the bullet struck his shoulder, his face contorted into a grimace of pain. He cursed—loudly.

"Stop!" she yelled. "Drop the gun!"

Despite his wounded shoulder, he held tightly to his weapon. Before she could fire again, he turned and ran back toward his car. Over his shoulder, he called out, "That kid is dead and so are you, lady cop!"

Juliette started after him. But a scream drew her attention. And a little voice called out urgently, "Mommy!"

The car peeled out of the lot, tires squealing against the asphalt. Juliette stared after it, trying to read the license plate number, but it was smeared with mud. From where? The weather here had been so dry.

He'd planned to obscure that plate. He'd planned to kill that woman.

Now he planned to kill her and Pandora. She moved toward the end of the tunnel and leaned over to peer inside at her daughter. "Sweetheart, are you okay?"

The little girl's head bobbed up and down in a jerky nod. "Are you dead, Mommy?"

A twinge struck Juliette's heart. "No, I'm fine, honey." But that woman was not. She pulled out her cell phone and punched 911. After identifying herself as a police officer, she ordered an ambulance for the shooting victim, an APB on the killer's car and her K9 team to help.

But she knew they would arrive too late. She doubted that woman could be saved, and she was worried that the killer might not be caught. At least not until he killed again...

And he'd made it clear who his next targets would be. Her and her daughter...

Pandora began to cry, her soft voice rising and cracking with hysteria as her tiny body shook inside the tunnel. Juliette's legs began to shake, too, then gave out so that she dropped to her knees. She crawled inside the small space with her daughter and pulled her tightly into her arms.

Pandora was Juliette's life. She could not lose her. She had to do whatever necessary to protect her.

What the hell am I doing back here?

There was nothing in Red Ridge for Blake Colton. He'd built his life in London and Hong Kong and Singapore—because his life was his business. And those were the cities in which he'd built Blake Colton International into the multibillion-dollar operation that it was.

That was undoubtedly why Patience had called him—because of his money—since he and his sister had never been close. He wasn't close to any of his other sisters, either, or to his father or mother. Maybe that was partially his fault, though, because he'd left home so young and had been gone so long now. But Patience hadn't called to see how he was doing; she'd called to ask him to help.

He didn't know how he could provide the kind of help his family needed, though. In addition to their father's business problems, she'd told him about a murderer on the loose. A murderer everyone believed to be a Colton, too—one of Blake's cousins.

Blake pulled his rental vehicle into an empty parking spot outside the long one-story brick building on Main Street—the Red Ridge Police Department. Maybe his cousin Finn, who was the police chief, could explain to him just what the hell was really going on in Red Ridge.

But only Blake could answer the question of what had compelled him to hop on his private plane and head back to Red Ridge. And he had no damn idea…

With a sigh, he pushed open the driver's door and stepped out. The sky was dark with the threat of a storm that hadn't come. Blake felt the weight of those clouds hanging over him like guilt.

He knew what Patience wanted—what she expected him to do. Bail out their father so that their sister Layla wasn't forced to marry some old billionaire to save Colton Energy. How like their father to care more about his company than his kids…

That was the Fenwick Colton whom Blake knew and had spent most of his life resenting. But he could understand his father a little better now. Blake didn't have any kids, but his company was like his child. If he withdrew the kind of money required to save Colton Energy, he could cripple his own business and put thousands out of work.

He couldn't do that—not for his father and not even for Layla. There had to be another way. Finn probably wouldn't have any answers to that, but he would know all there was to know about this crazy "Groom Killer" targeting men about to be married. At least the threat of dying had caused Layla's fiancé to end their engagement. But according to Patience, that threat was hurting her sister Beatrix's bridal shop business. It was also affecting their youngest sister Gemma's personal life because her boyfriend would not get as serious with her as she would have liked.

With a rumble of thunder sounding ominously in the distance, Blake hurried toward the doors of the police department. He didn't want to get caught in a deluge. A woman rushed toward the building, as well. She had one arm wrapped around a child on her hip and the other hand holding the leash of the beagle running ahead of her. He stepped forward and reached around her to open the door, and as he did, he caught a familiar scent.

He hadn't smelled it in years. Nearly five years…

But he'd never forgotten the sweet fragrance and the

woman who'd worn it. It hadn't been perfume, though. She'd said it had been her shampoo, so it had been light, smelling like rain and honeysuckle.

The scent wafted from the woman, whose pale shade of long hair was the same as the woman who'd haunted him the past five years. But it couldn't be her...

He'd looked for her—after that night—and hadn't been able to find her anywhere. She must have checked out of the hotel and left town.

She certainly hadn't been a Red Ridge police officer like this woman. She wore the distinctive uniform of a K9 cop and held the leash of her partner. But when she turned back toward him, her gaze caught his and held. And he recognized those beautiful blue eyes...

Remembered her staring up at him as he'd lowered his head to kiss her...

But no, it could not be her. Being back in Red Ridge, staying at the Colton Plaza Hotel, had brought up so many memories of her, of that night, that he was starting to imagine her everywhere.

He'd found her easily enough. But he couldn't take out her or her daughter here—outside the damn Red Ridge Police Department. Hell, after that bitch had shot him, he could barely raise his arm.

Blood trickled yet from the wound, soaking into his already saturated sleeve. He needed medical attention. But he'd have to find it somewhere other than a hospital or doctor's office. RRPD would have someone watching those places, waiting for him.

Damn the timing...

The park had looked deserted. He hadn't noticed anyone else around—until he'd heard the dog bark. Then he'd seen the little girl—but not before she had watched him fire those shots into that thieving dealer's chest. Did she understand what she'd witnessed?

She was old enough that she probably did. And because he hadn't known anyone else was around, he hadn't had his hood up or glasses on then. So she would be able to identify and testify against him. And so would her damn cop mama.

But that wasn't going to happen.

She and her mother were not going to live long enough to bring him down.

Chapter 2

Noooo...

Not now. Not ever…

Juliette had determined long ago that she would never see Blake Colton again. Even though she had heard that he'd recently returned to Red Ridge, she hadn't thought that she would actually run into him. It wasn't as if she worked at the Colton Plaza Hotel anymore.

And she hadn't expected him to show up at the Red Ridge Police Department.

What was he doing here—now?

She froze as their gazes locked. She should have been running instead—running away from *him* with Pandora. But she hesitated too long before stepping through that door. And his gaze went from her face to her daughter's.

While there was no mistaking that Pandora was her biological child, the little girl's blond hair was darker than Juliette's—more a dark gold like Blake's. Pandora's eyes were green instead of blue. Green like her father's eyes that stared at her now, widening with shock. She also had the same dimple in her left cheek that he had, but since neither was smiling now, it was just a small dimple and not the deep dent it became when they grinned.

Pandora wasn't grinning, though. She was sobbing; she hadn't stopped since the man had come after them despite Juliette's assurances that they were safe now. Juliette didn't feel safe, though.

Pandora must not have, either, because she buried her face in Juliette's neck, hiding from the handsome stranger who held the door for them. But she'd done that too late. He'd already seen the little girl just like he'd seen Juliette.

And from the expression crossing his handsome face, Juliette could tell that he'd recognized her despite the nearly five years that had passed. From the way he was staring at Pandora, with his brow furrowed as if he was doing math in his head, he might have also realized that the child in her arms could be his.

No. They were not safe.

He turned back to Juliette, and the look in his green eyes chilled her nearly as much as the look in the killer's dark eyes had. She shivered.

"It's you—" he murmured "—isn't it?"

She shook her head in denial. "I—I don't know what you're talking about…"

His eyes narrowed with skepticism and suspicion. "It is you. And she…" He raised his hand as if to reach for Pandora.

But Juliette spun around, keeping her child away from

him. "She's just witnessed a crime," she said, her voice cracking with regret and fear that her poor little girl had had to see what she had. A murder...

"I can't do this now," she told him. But before she could rush through those doors and get away from him, someone rushed out.

Like Juliette, the woman was clad in a RRPD uniform, her brown eyes dark with concern.

"Oh, my God," Elle Gage exclaimed. "I just heard what happened. Are you all right?" She focused on the little girl. "Is Pandora?"

"Pandora..." Blake murmured the name, drawing Elle's attention to him.

She gasped. "You—you're Blake Colton," she said. Then she glanced at Juliette. She was the only one who knew—the only one Juliette had trusted with the truth. "Were you at the park, too?" she asked him.

Blake's brow furrowed. "Park?" He turned toward Juliette. "Is that where the crime happened?"

She nodded. "I need to complete the report." But that wasn't all she wanted to do. She wanted to make sure she had a safe place for her daughter. Pandora needed protection from at least one man—the one who'd sworn she would die. She might need protecting from this one, too, if he had realized that he was Pandora's father.

"But I need to talk to you," he said through teeth gritted with frustration and anger.

Elle reached for Pandora, extricating the little girl from Juliette's arms. "Come here, sweetheart," she said. "Let you, me, and Sasha get something to eat and drink..." She took the beagle's leash from Juliette's hand, too, and with a crook of her neck gestured at

Blake. Since she'd learned he'd returned to town a couple of days ago, she'd been urging Juliette to talk to him.

But there really was no time. Not now...

Fear pounded in her heart as she watched her friend walk away with her daughter. She'd nearly lost her just a short time ago—at the park. If Juliette hadn't shot the man in the shoulder...

If she hadn't wounded him, he would have killed them both. She just had to convince her boss of the same. She had no time to deal with Blake Colton. But when she moved to follow Elle and Pandora, he caught her. Wrapping his big hand around her arm, he held her back.

Her skin tingled from his touch. It had been so long. But she could still remember how it felt...how he'd touched her that night...

She jerked her arm from his grasp. Just as he'd spoken through gritted teeth, she did the same. "I. Cannot. Do. This. Now."

"We need to talk," he insisted.

She knew it was true and not just because Elle had been badgering her to seek him out. She knew it was the right thing to do. But at the moment she needed to be with her daughter—needed to see for herself that her child stayed safe.

"She's mine, isn't she?" he asked, and his voice cracked slightly with the emotions making his green eyes dark.

Her reply stuck in her throat, choking her.

"She's the right age," he continued as if he was trying to convince himself. "And she looks like me..."

Juliette felt like she had when she'd stared into the barrel of the killer's gun. Trapped. Terrified. Desperate...

* * *

Frustration gripped Blake, twisting his gut into tight knots. He wanted to shake her, but when he reached for her again, she flinched as if she expected him to hurt her. He wouldn't have, of course—despite his feelings. But he dropped his hand back to his side.

"Tell me," he said, badgering her like she was a reluctant witness on the stand. "Tell me if she's mine."

"Yes!" she exclaimed, as if her patience had snapped. Or perhaps it was her conscience. "She's yours."

He expelled a sharp breath, like she'd punched him in the gut. All these years he'd spent thinking about her and about that night, he had never once considered that she might have gotten pregnant—that they might have made a child together. He was a father.

Anger coursed through him now, replacing the shock. "How—how could…"

Her lips curved into a slight smile. "The usual way…"

He glared at her. "How could you keep her from me?"

Her face flushed now, but she just stared at him with those damn beautiful eyes of hers.

"How could you?" he asked. "For years?"

"I—I—" she stammered. "You left Red Ridge right after…"

"You could have found me," he insisted. His family was in Red Ridge. They'd known where he was.

She tensed now and glared back at him. "You could have found me—even without knowing."

"I tried," he admitted. "You slipped out in the middle of the night, and I didn't even know your last name. Hell, right now I'm not sure you gave me your right first name, *Juliette*."

She flinched.

And he wondered. Had she told him anything that was the truth?

"Juliette is my real name," she said.

Someone from inside the police department called it now. She glanced back toward the building. "I—I need to go," she said. But when she started forward, he caught her arm again—stopping her.

"No—" He'd spent five years wondering what had happened to her. Where she was… He wasn't just going to let her walk away from him again.

"She needs me," Juliette said.

And he felt once again like she'd struck him. The child needed her *mother*. She didn't even know she had a *father*. Unless Juliette had passed off another man as the little girl's daddy. Blake glanced down at the hand of the arm he held—her left hand. Her fingers were bare of any rings. She wasn't married or engaged now.

But a lot could have happened over the last nearly five years. She might have had a husband. Hell, he'd thought she might have on their night together, and that was why she'd slipped away like she had, so nobody would spot them together.

She hadn't worn a ring then either, though. So maybe, as a cop, she'd just decided not to wear one.

How had she afforded that beautiful gown—those shoes and earrings—on a cop's salary—if she'd even been a cop back then? She looked younger now, without makeup, than she'd looked that night.

"Let me go," she said—once again through gritted teeth. She had beautiful teeth and lips and features…

He'd started to believe that he'd romanticized her and that night over the years. That she couldn't have been nearly as beautiful as he'd thought she was. He'd been wrong—about romanticizing it.

She was also stressed and afraid, her face pale and eyes wide with fear.

"I will let you go," he agreed because he had no choice. Her daughter—*their* daughter—needed her.

Before the little girl had hidden her face in her mother's neck, Blake had noticed her tears and, worse than that, her fear. His gut churned again—with a sense of helplessness even worse than when Patience had told him about his sister Layla's predicament.

"But you're going to come to my suite later," he told her.

Her eyes narrowed as if she thought he expected a repeat of that long-ago night. Of what had happened over and over that night…

His pulse leaped at the thought, but he was too angry with her to ever want her again. So he clarified, "Just to talk."

Someone called her name a second time, and she tugged free of him. But as she stepped through those open doors to the lobby, she turned back and nodded.

"I'm staying in the same suite as I was that night," he told her.

Color rushed back into her pale face, and she nodded again. She would be there. Eventually. But he suspected it might be a while before she could make it.

Still reeling from what he'd just learned, he no longer wanted to talk to his cousin—the police chief. Blake didn't want to step into that police department where she and their daughter were.

He just wanted to be alone. He wanted to think and

process and deal with all the emotions gripping him. The anger, the shock, the fear…

His daughter had witnessed a crime of some sort, and from the way both she and her mother had acted, they were definitely frightened.

Could they be in danger? Could he lose his child just as he had finally discovered her existence?

"He's back?" Fenwick Colton already knew that his son had returned to Red Ridge. The concierge at the Colton Plaza Hotel had confirmed that Blake had checked into a suite on the twenty-first floor a couple of days ago. But Fenwick hadn't seen him. And he sure as hell hadn't heard from him.

Patience, Fenwick's daughter and Blake's half sister, nodded in reply, but she had to understand what he was really asking. Why hadn't Blake come to see him?

The boy was Fenwick's only son. They should have been close. Fenwick had had primary custody of him, since a hyper boy had been more than his jet-setting mother had wanted to handle. But the kid had always acted like he couldn't stand to be near him. And as if to prove it, he'd spent the past five years living in other countries. Maybe that was just because he was like his mother, though.

"Why is he back?" Fenwick asked his daughter.

Patience lowered her head slightly, and her dark bangs shielded her dark eyes. She was staring down at her desk in her office at the Red Ridge K9 training center. If he wanted to talk to his daughter, he usually had to come to the training center, where she worked as a veterinarian. It was the same with Bea; he would have had to go to the bridal shop to see her. At least Gemma visited him, but it was usually to ask for money.

He ran his hands over his tailored suit, plucking a strand of dog hair from the expensive fabric. Then he touched his hair, making sure the blond piece hadn't slipped. As mayor of Red Ridge, he had to make sure he always looked good. "You called him," he surmised.

"I had to," she said, and her voice was sharp with resentment. Patience didn't understand business like Layla did. Like Blake did...

"He's not going to help," Fenwick said. It wasn't a question. He knew that with just as much certainty as he knew that Blake had returned to Red Ridge.

Patience looked up from her desk now. "He might. He will," she persisted, but she sounded more like she was trying to convince herself than she was him. "Why else did he come home?"

That was what worried Fenwick. If Blake hadn't come back to help his family, then he probably had another reason—a personal reason—for returning to Red Ridge.

"You shouldn't have called him," Fenwick admonished her.

"He's your son," she said. "My brother. He deserved to hear what's going on with the family from one of us."

Fenwick suspected the media had probably beaten Patience to the punch, though. Coltons were news. And a Colton scandal was even bigger news.

Damn his reprobate cousin Rusty and his equally disreputable kids for causing such a scandal. But it went beyond a scandal. Rusty's daughter Demi was a murderer. Evidence and witnesses proved—to him, at least—that she was the psycho killing grooms-to-be because she'd been dumped by her own one-week fiancé. Of course a

Colton being a killer wasn't news. Other Colton family members—very distant family members out of state—had committed murder, as well.

Fenwick didn't know what he might be forced to do if Layla wasn't able to carry out their plan of marrying to save the company. This damn Groom Killer nonsense was threatening their livelihood. But now that might not be all that was threatened.

"You shouldn't have called him," Fenwick repeated, "because you might have put him in danger."

Patience's dark eyes narrowed. "What are you talking about?"

"This maniac," Fenwick said, "is killing grooms. *Men.*" He was a little scared for himself—not that he had any intention of getting married again. Three times was more than enough. And he had more fun dating than he'd ever had being married.

"Blake isn't engaged," Patience said. "He's not marrying anyone. He didn't even have a serious girlfriend when he did live at home. So I doubt there's anyone in Red Ridge he would be tempted to propose to."

Fenwick wished he could trust that. "Couples are afraid to go public. Engagements have been canceled. Everyone is afraid of the Groom Killer. But that hasn't stopped anyone from coupling up in private."

He could think of at least six new couples in Red Ridge—some damn unlikely couples.

"And you know your brother," Fenwick continued. "If anyone tells that stubborn kid not to do something, he's twice as determined to do it."

Like build his own damn company. Fenwick had told the boy not to do it, that he didn't have what it took. Hell, he'd been fresh out of graduate school with his MBA and had no real business experience when he'd begun his "start-up." But Blake had had to go out and prove him wrong.

He was so damn stubborn it would be just like him to try to prove Fenwick wrong now about getting engaged. But then he wouldn't be risking just some money.

He would be risking his life.

Chapter 3

Juliette sat on one of the chairs in the row outside the chief's office. She'd given her report and she had helped Pandora give hers as well as a description of the shooter to Detective Carson Gage who would be working the murder case.

The last thing the Red Ridge Police Department could handle right now was another murder investigation. They were already spread so thin with the Groom Killer murders and the suspected criminal activities of the Larson twins. Did the RRPD have enough resources left to protect Pandora? That was what Juliette wanted to know, what she waited outside the chief's office to discuss with him.

But of course, Finn Colton was busy. So busy that she had to wait. The receptionist was busy, as well, taking one call after another. Usually they would have had time to talk while Juliette waited to see the chief. She would have asked Lorelei about her teenage kids, and Lorelei would have asked about Pandora.

Elle was with Pandora, coloring pictures in the conference room and trying to get her to eat the pizza she'd ordered for them. Elle was a good friend.

The only person Juliette had told about that night nearly five years ago. The night she'd felt like Cinderella being invited to the ball.

The invitation she'd received had come in the form of a tip from a hotel guest. Juliette had been cleaning the woman's room all week. She'd sought Juliette out a couple of times for more towels, to restock the minibar, and she'd talked to her like Juliette was a person and not just a maid. The woman had compelled Juliette to confide in her about working two jobs to pay off her late mother's medical bills and tuition for community college.

So later that week Juliette was disappointed that the woman had checked out before her business conference ended. She was even more surprised that instead of finding money as a tip, she found a note lying atop a glittering mound of a gown and some sky-high heels and long, dangling glittery earrings. The note read:

No cash for a tip, but take these as thanks. Had my heart broken in them and will never wear again.

Juliette wasn't so sure that was the case. The woman she'd met had seemed too strong and self-reliant to care much if her heart had been broken. She'd probably left her the items instead of cash because she'd known the cash would have just gone toward those medical bills. The shoes and earrings and that glittery gown were something Juliette never would have bought for herself. One, she couldn't have afforded them. And two, she wouldn't have needed them since she had no place to wear them. But lying beneath the note was a ticket granting her entry to the conference awards black tie dinner.

Because of her mom's long illness, Juliette had skipped her high school prom a couple of years ago. It hadn't mattered much to her then—not as much as it had meant to her mother, who'd felt so bad that Juliette hadn't attended it. But it wasn't as if Juliette had had a date anyway. And even if she had, she wouldn't have wanted to miss a minute left of her mother's limited time.

Juliette had already forgotten her father because he had died when she was very young. At least now her parents, who'd been high school sweethearts, were together again.

And Juliette was alone. Should she dress up and give herself the prom she'd missed? But instead of goofing around with high school kids who didn't understand how precious life was, she would be socializing with adults, with accomplished businesspeople.

The idea thrilled her too much for her to resist. The guest had been like a fairy godmother leaving behind that dress and heels and earrings. All that was missing were the carriage and the horses. But Juliette didn't need a pumpkin and some mice. She had her own vehicle.

When her shift ended, she left the hotel in her maid's drab uniform with her *tips* tucked inside her backpack. Her friend, who was going to cosmetology school, was thrilled to do her hair and makeup, so just a few short hours later, Juliette returned to the hotel where she worked. But not even her coworkers recognized her as she swept into the ballroom wearing those impossibly high and dainty heels as well as the long, nude-colored glittery gown. Her hair was half up and half down in some complicated style that defied gravity. And when she moved, the long dangling earrings brushed against her neck. For the first time in her life, Juliette felt like a princess. Even then she'd suspected it would be the last time she would ever feel like this.

So she'd vowed then and there to make the most of this magical evening. To experience everything that she could—because she knew very well how short life could be. Her *ball* wasn't exactly what she'd expected, though. Her fairy godmother must not have been the only one who'd cut the conference short, because the ballroom was not crowded, which made *him* impossible to miss.

He was younger than most of the other men in the room, and by far the most handsome in his black tuxedo. He was lean and muscular and just the right height that with these heels on, she would be able to stare into his eyes. Eyes that she knew were green and sharp with his keen intelligence. He wasn't much older than she was, but he already had his MBA.

Blake Colton. The only male heir of the wealthy branch of the Colton family. He was the prince of Red Ridge. And Juliette was…

For the night, Cinderella.

She felt the moment he noticed her—because her pulse quickened, and her skin began to tingle. She didn't even need to look up to know that he was coming toward her. Her heart beat faster and faster as he drew nearer to her.

"Hello," a deep voice murmured.

She turned and stared right into his eyes. And she knew in that moment, she never wanted to look away.

She didn't just see him; she saw herself in his eyes—the way she wanted to be: beautiful, interesting, happy.

He sucked in a breath, and she knew that he felt it, too—that instant and intense attraction between them. He extended a hand to her, and it shook slightly. "I—I'm Blake Colton."

She knew who he was. Hell, everybody in Red Ridge knew who he was. But he didn't know that she was from Red Ridge. She could have been from anywhere—could have been anyone. And for tonight, she could pretend that she was.

But her first instinct was to be honest, so she murmured, "I'm Juliette…" And she put her hand in his.

He cocked his head, and a lock of dark blond hair tumbled across his forehead. He was obviously waiting for her last name.

But instead of giving it to him, she just smiled.

He chuckled. "You're going to be mysterious," he said.

Her smile widened. "I'm going to be smart."

Just in case she got caught crashing the event, she didn't want to get fired from her job. Technically, since he was a Colton, and she worked for the Colton Plaza Hotel, he was her boss. He could even fire her.

"You don't trust me," he said.

"I don't know you," she said.

He uttered a sigh, as if that was a relief—that she didn't know him. But then he said, "Let's change that. Let's get to know each other." He entwined their fingers and tugged her along with him as he headed out of the ballroom.

"Where are we going?" she asked.

He stopped near the bank of elevators and pressed

the up button. While he didn't live in the hotel, he had a suite reserved on the twenty-first floor. Was this why? Because he could pick up women as easily as he'd picked up her?

He turned back to her. "I want to see you under the stars," he said. "There's a bar on the roof, and a band. A better one than the conference has. I suspect that's where everyone has gone."

So he hadn't just assumed she'd go to his room. That was good. But she had to acknowledge a flash of disappointment. She wouldn't have been upset at being invited to see his suite. The night wasn't over yet. She'd just left the ball, and she didn't mind since she was leaving with the prince. The elevator doors swooshed open to a full car of rowdy-sounding guests. They must have been abandoning the quieter bar in the lobby for the rooftop lounge.

She stepped back, willing to wait for the next elevator. But Blake pulled her inside with him. As crowded as it was, they had to stand very close to each other—so close that they touched everywhere. Arm, hip, thigh…

A guest jostled Juliette, and her heel twisted, nearly twisting her ankle, as well, but Blake's arm slid around her waist, pulling her more tightly against him. Even after the doors opened and they exited onto the roof, Blake kept his arm around her.

He led her onto the dance floor and pulled her closer yet as he held her in his arms. They danced slowly— slower even than the beat of the music. It was as if Blake, too, wanted to savor every minute of the evening like Juliette did.

He stared at her so intently that she lifted a hand to her face and asked, "What's wrong?"

Had her makeup run down her face? She usually didn't wear this much, but her friend had applied it heavily, to make Juliette look older—like the accomplished businesswoman her fairy godmother had been.

Blake lifted her hand from her face and replaced it with his, sliding his thumb along her jaw. "You are so beautiful—" he uttered a wistful sigh "—more beautiful than the stars themselves…"

She smiled. Her prince was definitely charming. Not that he was hers…except maybe for this night. A night she intended to make the most of—while it lasted.

They danced until the band stopped for a break. Then Blake, his arm still around her, began to steer her toward the rooftop bar.

But Juliette saw who the bartender was, a young man she'd turned down for a date several times. If he recognized her and—given how he always stared at her—he probably would, she knew he would blow her cover and destroy her evening. So she dug in her heels and propelled them to a stop.

"Don't you want a drink after all that dancing?" Blake asked.

"Uh, yes…" Despite the cool autumn air blowing around the roof top, she was hot and flushed, but that was more from his closeness than from the dancing. "But not here…"

Blake glanced down at her. "Then where?"

She knew what he would think, but she didn't care. She didn't want her ball to end at midnight. She was greedier than Cinderella. She wanted longer than a few hours and more than a few dances. She wanted Blake. "Your room."

He stared into her eyes, and as he did, his pupils dilated, swallowing the green. Then, his arm around her, he led her back to the elevators. But a line had already formed for them. So he pushed open the door to the stairs. "It's just one flight down," he assured her.

But when her heel slipped on one of the steps, he swung her up in his arms. "We can't have you breaking an ankle," he murmured.

"I can take off the shoes," she offered. She didn't want to break an ankle, either, because when this evening was over, she would have to go back to her real life and her two jobs and mountain of bills.

"I have you," he assured her.

A wistful sigh slipped through her lips. She wished he had her, but he didn't even know her. If he did, he wouldn't be carrying her; he would be asking her for extra towels. But she wasn't going to worry about that now. She was just going to enjoy being treated like a princess. So she linked her arms around his neck and snuggled against him, brushing her lips over his throat.

His pulse leaped beneath her mouth, and he tensed. "Now *I* might slip," he murmured. But he was already on the landing, pushing open the door with his shoulder. A few strides down the hall and he stopped outside a door. "You'll need to take the key card from my pocket," he said, and his voice sounded strange, strangled.

She smiled and slid one hand over his ass.

He nearly jumped and cleared his throat. "Not that pocket. Inside jacket pocket."

So she moved her hand between them, pushing aside his jacket to run her fingers down his dress shirt and over the rippling muscles beneath the silk.

"You need to find that key," he said through gritted teeth, "quickly."

"Why?"

He showed her why—with his mouth. He lowered his head and brushed his lips across hers before deepening the kiss.

Passion coursed through Juliette, and she kissed him back with all the desire she felt for him. Her hands moved through his short, spiky dark gold hair as she held his head to hers.

His arms tightened around her, and he shuddered slightly. Lifting his mouth from hers, he panted for breath and murmured, "The key card..."

She fumbled inside his jacket until she found it. When she pulled it out, the card nearly slipped from her fingers. Blake caught it and swiped it through the lock. Then he pushed open the door and carried her over the threshold.

The significance of the gesture must have sobered him a little because he set her on her feet and closed the door. And as he did, he ran his hand through the hair she'd tousled. "I—I got carried away," he murmured, his face flushed.

"Uh, technically I was the one who got carried away," she said. "Or carried down...the stairs."

His sexy mouth curved into a grin. But the humor didn't entirely reach his green eyes; he still looked troubled. Maybe he'd changed his mind about bringing her to his room. He left her standing by the door as he headed to the bar on the other side of the large suite.

"Don't worry," she assured him. "I know you carrying me over the threshold doesn't make me your bride."

He shuddered at the thought.

She'd been so hot earlier—in his arms, with his mouth on hers. But now she was chilled.

"I'm sorry," he said. "It's just that I want nothing to

do with marriage. My dad has had more than his share of marriages and I don't think any of them made him happy." His mouth pulled down into a frown now. "Actually I don't think anything makes him happy…except maybe his company and his money…"

"I'm sure that *you* do," she said. "That he loves you very much…" He had to be so proud of Blake; she'd heard that instead of going to work for Colton Energy with his oldest sister, Blake had launched his own successful start-up company straight out of business school.

He snorted. "You don't know my father," he said. "He doesn't love anyone but himself."

She'd heard that Fenwick Colton was one selfish son of a bitch. But how could he not love his own child?

She'd been feeling sorry for herself until now—until realizing that even though she'd lost her parents, at least she'd had no doubt that she had made them happy and that they had loved her.

His jaw was tense, a muscle ticking in his cheek. "I'm not going to make the mistakes he has. No marriage for me. No kids. Then nobody will feel like they don't matter as much as business does to me—because that is all that's going to ever matter to me."

He was warning her, but it wasn't a warning that she needed. She had no intention of getting married or having kids, either. She was taking criminal justice courses at community college because she wanted to be a cop, specifically a K9 cop. Her other job was helping out at the Red Ridge canine training center, and she loved working with the dogs.

"Maybe I'm more like my dad than I realized," he murmured. Along with Blake's words, she heard the pain and resentment in his voice. And she felt his pain, as well.

She stepped away from the door, crossing the room to where he stood by the bar with the wall of windows behind him, looking down on Red Ridge. Like she'd always thought he would look down on her.

But Blake Colton wasn't the spoiled, privileged prince she'd thought he would be. He was vulnerable and charming and incredibly handsome. He sighed and blew out a ragged breath. "I'm so sorry," he said. "I shouldn't be thinking about anything but how lucky I am."

She'd always thought he'd been born with a silver spoon in his mouth. But while he didn't have to worry about money, he had more emotional concerns.

He stepped closer and touched her chin. Sliding his fingertips along her jaw, he tipped her face up toward his. "I'm the luckiest man in Red Ridge that you came back to my room with me."

Her lips curved into a smile. And there was the charm again. Her prince…

She linked her arms around his neck again and pulled his head down for her kiss. She'd just felt his vulnerability, his pain, and she sought to soothe it with her lips and her passion. That kiss led to more—to making love the entire evening—over and over again.

But just before dawn, when Juliette had heard the creak and clatter of a cart in the corridor, she'd remembered who she was and that she had a shift to begin soon. So she'd slipped out of the arms of her sleeping prince, back into her dress and heels and into the hall.

Within minutes the dress and heels had been stowed in her locker, and she'd been back in her drab uniform of a Colton Plaza Hotel maid. Hours later, Blake had passed her in the hall while she was wearing that uniform, and he hadn't noticed her at all.

And she'd realized the night that had seemed so special to her was just a dream born of a silly fantasy. She was no Cinderella and Blake Colton was no prince charming. He would never try to find her and propose. He'd made it all too clear what he thought of marriage and that he never intended to make the mistakes his father had made—with women or children.

So when she'd missed her period and taken that pregnancy test, she'd been reluctant to seek him out with the news that he was going to be the father he'd sworn he never wanted to become. She'd known he would be furious with her—maybe even think she'd tricked him.

But before she'd been able to build up her courage to confront him, she'd seen in the *Red Ridge Gazette* "People" section that he'd left Red Ridge and not just for a vacation. He intended to launch his start-up company in other countries and call it Blake Colton International.

International…

So why was he back in town?

He wanted to talk to Juliette. Why? What did he want from her? Their child? He'd vowed he'd never wanted to be a father. That was why, even when Elle had been urging her to tell him, Juliette had hesitated to seek him out. She hadn't wanted him to reject his child.

But he hadn't looked at Pandora like he was going to reject her. Juliette closed her eyes as fear overwhelmed her. Why had he wanted to see their daughter now—when she'd just witnessed a crime?

Now Juliette had to worry about losing Pandora to her father as well as to a killer.

Chapter 4

Blake paced the suite on the twenty-first floor of the Colton Plaza Hotel. This was the same room where he'd spent that incredible evening with *Juliette*. He hadn't known her last name then. And after she'd slipped away from him, he hadn't even known if Juliette was her real first name or if she'd just been a Shakespeare fan. He'd had no idea who she really was. Hell, he still didn't know who she was or even if she would show up like he'd requested.

He stopped at the windows that looked down onto the lights of Red Ridge. He'd turned on only one of the lamps in the room, so his reflection stared back at him in the glass.

And he had to be honest. He hadn't requested that she come; he'd demanded. Maybe he was more like his old man than he'd thought—than he'd ever hoped to be.

But then, he had every reason to make demands of Juliette. She'd been lying to him—that night all those years ago and every day since, when she'd kept his daughter from him.

The fury he'd felt when he'd seen her—with that child in her arms—coursed through him again. He was not going to spend another day in the dark. Hell, he was not going to spend another minute. He'd give her a little more time to show up tonight. Then he would track her down, and at least this time—unlike last—he knew where to look for her. At the Red Ridge Police Department...

She'd been wearing a uniform. She worked there. He shouldn't have left the building. He should have talked to his cousin Finn, but not about what was going on in Red Ridge. He should have asked him about Juliette and about what the hell crime her—*their*—daughter had witnessed.

How much danger were she and her mother in? Was that why Juliette hadn't shown up yet? Had something happened?

Too anxious for answers, Blake turned away from the windows and headed toward the door. When he jerked it open, he found her standing in the hall—as if she'd been trying to work up her nerve or her courage to face him.

He glanced around her, but she was alone. She hadn't brought the little girl or her dog. She wasn't wearing her uniform anymore, either. She'd changed into a khaki skirt and a loose blouse. It didn't matter what she wore— that glittery gown from years ago, the uniform or casual clothes—like a blonde doll getting dressed up in different outfits, she looked beautiful in anything.

But she was the most beautiful in nothing at all...

"You're here," he murmured, and instinctively he

reached out to touch her, to see if she was real. Because when he'd thought about that night for the past five years, he'd always wondered if it had really happened or if it had just been some fantasy he'd conjured up.

Before he could brush his hand across her cheek, she flinched and stepped back. "That's not why I came here."

She must have thought he was making a pass. And he hadn't been—at least, not consciously.

"That's not why I asked you here," he said. He stepped back so she could enter the suite.

But she hesitated, as if she didn't believe him.

"Seriously," he said. "All I want from you is the truth. You damn well owe me that." She'd owed him that for the past five years.

She drew in a deep breath and stepped across the threshold, which reminded him of that night, of how he'd carried her across it and freaked out. She glanced up, met his gaze and nodded, as if she remembered it, too. "That's why," she said. "Even if I could have found you after you left town, I didn't think you'd want to know. You'd made it clear that you didn't want to be a father—ever."

He still didn't. But he didn't have a choice now. He was one. Wasn't he?

"So she is mine?"

She hesitated a moment, as if debating whether she could get away with lying about it.

"I'll ask for a paternity test," he warned her. No matter what she told him, he should do that anyway. But he didn't need one. That little girl looked like him—down to the dimple in her left cheek.

Color rushed to her pale skin as her face flushed. "She's yours."

He hadn't shut the door yet, so he looked into the hall again. Empty. "Why didn't you bring her?" he asked as he closed the door.

He hadn't chosen to be a father, but now that he was one, he wanted to know about his child. He wanted to see her, to talk to her, to hold her…especially when he remembered how upset she'd been at the police department. The tears, the fear…

Juliette's teeth sank into her bottom lip and she shook her head. And in her eyes were the same tears and fear that had been in her daughter's.

"What happened today?" he asked. "What crime did she witness?" He should have asked that earlier— should have demanded his answers then. But he'd been too stunned to think, to feel anything but shock.

"Murder," Juliette replied.

And that shock struck him again. He shook his head. "No…" He'd known there had been some murders in Red Ridge, but those had involved grooms. "Were you two at a wedding?"

Juliette shook her head. "We were at the park. She was sitting on top of the tall slide, and she saw a man and woman in the parking lot." She shivered. "She told me and the detective later what happened—that the woman opened a suitcase full of bags of sand and the man pulled out a gun and shot her. Then he threw the suitcase in the car and came after us." Her voice cracked with that fear.

And Blake instinctively reached for her again. But this time she didn't pull away. Instead she let him tug her into his arms and hold her as she trembled against him.

"What happened then?" he asked.

Obviously, she and the little girl had gotten away from the killer. But he wanted the details, needing to know how close he had come to losing them before he'd even known they were here.

"I hid Pandora in the tunnel under the slide..."

Pandora. That was the little girl's name.

"He didn't find her?"

"He found us," Juliette said. "But before he could shoot us, I shot him."

He shuddered now. He hadn't known her at all five years ago. She'd seemed so refined—so delicate—but she was much stronger than he'd known.

"I just grazed his shoulder, and he got away before I could arrest him," she said, her voice heavy with regret. "He told me that he'd get her, though. And I know that he will try. She saw him kill that woman."

That poor little girl. Nobody should have to witness something so horrific, let alone a child.

He pulled Juliette's trembling body even closer to his. But he wasn't sure whom he was trying to comfort now—her or himself. "Where is she?"

"The woman died."

"No," he said. "Your—our—" His voice cracked as he corrected himself, and he felt a rush of his own fear. "Our daughter," he continued. "Where is she?"

Juliette's breath shuddered out, brushing softly across his throat. Then she stepped back, out of his embrace, and wrapped her arms around herself. "I talked the chief into putting her in a safe house. The killer saw my uniform, so I'm sure he will be able to figure out who I am easily enough and where we live."

"You're in danger, too, then," he said, and he fought the urge to reach for her again, to hold her in his arms and keep her safe. "If he got close enough for you to shoot him, you saw him."

She nodded. "He was wearing sunglasses and a hood. But the hood blew back, and the glasses slipped down…" She shuddered again. "And I'll never forget that face, those eyes…"

He'd once said the same thing about her—that he would never forget her. And that had scared him, too, but no way near to the extent that she was afraid. She feared for her life. He'd feared only for his heart.

"So you can identify him," he said. Hopefully the Red Ridge Police Department could find the guy and put him behind bars for life for the life he'd taken.

"I looked through all the mug shots and—" she shook her head "—nothing. I thought he looked familiar, but I couldn't find any arrest or outstanding warrant for him." Her brow furrowed with frustration.

That same frustration coursed through him. Now there was more than one killer on the loose in Red Ridge. But this killer wasn't after just grooms. He was after Juliette and Blake's daughter.

"I'm going to hire private guards to watch that safe house," he said. He'd heard of a reputable security firm out of River City, Michigan. He would hire the Payne Protection Agency to guard his little girl. He hadn't known he was a father until now—but now that he knew, he was going to do the best he could by his daughter.

Juliette shook her head. "That's not necessary. Red Ridge PD will protect her. She has an officer staying with her inside the house and another one patrolling outside it. She has police protection 24-7."

And what about Juliette? Who was protecting her? Nobody had been in the hall with her when she'd arrived. Was there anyone waiting outside to protect her? Or had she come alone?

Blake shook his head. "The department is spread too thin right now. Surely you must realize that—with a serial killer on the loose and then this…murder involving drugs…"

What the hell had happened to Red Ridge since he'd been gone? When he was growing up here, it used to feel like nothing ever happened—except for that one night. But now too much was happening in Red Ridge.

Too damn much crime…

Juliette's face flushed again, and finally she nodded in agreement. "Our resources are limited right now…"

And they were about to get more limited. That was another reason Patience had called him. If their father lost Colton Energy, Red Ridge would lose their funding for the K9 program, as well. His late first wife's trust had originally funded the program, and he'd taken over when that had run out.

If the program ended, then Juliette would probably lose her job—her way of supporting their daughter, which she'd been doing alone.

Until now.

"You'll have to run it past the chief, though," she cautioned him.

That wasn't all Blake intended to run past the chief. He intended to make sure Juliette had protection, as well. But he didn't bring it up now because he didn't want to argue with her while she was upset.

"He doesn't even want me going to visit Pandora at the safe house," she remarked, and there was a little catch in her voice, as if she was choking down a sob.

Blake reached for her again, pulling her against him. His body tensed as attraction overwhelmed him.

"I've never been separated from her before," Juliette said. "She's never spent a night away from me…"

And his attraction cooled as his anger returned. Now he stepped back, breaking the physical connection with her. And physical was all they would ever have—if that. She was a woman he would never be able to trust—not after how she'd misled him five years ago.

Obviously she had not been the rich businesswoman he'd thought she was. And then to keep his daughter from him…

"I can't say the same," he remarked resentfully. "All I've been is separated from her. You should have told me…"

"I told you why," she said, and she gestured at the door and that threshold. "I didn't think you'd want to be part of her life."

He shook his head, rejecting her excuse. "I should have been given the chance to decide that for myself," he said. "You should have told me."

She shrugged. "You were already gone."

"But all my family is still in Red Ridge," he said. Except for his mother, who was always traveling. "You could have found me."

She snorted. "Like you tried to find me?"

"I told you, I tried," he said. "But after you snuck out in the middle night without even giving me your last name, I didn't have much to go on."

"You walked right past me," she said.

He laughed. Like that would have been possible. There was no way he wouldn't have noticed her, especially after that night. "When?"

"The very next day," she said. "Just out in the hallway." She gestured toward the door again. "But then, I didn't expect you to notice me. I was just the hired help."

He snorted now. "Yeah, right…in that dress, those heels…" The earrings. He still had those. She'd left them on the nightstand next to the bed.

"Those were a tip from a hotel guest," she said. "I was a maid here, putting myself through college."

He narrowed his eyes. "What was that night about?" Had she deliberately set out to seduce him? To get pregnant? But if that had been her plan, why hadn't she told him when she'd gotten pregnant?

If she'd been after money, that would have been the time for her to ask. But she'd never asked. She had raised their daughter all these years with no financial support from him. Unless she'd gotten it from someone else…

He narrowed his eyes and studied her face. "What were you after?"

Maybe it wasn't him at all. His father dated only younger women. Blake felt physically sick at the thought of her with Fenwick Colton.

"Nothing," she said. "I didn't want anything from you then and I don't want anything from you now."

"You already took something from me," he said. "My daughter—and nearly five years of her life."

Juliette flinched. "I'm sorry. I really didn't think you'd care…"

That night he'd told her so much—about his family—about himself. He'd been vulnerable with her in a way that he'd never been vulnerable with anyone else. Maybe she'd thought he was like his father despite his vow that he didn't want to be. Maybe she'd thought he was too selfish to care about his kids or anyone else.

"You should have let me decide," he said.

Her face flushed again, and she slowly nodded in agreement. "You're right. I'm sorry." Her voice cracked with emotion. "I can't give those years back to you, but I can show you pictures. Videos. Christmas and birthdays and Halloween parties."

His chest ached at the thought of all those milestones he'd missed. But photos and videos wouldn't tell him what he really wanted to know. "What is she like?"

Juliette's lips curved into a smile, and her already beautiful face became even more so as love radiated from within her. "She's amazing. So sweet. So generous. So funny…" She chuckled as if remembering something.

Something he'd missed. He'd missed a lot of somethings that nothing could bring back. No matter what she told him.

She shared stories with him. Story after story about something Pandora had done or said. And finally she must have noticed that while he listened, he said nothing. His heart ached too much over all the time he'd lost with his child.

She reached out now and ran her hand down his arm. "I'm sorry," she said again, and tears glistened in her blue eyes until she blinked them back. "I'm so sorry…" It was obvious she felt guilty now.

But Blake couldn't absolve her of that guilt. He couldn't change what had happened or get back those years he'd lost. And because of that, he would never be able to forgive her.

She had kept so much from him—his daughter and the truth about who and what she was. So he would never be able to trust her, either.

Finn looked pointedly at his wrist as he opened his condo door for his late-night visitor. He wasn't wearing a watch, though. He'd taken that off when he'd gone to bed a couple of hours ago. He was *not* happy that he'd had to leave his sexy, naked fiancée in that bed alone to answer the door.

Not that anyone knew he was engaged. Because of that damn Groom Killer, he and Darby were forced to keep their engagement secret. He suspected theirs wasn't the only secret engagement in town.

"What do you want, Blake?" He'd heard his billionaire cousin was back in Red Ridge, but he hadn't seen him yet. He could have waited until daylight for that. Maybe Blake was still on whatever time zone he lived in now.

"I need to talk to you about Juliette…"

"Walsh?" Finn finished for him. That was the only Juliette he knew.

Blake's handsome face twisted into a slight grimace as he nodded. "Yes, Walsh."

Finn wrinkled his brow. "How do you know that particular K9 cop?" Juliette's partner specialized in drug sniffing. Had Sasha gotten a hit on Blake?

A lot of spoiled rich kids got involved in drugs. But Blake, despite being the only male heir to the rich branch of the Colton family, wasn't spoiled. Finn knew he'd worked damn hard to establish his own business without his father's help. Maybe that was because he'd been trying to spite his father, though.

"I met Juliette before I left Red Ridge," Blake said—almost reluctantly.

"That was nearly five years ago," Finn remembered. "How would your paths have crossed? Juliette was working two jobs back then to pay off her mother's medical bills and put herself through college." He had a lot of respect for the young woman's work ethic. That was why he was damn happy to have her as part of his police force.

A ragged breath escaped Blake's lips. "I—I didn't know that…"

"So you didn't know her well, then," Finn said. Sounded like he hadn't even known her last name. "What's with your sudden interest in her now?"

"I—I know she and her daughter are in danger," Blake said. "And I want to help."

Finn furrowed his brow again. "That's not necessary." A civilian like Blake would only get in Finn's way. "I've got it handled. The little girl is in a safe house with around-the-clock protection—"

"Juliette should be in the safe house, too," Blake said. "With the child."

Finn nodded. "I tried that. She refused to go into hiding." He suspected she wanted to personally catch the killer who'd traumatized her daughter. "I'll have other officers watching her at all times."

Blake shook his head. "That's not enough. With all these murders, the Red Ridge PD is spread too thin."

Finn couldn't argue with that. He was damn tired of not being able to find Demi. He would have rather she was the cousin who had paid him this late-night visit, so he could figure out whether or not she was the Groom Killer. He suspected not, and there was a psycho on the loose in Red Ridge.

Then he also had the Larson twins and all the criminal activities he suspected they were behind to deal with, as well. He needed more than suspicions to nail them, though. He needed proof. But the officers he'd put on surveillance of the twins' real estate company hadn't come up with anything yet.

"We're spread a little thin," he reluctantly admitted. "But we protect our own. Nothing will happen to Juliette or her daughter." He would make damn sure of that.

Blake shook his head again, and there was a slightly wild look in his green eyes. Fear. He was really afraid for Juliette and Pandora. But why did a woman he'd barely known years ago matter so much to him?

"I'm hiring a private security company out of Michigan," he said. "I want to have bodyguards backing up the police at the safe house and the car following Juliette around."

Finn groaned. He didn't need outsiders getting in his way any more than he needed billionaire Coltons. He already had Blake's father breathing down his neck to find Demi; he didn't need Blake breathing down his neck, too. At least his father had a reason; he was worried about his business. Apparently his daughter was supposed to marry a zillionaire to save Colton Energy in a merger. But because of the Groom Killer, Layla Colton's fiancé had called off the necessary wedding.

What was Blake's reason?

So Finn asked, "Why do you care so damn much about a woman you must not have seen in five years?"

Blake's jaw clenched so tightly that a muscle twitched in his cheek—in his left cheek with the deep dimple in it. The same one Juliette's little girl had.

"She's yours," Finn said with sudden realization. "Juliette's daughter is yours."

Blake nodded.

"I didn't know…" Finn murmured. How had the Red Ridge rumor mill missed that juicy bit of gossip? Hell, how had the media?

"Neither did I," Blake replied.

And Finn flinched for him. Obviously, his cousin had just learned that he was a father—as his daughter was in danger. He reached out and squeezed his shoulder. "I don't know what to say, man…"

"Say that you'll accept my help," Blake said. "These bodyguards are the best."

Finn sighed.

"And along with the bodyguards, I intend to protect Juliette myself," Blake said.

Finn snorted.

Blake tensed, looking offended.

"Come on," Finn said. "You're no bodyguard." He was a billionaire.

"The bodyguards will be there, too," Blake pointed out. "So will your officers."

"Yeah, so you don't need to be," Finn said.

"Yes, I do."

And from the determination in his cousin's voice, Finn knew there would be no arguing him out of it. Even if he flat-out told him not to, he suspected Blake would follow her around anyway.

"Why?" he asked again. Blake's revelation explained why he wanted the extra protection on Pandora but not on Juliette. "Why would you put your life in danger for someone who didn't even tell you that you had a kid?"

Blake sighed. "This isn't about me. It's about that little girl. She can't lose the only parent she knows."

Finn echoed Blake's sigh in agreement. But he had to point out, "She might lose both of you since you're putting your life in danger, too."

Chapter 5

"Why can't you come tuck me in, Mommy?" The question emanated from the speakers in Juliette's personal vehicle since her cell had connected via Bluetooth.

She wanted more than anything to be with her daughter, to hold her in her arms. She had only missed that first night of tucking Pandora into bed, but Elle had assured Juliette that the little girl had been so exhausted she'd fallen immediately to sleep. That was not the case tonight. Tonight, she was so upset that Elle had had to call Juliette to settle her down.

Pandora seemed to be getting more and more upset. She wanted to be with Juliette as badly as Juliette wanted to be with her. They were all each other had ever had. And it was killing Juliette to be away from her.

Last night Juliette had had a distraction—that meeting with Blake. It had gone better than she'd expected it would. While he had been angry with her, he hadn't been as furious as he could have been with her, as he probably should have been with her.

But he'd been too concerned about the danger she and Pandora were in to focus too much on what she'd done. On how she'd betrayed him. She had no doubt that, despite her apologies, he hadn't forgiven her, though.

He had just made keeping Pandora safe his top priority. But what would happen once the killer was caught? What would Blake do then?

He would want to meet his daughter. He deserved to meet his daughter. Yet right now that would be putting her at risk—just like Juliette visiting her would. That was why the chief had insisted that if she was determined to keep working, she couldn't go to the safe house. They couldn't risk the killer following Juliette to her daughter.

But when that soft voice emanated from the car speakers, breaking with sobs as she pleaded, "Mommy, come tuck me in…" Juliette worried that she'd made the wrong choice. Her heart ached with missing her little girl.

She'd thought that if she stayed on the job, she would be able to find the killer faster than her coworkers. After all, she'd seen him; they hadn't. Hell, she'd even hoped to draw him out, so that this would all be over soon. So that she and Pandora could go back to their everyday, perfect life together.

But even after the killer was caught, they wouldn't be able to do that—because of Blake Colton. No matter what, he would be part of their daughter's life now. And that would make him part of Juliette's. He wouldn't be just a nearly five-year-old memory. Juliette focused on her daughter again. "Sweetheart, I wish I could be with you right now…"

But she loved her too much to put her in any more danger than she already was.

"I'm working right now, though, baby…"

A little hiccupping sob echoed throughout the car. "Did you get the bad man, Mommy?"

"Not yet, honey," she said. "But I will find him pretty soon. Then we can go home."

"I wanna go home now, Mommy!" Pandora said, and now her sobs became wails of frustration and anxiety.

Juliette's already aching heart threatened to break. She hated when her daughter cried, which, until the day before in the park, had been very rarely.

"Shh, shh," she tried to soothe the child. "Don't cry, sweetheart. We will be together again soon." They had to be. It was hurting Juliette as much as it was Pandora for them to be apart.

However, she didn't know if putting the killer behind bars would guarantee that they would never be separated again. What if Blake wanted visitation? What if he would be the one putting their daughter to bed on some nights? But his life wasn't here in Red Ridge; it was overseas, in various other countries, according to the tabloids. The same tabloids that had published photos of him with models and actresses and foreign royalty.

If not for Pandora, Juliette wouldn't have believed that night had happened, because guys like Blake never noticed women like her. She wasn't famous or rich or well connected.

"You gotta catch the bad man, Mommy," the little girl pleaded. "You have to make sure that he doesn't make us dead like he said…"

"You are safe," Juliette promised her. "Nothing will happen to you."

"Are you safe, Mommy?"

Juliette had thought she was. She'd had a very uneventful day despite spending it on the streets, talking to informants, trying to find out if anyone knew anything about the man Pandora had witnessed committing a murder or at least about the purple-haired woman he'd killed. Since Pandora had seen her with a suitcase of drugs, she must have been a dealer. But nobody had been talking.

Yet. She would keep at them until they did.

But while she'd felt safe during the day, she had an odd sensation now. And Sasha, sitting in her harness in the back seat, must have felt it, too, because the beagle suddenly sat up and strained against the pet safety belt.

"Yes, of course I'm safe," Juliette assured her daughter. But then she noticed the glimmer of lights in the rearview mirror. She'd been driving for a while as she'd internally debated whether or not she should go to Pandora. So the routes she'd taken had been circuitous, leading toward neither her house nor the safe house. She'd just turned onto random roads until she found herself on the outskirts of Red Ridge in an area of greenhouses for one of the bigger plant nurseries. In July the greenhouses would be empty—too hot to use for the summer. So why were there lights behind her?

Who would be heading out this way? She didn't think the road led to any housing developments.

A knot of apprehension tightened in her stomach as she faced the likelihood that the vehicle was out there only because it had followed her.

Who? Was it the shooter? Or one of those people Juliette had questioned today? Maybe one of them was ready to talk to her.

She hoped that was the case, but she had to be prepared that it was the former. The killer carrying out the threat he'd made on the playground.

Her pulse quickened. While she was afraid, she was also—oddly—hopeful. Maybe she wouldn't have to search any longer to find him. Maybe he had found her.

The challenge was going to be taking him out before he could take out her. She couldn't leave her daughter alone. But then, Pandora wouldn't be alone. She had a father—a man she had never officially met, though.

"I have to go for now, honey," Juliette told her daughter as she flipped off the headlights and made a sharp turn around one of the empty greenhouses. "But I will see you soon."

As the vehicle following her also made the turn, she swallowed the fear that had rushed up on her. She hoped she would be able to keep that promise to her daughter. She hoped she would be able to see her again.

"Where the hell did she go?" Blake asked himself.

She'd suddenly shut off her lights. But despite that, with the moon shining brightly, he'd been able to see her vehicle turn into the plant nursery. He'd followed it between two greenhouses. But her car was gone.

At least, he couldn't see it.

She couldn't have gone far. His lights shone onto the fields behind the greenhouse. The trees in it were seedlings—not big enough to hide a vehicle, even one as small as her economy sedan.

He drove a little farther—to the end of the greenhouse. Then he rolled down his window to peer around the back of the long building. He felt a sudden presence. From the corner of his eye, he caught the glint of moonlight shining off the barrel of a gun—the one pointed right at his head.

Maybe his cousin Finn had been right. Maybe he should have left the security detail to the professionals. But he hadn't even seen them following Juliette. He'd worried that she'd been left all alone.

"What the hell are you doing?" a female voice asked.

And now he kind of wished he'd left her alone. Juliette sounded furious with him. She pulled her gun back, sliding it into the holster on the belt of her uniform. She hadn't changed even though her shift had ended a couple of hours ago. But with the threat against her and her daughter, she would always be on duty.

Until the killer was caught.

"I'm following you," he said. He'd followed her all day as she'd gone from drug house to drug house. He knew she'd been looking for the killer or for information that would lead to him.

He was stunned that Red Ridge had areas like the ones where she'd gone. Had things changed that much in the past five years? Or had he been so sheltered and self-involved all those years ago that he hadn't known those areas existed?

She uttered a sigh of pure exasperation. "I know you're following me. But why?"

"To protect you." His face heated now with embarrassment that he'd thought he could keep her safe. She was the one with a gun. His only weapon was his cell phone to call for help. For backup from the bodyguards and the police who were supposed to be following her. Where had they all gone?

She snorted. "How? By distracting me so I'll miss seeing the killer if he finds me?"

How was Blake a distraction to her? Was it just his presence? Or was it because of their past? Because of what they'd shared that night and what they had, unbeknownst to him, created? A child…

"I didn't mean to distract you," he said.

"Well, you did…" Then she muttered something else, something that suspiciously sounded like, "You've been doing it for years…"

But he hadn't been around for years. Had she thought of him as often as he'd thought of her? Probably not—because he'd thought about her all the time.

He pushed open the driver's door to step out of his car. But she caught and held it.

"Get back inside," she told. "Turn this car around and leave me alone."

He sucked in a breath, not at her rejecting him—or at least not entirely because of that—but because of the thought of her being alone. Physically he was stronger than she was, so he managed to open the door. But he was careful that he didn't hit her with it; he did propel her back a bit, though. Then he stepped out and shut the door—so there was nothing between them but a few feet of night air. He wanted to wrap his arms around her to protect her, but he was also furious with her.

"What the hell are you doing?" he asked her. "Why are you out here alone?"

Where were the bodyguards and the patrol car? he wondered again. They were supposed to be following her, too, and because of that, they were all aware of the make, model and license plate number of his rental vehicle.

He glanced around and noticed a faint glow of lights on the other side of one of the green houses. The tightness in his chest eased a little. They were here. She had backup.

She hadn't answered him. Had she noticed the glow of lights, too? Maybe those were from her car, though. He still couldn't see where she'd parked it. But it must have been close because he heard the low growl of her dog.

She must have, too, because she cocked her head and listened. And in the moonlight her brow furrowed.

"You aren't meeting someone out here, are you?" he persisted. "I thought your shift ended hours ago."

"It did," she said. "But I didn't want to go home…"

To an empty house. He could hear the pain in her voice, the ache of missing her daughter.

He felt both a twinge of sympathy and one of resentment. She knew their daughter enough to miss her. He didn't even know the child.

"And Elle called me for Pandora," she continued. "She wants to see me."

"Finn thinks it's too dangerous," Blake said, "that someone could follow you."

She sighed. "I guess he's right. You followed me."

"But you noticed me," he pointed out.

Her lips curved into a slight smile as the moonlight bathed her face with a golden glow. "You're not a professional," she said. "You shouldn't be trying to protect me. You're only going to get hurt."

"Too late," he murmured. He already was—hurt over all the years he'd missed with his daughter.

The smile slipped away, and she closed her eyes. "I'm sorry…"

She knew what he was talking about—what he would probably never get over—because no matter what, he couldn't get back those years he'd lost. He just had to make sure he didn't lose any more with her.

"Do you think Finn would let me see her?" Blake asked.

Juliette gasped. "The chief knows? You told him?"

That twinge of resentment spread to an ache. "I'm not keeping a secret that never should have been one in the first place."

Juliette's teeth sank into her bottom lip as if she was physically holding back a protest.

"What are you worried about?" he asked. "What people will think of you?"

She shook her head. "I don't care what people think. I didn't grow up like you. I grew up in the poor area of Red Ridge. People always thought I was trash. So they can't think any worse of me than that."

Trash? He could not reconcile that impression with the one he'd carried of her the past nearly five years— of her in that glittery gown with those high heels and dangling earrings. She'd looked like a movie star. Or a princess...

Cinderella. That was who she'd been. His Cinderella...

But he hadn't been able to find her. Until now...

"I'm worried about Pandora," she said. "I don't want her in any more danger than she already is."

"So you want to keep me away from my daughter even longer?" he asked.

"I want to keep the killer away from her," Juliette said. "If he learns that you're her father—and once word gets out it will be all over the news—then he could follow you to her if you try to see her."

And he couldn't deny that he could probably be easily followed. But Juliette wasn't the only one missing their daughter. She was missing her after just one day. He was missing five years.

But could he take the risk that he might put her in more danger than she already was? No.

This was a hell of a risk. But he had to take it; he had no choice. The longer the K9 cop and her little kid lived, the greater the chance they would identify him. He needed to get rid of her now.

She wasn't alone, though.

He wasn't the only one who'd followed her to the plant nursery. She'd led a damn parade here. So he had to be very careful when he took the shot. He had to make sure it counted—that it killed her—and that he had time to get away before anyone saw him.

Like those other guys, he'd been following her the whole damn day from the time she'd left the Red Ridge Police Department that morning. She'd spent the day shaking things up—talking to informants, visiting drug houses.

He knew why.

She was trying to find him, or at least someone who would tell her who he was. Hopefully all those people were too scared, not just of him but of the people who'd hired him, to talk. But they were drug users, and so they were unpredictable.

He couldn't risk that someone might talk to her. He had to get rid of her. *Now.*

He stared through the scope of the long gun, trying to center her in the middle of it. But that damn guy kept getting in the way...

Who the hell was he? And why was he following her?

Beyond some mild curiosity, it didn't really matter to him who the guy was, though. If he got in the way of the shot, he was going to be dead—like the beautiful K9 cop. And soon her cute little kid would be dead, too.

He put his finger on the trigger.

Chapter 6

The rumble of Sasha's low growl rose to a howl. And Juliette reached for the weapon she'd holstered—apparently too soon.

"Somebody already followed you here," she said as she gazed around the shadows the greenhouses cast.

She'd seen a faint glow a while ago—other lights shining on the premises. It could have been a motion light clicking on, or a vehicle's low beams from the other side of one of the greenhouses.

If someone had followed him here, there was no way she would let Blake anywhere close to Pandora's safe house—she didn't give a damn what her boss said about it. The little girl was not the chief's kid. But she was his cousin...

Juliette sucked in a breath with that sudden realization. And now her boss knew—thanks to Blake going to him behind her back.

"They didn't follow me," he replied. "Finn has a patrol car on you."

Members of her own team...

Juliette expelled the breath she'd sucked in—feeling like she'd been punched.

"And I hired that private security company like I told you I would," he said.

But she hadn't thought the chief would actually agree to Blake bringing in outsiders. And how had they gotten to Red Ridge so quickly?

"There are extra guards on both Pandora and you," Blake said.

She flinched. Did nobody think she could take care of herself? Not even her own coworkers, who should know her best? Sure, all the male ones were big and muscular, and she was not. But they shouldn't underestimate or think she was weak just because she was short and small-boned.

"You can come out!" she called to them. "I know you're all there..."

Nobody rushed out of the shadows, though, as if they weren't sure they were supposed to show themselves. What kind of orders had the chief given her fellow officers? And what had Blake told the bodyguards?

She could understand his hiring extra protection for their daughter. But why had he hired guards for her? And why the hell was he following her around himself?

He wasn't a cop or even a bodyguard. He was going to get himself killed.

And just as she thought it, she glimpsed the flash of a gun blast in the dark. The bullet struck the metal of his rental car just as she knocked Blake to the ground. Another bullet struck the mirror, raining shards of glass down on them. More bullets followed, striking the side of the car right above where they crouched.

He rolled so that she was under him, so that he was protecting her. But she was the cop.

"Let me up," she said.

Despite the situation, despite her frustration, she noted the heat and hardness of his muscular body. Maybe he was more capable of protecting her than she'd realized. He wasn't some soft billionaire. He was strong.

But so was she…

She shoved him off and turned her gun toward the direction from which the shots had come. She knew none of her fellow officers had fired those shots. Nor would bodyguards who'd been hired to protect her.

The shots had to have come from the killer. Along with everyone else, he must have been following her. She fired into the darkness and heard glass breaking as she struck a greenhouse. He must have gotten inside one of them. Or maybe he'd been on top of it.

She needed to check. But when she tried to get to her feet, Blake grabbed her and held her down. "You can't go after him," he said.

"It's my job," she reminded him.

"You're not going after him alone," another voice chimed in as K9 cop Dean Landon rushed up around the rear bumper of Blake's now bullet-ridden rental. He was the explosives expert, but since they didn't often have to deal with bombs in Red Ridge, it wasn't a surprise that the chief had tapped him for this secret assignment.

Tailing Juliette…

Like her, he must have left his dog in his vehicle. She would have released Sasha from her harness and taken her from the car if she thought the beagle could help locate the shooter. But she wasn't sure Sasha had been close enough to him in the park to recognize his scent.

Dante Mancuso joined them near the rear bumper. Unfortunately, he hadn't brought his dog, either. Flash, the bloodhound, was their evidence recovery dog. He'd been brought to the murder scene at the park. "I nearly just took out a couple private security guards," Dante said. "What the hell is going on here?"

"He hired them," Juliette said, gesturing at Blake.

"Well, they're going after the shooter," Dante said.

Juliette shook her head. "No, he's mine."

He'd threatened her and her daughter. She wanted to be the one to put the cuffs on him. She couldn't take the time for Dante to get Flash or even for her to get Sasha. She had to find the killer before the bodyguards did.

"You stay with Colton here," she told Dante. "Make sure he keeps his head down and doesn't get it blown off…"

"Juliette!" Blake protested. "You can't go out there! You're the one he's trying to kill."

"Exactly," she said.

When Blake reached for her again, Dante stepped forward and pushed him back onto the ground. She trusted that her coworker would protect the civilian. And as she headed out, crouching low and keeping to the shadows, Dean Landon crept along beside her. Like a bodyguard, he kept his body between hers and that greenhouse.

The shooting had stopped. The bodyguards must not have found him yet. Or he'd gotten away just like he had in the park even after she'd put a bullet in his shoulder. Damn it…

Juliette couldn't have come this close to capturing him and he had already slipped away because of Blake because he'd held her back. If Blake truly wanted to help her and their daughter, the best thing he could have done was stay the hell out of her way.

"You can't let her go!" Blake yelled in protest as he strained against the hands holding him back. But this cop was a big guy. And he was armed.

"No," the police officer replied. "I can't let *you* go."

Frustration and fear gripped Blake in equal force, threatening to tear apart his madly pounding heart. He'd never been shot at before. And the bullets had come close, breaking the side mirror that had been just above his head and piercing the metal of the rental vehicle.

Juliette had saved his life. But now she was putting her own in danger.

"She can't go out there!" Blake protested. "He's going to kill her!" Those bullets had been meant for her—not him.

"Walsh is a good cop," the guy replied in her defense. "She knows what she's doing. Unlike you…"

Blake flinched. He had never been more aware— when those shots had rung out—that he was out of his element. His element was business, making deals and making money. Not getting shot at…

"The chief warned us that you were probably going to get killed," the guy continued.

Since the police officers backing her up had known about him, why hadn't she? Before Blake could ask him why the chief would have kept such a secret from her, shots rang out again.

Blake jumped up, his every instinct compelling him to run in the direction Juliette had gone and make sure she was all right. But he'd made it only a few feet when the cop knocked him to the ground. And when he tried to get up, a knee settled into his back.

"Stay the hell down," the guy told him. "Or I will damn well cuff you to this car."

That could have been just as dangerous as Blake going after Juliette. But the shots weren't coming anywhere near him now. They were on the other side of the greenhouse—maybe even on the other side of the one next to that one—because they weren't as close or as loud as they'd been when those bullets had nearly struck him.

He closed his eyes and hoped like hell those bullets weren't striking anyone now. Unless that anyone was the killer who'd threatened Juliette and their daughter. Blake didn't care what happened to that man as long as he was stopped.

But he was worried about Juliette and the others.

"Go," he urged the police officer. "Go help them. I'll stay here."

The officer rolled him over and studied his face through narrowed eyes. "I don't think I should trust you."

"I won't get in the way," Blake promised. Not any more than he already had. If Juliette hadn't noticed him following her, she never would have led him to this area—which had presented the killer with the perfect place to go after her.

More shots rang out. And the officer must have been more concerned about his coworkers than he was Blake, because he eased off him. Withdrawing his weapon from the holster on his belt, he headed toward the direction of all that gunfire.

Before Blake had left Red Ridge, he'd held a concealed weapons permit. He'd only applied for it so he would have something in common with his father. He'd thought that once he'd gotten it, his father might take him shooting like he did his business associates. But Fenwick had never invited him along to the range. No matter what Blake had done to get his attention, his father had never given it to him. When Blake had left Red Ridge, he had left the gun and the permit in the safe at his father's house.

He needed them now. He needed to be armed so he could protect Juliette. He only hoped that it wasn't already too late.

For the second night in a row, Finn's sleep was interrupted. But it was his phone ringing, not his doorbell. He fumbled around the bedside table until he grabbed up his cell and accepted the call.

"Chief Colton," he murmured groggily as Darby murmured in her sleep next to him. He slipped out of bed and walked into the hall so he wouldn't wake her.

She worked so damn hard that she needed her rest.

What the hell time was it?

Who would be calling him now?

If it was Blake or, worse yet, Fenwick…

But the voice on the other end was the gruff one of Frank Lanelli, the Red Ridge dispatcher. "Chief, we've got an officer down…"

And Finn's heart lurched in his chest. This was the call he'd never wanted to receive.

"How bad?" he asked, and his voice cracked slightly as concern overwhelmed him.

Lanelli's voice was gruff, too. "I don't know. It didn't

sound good when the call came in. I dispatched the clos-
est ambulance to the scene."

What scene? What the hell had happened? He wanted
all the details, but most important, he wanted to know
if his officer would survive.

"Do you have ETA?" Finn asked. Fortunately he'd
left his clothes in the living room from when Darby had
undressed him earlier. So he was able to pull them on
without disturbing her.

"Hopefully they're en route to the hospital now."

And not the morgue...

He wanted to ask who the officer was, but he was
afraid that he might already know.

Juliette...

She shouldn't have insisted on staying on the job. She
should have gone into the safe house with her daughter. Now she might not ever get the chance to see her
little girl again.

Chapter 7

The minute the waiting room doors opened—everyone jumped up from their seats and rushed toward the chief, who had just arrived at the hospital. But Juliette was already on her feet since she'd been pacing back and forth across the tile floor. So she beat everyone else to Finn Colton.

His blue eyes widened in surprise at seeing her. "It's not you..." he murmured. "The officer down..."

"Dean Landon," she replied. But it should have been her. That was who the killer had been aiming for, but Dean had been in the way. Just like Blake had been when the first shots had rang out.

"How is he?" Finn asked anxiously, his face tight with concern.

Juliette shrugged, her shoulders aching with the

weight of her guilt on them. "We don't know yet. He's still in surgery."

"What about Mancuso?" the chief asked as he glanced around the waiting room. "Is he okay?"

"He stayed behind with Flash to process the scene and collect whatever evidence the shooter might have left behind." She doubted he'd left any. He hadn't at the park. They had nothing but her and Pandora's description of him in order to identify him.

Because of the other officers gathered around, she lowered her voice and said, "You shouldn't have put a patrol on me." She glanced toward where Blake stood apart from everyone else, leaning against one of the brick exterior walls of the waiting room. "And you shouldn't have let him follow me around, either…"

"There was no stopping him," Finn replied. "Just like there was no stopping you. You need to be in that safe house with your daughter."

"I would have been fine," she insisted. "If I'd known I was being followed, I wouldn't have stopped."

Finn flinched, but he didn't acknowledge that she was right—even though they both obviously knew she was.

"You didn't know you were being followed," he said.

She flinched as she realized what she'd admitted. But she had been distracted—thanks to Blake—not inept.

Her boss must have thought she was the latter, though, because he added, "That's why you need backup."

She glanced again at Blake. Despite the dark circles of exhaustion beneath his eyes, he was still so damn handsome that her heart skipped a beat with the attraction that had never died—despite all the years. "I don't need *him* getting in my way. Why would you allow a civilian…"

Finn held up a hand to stop her protest. And he reminded her, "I'm the chief."

He was also Blake's cousin. Was he angry with her, like Blake was, for keeping Pandora a secret?

"I'm sorry," she said. And she was—sorry about so many things. At the moment, she was sorriest about Dean getting hurt. "It's my fault…"

"It's the shooter's fault," Finn said. "We need to find him."

"That's why I want to stay on the job," she said. "Why I don't want to stay at the safe house."

"You need to," a deep voice said, close to her ear.

The man's warm breath made her shiver. Then she tensed as she realized Blake had crossed the room without her noticing. He stood beside her now, so close that she could feel the tension in his body. The same tension that was in hers.

She shook her head. "And lead the killer right to…" *my daughter*… She couldn't say that at the risk that he might correct her and say she was *their* daughter—right in front of most of the Red Ridge Police Department. "…Pandora."

His handsome face was tense, as if it was killing him not to claim the child. But he had to be aware that everyone was watching them, already wondering what the hell he was doing there and what he was to Juliette.

"The bodyguards—they can make sure you get to her safely—with no one following you," he assured her.

She knew they were good. Right before the shots had started, Dean had been telling her that while he and Dante had easily made Blake's tail, they hadn't noticed the bodyguards until the guys had started to approach them at the plant nursery.

"She called you," Blake reminded her. "She wants to see you."

And her heart ached to see her little girl—especially after what had happened tonight. If Dean hadn't taken that bullet, she might not have had the chance to be with her daughter again.

"Those guards are good," the chief agreed. "They can take you to see her—if you want..." But he wasn't talking just to Juliette now. He was looking at Blake, as well.

She felt a twinge of panic that Finn knew. Who else had he told? Anyone? Everyone?

She felt like a fool over that night—over ever thinking that billionaire Blake Colton could be her Prince Charming. Or that she was Cinderella.

She was no princess. She was a cop. "I'm not going to stay there," she warned them both. "I have to find this killer..." Now more than ever, after one of her friends had been hurt because of him—because of her. "And I have to make sure Dean will be okay..."

Like everyone else, she was so worried about the fallen officer. Maybe that was why nobody asked her about Blake and what was going on between them. Or maybe some of them had already put it together—how long Blake had been gone and how old Pandora was...

It was inevitable that the little girl's paternity was eventually revealed. Juliette had already had to tell the child that her daddy wasn't dead—just that he lived very far away.

He wasn't far away anymore, though.

In fact, he was much too close. So close that he could have been in surgery just like Dean Landon. If she hadn't seen that muzzle flash in the dark...

If she hadn't knocked him to the ground...

She shivered, and he slid his arm around her, as if to warm or comfort her. But conscious of everyone watching them, Juliette pulled away. While she didn't want him dead, she was furious with him for putting himself in that position—for putting himself in danger.

The officer's surgery had taken a long time—so long that the sun was already coming up as Blake and Juliette left the hospital. Not that they could see much more than a glimpse of it since they'd been zipped into black bags. They were rolled on stretchers out of the morgue and lifted into the cargo area of a long van. The minute the double doors closed, Blake jerked down the tab of the zipper and freed himself. Usually small spaces didn't bother him, but being zipped alive into a body bag was something from his worst nightmares.

He shuddered as he pushed it down around his shoulders and sat up. Juliette had unzipped hers, as well, and she sat across from him with her back against one of the metal sides of the van. There were no windows in the back and a solid partition between the front seat and the cargo area, so nobody could see them. He kicked off the bag and shuddered again.

"You could have wound up in one of these for real," Juliette warned him, her blue eyes suspiciously bright, as if she was about to cry.

But he doubted she cared enough to cry over him. She was probably upset about her friend.

"Officer Landon is going to be okay," he reminded her.

She sighed. "Not for a while."

The doctor had warned all his coworkers that he had a long recovery ahead of him. While Finn and Juliette had griped about the security agency Blake had hired, he was even happier that he had since the Red Ridge PD was going to be stretched even thinner than it had already been. He was also glad that the security firm could help reunite mother and child.

While he was determined to stick close and protect Juliette, he wasn't convinced that his meeting the little girl was a good idea. His stomach knotted with nerves. He trusted that the security firm would make sure the killer didn't follow them. He was nervous about meeting the child—his child. He had no experience with kids. He didn't know what to say to her, how to act.

Hell, he didn't know what to say to her mother or how to act, and Juliette was an adult. She was stubborn but also strong and brave. She'd been that way all those years ago—confident beyond her years.

Was that because of her mother's illness? He wanted to ask her about it—about all the medical bills Finn had said she'd been working two jobs to pay. Why hadn't she asked him for money back then? She could have, and he would have given it to her. Hell, after that night, he would have given her anything.

But his heart…

After watching his father's failed attempts at marriage and love, Blake knew they weren't for him. He'd also decided never to be a father, but now he was. He didn't have to get involved, though.

He didn't have to be part of her life. She and Juliette had done just fine without him all these years. But now that he knew…he couldn't just walk away. He couldn't pretend that he didn't have a child—like his father had pretty much done Blake's entire life. Sure, he'd acknowledged him and his sisters from time to time, but never with any real attention.

Even if he was bad at this, he still had to be better than his father was. But would he be good enough for a little girl who'd already been traumatized?

Juliette stared at him, as if she was watching all those doubts and fears cross his face. "Do you want to do this?" she asked him.

Those doubts and fears rushed up, choking him, so that he could only nod in response.

"What do you want to tell her?" she asked.

"The truth," he replied as he internally battled back his doubts and fears. "It's been kept for far too long."

She flinched but then persisted, "And what is the truth, Blake? Do you want to be part of her life? Do you want to be a father?"

"I am a father," he said. He wasn't certain how to be one, but he would have to figure it out.

"I'm not sure this is the best time to tell her that," Juliette said. "Not after what she's been through, the danger she knows she's—"

"Maybe having a father will make her feel safer." Having a father hadn't meant a whole hell of a lot to him. But then, he hadn't meant a whole hell of a lot to his father, either.

"She knows she has one," Juliette said.

At least she hadn't told the child he was dead.

"She just doesn't know who he is," Juliette continued.

"Then I would say that it's time she found out who I am, and that I will be here for her," Blake said.

Juliette narrowed her eyes. "For how long? Are you staying in Red Ridge?"

He flinched now. He hadn't even wanted to come

back for a visit, but Patience had convinced him. "I can be her father whether I'm here or abroad."

Her lips drew into a tight line of disapproval. And he knew what she was thinking—the same thing he was— that he was going to be about as involved in Pandora's life as his father had been in his.

He flinched now. Maybe the best thing he could do for the little girl was continue the lie. But he knew how he felt over the truth being kept from him all these years— how betrayed he felt. He couldn't do that to the child.

The van stopped, idling, as something rattled open. Then the van lurched forward before stopping again. The ignition shut off. And something rattled closed. Moments later those back doors opened, but there was still very little light. They were in a garage, parked next to another vehicle. It must have belonged to the officers guarding Pandora.

"We're here?" he asked.

The bodyguard—a burly former Marine—nodded. "Yes, Mr. Colton." The guy reached up to help Juliette down from the back, but she ignored his hand and leaped down on her own.

She was so independent. Too independent.

Why had she never told him about their daughter? She'd already been struggling with her mother's bills. Why hadn't she at least sought him out for financial support?

He ignored the proffered hand and jumped down, as well. "Is it too early?" he asked her. "Will we be waking her up?"

Juliette smiled, transforming her already beautiful face to breathtaking. "She's an early riser. Even on my days off, she doesn't let me sleep in."

The door between the house and the garage opened, and a young woman breathed a sigh of relief before re-holstering her weapon. "I'd hoped that was you!"

The two women embraced.

Blake recognized her as the Red Ridge officer who'd helped Juliette with Pandora at the police department. They seemed like more than coworkers, though. It was clear they were very close friends, especially when the woman glanced at him, and said, "You told him."

Juliette nodded.

And Blake stepped forward with his hand out-stretched. "Yes, she told me," he said. "I'm Blake Colton." He was certain that she already knew, though.

There was an ironic twist to the curve of her lips when she replied, "Yes, I know. I'm Elle Gage." She took his hand and squeezed it. Like Juliette, she was stronger than she looked, and she was obviously trying to send him a message.

Probably not to hurt her friend.

He couldn't hurt someone who didn't care about him. If Juliette had cared, she wouldn't have kept his daughter from him for all these years. But he doubted Elle had had anything to do with that.

She had enough troubles of her own.

He extended his condolences to Elle. "I'm sorry to hear about Bo." When Patience had called to compel him to come home, she'd told him about everything that had happened in Red Ridge—about Bo Gage, the first victim of the Groom Killer, getting murdered the night of his bachelor party. "Was he a very close relative of yours?"

"My brother," she said, and sadness darkened her brown eyes. "I'm surprised you heard about it with how far you live away from here."

"My sister Patience called and told me about it," he explained.

"Everybody thinks Demi Colton did it," she told him, and there was an almost accusatory note in her voice. "She and Bo had been a couple until he broke up with her for another woman."

Oh, God, the last thing Red Ridge needed was the old feud between the Coltons and the Gages firing back up. But that sounded exactly like what Bo's murder had started. Blake just shrugged.

He wasn't part of that. He didn't live in the past like most of this town did. But as a little girl peeked around Elle, he felt a pull to the past—wishing he could go back and reclaim the years he'd lost with her.

"Mommy!" she cried out, and she slipped around the female cop to throw herself into her mother's arms.

Juliette picked her up and spun her around, holding her close. And the look on her face...

It took Blake's breath away. He had never seen such a look of love. It stunned him.

"Mommy! Mommy!" she said as she pulled back and put her tiny hands on either side of Juliette's face. "I missed you..."

The wealth of emotion in those three words pulled at Blake, making his chest ache. He could see how true it was as tears sparkled in the little girl's eyes.

Juliette leaned her forehead against her daughter's and said, "I missed you, too, sweetheart." Then she kissed the little girl's nose.

Pandora wrinkled her nose and giggled. "Can we go home now, Mommy?"

Juliette's lips lowered in a frown. "Not yet, baby..."

"You haven't caught the bad man yet?" the child

asked, and now the tears in her green eyes were tears of fear.

Anger surged through Blake. He wanted to take down that killer himself. And now he understood Juliette's insistence in staying on the job—in trying to find the man who'd threatened their daughter.

"Not yet, honey, but we're getting closer…"

He wasn't so sure about that. The killer had gotten close to her last night—too close when he'd shot the man right next to her.

"I heard about Dean," Elle remarked. While she kept her voice calm for the little girl's sake, anger shone in her eyes.

If the killer was smart, he would get the hell out of Red Ridge now. He was an even more wanted man than he'd been from the shooting in the park. Now he'd shot an officer.

"Dean will be fine," Juliette assured her friend.

Blake glanced back at her and noticed Pandora was staring at him. Was this it? Was this when he needed to introduce himself? What the hell would he say?

But then she asked, "Are you my daddy?"

And everyone gasped in surprise.

"I heard Auntie Elle say you live far away." Apparently the little girl had been standing behind the officer longer than they'd realized. She continued, "And my daddy lives far away."

So Juliette hadn't lied to their daughter.

All three females stared at him, waiting for his reply. He swallowed hard, choking down the emotion rushing up on him. "Yes," he answered her. "I am your daddy."

A long silence followed his acknowledgment. Then Pandora extended her arms toward him, angling away from her mother. For a moment he didn't know what she wanted—until he realized she was reaching for him.

He lifted her from Juliette's arms.

He didn't know much about children, but he suspected Pandora was small for her age. She was so light. He barely felt the weight of her in his arms, but he felt it in his chest, weighing heavily on his heart.

As she had with her mother, she reached up and planted each of her tiny hands on the sides of his face. And she studied him intently as if trying to figure out if they looked alike. And they did.

Or maybe she was trying to discern what kind of man he was. A bad man like the guy who'd killed the woman in the park. Or a good man.

Blake wasn't always sure what he was. He wasn't a killer. But he could be quite cutthroat in business. Some women might claim he was the same with personal relationships. But before and after that night, no one had ever affected him like Juliette had.

A little finger traced over the dimple in his cheek. "I have a dent in my face, too," Pandora said.

"It looks better on you," he said.

"You're handsome," she said. "Just like Mommy said…"

He glanced at Juliette, who flushed a bright red while Elle chuckled. Curious, he asked, "What did Mommy tell you about me?"

"She told me that my daddy was a handsome prince who swept her off her feet." Her mouth curved down into a frown of disapproval. "Why would you knock Mommy down?"

"I picked her up," he said. "I didn't knock her down."

Elle laughed harder and murmured, "That might be a little too much information…"

"He carried me," Juliette clarified. "Because I almost tripped on some stairs…"

Pandora wasn't paying attention to either of the women. She was totally focused on him.

So he felt compelled to say, "I would never hurt your mommy. Or you…"

"Mommy said you left Red Ridge before she could tell you about me."

He glanced at Juliette again, wanting to convey his appreciation that she hadn't lied to their daughter. She could have let Pandora believe that he'd wanted nothing to do with her, especially since that was what she'd thought after the things he'd said that night, that he never wanted to be a husband or a father.

But Juliette wouldn't look at him.

So he focused on their daughter again. "I would have come back sooner," he said, "if I'd known about you." And he gently tightened his arms around the little girl, holding her close to his heart.

She settled her head onto his shoulder and emitted a soft sigh. "I'm glad you're back now," she said. "You can protect me and Mommy from the bad man."

He would damn well try his hardest to guard them— even if his efforts had him ending up in one of those body bags again.

Chapter 8

"By now you've all heard about Officer Dean Landon," the chief said as he began the morning meeting.

Juliette glanced around the squad conference room. Every Red Ridge PD officer had been at the hospital the night before—whether they'd just stopped to check on him during a shift or they had come in while off duty. They had definitely all heard about Landon getting shot.

Did they blame her for it? Nobody was looking at her, but it was almost as if they were making a conscious effort not to. Maybe they knew she already felt guilty enough over what had happened to their coworker.

"Officer Landon is expected to fully recover from the gunshot wound," the chief assured them. "However, it will take some time, so I will be actively looking for a temporary replacement for him during his recovery."

Juliette expelled a breath. That was good. They couldn't be shorthanded right now.

"Until I find that temporary replacement, I need you all to pull together like never before," the chief continued. "No more infighting."

Juliette felt no guilt over that; she wasn't part of the feuding going on within the department because she was neither a Gage nor a Colton. It seemed as if, with a few exceptions like Dean Landon and Dante Mancuso and her, everyone in the K9 unit of the RRPD was related to one or the other.

"Have you heard from your sister?" Detective Carson Gage asked Brayden Colton, who was sitting in the chair in front of Juliette in the briefing room.

Brayden didn't answer him. Everyone knew Carson was romantically involved with a Colton—Serena, who'd become close to Demi before she'd fled. Serena believed in her innocence. But Carson was ambivalent. Unlike the detective, though, Brayden was sure his sister was not the Groom Killer. He thought she'd been framed.

From what Juliette knew of Demi Colton, she had to agree with him. If Demi had killed someone, she would have done a better job of covering her tracks. Not that she hadn't had a motive to kill Bo Gage. Apparently, he'd gotten her pregnant and then become engaged to another woman.

"Have you heard from her?" the chief asked now. "Any texts? Calls?"

The last time Demi had texted one of her brothers, she'd insisted she was innocent—and had said the baby was fine. No one could she be sure if she'd actually given birth yet, though the timing was right. Brayden shook his head. "No. And it's been a while…"

Juliette could hear the concern in his voice. His sister was on the run—alone, heavily pregnant or traveling with an infant, and desperate. Juliette knew how that felt. Compassion compelled her to reach out and squeeze his arm.

"I'm worried something could have happened to her," he admitted. "To them…"

"And whose fault would that be?" Carson asked.

"Her baby is a Gage, too," Brayden reminded the detective. "Do you want to lose another one?"

Carson flinched.

"Knock it off," the chief said. "After what happened to Dean last night, we all have to trust that we have each other's backs. I can't send any of you out there until I know that for certain."

Carson closed his eyes and nodded. "I'm sorry. Of course, I know that. And I do…" He looked across the aisle of chairs at Brayden. "I have your back."

"Juliette's the one we need to watch right now," the chief directed.

"You should be in witness protection with your daughter," Carson told her. "Not out trying to do my job to track down that killer."

"I will be able to recognize him," Juliette pointed out. "And maybe my being out there will flush him out…" Because this had to end soon. Pandora wanted to go home—to her bedroom with all its stuffed toys and to her familiar bed.

And to her daddy…

This morning she'd asked if he was going to come live with them when they went home. Blake had told her that was her and Mommy's house, not his. His home wasn't in Red Ridge anymore. Would he leave once the killer was caught?

Of course he would. His business was called Blake Colton International. Not Blake Colton Red Ridge, South Dakota. He would have to return to his headquarters in London or his other branches in Hong Kong and Singapore.

Her face flushed as she realized how well she'd kept apprised of him in the past. She told herself that it was just because he was Pandora's father. But Juliette had been keeping track of him even before that night they'd conceived their child.

She'd had a crush on Blake Colton for a long time.

But a crush was all it was. Nothing could ever come of it. They were too different. Her life was in Red Ridge as a K9 cop. His was in international cities with his business and his models and actresses.

She doubted he was going to give any of that up—even for his daughter. But she was worried that Pandora, after just that one meeting, had already gotten attached to her daddy. And Juliette was worried that after watching him during that meeting—watching him play and speak so sweetly with their little girl—that Juliette was getting too attached, as well.

"Walsh!" the chief shouted her name.

And she realized she'd missed whatever he'd been saying—to her. Her face flushed even hotter with embarrassment. "I'm sorry," she murmured. "What were you saying?"

"That you are not going to use yourself as bait to flush out this lunatic," the chief said. "That's too damn dangerous."

If he wasn't the boss, Juliette might have dared to call

him a hypocrite. Not too long ago he'd used himself as bait to flush out the Groom Killer. He'd drawn out an obsessed stalker instead.

"I don't have to," she said. "I just need to do my job. He must be involved with the drug problem in Red Ridge since he killed that woman in the park to take that briefcase of drugs from her. My partner is the drug sniffing expert. I need to keep going to the train terminal and the airport and the bus terminal…"

The more people she caught smuggling drugs in and out of Red Ridge, the better the chance that she would get a lead on the killer during one of those arrests.

"You're going to have another patrol car on you at all times," the chief said.

She shook her head. "That's not necessary. We're already spread thin—with the Groom Killer on the loose."

"The killer hasn't acted in a while," the chief reminded them.

"About the same amount of time since anyone's heard from Demi…" Carson muttered. But his comment was loud enough for Brayden to overhear and tense with anger.

So much for the détente…

Then Carson shook his head and murmured an apology before adding more loudly, "Probably because everybody's scared to even think about getting married…"

But Juliette knew many of her coworkers were already thinking about it. Even the chief had recently fallen in love and moved in with the first murder victim's ex-wife, Darby Gage. And Juliette knew her best friend Elle Gage had fallen in love, as well—with a Colton, no less. Juliette suspected there were probably quite a few secret engagements in Red Ridge. She figured that was one secret that she and Blake would never have between them.

Unless he was already engaged to someone else— to one of those models or actresses he dated. But then, she would have already read about that in the tabloids.

No. He probably meant what he'd told her nearly five years ago about never wanting to get married. And she knew that she would not be the one to change his mind.

Blake had been quiet when they'd left the safe house with just enough time to spare so Juliette wouldn't miss the morning meeting. Maybe he'd just been tired since they had not slept at all the night before. She was tired. But she didn't think that was why he hadn't talked to her. It probably hadn't been because he had been worried that the bodyguards might have overheard their discussion, either.

She suspected he'd been angry. After meeting their amazing little girl and realizing what he'd missed, he was probably so furious with Juliette that he wouldn't care anymore if the killer got to her.

Because when she stepped out of the meeting, she didn't find him waiting in the hall for her. The only person in the reception area was Lorelei Wong. She glanced up from her desk and smiled at Juliette. Her silver-framed glasses had slipped down her nose. She pushed them up and blew a breath through her black bangs as she spoke on the phone.

She was too busy again to talk—probably fielding calls about the Groom Killer.

Juliette just waved at her as she and Sasha headed out to their patrol car. As she put the beagle in her harness in the back of the vehicle, she glanced around and still caught no sight of Blake. Of course, she hadn't noticed him the day before, either—until after work. So he might have been out there—with the bodyguards whose presence she didn't notice.

Despite the heat of the July day, she shivered. The killer could be out there and undetected, too. If he was smart, though, he'd be lying low—because he'd made a serious mistake when he'd shot a Red Ridge police officer. Now the entire department was even more determined to find him.

"Dad wants to see you," Patience told Blake.

"He knows where to find me," Blake reminded her. Even if he didn't own the hotel anymore—with all the financial difficulties he was currently having—he would know it was where Blake would stay.

"And I already told you that I can't help him," Blake reminded her. Withdrawing the amount of cash from his corporation that his father needed could cripple his business and cost too many of his loyal employees their jobs. He couldn't do it—not even to save Layla from marrying some old wealthy guy who'd struck a deal with Fenwick Colton. What he'd rather see was Layla standing up for herself, choosing her life and her heart over business. For once.

Patience's sigh rattled the cell phone Blake held. The rental car didn't have Bluetooth. After he'd brought back the damaged one, the company had been willing to loan him only one of their older models. He hoped it was reliable enough to follow Juliette's patrol car. Maybe he just needed to buy a vehicle—something like the SUVs the bodyguards he'd hired drove. Not that he could see them…

He could see the other patrol car, though, the one the

chief had following Juliette. She must have been headed toward the bus terminal. That was better than the places she'd gone the day before.

"Dad wants to see you because he's worried about you," Patience said.

And Blake snorted in derision. "Yeah, right…"

Even if his father had, by some odd chance, heard that Blake was present at the shooting the night before, Blake doubted he would have been all that concerned about his safety. They'd barely spoken the past five years.

"I told you about this Groom Killer," Patience said.

"Yeah, that's why Dad can't marry off Layla to some old guy and save his company," Blake said.

Patience expelled another sigh that was clearly of exasperation. Blake wasn't certain if she was exasperated with him or with their father, though.

He tried to focus on their conversation. But it was hard when he was watching Juliette at the same time. She was so damn beautiful—even in the drab Red Ridge Police Department uniform. She and the beagle moved with confidence through the crowd of people in the bus terminal.

"I'm sorry," he said. "Why would Dad be worried about me?" Had he heard about him and Juliette? About his grandchild? Maybe Blake did need to speak with his father. But he hesitated even to tell his sister.

"I don't know," Patience said. "I assured him that you were in no danger."

He flinched as he remembered the night before—the bullets hitting the rental car so close to where he'd been standing. If Juliette hadn't knocked him down, if she hadn't saved his life…

Had he even thanked her?

Everything had happened so quickly at the plant nursery that he didn't think he had. And then after...

The hospital and the safe house and meeting Pandora...

His heart contracted, affection for the little girl
squeezing it. He'd been so overwhelmed after meeting
her that he hadn't been able to think, much less talk to
Juliette. He should have thanked her for how well she'd
raised their daughter. But he hadn't been entirely able to
let go of his anger with her, of his resentment over her
keeping him from being part of his child's life.

"It's not like you're about to get married or anything,"
Patience continued.

Blake opened his mouth to laugh, but the chuckle
stuck in his throat as he wondered, should he be? Then
he wouldn't have to worry about Juliette keeping him
away from Pandora anymore. But that was crazy. He
didn't have to marry Juliette to make sure any of that
happened. He could legally claim his child without legally tying himself to her mother—to her lying, secret-
keeping mother.

"No," he said. "I'm not about to get married..." Especially not to a woman he couldn't trust. And no matter how well she'd raised their daughter, Blake could
not trust Juliette. Five years ago she'd led him to believe she was someone she wasn't and then she'd kept
a secret from him.

Kept Pandora from him...

"That's good," Patience said. "I don't want to have
to worry about you, too." Like she worried about Layla
marrying a man she didn't love and about their father
losing what mattered most to him—his company. She

was worried about Bea, too. Their sister loved the bridal shop she'd inherited from her grandmother.

Blake understood his sister's concerns. And he didn't want to add to them. He knew he needed to tell her that she was an aunt. But then he would also have to tell her that the little girl had witnessed a murder and was in danger.

"Nope, you don't have to worry about me," he said. And he clicked off the call to quickly make another.

The bodyguard picked up on the first ring. "Yes?"

"Any sign of him?" Blake asked.

"We didn't get a look at him last night," the bodyguard reminded him. "But there's no one suspicious-looking hanging around…"

Just as the man made the claim, Juliette's canine partner reacted to someone boarding a bus.

It would make sense that the killer would be trying to leave town right now.

Was it him?

He had been told to leave town—actually, to get the hell out of it. His head still rang with the way his current employer had shouted the order at him. "What the hell were you thinking—shooting a cop?"

Juliette Walsh was a cop. If he hadn't missed and struck the male officer instead, he would have *killed* a cop. But he hadn't bothered pointing that out.

"You've brought the heat of the entire department now," he'd been warned. "So you need to get the hell out of here!"

It was probably good advice. But he had unfinished business in Red Ridge. He had never left a witness alive

before and he didn't intend to do that now. He had to find
that little girl. He already knew where her mama was.

He also knew he wasn't the only killer in Red Ridge
right now. "The police are all preoccupied with that
Groom Killer," he reminded his boss. "I'm not their
only focus."

"You are now," he'd been told. "No grooms have died
lately. They probably think that killer's moved on. You
need to do the same. Get the hell out of Red Ridge."

He'd reached for the back door to the realty company
office. But a shout had stopped him. "And for God's
sake, make sure nobody sees you leaving here!"

Anger twisted his guts. They'd begged him to come
work for them. Luring him with the promise of big
money for carrying out their dirty work. But now that his
hands were dirty, they wanted nothing to do with him.

He was tempted to end not just his association with
them but them, as well. He'd forced a smile instead.

"Nobody sees me come and go," he'd promised.

And the boss had snorted. "Except a little girl…"

He'd held on to his smile because he'd known that
little girl would never be getting any bigger or any
older than she currently was. Because she would soon
be dead—right along with her cop mama…

Chapter 9

Zane Godfried studied his face in the reflection of the rearview mirror of the Corvette his fiancée had given him as an engagement present. With his black hair slicked back and his teeth whitened to a brighter shade than his tuxedo shirt, he looked damn good—so good that it was a shame they had to keep this wedding on the down low. But it was the only way he had been able to convince Marnie Halloway to marry him.

Not that she hadn't wanted to. Since he'd connected online with the lonely, rich widow, she had been anxious to spend as much time as she could with him. First she'd sent him plane tickets to Red Ridge. Then she'd bought him his sweet ride. But when the whole Groom Killer crap had started, she'd been too worried about him to accept his proposal.

Fortunately for him, she was easily manipulated, and

he'd been able to use those deaths as evidence that life was too short. More so for her than him. She was pushing seventy. He had to get her to do this now—before anyone figured out who Zane Godfried really was and where to find him.

He was in more danger from previous marks and loan sharks than he was from some serial killer. Of course, he didn't think it was really a serial killer on the loose. Wasn't it just some crazy broad who'd found out her baby daddy was going to marry someone else?

She'd killed him and then maybe a few more because she'd still been pissed. No more grooms had been killed lately, so she must have cooled off. Or left Red Ridge or the country.

Just like he'd told Marnie, nothing was going to happen to him. Though getting someone to perform their wedding ceremony hadn't been easy. He'd had to go online again to find somebody willing to do it. Fortunately for him again, pretty much anyone could get a license to marry people now, so he'd been able to find someone.

He glanced at the motel where the person had said for them to meet him. It looked a little seedy. Marnie probably wouldn't like this. Despite her age, she was acting like a blushing bride. The old chick probably had dementia, which was another reason Zane needed to push for this quickie wedding. He needed to clear out her bank accounts before someone figured out she'd lost her marbles.

And all her money…

He chuckled as he straightened his bow tie. Yeah, he looked good. Who gave a crap what the motel looked like? He pushed open the driver's door and stepped into the parking lot.

It was early. So nobody was in the lot but him. Marnie was late. She was probably still trying to get beautiful. No matter how long she worked at that, it wasn't going to happen, though. He grimaced as he thought of his elderly bride. Then he looked again at the sexy red Corvette and smiled. At least he would have enough money to buy himself beautiful things. Like cars. And women...

A shadow reflected back from the side of the 'Vette as someone walked up behind him. He turned around, but instead of focusing on the person, he saw only the gun barrel pointed at him.

A shot fired, striking his chest with such force it knocked him back against the car. His last thought, as he slid down the side of it, was that he hoped he hadn't dented it. He didn't even get the chance to think that Marnie had been right; he was dead before he fully hit the ground.

Juliette stared at the body propped against the side of the Corvette. The pleated shirt, which had probably once been white, was stained red—with a gaping hole through the heart. And a black cummerbund spilled out between his open lips. His eyes stared up at them, glazed in death.

She resisted the urge to shudder. She should have been used to the sight by now. The Groom Killer had struck again.

"Who is he?" the chief asked as he joined them at the scene.

Detective Carson Gage had the guy's wallet, which he held out to his boss. "Your guess is as good as mine. He's got a few IDs in here."

"She says—" Juliette pointed toward the woman sitting in the back of an ambulance "—that his name is

Zane Godfried." Juliette had been the first officer on the scene since the motel was near the train terminal where she and Sasha had been heading. She'd hoped to make more arrests like the one at the bus terminal.

She'd gotten that person only on a small amount of a controlled substance, though, which hadn't given her enough leverage to get him to talk about the killer from the park.

If he'd even known who he was…

He hadn't reacted when she'd described the killer to him.

"Marnie Halloway?" Finn asked as he peered into the ambulance.

Her makeup had run down and smeared her face. Some of it had even dripped onto the bodice of her white wedding gown.

"She met Godfried online a few months ago, and he convinced her to marry him," Carson said.

The detective had arrived soon after Juliette had—so soon that he'd probably been in the patrol car following her. Brayden Colton had been out riding with Carson, probably to prove to the chief that they were unified now.

Maybe something good had actually come of her being in danger and Dean getting shot: the K9 unit had come back together as the family they'd always been before the Groom Killer had first struck Red Ridge.

She would have rather they'd put aside their differences and resentments without her daughter having to witness a murder and Dean having to take a bullet.

Carson and Brayden weren't the only ones who'd been following her, though. Blake had, too. He stood on the other side of the crime scene tape she'd strung up, around lamp posts in the parking lot, to keep out the reporters and morbidly curious gawkers who crowded all around Blake. Despite the crowd, he easily stood out. He was so damn handsome with his dark blond hair and those piercing green eyes.

"They were going to get married here?" the chief asked with a glance at the seedy motel. His brow furrowed as if he was confused.

Juliette shared his confusion. Marnie Holloway was a wealthy widow. She could have afforded a much more expensive venue. She could have—and probably should have—sprung for a destination wedding.

"The groom had found someone online who'd agreed to perform the ceremony," Carson said.

As chief, Finn had put out a warning weeks ago that nobody should attempt to get married until the killer was caught. Between sobs Marnie had said that she'd warned her groom it wasn't safe, but he'd been too eager to wait.

Probably too eager for her money.

"So this wedding was kept really hush-hush," the chief mused.

Juliette knew where he was headed with this—toward his cousin's innocence, although he'd done his best to appear impartial since that first murder. Bo Gage's.

"Demi couldn't have heard about their engagement," Juliette said for him. "It had to be someone right here in town." Someone watching and listening…

She shivered as she considered that idea—two killers out there now…

She was glad that Pandora was in the safe house with Elle protecting her. But the little girl wasn't the only person Juliette was worried about.

She glanced again at Blake. He had to stop following her around; it was too dangerous. His near miss at the plant nursery should have proved that to him. As she'd told him that night, he could have wound up in a body bag for real or, like Dean, in a hospital bed.

"It wasn't Demi," Brayden said, to Carson more than anyone else.

Carson looked like he was about argue, but then he just shrugged and turned away from Brayden. He called out to Dante Mancuso, who was guiding Flash around the parking lot, looking for evidence. "Any scent of…"

"Demi?" Brayden finished for him.

Dante didn't deny having Flash check for it. He just shook his head.

"That proves she hasn't been here," Brayden said. "Demi had nothing to do with this murder."

There had been evidence tying her to the other ones, though—evidence that not even her loyal brother had been able to explain. Of course, it could have been planted; he had raised that possibility.

"Demi knows dogs," Carson reminded him. "She knows how to get rid of or change her scent."

"That's a reach and you know it," Brayden said.

"We need to focus on this murder, this victim," Finn advised them. "Sounds like Godfried or whoever the hell he really is might have made some enemies of his own."

Carson nodded. "A person usually has a reason to use a bunch of different aliases. He or *she* either doesn't want to be found or caught…" He was obviously wondering if Demi Colton had changed her name. Maybe that was how she'd eluded all the people looking for her.

"We also need to have Katie check out all those identities of our victim," Finn said, referring to their tech whiz, Katie Parsons, "and see if he was ever romantically linked with Hayley Patton."

Was the chief beginning to suspect Hayley? Juliette wasn't a big fan of Bo Gage's *grieving* fiancée. They'd gone to the same school and Hayley had always treated Juliette like she was trash—even though they hadn't come from all that different backgrounds. Not like she and Blake had...

Just like she'd told Pandora, her daddy was a prince—or at least Red Ridge's equivalent of one. Her face heated with another rush of embarrassment that the little girl had shared that story with him. For that one night, when they'd created their daughter, Juliette had been his Cinderella. But unlike in the fairy tale, she and Blake were not going to wind up together.

He must have still been furious with her. He hadn't sought her out last night. He hadn't joined her when his bodyguards had slipped her into the safe house to tuck in Pandora for the night, either.

The little girl had asked about her daddy—had wondered where he was. From just that one meeting, she had gotten attached. Juliette never should have let them meet—not until she'd known how much a part of their daughter's life he wanted to be. She had a feeling that he didn't know that yet either, though.

"You all need to be extra careful out there," the chief cautioned the officers in the parking lot. He stepped closer and said to Juliette, "Especially you..."

She understood. Since the Groom Killer had struck again, the department would need to focus on finding that killer and not the one who had threatened her and Pandora.

"I'm glad now that Blake hired that security agency," Finn added.

She couldn't deny that they'd helped her—by getting

her to see her daughter. But those visits were bittersweet because they were so short. She needed to be with Pandora again—home with her again.

She pointed to Blake. "You need to order him to back off."

"He's bothering you?" Finn asked.

Blake wasn't even talking to her. But Juliette nodded. "I can't worry about him while I'm watching out for the killer."

"Then maybe you need to go into that safe house with your daughter," the chief said.

How could he make such a suggestion when there had just been another murder? Or maybe that was why he had.

But everyone else would be focused on finding the Groom Killer now, and the man who'd threatened Pandora could get away with murder. Maybe even theirs... if he managed to carry out that threat he'd made.

Chapter 10

Blake hadn't slept for the past couple of nights, so he should have been exhausted. But every time he closed his eyes he saw that dead man, propped against the red Corvette with blood soaking his shirt and pooled all around him. And he also saw Dean Landon, the injured officer...

Blood oozing from his belly wound which was where one of the killer's bullets had struck him right beneath his vest. That injury had looked bad, too. Like it could have been fatal.

But that bullet had been intended for Juliette. The killer was out to get her and their child...

He shivered. But instead of pulling up his covers, he kicked them off. He couldn't stay in bed. He should be parked outside Juliette's house, making sure she was safe.

For Pandora's sake. The little girl could not lose her

mother. Blake didn't want to lose her, either. Not that he had her...

He just didn't want anything bad to happen to her. But with the job she had, it was almost inevitable. As a police officer, she put herself in danger every day. And now, with the killer on the loose, she was in danger every minute of every day and night.

He jerked open a dresser drawer and reached for a pair of jeans. But before he could step into them, a knock rattled the door in the living area of the suite. He quickly pulled up the jeans and headed toward the door.

It was late. Who could be visiting him now?

Finn trying to once again talk him out of tailing Juliette? His cousin had tried that morning—at the crime scene. He'd said that Juliette was not appreciative of his constant presence. That Blake was more a distraction than a help...

He couldn't be any help in finding the killer. But he could be an extra set of eyes, so that she didn't get hurt trying to find the murderer. And for some reason, he just needed to be near her—to assure himself that she was all right.

He paused at the door, which rattled with another knock. He would be lucky if his visitor was Finn. It could be his dad or Patience at the door. He drew in a deep breath then pulled it open...and expelled that breath as if he'd been punched.

He'd expected anyone else at the door but her—but Juliette.

"Miss me?" he asked as he stepped back.

She walked in and slammed the door behind herself, then winced as she must have realized how loudly it had closed. Her face flushed, but then, her skin had already looked red when he'd opened the door to her. Maybe she'd gotten sunburned in the parking lot earlier that day.

But when he noticed she was glaring at him, he realized she was angry—really angry.

"What's wrong? What happened?" he asked.

She pointed her finger at him. "You are. You're what's wrong."

He shook his head. "You're wasting your time. Finn already talked to me today. And like I told him, I'm not backing off. I'm going to keep following you."

"To your death," she said.

"That's my choice," he said. "I'm a big boy. I know the risks."

"Death," she said. "That's what you're risking. You saw it today. Do you want to wind up like that murder victim? With a bullet through your heart?"

He wasn't worried about a bullet. He was worried about her. Their daughter needed her. He was also beginning to worry that he did, too. She was so damn beautiful that his blood pumped hot and fast through his veins. He wanted to be with her—badly.

Like they'd been together that night so long ago...

His lips curved into a grin, and he teased her, "I didn't know you cared so much about me."

Her eyes narrowed more in an angrier glare. "I don't care and apparently neither do you!"

His head was beginning to pound—from her yelling and from her confusing him. He was following her around—didn't he care too much?

"What are you talking about?" he asked.

"I'm talking about Pandora."

He sucked in a breath. "What about her? Is she okay?"

Juliette shook her head, tangling her blond hair

around her face. When she was working she wore it in a ponytail. Otherwise it was down and loose around her shoulders like now.

Blake felt the silky strands of it when he grasped her shoulders. "What? What happened? Did he find the safe house?"

Maybe it hadn't been a good idea for her and him to visit the little girl. Maybe despite the bodyguards' best efforts, they had been followed.

"No," she said. "That's not the issue. Neither is the killer. *You're* the issue. *You* haven't found your way back to the house again."

He furrowed his brow as confusion rushed over him. "I don't understand…"

"And neither does Pandora," she said. "She doesn't understand why her *daddy* hasn't come back to see her. She doesn't understand why I'm the only one tucking her in at night."

Blake grimaced at the twinge in his heart. "I—I didn't think…"

She shrugged off his hands as if she couldn't bear to have him touching her. "No, you didn't think of Pandora—of how you could disappoint her."

"I thought of that," he said. "That's why I haven't been back. I didn't want to disappoint her." Like his father had disappointed him so many times.

Even now…

Patience had claimed Fenwick wanted to see him, but he hadn't come by the hotel. He hadn't called. That was just Blake's sister's wishful thinking—that their father had enough heart to actually care about any of them.

And if his father didn't have enough heart, Blake wasn't sure that he did either.

"You disappointed her by not coming back," Juliette said. "She keeps asking me where you are…" Her voice cracked with emotion.

And Blake's heart felt like it cracked with regret. "I'm sorry. I didn't think she would care that much."

"For years she has asked me about her father," Juliette said.

"And you told her I was a prince," he said.

Her face flushed again, but this time it was definitely with embarrassment. Then she lifted her chin and replied, "Well, you are."

He snorted.

"You're the only male heir of Fenwick Colton," she said. "Doesn't that make you the prince of Red Ridge?"

"Hell, no," he said. "My father doesn't care about having a son or a daughter. He doesn't care about his kids at all or he wouldn't be trying to marry off one of my sisters to some rich old man to save Colton Energy."

"Is that why you came back to Red Ridge?" she asked.

He shrugged. "I don't know why I came back. I can't bail him out."

"Can't or won't?" she asked.

"Can't," he said. "Not without a lot of my employees losing their livelihoods." And he wouldn't do that to people who'd been loyal to him. "Fenwick will need to find another way to save his business—besides selling my sister Layla to the highest bidder." Which sounded pretty much like what he'd done.

"Fenwick Colton is Pandora's grandfather," she murmured, as if the fact had just occurred to her. She shuddered.

He reached out again, settling his hands on her shoulders to offer a reassuring squeeze. "You don't have to worry. I will never let him hurt her."

"I wish you could say the same about you," she said.

And that twinge struck his heart again. She'd made it clear that he had already hurt the little girl. He stepped back, dropping his hands from her shoulders. Then he ran one, which was shaking slightly, over his bed head tousled hair.

"That was the last thing I wanted to do…" he murmured. "That's why I stayed away the past couple of nights. I didn't want to screw this up…"

But he had. He turned and headed to the glass exterior wall that looked out over the glittering lights of the city below. There weren't many—not in comparison to his places in London, Hong Kong or Singapore. He was like his mother, too, and she hadn't known how to be a parent any more than his father had. "I don't know how to do this…"

"What?" she asked. And he saw her reflection in the glass as she walked up behind him. She was wearing another skirt. This one was a dark denim, and it was short—probably in deference to the heat. And probably also because of the heat, she wore a sleeveless blouse with it. She looked so damn beautiful—no matter what she wore.

He wanted to see her again in nothing at all. But she was too angry with him. And he was…

He reached for the resentment, trying to pull it up again. Trying to be angry with her for keeping him from his child. But the past couple of nights he'd kept himself from her.

He was scared.

"I don't know how to be a father," he said. "I don't know anything about kids—about how to talk to them or relate to them…"

"What!" she said again. But it sounded more like an exclamation than a question. And she grabbed his arms and spun him around to face her. "You were great with her that first time. That's why she misses you—that's why she wants to know everything about you. And she wants you to know everything about her..." She bit her lip now and tears pooled in her eyes.

And his heart lurched in his chest again. It wasn't just the child he'd hurt; he'd hurt the mother, too. "I'm sorry," he said again.

She shook her head. "I shouldn't be jealous, but I am. It's been just her and me all these years."

He felt that twinge again, and it must have shown in his face because she squeezed his arms.

"I'm sorry," she said. "I know that was selfish."

Selfish. Or selfless? He wasn't sure now. She'd already been struggling to pay off her mother's medical bills—according to Finn—and to put herself through college. And then she'd taken on the expense of raising a child alone. How the hell had she managed?

She was incredible.

"I'm so sorry I kept her from you," she continued. "I should have told you. I could have tracked you down through your family. I know that..." But her face flushed again with the embarrassment Blake knew that would have caused her.

And he honestly wasn't sure they would have believed her. He'd never talked about her, had never talked about that night. "I still need to tell them," he said.

She tensed. "You haven't?"

He shook his head. "I said before—I'm not close to my family..." And he was beginning to see maybe that was as much on him as on them. He'd even pulled back from his daughter just days after realizing he had one. He drew in a deep breath. "But I'll do better. I'll do better with Pandora."

She tilted her head and studied him, as if wondering if she should believe him.

Apparently he wasn't the only one struggling with trust.

"I don't want to hurt her," he said. "That's why I stayed away the past couple of nights."

"I was surprised," Juliette said. "You've been following me everywhere—but there. It seems like you would rather put yourself in danger than see your daughter."

She had no idea how dangerous seeing that little girl was for Blake. He wasn't just afraid of screwing up and hurting her. He was afraid of getting hurt. It was easier for him to risk his life than his heart.

"It's hard to see her," he said, "and think about what I missed."

She flinched now, and the tears that had glistened in her eyes spilled over, sliding down her cheeks. "I'm sorry. I can't give those years back to you."

She couldn't.

He would just have to accept that and let go of his anger. "Just like how you were jealous tonight when she asked about me," he said. "It's hard to see the two of you together—that bond you share. It's beautiful, but it's something I will never have with her."

"That's not true—"

"I'm a stranger she wants to get to know. You're the parent who was always there." And his voice cracked with emotion.

Juliette closed her eyes, but the tears kept sliding down her face. Her emotion moved him to put aside his resentment to comfort her. He pulled her into his arms and held her close.

She tilted her face up to his. "I'm sorry. I really am sorry…"

He slid his fingertips along the delicate line of her jaw. She was so beautiful, so fragile-looking, but that fragility was just an illusion. She was incredibly strong—to survive what she had with losing her mother at such a young age and to do the work that she did as a K9 officer.

"I know," he said. And he had to stop beating her up about it.

She couldn't change the past any more than he could.

He closed the short distance between their faces and brushed his mouth across hers. Her breath escaped in a sweet sigh across his lips. Then she kissed him back.

It was like that night so long ago in this very suite. The passion between them ignited, burning so hot. He'd never felt an attraction like this to anyone else—never before or since Juliette.

She ran her hands over his chest, and he realized he'd never put on a shirt. Her skin touched his, making him tingle—making him hard.

"I want you," he said, and his voice sounded so deep and gruff as desire nearly strangled him. Want didn't even seem adequate to describe the hunger burning inside him, making him ache.

She kissed him again with a hunger of her own, a hunger that almost matched his.

He groaned, and her tongue slid between his lips, mating with his. She tasted so damn sweet…

And she smelled like honeysuckle and sunshine, yet he didn't think it was just the shampoo. It was like it was her essence because he could taste the sweetness on her lips and feel the heat of her mouth.

She pulled back, gasping for breath, and murmured, "I want you…"

He swung her up his arms, like he had that night on the stairs. Like that night, she slid her arms around his neck, holding him as he held her. He turned toward the bedroom.

But as he turned, the door to the hall rattled. It wasn't with a knock, though. It was just a faint noise as the handle jiggled.

Someone was at the door. Someone was trying to get in without alerting them to his presence. The officers or bodyguards wouldn't do that. Probably only the killer would. Just like that night at the plant nursery, he must have been following Juliette tonight.

He was going to try to kill her—right here.

Chapter 11

Juliette had been so careful to make sure that she wasn't followed. She'd been certain she'd lost the killer and the bodyguards since neither could have been all that familiar with Red Ridge. She'd even lost the patrol car stationed outside her house because she hadn't wanted her coworkers to know where she was going—to see Blake.

She figured that they already suspected Pandora might be his child. So if they followed her to his hotel suite, they would have speculated that something was going on between them again.

And that wasn't why Juliette had come to him. Nothing had been going on between them. Well, clearly that had changed. She'd told herself she'd only come here to confront him about disappointing their daughter. But when he'd kissed her...

She'd forgotten about her anger. And she'd forgotten about that killer...

Until now. That had to be who was messing with the door, trying to get inside the suite undetected. She reached inside the bag slung over her shoulder and pulled out her service weapon. Sliding off the safety, she pointed the pistol toward the door.

Her instinct was to let him get inside the suite. Then it would be easier to apprehend him—even if she had to put another bullet in him to do that.

But Blake might get hurt...

She gestured at him to go into the bedroom and close that door. But he just shook his head. And then his cell phone rang. He must have had it in the pocket of his jeans because the bells pealed loudly, echoing in the living room.

The rattling at the door stopped.

"Damn it..." she murmured.

As he accepted the call, she headed toward the door. "The bodyguards are in the hotel, looking for the man they saw following you," Blake related. "Once they caught up to you."

She'd been so careful that she was surprised that they had. But they weren't the only ones. The killer had caught up to her, too.

Juliette knew where he was—or where he'd been. He couldn't have gotten far. Or he might not have left yet at all. She kept her back against the foyer wall as she neared the door. Then she reached out, jerked open the handle and swung her gun into the hall.

"Wait!" Blake called after her.

But she had already slipped into the corridor, once again keeping her back against the wall.

"Wait for them!" he called out.

"Stay here!" she yelled at him as she headed down the hall. She heard a door closing. At this hour, she didn't think it was a guest. And none of the elevators she passed were at the top floor, so it must have been to the stairwell at the end of the hall. She rushed toward it.

She had to catch him. She had to end this.

So she wasn't even thinking as she pushed open the door to the stairs. She wasn't thinking that he might have been standing behind it, waiting for her—until a big hand wrapped around her wrist and struck it against the top railing to the stairs.

Pain radiated up her arm. But she didn't loosen her grasp on her weapon. If she dropped it, then she had no chance of surviving. Even with his wounded shoulder, he was so much stronger than she was.

She couldn't lose her weapon.

But then his hand moved from her wrist to her shoulders, and he pushed—trying to send her over the railing and down twenty-one stories. Now she dropped the gun as she struggled to hold on to the railing. It clattered as it hit the stairs below her. But it didn't fire—fortunately.

As she tried to hang on, she looked up—and into those cold eyes of the killer. His hands moved from her shoulders to her throat. He squeezed, cutting off her breath, and his mouth curved into a cruel grin as he told her, "Your kid is next, bitch!"

Blake's heart stopped beating entirely as he pushed open the door to the stairwell. He'd been only seconds behind Juliette. But he was too late—just like the bodyguards would be when they made it up to the twenty-first floor. The killer had his hands on her—around her throat now—trying to choke the life out her.

Blake balled his hand into a fist and swung it at the guy. He caught him by surprise—enough that the guy loosened his grip. But so did Juliette, her hands sliding from the stairwell railing. Blake lunged for her, catching her. But he missed a few steps and slammed into the brick wall of the stairwell before regaining his footing.

"I'm going to make sure you stop playing her hero," the man said as he raised a gun, pointing the barrel down the stairwell—right at Blake.

Juliette had regained her footing, as well, and she grabbed Blake's hand—pulling him down the stairs. As they ran, shots rang out—the blasts echoing through the stairwell. Bullets struck the wall near their heads, sending chips of brick back at them.

One caught Blake's cheek, stinging. He ignored the pain and hurried along behind Juliette. But he collided with her as she stopped on a landing. Then she was moving around—back up the stairs.

Her gun gripped tightly in her hands, she began to fire back. Her shots were even louder, the blasts ringing in Blake's ears, and his head began to pound. While there had been shooting a couple of nights ago, he hadn't been this close—with his head nearly next to the weapon.

But then it stopped firing as Juliette emptied the clip. "Run!" she yelled at him as she fumbled inside the back-pack-style purse swinging from her shoulder. She was probably looking for more ammunition.

Blake didn't move. He couldn't go without her. He couldn't leave her behind and unprotected.

She shoved at him, trying to get him out of the way as more shots rang out.

These were not hers. These were the killer's bullets coming at them—at him.

Finn had seriously just about had it with late-night visits and phone calls. Nothing good ever came of either. And this one was no exception. But this call had summoned him out of his house—to the Colton mansion on Bay Boulevard.

He drove past the Larsen twins' mansions, trying to peer beyond the gates. Despite the late hour, the homes were all lit up. Who the hell knew what was going on inside them? Parties? Clandestine meetings?

If only he could get some evidence that they were behind all the drugs coming in and out of Red Ridge...

But they were too smart for anything to stick. Finn had nothing but rumors and speculation, and no prosecutor could use those to convince a grand jury to indict. They were probably involved with that killer from the park, too, the one threatening Juliette and her daughter. He suspected that anything involving drugs in Red Ridge also involved them.

And that suitcase full of *sand* the little girl had seen the shooter take from the victim—that had to have been drugs. Once they'd ID'd the young woman, they'd found her prior arrest for some low-level dealing. Had the woman stolen the drugs and been trying to resell them? Had the killer murdered her to reclaim the drugs or to send a message to other dealers?

Whether intended or not, that message had been received, because no one was talking. Finn sighed as he drove past those mansions.

He had nothing on the Larsons. Yet. But hopefully that would change soon.

He also had nothing on the Groom Killer. That was what he'd already told Fenwick Colton when the man had called him. But the mayor of Red Ridge had insisted that Finn come out to his estate anyway.

The gates were open, so he drove right through and around the circular drive to the front door. Like the Larsons' mansions, this one was all lit up.

Didn't rich people sleep?

But then, it wasn't as if they had to punch clocks like working stiffs.

Finn shut off the ignition and headed up the walk to the front door. Fenwick must have been watching for him because the tall mahogany door opened before Finn could even ring the bell. "You took your time," the older man remarked.

And Finn grimaced. No thank you for agreeing to this late-night visit. No appreciation at all. Fenwick Colton had always been a loud blowhard. Rich and entitled. But he was even worse now than he'd been before—because now he was desperate.

Finn could see it in his eyes. They were glassy, too, as if he'd been drinking. It probably didn't take much for a guy as short and skinny as Fenwick to have had too much, though. The man turned from the door and walked away, expecting Finn to follow. And of course he headed, albeit a bit wobbly, to the den and straight to the bar in the corner of it.

"Drink?" he asked as he lifted a decanter of liquor.

Finn shook his head.

"So you're on duty?"

"No," Finn said. "I told you that when you called. I was home in bed." With the most beautiful woman…and once again he'd had to leave her. He'd known being police chief was a full-time job, but with the Groom Killer on the loose, it had become an around-the-clock position.

"How can you sleep with what's happening in Red Ridge?" Fenwick asked, his face tight with disapproval. "Killers on the loose, spoiling weddings."

Once Katie Parsons had dug up more on the latest murder victim, Finn wasn't so sure that the killer hadn't actually done Marnie Halloway a favor. Neither Zane Godfried nor any of his other aliases had been a good person. Marnie was probably better off that the wedding had never happened.

But as someone who longed to get married himself, Finn was frustrated that they had yet to catch the Groom Killer.

"You need to step up your efforts to track down Demi Colton," Fenwick told him.

It wasn't the first time the businessman had told Finn how to do his job. Even if Fenwick wasn't also the mayor of Red Ridge, Finn suspected he still would have tried steering this particular investigation. "Finding Demi is not our only concern right now," Finn said.

Especially when Finn wasn't even sure she had anything to do with the Groom Killer except for having once been involved with the very first victim. She couldn't have even known about the last one since the FBI had reported sightings of her far from Red Ridge. So how would she have had anything to do with his murder?

His path had never crossed Hayley Patton's, either. So that hunch Finn had started having about the first victim's fiancée hadn't panned out. He didn't necessarily think she was guilty—just someone involved, however indirectly, with the murders.

Fenwick waved a hand dismissively and said, "I hope

you're not wasting your limited resources on finding a drug dealer's killer."

The mayor, once again, seemed to already be apprised of everything happening within the department.

"How'd you know she was a dealer?" Finn asked.

Fenwick winked. "I have my sources..."

Lorelei?

The receptionist was fiercely loyal, though. Finn doubted the mayor could have charmed her. But there were plenty of other people within the department who could have told him.

"It doesn't matter what the young woman was doing," Finn said. "She didn't deserve to die."

Fenwick snorted. "She knew the dangers. That kind of stuff happens all the time with their kind shooting each other over disputes."

"That killer also shot one of my officers and is trying to kill another one, as well as her daughter, who witnessed that murder." Her daughter. *Your granddaughter.*

It wasn't Finn's place to tell Fenwick Colton that he was a grandpa—although he would love to see the vain playboy's face when he heard the news. And that was news he must not have heard yet or he wouldn't have been so quick to dismiss the importance of finding the man who'd threatened his granddaughter.

Fenwick shrugged. "The Groom Killer still needs to be your top priority."

"Finding the guy shooting and threatening my officers is my top priority," he said. He hated that he'd come so close to nearly losing one of them. He didn't want that to happen again—with Juliette Walsh.

"You need to remember, Finn," the mayor persisted,

"that if Layla can't get married and save my company, your resources will be even more limited."

Finn flinched—even though it wasn't the first time he'd heard the threat. He knew where Fenwick was heading with this.

"I subsidize the K9 program per my late wife's wishes," the older man continued. "But I won't be able to afford to do that much longer…"

Finn had nothing to do with business, so he didn't know how Fenwick had gotten into his current predicament. He also didn't know how a man could barter one of his children's lives as a way to get out of it.

And now he realized why Blake hadn't told his father that he had a granddaughter. Hell, if Finn had a daughter, he wouldn't want Fenwick Colton to know it, either.

Before he could even decide if or how he wanted to reply, his cell phone vibrated in his pocket. He pulled it out, which caused Fenwick to grumble at the rudeness. Ignoring him, he accepted the call, "Chief Colton…"

"Chief, it's Frank," the dispatcher said. And he sounded nearly as upset as he had the night Finn had had an officer down.

"What is it?" Finn asked, as his heart pounded heavy and hard with dread. "Not…"

"There's been a shooting at the Colton Plaza Hotel," Frank replied.

"Any casualties?"

"Not that have been reported," Frank replied. "But it is officer-involved."

"Which officer?" he asked this time.

Last time he'd made an assumption and he'd been wrong. But it had been a safe assumption to make since he had only one officer a murderer was determined to kill.

"Juliette Walsh," Frank confirmed.

"Was she alone?"

"No," Frank replied. "Blake Colton is with her."

Finn flinched. "I'll be right there." He clicked off the call and slid the cell into his pocket. But he hesitated before turning toward the older man.

Had Fenwick overheard any of the conversation?

Did he know that his son had been involved in a shooting? And while there had been no reports of casualties yet, that didn't mean that there wasn't one.

Or two…

Chapter 12

"Where the hell did he go…?" Juliette murmured as she followed Sasha around the perimeter of the hotel. Animals were not allowed in the hotel, so she'd left Sasha in the car when she'd arrived. Despite being July, the evening was cool. So Sasha had been fine with the windows down and a bowl of fresh water on the back seat with her. Juliette hadn't intended to stay longer than the time it would have taken to give Blake a piece of her mind over not seeing their daughter again. But then he'd kissed her…

If not for the killer interrupting them, they would have done more than that. So it was probably good that he'd interrupted them. But trying to kill them…

Fortunately the bodyguards had shown up in the stair-well and the killer had fled out a door on another story.

The bodyguards had then moved to cover all the exits—to catch him when he tried to escape.

But they hadn't seen anyone leaving the hotel. Not even a guest or employee.

It was in the middle of shift, so an employee wouldn't have been leaving. And it was so late that guests were probably already settled in for the night.

While she and Sasha were checking the perimeter, Dante Mancuso and Flash were inside—trying to track the killer to a room. The man had nearly opened the door to Blake's suite, so he might have been able to open another one and slip inside to hide.

Once she'd slid in another clip and started firing back at him, he'd taken off onto a floor above where she and Blake had been.

Blake...

He was okay—but for a scratch on his face. He'd claimed that wasn't because of a bullet directly but from a bullet breaking off brick that had struck his face.

His handsome face...

He'd looked so worried when she'd insisted on retrieving Sasha from her car to search the lot. He'd been concerned about her.

She was worried about him. He was the one still in the hotel and, unless the bodyguards had missed him exiting, so was the killer.

But Flash was the best tracker in Red Ridge. If the killer was inside the hotel, he and Dante would find him. And Blake was not alone in his suite. The chief was inside with him.

And so was his father...

The mayor of Red Ridge hadn't even acknowledged her when she'd walked past him. It had reminded her of how Blake had walked past her that morning after their incredible evening together. Because she'd been dressed as a maid, he hadn't even noticed her. No. She would never be a Colton—never be Blake's Cinderella. But the truth was that she had given birth to a Colton.

Would her grandfather accept Pandora? Or would he ignore her like Blake claimed the man had ignored his own children? Maybe that would be best for the little girl, though.

"Find anything?" Dante Mancuso asked through the radio Juliette held.

She pressed down the button. "No. You?"

"No."

She wasn't surprised at his response—not after his asking her. "Nothing?"

"Flash tracked him from the stairwell to the corridor of the eighteenth floor. He walked down it to a service elevator. We stopped on every floor to see which one he got out on," Mancuso wearily continued. "He appears to have taken it to the basement."

"So he must still be down there," she said hopefully, and she turned back toward the building. "Blake's bodyguards were on the exits and didn't see him leave."

She suspected they were watching her now, though, so the killer could have slipped out of the basement recently. She hoped like hell he hadn't, though. She wanted to catch him so badly—for terrorizing her daughter and for shooting at Blake and injuring her coworker. Not to mention murdering that woman in the playground parking lot.

He had to be stopped before he hurt anyone else.

Mancuso's voice emanated from the radio. "I don't

think he's here. Flash just stopped at some kind of manhole in the floor—it looks like it goes into the sewer."

So he'd made it out.

And he could be anywhere in Red Ridge by now.

Despite the warmth of the July night, Juliette shivered at the thought of the killer still being on the loose. She had no doubt he hadn't gone far, though. He was too determined to carry out his threat to kill her and Pandora.

Frustration gripped Blake. He did not have time for this—for whatever the hell this ambush was with Finn bringing his father to his hotel suite.

Finn pointed toward Blake's face. "You should get that checked out."

"I told you I did not get shot." He'd told Juliette the same thing when she'd noticed the cut and had been concerned. She'd also been angry with him, though. Angry like the chief and his father were—for putting himself in danger.

But if he hadn't chased her down the hallway, if he hadn't intervened in the stairwell…she would have been dead or at least severely wounded.

Anger surged through him now. He needed to be talking to the security agency he'd hired—not Finn and definitely not his father. While they had intervened and saved them in the stairwell, they'd still let the killer get away. And earlier that evening, they'd let Juliette slip away from them. Sure, they'd found her, but unfortunately, the killer had found her first.

His father hadn't actually said a word yet, though. He just looked angry—his face pinched and flushed. But then the words he must have been holding back finally burst free. "You're damn lucky you didn't get shot—what with all the bullets flying around the hotel. I heard all the guests complaining about the ruckus."

That was it. His father was worried about the Colton Plaza Hotel—not his son. Probably concerned that he'd have to refund money to those complaining guests.

"Don't worry, Dad," Blake replied, his voice sharp with bitterness. "There was no real damage—just a few chips out of the brick wall in the stairwell."

He touched his cheek again and winced at the sting of it. A few crumbs of that concrete were embedded in his skin. He probably should head to the ER. But first he wanted to check on Juliette.

She'd sworn she was fine. But how could she be after that close call?

Blake was still shaking—not with fear but with adrenaline. It coursed through him, making his pulse race and sweat trickle down between his shoulder blades. He'd pulled on a shirt when he'd returned to his suite, which was probably good so nobody had noticed he had a few more scratches on his back and chest from those concrete chips.

But he would be fine.

The killer hadn't really been aiming for him. Juliette had been his target. She was the one in danger. She and their daughter.

"I'm not worried about the damn hotel!" Fenwick replied. But his face had flushed an even brighter shade of red and Blake knew he'd touched a nerve. The old man cared about the business—hell, it was all he'd ever cared about. "I'm worried about you!"

Blake glanced at Finn now and narrowed his eyes. What had the police chief told his father?

Everything?

Anything?

As if he'd read his mind, Finn shook his head.

And the pressure in Blake's chest eased slightly. But maybe it would have been easier if Finn had told the old man and spared Blake the scene he anticipated.

He assured his father, "You don't need to worry about me."

Fenwick gestured at Blake's face, and his hand was shaking. "You could have been killed."

"By a concrete chip?" Blake snorted. "Not likely."

"By a bullet. Someone was shooting at you. Why was someone shooting at you?"

"He wasn't shooting at me," Blake said.

"He just got in the way," Finn added, and there was bitterness in his voice. "That's why I didn't want you following her around. I knew you were going to get your head blown off and it damn near happened!"

"Who?" Fenwick asked. But his question was for the police chief now as if he didn't trust Blake to answer him. "Who is he following around?"

Finn glanced at Blake and raised his eyebrows. "You want me to answer him or are you going to do it?"

"Who?" Fenwick asked, and he turned to Blake now.

Blake wasn't sure how to answer his father. What was Juliette? A one-night stand? His old lover? If the killer hadn't interrupted them, she would have been his lover again.

Whatever else she was to Blake, she was the mother of his child.

"Who?" Fenwick asked impatiently, and he'd turned back to Finn again.

"One of my officers," Finn replied. "The one whose life is in danger."

Fenwick sucked in a breath. His brow furrowed, he focused on Blake again. "Why are you getting involved in this? You've only been back in town a few days."

It had been longer than that, but Blake wasn't about to point out that he'd been home a while and hadn't contacted his father. The man was already angry and confused enough.

Which struck Blake as odd…

Could the old man care more than he'd realized?

"You can't know this woman," his father continued. "She's just some cop…"

Nope. His father hadn't changed. He was still an entitled snob. That was what Juliette had thought he was all those years ago when he'd walked past her in her maid's uniform and hadn't even noticed her. How could he have done that?

Was he his old man's son? A rich and entitled snob?

"She's the mother of my child," Blake said. "The mother of your grandchild."

Fenwick's eyes nearly bugged out of their sockets. "What? What the hell did you just say?"

Finn headed toward the door. Blake gestured him back. But Finn shook his head and quietly murmured, "This is a private family matter."

Finn was family, too. Blake was probably closer to his cousin than he was any of his sisters or his dad. And he hadn't seen his mom in years, either, since she was always traveling.

He glared as the police chief headed out the door. Before it closed, Blake mouthed the word, "Coward" at him. Finn grinned as he shut the door.

Silence fell over the room for a long moment while Fenwick digested the news.

But just in case he hadn't understood, Blake rubbed it in. "You're a grandpa."

That would probably kill his vain father. The guy wore a blond toupee to hide his thinning hair and dated women Blake's age rather than his own. He was desperately trying to appear younger than he was.

"I want to see her," Fenwick said.

Blake shook his head. "Nope."

"*If* she's my granddaughter," he said with suspicion, "I have the right to see her."

Blake sighed. Of course, his father would think to question paternity. "As long as I'm yours, she's your granddaughter." That dimple in her left cheek was DNA enough to prove it to him.

"Don't be naive," his father admonished him. "A lot of women would like to have a Colton heir."

Blake snorted now. "Her mother didn't even tell me about her. If she wanted a Colton heir, she would have told me she'd borne one before now."

"How old is this kid?" his father asked, his voice still sharp with suspicion.

His little girl wasn't just *this kid*.

"Pandora," Blake told him her name. "And she's four."

"You left five years ago."

"Not quite five yet, and the timing is right," he said.

But his father's eyes were narrowed in skepticism. He probably really did not want to be a grandfather. Or he thought Blake was a fool.

"Why can't I see her?" he asked.

"She's in danger," Blake said, and he touched his cheek again and shuddered at the thought of the little girl getting hurt. "She witnessed a murder, and the murderer wants to kill her."

Fenwick sucked in a breath. "And she's only four …?"

"She's too young to have seen what she did," Blake said. After visiting that crime scene in the parking lot, he understood more about what his daughter had witnessed. He'd only seen the aftermath, though—the death. She had seen the actual murder as it had taken place.

"Where is she?" his father asked.

"A safe house."

"I can't go to this safe house?"

Blake shook his head. "No. It's too risky." He could have had the bodyguards smuggle in his father like they smuggled in Juliette. But his father had never been good at sneaking around—that was why he'd been divorced three times.

"Is that the only reason you don't want me to see her?" Fenwick asked, and now he was suspicious of Blake.

Here was his chance to lobby for his sister. "With what you're doing to Layla—forcing her to marry a man she doesn't love to save your business…" He shuddered. "I'm not sure I want you anywhere near my daughter."

Fenwick's face flushed bright red now. "How dare you speak to me this way!"

And this was why Blake hadn't sought out his father when he'd returned to Red Ridge—because usually every conversation between them dissolved into a shouting match.

"I don't have time for this," Blake said. And he grabbed the keys for his rental car and headed toward the door.

"You're not going anywhere!" Fenwick yelled at him.

But Blake just kept walking—right out the door. He didn't have time to waste arguing with his father. He needed to check on Juliette. To make sure she was really okay and that she was safe…

But he had a horrible feeling that until the killer was caught, she wouldn't be safe—no matter how many people were trying to protect her.

The killer was too damned determined.

Fenwick gasped as the door slammed closed behind his son. He'd just walked away. Last time Blake had done that, he'd stayed away for five years. Fenwick shouldn't have been surprised that he had, though. Blake had always been his own man—even when he was just a little boy.

He was headstrong and stubborn.

And Fenwick worried those traits just might get him killed. He was determined to protect this woman—some old girlfriend—and a child that he didn't even have proof was actually his.

Why hadn't he demanded a paternity test the second she had made the claim? He was probably being taken advantage of…

And it wasn't just his money he was risking for her and this kid. He was risking his life for them, as well.

"Damn fool…" Fenwick murmured, his eyes stinging.

What if that had been the last time he saw his son?

Chapter 13

Juliette stared at the clock beside her bed. If she closed her eyes now, she would get a couple of hours of sleep before the alarm went off.

If she could sleep...

But she closed her eyes, and nothing happened. She was too wired, her pulse still pounding, her blood still rushing quickly through her veins...

She had been so close...

To dying.

If Blake hadn't charged into the stairwell when he had, the killer would have thrown her down those twenty-one stories. She'd been losing her grasp on the railing and on her breath as he'd closed his hands around her throat.

But she'd lost something before that...when she'd nearly made love with Blake. She'd lost control of the attraction she felt for him. It was even stronger now than it had been five years ago.

Maybe that was why her pulse kept pounding—because of the excitement of those kisses, the heat of the passion...

She kicked off her sheet and uttered a groan of frustration. It was no use. She was not going to sleep. But maybe that was a good thing, because she was awake enough to hear the creak of the floorboards of her front porch as someone headed toward her door.

Juliette was ready. She picked up her weapon next to her alarm clock. After flicking off the safety, she rolled out of bed. Her house was small—so small that it was just a few steps from her bedroom to the living room.

A knock sounded at the front door now. Maybe the killer had decided to forego trying to pick the lock. But then a voice called out, "Open up, Juliette. It's me."

Her pulse quickened even more than it had already been pounding as she recognized the deep voice. Blake.

Was that why Sasha hadn't joined her at the door? The beagle had been exhausted when they'd come home. She was also missing Pandora and had gone into the little girl's room and crawled onto her bed. The bodyguards and patrol officers must have realized it was him, too, since they'd let him get to the front door.

She hesitated a moment before reaching for the lock. And he knocked again.

"Come on," he said. "I doubt you're sleeping."

She turned the deadbolt and opened the door. "Who can sleep with all the noise you're making out here?" she asked.

Hopefully he had not awakened her neighbors. Mrs. Ludwick might come over wielding her rolling pin as a weapon. While the rolling pin might hurt Blake, it would be no protection against the killer's gun.

Maybe she shouldn't have insisted on staying in her home. It wasn't just herself she was putting in danger but maybe her neighbors, as well. Of course the patrol car was parked out front, though—watching. And the bodyguards were somewhere…

The killer wouldn't try for her here.

"What the hell are you doing here?" Blake asked as he stepped through the door. "Are you trying to get killed?"

"No," she said. "That's what you do—when you keep putting yourself in danger."

He glared at her and sarcastically remarked, "You're welcome."

Heat rushed to her face. She hadn't thanked him yet. She'd just remembered that. "You did save me tonight," she said. "If you hadn't stopped him…" She shuddered. "He would have pushed me down the stairs. I didn't thank you then."

"You didn't have time," Blake said. "And I'm not here looking for gratitude. I'm here to point out that you nearly died tonight and then you come back here alone."

"Thanks to you and the chief, I'm never alone," she said. "You have bodyguards on me. And he has a patrol car following me around."

"And you still nearly got killed tonight," he pointed out. "You're still not safe." He glanced around the house and gestured toward the big picture window in the living room. "Especially not here."

With all the backup she had at the moment, she wasn't concerned. After tonight, she'd learned to not try to lose them again. She also didn't think that the killer would risk another attempt on her life right now. He would know she had extra protection. She was actually surprised that Blake had gotten past everybody. But then, the bodyguards worked for him. And the police officers—her friends—must have realized that there was something going on between her and Blake.

"Then leave," she said. "If you don't feel safe here."

"I don't," he said. But he was staring at her so intensely—like she was the threat—not the maniac who'd shot at them in the stairwell.

"You claimed the bodyguards you hired are the best," she reminded him.

"They are, as long as you don't purposely try to lose them," he said. "But I'm not worried about the killer trying to shoot you again right now."

Probably because he'd read his security firm the riot act for letting the killer nearly get to her tonight. But that had been her fault. She'd tried really hard to lose them and the patrol car when she'd left her house earlier to confront Blake over disappointing their daughter. She hadn't wanted anyone to know that she was going to see him.

"So what are you worried about?" she asked.

"You getting to me," he replied. And he stepped closer to her, his chest nearly brushing against her breasts.

Because of the heat and her temperamental air conditioner, she wore a light nightgown with thin spaghetti straps. The material was so thin that she could feel the heat of his body through it, and her nipples tightened and pushed against it.

Blake lifted his hand to her face. As he cupped her cheek in his palm, he ran his thumb across her mouth. "You are so beautiful…"

Her lips tingled from the contact with his skin. Her

breath stuck in her throat. She wanted him to kiss her. She wanted him to touch her.

She glanced at the door and tilted her head to listen intently. Was anyone going to interrupt this time?

Nothing moved. There was no sound but the pounding of her own heart.

Then he slid his thumb from her lip and leaned forward—pressing his mouth against hers. The kiss was gentle at first then deepened with his groan. She delved into his hair with her fingers, clutching his head to hers as their mouths mated. Their lips nibbled at each other's, clinging in hungry kisses.

She didn't want to stop—knew they couldn't stop—even if the killer showed up at the door again. So she grasped his shirt and walked backward, tugging him along with her toward her bedroom. They didn't stop kissing, didn't even look to see where they were going. But they made it through the door and to the bed. When her legs hit the edge of the mattress, she tumbled down onto it, and Blake tumbled with her, sprawled across her.

She giggled. And he chuckled. Then he moved his weight off her, and she murmured a protest as she reached for him. She caught the waistband of his jeans. They were buttoned now, unlike when she'd shown up at the hotel and they'd been riding low on his lean hips. And he'd worn no shirt. He'd looked so damn sexy. Then.

And now.

His dark blond hair was tousled, and his green eyes were dark with desire as he stared down at her.

She unbuttoned his jeans and reached for his zipper. But he caught her hand in his and held it. His chest expanded with his sharp pants for air.

"You're driving me crazy…" he murmured.

"I haven't done anything…" Yet. But she intended to make love to him—like they had that night—like they were the only two people in the world. She knew they weren't, but she needed this moment—needed to escape from all the fear and stress overwhelming her.

Then he overwhelmed her—with his touch, his kisses…

As he pressed his mouth to hers, he trailed his fingertips down her shoulders, pushing the straps and the front of her nightgown down. Then he traced her collarbone before moving his hands to the swell of her breasts, cupping them in his hands and brushing his thumbs across the nipples.

She squirmed and moaned as heat streaked through her, from her breasts to her core. She pressed her legs together as she began to throb inside—where she wanted him to be.

With his hands busy on her body, she was able to tug down his zipper and free him. Her fingers slid over the erection straining against his knit boxers.

He groaned and pressed against her hand. And she knew he needed her as much as she needed him. But he pulled away from her to move down her body. He kissed her shoulder and the swell of her breast before closing his lips around one of her nipples. He tugged gently on it, and she arched off the bed.

"Blake!" she called as pleasure coursed through her. It wasn't enough, though. She was still full of tension, still full of desire and need.

She pulled on his shirt, dragging it up and over his head. He let her pull it off. But he didn't move back up. Instead he moved lower, and as he did, he slipped off her nightgown and tossed it onto the floor. Then he made love to her with his mouth.

She cried out as pleasure overwhelmed her. But still it wasn't enough...

When had she gotten so damn greedy?

Maybe it was because she knew that he could give her more pleasure than even that, than anyone else ever could...

She clutched at his bare shoulders, trying to pull him up. Instead, he got off the bed entirely.

Was he leaving her?

Was that all he intended to do? Give her pleasure yet take none for himself?

But he'd only stood to push off his jeans and boxers. Then he pulled a condom from a pocket of his jeans and rolled it over his shaft. He joined her on the bed, but he didn't immediately join their bodies. Instead he held his weight off her, their naked bodies just brushing against each other, as he kissed her. Tenderly...

Almost reverently...

Then the passion between them ignited, burning so hot that Juliette's skin heated. She reached up and locked her arms around his neck and her legs around his waist, pulling him down on top of her.

And finally he joined their bodies, easing inside her. She shifted and arched, taking him deeper. Then he began to move, and she bit her lip as the tension and the pleasure intensified. Each thrust brought her closer and closer to the edge of madness. She clutched harder at his back, his muscles rippling beneath her fingers.

She met each thrust, rising up from the mattress—pushing her hips against him. The tension spiraled inside her—out of control—until it finally broke. Her body shuddered, her inner muscles clenching and rippling as the orgasm overwhelmed her. She screamed his name.

Then he tensed and uttered a deep, almost guttural groan of pleasure. He leaned his head down, against her shoulder, as he panted for breath.

She was panting, too. She'd never felt anything as powerful—not even with him.

Finally he moved again, trying to ease out of her. But she clutched him, not wanting him to pull away. He felt so good—so perfect—inside her. As if they'd been made for each other...

But they had no more in common now than they'd had five years ago, except for their daughter. Pandora was the only bond they shared. Their lives were too different, were even in different countries.

She had to remind herself of that—he was only home for a visit. He wasn't staying. So she could not get attached—or let Pandora get too attached—because they would both wind up with their hearts broken.

Blake opened his eyes, then squeezed them shut again as the sunlight pouring through Juliette's bedroom window blinded him. He reached across the tangled sheets, looking for her, but the sheets were empty and probably warm only from the sunlight streaming through that window.

How long had she been gone?

How long had he been asleep?

He opened his eyes again, squinting, and peered at the clock beside the bed. It was nearly noon. All those sleepless nights must have finally caught up with him.

But where was Juliette?

He listened but heard no movement inside the

house—just the sound of birds chirping outside the bed-room window. She was gone.

To work, probably.

At least the bodyguards he'd hired and some of her coworkers would be following her—because Blake was making a piss-poor protector.

But then, he wasn't a bodyguard. He was a business-man. He'd proved that last night. While he'd saved her from the killer pushing her down the stairs, he hadn't been able to catch the guy.

Neither had the bodyguards or the police officers, though. So he probably wouldn't have felt too bad about his efforts to protect her—if Juliette hadn't managed to sneak away from him while they'd been sleeping in the same bed. He needed to be more alert to keep her safe.

Maybe she hadn't slept, though. He couldn't remem-ber much after they'd made love…the third time…

They hadn't been able to get enough of each other—just like that night nearly five years ago. That night had had a once-in-a-lifetime feel to it, though—like it was just a stolen moment they'd needed to make the most of. Blake had already known then that he was going to leave Red Ridge. That the only way he could truly make it on his own was if he was somewhere that being a Colton didn't matter.

Maybe that was why he hadn't noticed her in her maid's uniform. He hadn't wanted to see her—hadn't wanted to have to say goodbye.

Was that why Juliette had slipped away from him today—just as she had after that night so long ago? She didn't want to say goodbye?

He could understand that five years ago. She'd been all hung up on the fact that she was a maid and he was the son of a millionaire. She'd thought they had nothing in common. And they hadn't.

. They still didn't. Following her around the past few days had proved that to Blake. He was nowhere near as tough and brave as she was. He had no interest in risking his life day after day to serve and protect Red Ridge.

And Juliette was risking her life even more because there was a man on the loose determined to kill her. She should have woken him up—should have said goodbye—because Blake worried that she might not have the chance if the killer got her before he saw her again.

Chapter 14

Sometimes Juliette wondered which of them was the handler. She or Sasha?

The beagle was the one leading her around the bus terminal. After another sleepless night, Juliette was too distracted to focus on the job. It might not have been lack of sleep that was distracting her, though, but thoughts of what she'd done with Blake Colton.

What the hell had she been thinking?

She hadn't been thinking. She'd just been feeling— so much passion for him. But if it had only been desire, she might not have been worried. Her feelings for Blake went deeper than lust, though.

Gratitude...

Not just for saving her life the night before but for giving her Pandora, as well. Their daughter was the greatest gift Juliette had ever received. At the time she'd learned she was pregnant, she'd been scared and over-whelmed.

But now…

She couldn't imagine her life without her child in it. Couldn't imagine not having Pandora to hold. Or seeing her smile.

Just as Mama had said, there was a reason for everything. Pandora was the reason for everything Juliette did now.

She needed to find this killer and put him in jail. She needed her child and her life back. That life hadn't included Blake.

Would it?

She doubted he would stay in Red Ridge, but would he come back more often to see his daughter? Or once he left, would they be out of his sight, out of his mind?

That must have been the case last time. He couldn't have looked for her very long before he'd left Red Ridge. And he had never come back to look for her again within those five years. That night—and she—had not meant as much to him as it and he had to her.

She was glad she'd slipped out of bed without awakening him. It would have been even more distracting had he been following her around today.

Sasha emitted a sound deep in her throat, and her hair began to rise on her neck. She'd caught the scent of something…

She'd also caught Juliette's attention. She shook her head, shaking off the sleepiness and distraction. She had to be focused now. Her life depended on it.

"What do you smell, girl?" Juliette asked.

And the white-and-brown dog turned back and looked

at Juliette, as if asking if she was new. What the hell did Juliette think Sasha smelled?

Of course it was drugs. Sniffing them out was Sasha's specialty.

The beagle had found that small amount of marijuana on someone a few days ago. But this seemed bigger—Sasha seemed more excited, her little body trembling with it.

Juliette and Sasha weren't the only K9 team at the bus terminal. Carson Gage walked around the lines of people waiting outside for buses, as well. His German shepherd, Justice, was more a tracker than a drug sniffing dog, though.

She could have used them last night to find the killer. But once he'd disappeared into the sewer, probably not even Justice would have been able to track where he'd gone after that.

To her house?

Had he been watching her place last night? Waiting for another chance to shoot at her?

She shivered despite the afternoon heat.

Then Sasha stopped moving down the row and sat down next to the suitcase of a woman in line for the bus to Spearfish. The young woman dropped the handle of the small case and stared straight ahead, apparently trying to pretend that she was unaware of Juliette and the canine. Sweat beaded on the woman's brow and upper lip. She was young—with several tattoos covering her skinny arms. Her hair had been dyed purple but black roots showed at her scalp.

She looked familiar to Juliette. But then, she'd spent the first day after the murder in the park rousting drug houses. She could have seen her there. She looked like a user. The ivy vine tattoos on her arms did not hide her needle marks.

The woman from the park had had those same tattoos. And the same purple hair. Carson had made the notification to the woman's next of kin; did he recognize this woman? Was she related to the murder victim?

Juliette looked up to try to catch his attention, and the girl took that second to try to run. She leaped over the suitcase that Sasha had gotten the hit on and ran past the line for the bus.

"Gage!" Juliette yelled at her co-worker.

Without waiting to see if Carson followed, Juliette dropped Sasha's leash, knowing she'd stay with the suitcase, and started running after the girl. She couldn't let her get away. This woman—who looked so much like the murder victim—might be the best clue to finding the killer.

This was not good.

The bitch should have left town days ago—right after her sister's death—if she'd wanted to live. Hadn't her sister's murder been a lesson to her?

Don't cross your bosses...

Sure, he'd been told to leave town and he hadn't yet. But they didn't understand he had unfinished business. He was not about to leave witnesses alive.

And apparently, they'd been relieved, too, that he hadn't left when they'd realized the dead woman had not acted alone. They wanted their loose ends cleaned up, so maybe they would understand that he had to clean up his, as well.

They also wanted to send a message to their other associates: *You stole product from them and tried to sell it to someone else, and you were going to wind up dead.*

He stared through the scope of his long gun as he moved the barrel around—trying to find her.

Her purple hair made it easy enough to pick her out of the crowd. That and the fact that she was running.

He groaned. He wasn't the only one who'd made her. Those damn Red Ridge cops were getting in the way again. Then he saw the blond hair of the female officer who pursued her.

And he grinned with happiness. Maybe his luck had begun to change.

He was about to hit two birds with one stone…

After waking up alone in her house, Blake had called the bodyguards on her protection duty. They had assured him that they were close to Juliette, and that they wouldn't let anything happen to her.

But Blake had been compelled to join them again.

It wasn't just that he'd lost a little faith in them after the night before. It was also that he had an odd feeling he might not see Juliette again. So he was driving to the bus terminal where the bodyguards had told him they'd followed her from the police department.

Why did Finn keep sending her out in the field? While he might not have been able to force her to stay in the safe house, he could have assigned her desk duty. Or suspended her completely until the killer was caught.

The man had not let up any on his attempts on her life. In fact, he'd seemed to get bolder. That attempt last night…

Blake shuddered as he remembered rushing into the stairwell to find the man's hands locked around Juliette's throat. She was strong. But the man had been stronger. If Blake hadn't shown up, he would have killed her for certain.

It was too dangerous for her to be anywhere but that safe house with their daughter.

That was where she needed to be—with Pandora.

A twinge struck his heart when he remembered that the little girl was why Juliette had come to see him at the hotel the night before.

Because he'd disappointed their daughter...

Already.

Evidently, he was his father's son. He remembered all the times he'd waited by the door for Fenwick to pick him for some promised outing. Only to have his father never show up...

All the times he'd searched the stands during football, basketball or baseball games to see if his father had come to watch, like he'd promised. But even on those rare instances when Fenwick had shown, he'd been on the phone with someone—too preoccupied with business or women to actually watch Blake play.

That long-ago disappointment in his father turned into disappointment in himself now. Had he made Pandora feel like that—the way his father had made him feel?

He was also frustrated because he didn't know what to do. Did he get closer to the child and risk disappointing her even more than he already had?

Or did he figure out how to be a better father than Fenwick Colton had been to him and his sisters?

Maybe Juliette could teach him how. For the little girl's entire life, Juliette had been her father as well as her mother. She'd been everything to Pandora.

So why wasn't she with the child now? Why did she keep putting herself at risk to catch this killer?

He sighed again—because he knew. She needed to make sure the little girl was safe, and the only way to do that was to catch and put away the killer who'd threatened her.

He pulled his rental vehicle into the parking lot of the bus terminal and looked around for the bodyguards. As usual, he couldn't see their SUV; Finn had said he would only allow them to follow Juliette if they stayed out of the way of his officers. Blake saw two Red Ridge K9 unit patrol cars.

Juliette was not here alone.

He should have felt better, but he still had a heavy pressure in his chest. Maybe that was just his disappointment over how his parenting had started off.

Or maybe it was still that fear that he might not see Juliette again.

But then he did—as she ran through the parking lot— chasing some girl with purple hair and torn jeans. Instinctively he reached for the door handle to push it open and step out.

The woman was obviously not the killer. So Juliette was chasing her for another reason. And he shouldn't intervene in police department work. He might jeopardize the arrest.

And infuriate Juliette even more than his presence usually did. But he couldn't stay in the car and just watch, either. He pushed open the door and stepped onto the parking lot. Heat radiated up from the asphalt.

The temperature didn't seem to bother the two women—who ran flat-out across the lot—in his direction. The purple-haired girl seemed desperate to escape the officer. But Juliette was determined, too, and closing the distance between them. Just as Juliette leaped toward the runner, shots rang out. Both women fell to the hot asphalt.

Had Juliette knocked them to the ground?

Or had a bullet?

Chapter 15

Blood spatters dripped down Juliette's face. She wiped them away with a trembling hand. What the hell had just happened? She'd heard the gun shots—just as she had already been falling, knocking the woman to the ground.

She hadn't acted fast enough, though. She hadn't been able to draw her weapon from her holster to return fire. But she hadn't needed to. The bodyguards had jumped out of wherever they'd been hiding to return fire. They'd undoubtedly saved her life, just as they had the night before.

Once again, the killer had chosen a higher vantage point, like the roof of the greenhouse at the plant nursery from where he'd shot at her and had hit Dean instead.

Blake was standing over her now, staring down at her. "Are you okay?" he asked, his voice gruff. His gaze appeared focused on her face and the blood droplets she'd smeared across it.

She nodded and tried to see where the killer might have shot from. He must have been on the roof of the hotel near the bus terminal. The bodyguards had gone after him. But she suspected that just like last night, the killer would have already escaped.

He moved so quickly. His wounded shoulder—which she'd shot in the park—must not have bothered him at all. She wished she'd shot him somewhere else that day—that she'd been able to stop him from hurting anyone else.

Like Dean...

And Blake...

And this poor girl...

"But there's blood..." Blake murmured.

"It's not mine." She glanced down at the prone body of the girl she'd been chasing. There was no need to check for a pulse. The girl had been struck in the head. She hadn't had a chance.

But had she been the intended target? Or like Dean Landon, had she taken a bullet meant for Juliette?

I'm sorry...she silently told her.

Juliette had only meant to arrest her. Not for her to die...

"Are you okay?" Carson Gage asked as he and the German shepherd joined her. Sasha was also with him, following the suitcase he carried. The girl's suitcase.

She would not be needing it anymore.

Juliette nodded. "I'm fine. You should take Justice and see if you can track the killer."

Carson nodded, but he didn't rush off. He must have thought the same thing she did—that it was too late. The killer was long gone again. "I called it in," he said.

"But it doesn't look like an ambulance is going to be necessary."

"No." Instead of leaving in the back seat of a police car, the girl would be leaving in a body bag.

"This suitcase was hers, I'm assuming," Carson remarked. His eyes narrowed as he stared down at the body, focusing on the woman's face. "She looks familiar…"

"She looks like the woman from the park," Juliette said.

And Carson nodded. "I think it's her sister. I didn't get a good look at her when I notified the parents about the first victim. She wouldn't come out onto the porch where I was talking to them."

Like maybe she hadn't wanted him to get a good look at her. Or maybe she hadn't been curious about what had happened to her sister because she'd already known. Maybe she'd even known her sister's killer…

Damn it!

A potential real lead to the killer was gone. So maybe the woman hadn't just been in the wrong place at the wrong time. Maybe the bullet she'd taken had actually been meant for her and not for Juliette instead.

But still she felt a twinge of guilt along with her disappointment in losing the lead.

She had a feeling the girl would have been alive if Juliette hadn't been the one who'd discovered her standing with that suitcase in line for the bus.

Blake had witnessed a murder himself now, so maybe he could relate to Pandora—if she brought up what she'd seen that day in the park. As he did for business meetings, he had prepared himself for every possible scenario that might happen during his visit with his daughter.

He'd had time to think about it while the bodyguards had smuggled him into the safe house. But now, standing in the doorway of the bedroom in which she was staying, he could only stare at her.

She played with some dolls. A trio of them sat in miniature chairs around a miniature table in the corner of the room. Pandora poured them each imaginary tea from a small plastic teapot.

Before he could think of anything to say, she glanced up and noticed him in the doorway. "Daddy!" she exclaimed. She leaped from her chair and rushed toward him.

And his heart stopped. Nobody had ever been as happy to see him as she was. And she didn't even know him...

But maybe that was why she was so happy.

She held up her arms, and for a second Blake froze, uncertain what she wanted. He had never been around little kids before. Then, just as disappointment was beginning to flash across her face, he lifted her in his arms and drew her close to his chest.

She threw her arms around his neck and pressed her cheek to his. And his heart lurched with the overwhelming force of the love rushing through him. He'd never felt anything like this before.

She leaned back and stared at his face, as if trying to memorize it. Maybe that was because she'd seen it only once and then he hadn't come around again.

He'd been such a fool. And a coward...

Sure, she was in danger. But the bodyguards took extra precautions to make sure there was no way anyone would realize they were heading to the safe house.

They never drove their SUVs—always some other kind of vehicle they found, like that van from the hospital or utility trucks.

Right now, the killer, if he was for any reason following Blake, would think he was back in his hotel suite. But Blake suspected the killer was instead parked somewhere outside the Red Ridge Police Department, which was where Juliette had been heading after leaving the crime scene at the bus terminal.

She had to be safe at the police department. But Blake had a team of bodyguards stationed outside it, as well. He'd brought in more guards from the security agency to make sure there were enough to keep her and Pandora safe.

"I'm so glad you're here," the little girl told him. "You're just in time for the party." She wriggled down from his arms but grabbed his hand with her tiny one and tugged him toward the table of dolls.

He had sisters, so he was not unfamiliar with tea parties. But it had been a long while since he'd been forced to participate in one. Pandora had a sweeter way of manipulating him than his sisters had had, though. There was no one holding his matchbox cars hostage until he drank several cups of fake tea.

He was here willingly. "I'm glad I didn't miss it," he told her.

She reached for one of the dolls to move it from the chair, but he knelt next to the table instead. "I can't take a seat from a lady," he told her.

"Why not?" she asked.

Of course her mother, who was tough and independent, would be teaching her daughter to be a little feminist, as well.

"It's just not the gentlemanly thing to do," he explained. "A gentleman always gives his seat to a lady."

Her little brow furrowed with confusion. Then she nodded. "And princes are gentlemen, right?"

Not some of the ones he'd met—the ones who were real royalty. Blake was just Red Ridge royalty—according to Juliette. And right now, with his cousin suspected of murder bringing to attention the horrendous crimes some of his other family members had committed, there was nothing advantageous to being a Colton.

Maybe that was why Juliette had never told him about his daughter. She hadn't wanted Pandora to be acknowledged as a Colton. At the moment, he couldn't blame her.

"Daddy?" she prodded him.

And he realized he hadn't answered her question. Because he wanted to be honest but appropriate with her, he replied, "All princes should be gentlemen."

She smiled and nodded in agreement. Then she handed him a cup of tea.

He passed the little plastic cup from hand to hand. "Ow, ow, that's hot!"

She giggled and acted as if her cup was too hot, as well. Then they kept playing like that—following each other's lead until they both collapsed into fits of laughter.

Blake had never felt the way he did with his daughter. Had never felt so much love...

Then he looked up and noticed that they were no longer alone. Someone leaned against the doorjamb, watching them. It wasn't the female cop, Elle Gage, who must have been assigned to protect Pandora 24-7. After letting him into the house, Elle had left him alone with his daughter.

The woman standing in the doorway was Juliette.

Her lashes fluttered as she blinked rapidly, as if fighting back the tears that glistened in her eyes. Then Pandora noticed her, too, and jumped up to throw herself into her mother's arms.

Juliette did not hesitate for even a fraction of a second. She clutched the little girl close and spun her around like they'd been separated for weeks instead of hours.

"Mommy, Mommy!" Pandora said. "You're just in time for our tea party! The tea's still hot."

"I see that," Juliette murmured. She must have been watching them for a while.

But Blake had been so enthralled with his daughter, he hadn't noticed Juliette's arrival. He noticed her now, though. She looked so beautiful, her hair down and loose around her bare shoulders. She wore another sleeveless blouse with a short skirt. This one was an off-white color that complemented her orange blouse.

Unlike him, Juliette settled onto one of the chairs—with the doll she'd displaced in her lap. The chair didn't break beneath her weight like it would have Blake's, but then, Juliette was so petite and light that he'd easily lifted her.

Pandora looked around the table, and a big smile spread across her face, making the dimple in her left cheek deepen. "The whole family's here now."

Blake felt another twinge in his heart, but he wasn't sure if it was love this time.

Or pure panic.

"She's supposedly my family!" Fenwick Colton bellowed. "I should damn well be allowed to see her."

Finn was the police chief. Not a family counselor. "I'm not getting involved in this," he told the man.

Fenwick was so fired up that instead of summoning Finn, he'd come down to the police department himself. He must have either bullied or charmed his way past Lorelei back to Finn's office.

Fortunately Juliette had already left for the day, or the older man might have demanded to see her, as well. Right now he was just focused on her daughter, though.

"You have her stashed away in some safe house," Fenwick said. "So you are involved."

"I'm protecting a witness to a murder," he said. And he was damn glad that he had. With all the attempts made on her mother's life, there was no way the child would have been safe if she hadn't been hidden away from the killer.

"She's a little girl," Fenwick said, and for once there seemed to be almost genuine empathy in his voice. But then he cleared his throat and mused, "It's just not for certain that she's Blake's little girl."

And the empathy was gone.

Finn swallowed a sigh of frustration as his head began to pound. Was he really related to this man? At least he wasn't his son—like poor Blake was.

"What do you know about her mother?" the mayor asked.

"That she's a damn fine officer," Finn said. "One of my finest."

"How *fine* is she?" The older man's eyes narrowed with suspicion. "Have you been involved with her, too?"

"Absolutely not." That was a line Finn would have never crossed—with any of his officers.

"What about anyone else? Has she ever been married or engaged?" Fenwick fired the questions at him. "Has she ever dated anybody else around here?"

Finn wasn't about to discuss Juliette Walsh's personal life—not that he thought she'd ever had much of one besides her daughter. Her life revolved around that little girl.

That was probably why she was so determined to catch the man who'd threatened the child. Even if her efforts cost her own life.

"I don't get involved with my officers," Finn said. "And I don't get involved in their personal lives, either. You need to talk to your son about this."

Fenwick didn't bother swallowing his sigh; he expelled a long and ragged one. "Blake and I don't talk. We argue."

No wonder Blake had stayed away from Red Ridge for so many years. Finn didn't know what to say, so he remained silent. Maybe the mayor would get the hint that he was not going to participate in this conversation and leave.

"And why is Blake following this police officer around?" Fenwick asked. "He's not a cop or a bodyguard."

Finn shrugged. He'd already pointed that out to Blake to no avail. Maybe that was why father and son argued so much; they were too much alike. Stubborn and headstrong.

"She must mean something to him," Fenwick said, and now there was fear in his voice. "Maybe too much…"

Finn suspected the same. If a man was willing to put his life at risk for a woman, he must care about her.

"You don't think he'd do something crazy like propose to her, do you?" Fenwick asked, his voice cracking with very real fear and horror.

Finn shrugged again. "Like I said, Blake's the one you need to have this conversation with."

The older man shook his head. "No, you're the one who needs to catch Demi Colton and stop these killings of innocent men about to be married."

And now Finn understood why Fenwick was here. He was worried that his son might become the next victim of the Groom Killer.

"I don't think you have to worry about Blake becoming a target," he said.

Juliette wasn't happy to have Blake following her around. And she had never told him about his child until he returned to Red Ridge.

No. Fenwick didn't need to worry about the Groom Killer going after his son; he needed to worry about the killer that was after Pandora and Juliette taking out Blake, too.

Chapter 16

Standing in that doorway, watching Blake play and laugh with their daughter, had caused Juliette physical pain. She'd felt the pressure of guilt weighing so heavily on her that her heart ached with it. She never should have kept his daughter from him.

She should have told him. He'd had a right to know. And then, if he hadn't wanted to be involved in Pandora's life, it would have been his choice.

She never should have made that choice for him. Or for Pandora...

But along with the guilt, Juliette had felt another kind of pain as her heart had swelled with so much love she'd thought it might burst.

Pandora was so funny and sweet and smart. She was an amazing little girl. And Juliette was so lucky she was hers. She had to make certain nothing happened to her.

But she didn't want anything to happen to Blake, either. He could have died the night before—when the gunman had fired all those shots in the stairwell.

"What's wrong, Mommy?" Pandora asked.

The tea party had ended a while ago, and the little girl was lying in bed now, her head on her pillow. Juliette knelt on one side of her twin bed, and Blake knelt on the other. Sasha had jumped onto the foot of the bed, spinning in circles like a cat until she settled onto the little girl's feet.

Sasha was missing Pandora nearly as much as Juliette was. That was why the beagle hadn't budged from the little girl's empty bed last night when Blake had arrived. She wondered how she would get her canine partner to leave her daughter tonight. She would have left the dog here—if she didn't need Sasha so much herself.

Pandora reached out and touched Juliette's forehead. "You have worry lines," she murmured.

And Juliette smiled with that love bursting inside her. Her little girl was so precocious.

Pandora turned to Blake. She reached out and touched the cut on his cheek. "Daddy has a line, too."

"It's just a scratch," he assured her. "No worry line."

But Juliette's were. She was worried that he could have been hurt so much worse than the concrete chips he must have had flushed out before he'd come to see her the night before.

Pandora smiled. "You are still handsome," she assured him. "Don't you think so, Mommy? Don't you think Daddy is a handsome prince?"

The little girl knew that Juliette did because she'd told her so in the stories she'd shared about her father. The imp was playing matchmaker.

And now panic struck Juliette's heart. Pandora had already called them a family during her tea party.

Was she setting her heart on them all being together?

Juliette smiled back at her daughter. But as a mother, she had to caution her. "Remember that Daddy doesn't live with us," she told her. "Daddy doesn't even live in Red Ridge."

Blake sucked in a breath. Then he forced a smile and remarked, "Would I be better-looking if I did?"

He would be—then Juliette wouldn't be so worried about him breaking her and Pandora's hearts.

"I just want to remind Pandora that we can't have family tea parties every day. Eventually you'll be going back to your home."

"Where do you live, Daddy?" the little girl asked. "In a castle?"

"Right now I live in a hotel suite," he said.

And Juliette wondered about his home in other countries. Did he just live out of hotel suites in them, too?

That was no kind of life for a child. But then, because of her, he hadn't known he had a child.

"What's a hotel sweet?" asked the little girl. "Is it made of candy?"

He chuckled and leaned forward to press his lips against her forehead. "No. Then little girls like you would eat it all up."

She smiled. "Yes, I would."

How had he gotten to know their daughter so quickly? How had they bonded already? Was it because they had always had a bond but never known about it—because of her?

The guilt pulled heavily on Juliette again. But she

pushed it aside to focus on what was best for Pandora. And she—and the life they'd built in Red Ridge—was.

"I love our house," Pandora told her father. "I love my room. And my toys. And Mommy tucking me in with Sasha sleeping on my bed."

Sasha was on the bed now. That was why she and Blake had had to kneel on the floor. While neither the beagle nor the little girl was that big, combined they took up the entire twin.

"When can we go home, Mommy?" she asked. And finally her eyelids began to droop as she struggled to stay awake. No doubt the little smarty had figured out that once she fell asleep, Juliette left.

"As soon as we put the bad man in jail, we'll go home," Juliette assured her.

Despite the blankets and the dog covering her, the little girl shivered.

And Juliette regretted bringing up the bad man. Pandora didn't have imaginary monsters to fear; she had a real one.

"It'll be soon," Juliette promised. She would make sure she wasn't lying. She would keep that promise to her daughter. She had to—for all their sakes.

As if taking her at her word, Pandora slipped into slumber. A breath sighed out between her lips.

Juliette kissed her forehead and rose from the floor. Blake stood up, too, and reached for her across the bed. But Juliette pulled away and walked into the hall.

"You don't have to be the one to get him," Blake said. "You can let someone else catch him."

"Like they caught the Groom Killer?" She shook her head. "We're already spread too thin. I need to stay on the job. I need to stay focused."

So she couldn't get involved any deeper with him. He was messing with her sleep and her head and her heart.

Blake gestured toward the bedroom door she'd pulled mostly closed. "She's the one you need to focus on," he said.

She sucked in a breath. "How dare you critique my parenting! I've been doing it alone just fine all these years."

"That was your choice," he said. "Not mine."

"What is your choice?" she asked. "Are you going to stick around and be a real parent? Or will you be taking off once she's no longer in danger?"

He sucked in a breath now. But he just shook his head. "We can't talk about that here."

He was right. She didn't want Pandora or Elle to overhear their argument. And she knew they were going to argue. But that was all they were going to do.

She couldn't make love with him again—because she was starting to fall in love with him. And she wasn't about to risk her heart on a man who was leaving—again.

The bodyguards smuggled out Juliette and Blake as carefully as they'd smuggled them into the safe house. Blake wasn't worried that anyone would find the place where Finn had stashed their daughter. That was why he wished Juliette would stay there.

Instead she'd insisted on coming back to her little house on that suburban street in Red Ridge. He was worried that the killer would find her here—easily.

She was making it even easier for him when she sat down on her front steps instead of unlocking the door to go inside. The beagle, off her leash, meandered around the small front yard, sniffing the grass.

"You should come back to my hotel suite," he said.

"Because it's so safe there?" she asked with a disparaging roll of her beautiful blue eyes.

"It will be now," he promised. He'd brought in more bodyguards from the protection agency. "The hotel stepped up security."

She pointed at Sasha and in a snobbish-sounding voice remarked, "The Colton Plaza Hotel does not allow animals in their rooms."

Blake chuckled at her tone. "They make exceptions for service dogs and that's what Sasha is. She does an incredible service by getting drugs off the street."

Juliette sighed. "That wasn't all we got off the streets today."

"The girl…" Blake said. She'd looked so young. He'd overheard Juliette and the detective talking about her being the sister of the murder victim from the park. "Why do you think he wanted them both dead?"

She shook her head. "I think someone else wanted them dead. Whoever she'd taken that suitcase of drugs from, just like her sister had. The man was just carrying out the order…"

"A hired assassin? That's what this guy is who's after you and Pandora?" He shuddered. But of course, it all made sense. That was why he was so good that last night he'd slipped past even the renowned security agency Blake had hired.

Maybe he was too good…

"You're not safe here," he persisted. "You and Sasha need to come back to the hotel with me."

"No," she said. "I need to sleep tonight."

"You'll sleep better when you know you're safe," he insisted. And so would he.

She shook her head again. "You and I both know we won't sleep if I go back to your suite."

His body tensed thinking about it—about being inside her again. He fit so perfectly, as if they'd been made for each other.

"And that's a problem?"

Now she nodded. "Yes. It's bad enough that I'm worried you're going to break my daughter's—"

"*Our* daughter's," he interrupted her as a fierce possessiveness overcame him.

"Pandora," she said instead. "I think you're going to break her heart. I don't want you breaking mine, too."

Frustration nagged at him. "I don't understand you. Last night you were mad at me for not going to see Pandora. And now you're mad that I did."

She uttered a weary sigh. "I just don't want her getting hurt."

"Neither do I." But he was very afraid that he might—inadvertently—hurt her just because he had no damn idea how to be a father.

"If you're going to leave soon and not come back very often, it might be best if you don't see her now," Juliette said. "If you just let her go…"

The thought gripped his heart in a tight vise, painfully squeezing. He shook his head. "No."

Now that he knew he had a daughter, he couldn't just walk away. He could never return to the life he'd had before he'd learned the truth. So what the hell was he going to do? Not about just Pandora but also about his business?

He needed time to think, and that was impossible to

do around Juliette. She was too beautiful, too sexy, too damn distracting...

She was smart not to come back to his hotel suite. But he didn't think she should stay here, either.

She stared up at him through eyes that were heavy with exhaustion. "Please," she implored him. "Think about what's best for her."

"I don't have to think about that," Blake said. "You are. She can't lose her mother, so you need to stop putting yourself in danger."

He grimaced as he remembered watching her fall in the parking lot today and then running up to see that blood spattered across her face. For a long, horrifying moment, he'd thought she'd been hit. Then she'd moved, and relief had rushed through him.

"I have the training and experience to handle the dangers of my job," she said. "You don't. You have no business following me around all day."

"You don't want Pandora to get hurt," he said. "Neither do I. You getting hurt will hurt her." Far worse than if he left Red Ridge.

"It would hurt her to lose you, too," Juliette said. "And that's more likely to happen if you insist on sticking so close to me. You saw what happened to that girl today."

He flinched. "Yes, but that was because of the drugs she was carrying."

"We don't know that for certain," Juliette said. "The bullet could have been meant for me—not her."

True. And that was what he'd thought when it had happened. "You need to go into that safe house with Pandora," he said.

"What I need to do is sleep," she said. And she rose from the porch steps.

He couldn't argue with her. Being exhausted was not going to help her find the gunman—or survive his next attempt on her life.

And Blake knew there would be another attempt. This assassin was obviously determined to get rid of her.

He glanced around, but it was so dark beyond the circle of light from the streetlamp in front of her house. While there was no patrol car yet, the bodyguards were out there—somewhere. They would make certain nothing happened to her.

He hesitated before turning away from her, though. Maybe it was because he wanted to kiss her good-night. But this wasn't a date. And he knew if he kissed her, that the night would not be over—or at least, he wouldn't want it to be over. He would want to make love to her again and again like he had the night before and that night five years ago when Pandora had been conceived.

"Sasha," Juliette called to the beagle. The dog immediately headed up the porch steps with her.

She had the bodyguards and her canine partner. She didn't need Blake.

But he was beginning to feel as if he needed her.

"Good night, Blake," she said.

She was dismissing him. He knew that. But he wondered if it was just for the night or for always. She'd made it clear that she didn't want him following her anymore, and he didn't think it was just because that girl had died today.

She was determined to protect her life herself. Now she was also determined to protect her heart. From him…

"Good night," he murmured back, but she was already unlocking her door to step inside the house. The dog rushed through before Juliette could enter. She followed Sasha inside and closed the door without so much as a glance back in Blake's direction.

He stayed on the front walk for another long moment, staring up at the house. So he noticed the flash even before he heard the shot.

Someone had fired a gun inside the house.

Chapter 17

The way Sasha had hurried inside the house had fore-warned Juliette that it was not empty. That was why she hadn't looked back at Blake. She hadn't wanted him to interfere and get caught in the middle as she drew her weapon and returned the fire of whomever had started shooting the minute she'd closed her door.

Glass shattered behind her as bullets struck the picture window. She hoped Blake was no longer standing out there, that he'd turned and walked away. Far away...

"Put down your weapon!" she shouted—even though she couldn't see the intruder. "You're under arrest!"

A chuckle rang out of the darkness. And she fired in its direction. Glass broke. She hadn't shot in the direction of a window, so it must have been a picture frame or a mirror. She hoped the former. The last thing she needed was any more bad luck.

"Put down your weapon!" she shouted again.

There was no chuckle this time. No response at all. Had she hit him?

Sasha's barking, which had been incessant since she'd pushed ahead of Juliette through the door, finally stopped. Had the beagle been hit?

Juliette could see nothing in the darkness. But before she could fumble around for a light switch or a lamp, she heard a noise behind her.

Had he circled around her?

Her finger twitched on the trigger as she prepared to pull and fire again. But then a deep voice called out, "Juliette! Are you okay?"

And she cursed and lowered the barrel.

But more shots rang out.

She fell from the heavy weight on top of her as she lay back on the hardwood floor. But the shots weren't close. Someone was firing outside her house. Blake was the one who'd knocked her to the ground.

The killer and the bodyguards must have been exchanging gunfire. And she could hear Sasha barking, too.

"Are you all right?" Blake asked.

"No, thanks to you," she murmured as she struggled to get up. She needed to get outside—to handle Sasha and to find the killer.

And maybe that was why Blake remained on top of her, his hard body heavy on hers—because he didn't want her confronting the killer again.

She shoved his shoulders, trying to push him back. "Get off me! I need to get out there!"

"You need to stay here," Blake said.

The gunfire had stopped. But she heard sirens now,

wailing in the distance. And she felt like wailing in frustration. He'd been right here.

So close…

And yet he'd escaped her once again. She had no doubt that he had escaped the bodyguards, too—because she could hear Sasha's barking grow fainter and fainter. She was still pursuing the intruder.

She shoved harder. "Blake, let me up. I need to back up Sasha." So many canines were injured or killed just doing their jobs—because they wouldn't stop until their handlers told them to.

Sasha wasn't as big as some of the other breeds in the K9 unit, but she was every bit as fearless.

Finally Blake budged, and Juliette squirmed out from beneath him. Then she rushed out the back door. The killer must have left it open when he'd run out.

"Sasha!" she called out, her heart pounding with fear for her partner. "Sasha! Heel!"

She could hear the dog whimpering somewhere in the dark. Had she been hurt?

She started across the backyard, but she wasn't alone. Blake had followed her from the house, and he kept reaching for her arm, trying to pull her back.

"Juliette, it isn't safe."

"He's gone," one of the bodyguards remarked as the burly man rushed up to join them. "He fired off a couple of rounds as he came out of the house, but he kept running."

So Juliette had not hit him inside the house. He wasn't injured other than his previous shoulder wound. And that hadn't slowed him down at all yet.

The guy just kept coming.

She sighed with frustration and tugged away from

Blake's hand on her arm. "I need to find Sasha." She met the beagle halfway across the backyard. The dog whimpered when Juliette touched her side. Had she been shot?

"I need to get her to the vet!" Juliette said as concern gripped her. "She's hurt."

Before she could lift the animal, Blake was there, gently picking up the dog.

"Be careful with her," Juliette implored him as she blinked against the tears stinging her eyes. "Please, be careful!"

"I will," he said.

And he was, because the dog didn't whimper again even as he loaded her into Juliette's car. They were just backing out of the driveway when the first patrol car arrived. Where had it been?

Had there been another murder tonight? Was that why her coworkers hadn't been watching her? Of course, the bodyguards were the ones who'd been getting her in and out of the safe house, and they did their job so well that they must have lost the patrol car, too.

Maybe her coworkers had thought she would return to the Colton Plaza Hotel after seeing Pandora.

"Sasha's hurt," she told the dark-haired officer when Dante Mancuso rushed up to her car. "We need to get her to the vet."

"Go! Go," he urged her.

"The bodyguards can tell you what happened," she said as she eased her foot off the brake and started backing into the street.

Mancuso murmured something as she drove away. Something that sounded like, "I can guess…"

Everybody could—because it seemed as though anyone close to Juliette got hurt. She glanced across the console at Blake. He'd nearly been shot the night before. It was only a matter of time before he got hurt again.

Or worse…

Patience Colton had no life. At least no social life. Her life was her job, and the top priority of her job was to take care of Red Ridge's canine force. She rushed around her office, making sure she had everything ready.

She hoped it wasn't a bullet that had injured the dog. If it was, she would be prepared. But she wasn't prepared to turn around and see her brother carrying in the wounded beagle. She stared, stunned, at his sudden appearance. "Blake, what the hell…"

"Where do you want her, Patience?" he asked.

She gestured to the stainless-steel examination table. "There. What happened?" And what did her brother have to do with it?

A blond-haired woman followed him into the office. It took Patience a few seconds to recognize her without her uniform. But then she glanced at the dog again. "Sasha…" And Juliette Walsh was her handler.

"What happened?" she asked the female officer.

"I don't know," Juliette replied. "She went after a perp. I don't think he shot her because I don't see an entrance wound."

Patience turned her attention to the dog. She would deal with her brother later. "No blood…"

Juliette's breath shuddered out. But a lack of blood wasn't always a good thing. There might have been no blood because the injuries and bleeding were all internal.

Patience ran her hands along the dog's side, and Sasha whimpered softly and arched her neck. Patience rubbed the dog's head between her ears. "It's okay…"

she soothed her. To Juliette, she said, "I'm going to take some X-rays. You two should step outside."

Juliette hesitated, clearly unwilling to leave her partner alone. But Blake slid his arm around the slight woman and escorted her toward the waiting room.

And Patience drew in a deep breath. She wasn't just worried about the dog. Now she was worried about her brother, too. She had never seen him look at anyone the way he'd looked at Juliette—with such caring and concern.

Had her father been right? Should she not have called Blake to come back to Red Ridge? Because if he had fallen for the beautiful K9 cop, he would be putting his life in danger—from the Groom Killer.

But that wasn't all the danger he faced if he was involved with Juliette Walsh. She'd heard about the murder in the park—the one Juliette's daughter had witnessed.

She tensed as she suddenly understood the message her father had left her. The voice mail had told her that she needed to talk some sense into her brother. She hadn't had a chance or the inclination to call him back yet.

But now she knew what he was talking about...

Juliette Walsh.

She pushed concern for her brother aside, though, as she focused on the beagle instead. Once she read the X-rays she'd taken, she finally blew out the breath she'd been holding. She opened the door to her exam room and gestured for Blake and Juliette to step back inside.

"How bad is it?" Juliette asked, her blue eyes glistening with unshed tears. She really loved her partner.

How did she feel about Patience's brother?

Patience smiled reassuringly. "She's fine. Just bruised. I would say someone kicked her side."

Juliette leaned over her dog and pressed her head against the dog's as she rubbed her neck. "You are such a good girl. You tried to get him…"

"Do you think she got a piece of him?" Blake asked.

Juliette stepped back, and Patience looked in the dog's mouth. A few strands of denim were stuck between her teeth. "Looks like she might have gotten his jeans."

"Good dog," Blake praised the canine, too.

"What's going on?" Patience asked. And she wasn't asking about just what had happened to Sasha. She suspected it was that other killer on the loose who'd kicked her. She was asking what was going on with them. How did Blake even know Juliette Walsh?

"The man who killed the woman in the park was in my house," Juliette told her.

And apparently so was Blake.

"Sasha alerted me to his presence," Juliette said as she lovingly ran her hand over the dog's head again. "If she hadn't, I might not have survived."

The color drained from Blake's face, leaving him looking pale and shaken. The thought of losing Juliette obviously upset him. What did she mean to him?

"Are you okay?" Patience asked her. She narrowed her eyes and studied the woman. She looked as upset as Blake was. She truly had had a close call.

Juliette nodded. "Yes, I'm fine—as long as she will be…" She stared down at her dog.

Patience smiled. She loved how close every K9 officer was to his or her canine partner. But then, that was bound to happen when they trusted each other with their lives. Patience's smile slid into a frown. "I heard you're in danger. And your daughter, too." She glanced at her brother. "I'm sorry…"

"We'll catch him," Juliette said, but she still sounded scared and uncertain.

"We will," Blake insisted.

"We?" Patience asked, and her control on her curiosity snapped. "What the hell are you talking about? You're a businessman, not a police officer!" She hadn't called him to Red Ridge to lose him.

"That's what I keep telling him," Juliette said. "He needs to stop trying to protect me."

Blake shook his head. "I can't."

"Why not?" Patience asked. Was he in love with the beautiful K9 cop?

"Because she's the mother of my daughter."

Patience's knees shook for a moment, and she nearly dropped. But she clutched the edge of the exam table and stayed upright. Sasha licked her hand, as if in commiseration or out of gratitude.

Her brother was a father? She was an aunt?

"No way," she murmured.

And she couldn't help but think that her dad was finally right about something. She never should have called Blake back to Red Ridge—because it was clear to her now that he was in danger.

Blake waited for Juliette to step across the threshold and enter his suite. She hesitated so long that he was tempted to pick her up like he had that night so long ago and carry her across it.

But he'd freaked himself out when he'd done that because it had felt too much like a honeymoon. And he'd never intended to get married. Then.

That hadn't changed, even though he knew he had a

daughter now. Sure, he'd never intended to be a father, either, but that choice had been taken from him.

And he wasn't mad about that at all.

Juliette seemed mad, though. But then, she hadn't wanted to come back here when he'd asked her earlier. It had taken her house getting shot up and her canine partner hurt for her to agree to return to the suite with him.

"You hadn't told her," she murmured as she finally stepped inside with him.

Before he closed the door, he glanced into the hallway and expelled a breath of relief to see one of the bodyguards standing sentry. They would be safe tonight.

"What?" he asked, his brow furrowed. He couldn't figure out why she was angry.

"You hadn't told your sister about Pandora," she said.

He shrugged. "I'm not that close to my family. You realize that…" She knew more about him than anyone else—especially his family.

"Is that the real reason you didn't tell her?" she asked.

He nodded. "What other reason could I have?"

"You're ashamed of her. Of us…"

Now he understood why she was angry. But her accusation made him angry, too. "Stop calling me a snob," he said. "I don't care that you used to be a maid. I respect that you have always been a hard worker. And there is no way I would ever be ashamed of Pandora." His voice cracked with emotion when he added, "She's amazing…"

And not just because she was his. He would have thought she was special even if he wasn't related to her.

"Yes, she is," Juliette agreed. And there was so much pride and love in her voice.

"My father knows," he admitted. "I thought that he'd probably told my sisters." He was surprised that he hadn't, but then, his father wasn't convinced that the little girl was Blake's. He wanted to see her first.

And even then, he probably still wouldn't believe it.

He stepped closer to Juliette and tipped up her chin so that he could stare deeply into her beautiful eyes. "You have to stop this…thinking I would be ashamed of you," he said. "You and Pandora should be ashamed of me."

Her lips curved into a smile. "Really?"

"Yes," he said. "I'm a Colton."

She tilted her head.

"Being a Colton isn't always exactly a source of pride," he told her. "My cousin's wanted for murder."

"It's looking less and less like Demi is the Groom Killer," Juliette said.

He shrugged. "It doesn't matter. Other members of distant branches of the Colton family have been killers."

"So what are you telling me?" she asked. "That I should sleep with one eye open?"

"Maybe you shouldn't sleep at all," he told her.

She narrowed her eyes with suspicion, but she grinned. "You told me that I would be able to sleep here."

He had—when he'd finally convinced her to come back with him. Patience had had her leave Sasha with her for the night—just to make sure the beagle got a chance to rest and recover.

"Do you want to sleep?" he asked. She looked exhausted—with dark circles beneath her eyes. He really should let her sleep.

But she shook her head, stepped closer and pressed her lips to his. Against his mouth, she murmured, "I want you…"

He wanted her, too—so badly. But he was worried that she was totally exhausting herself trying to catch this killer, so he pulled back and stared down at her. "You should sleep. You need your rest."

"I need…"

He waited for her to say—to say that she needed him. But instead she said, "I need this…" She yanked up his shirt and pulled it over his head. "I have all this adrenaline…"

He could understand that—after the shooting. His pulse was racing, too, but it wasn't because of the bullets that had been flying. It was because of her.

She unbuttoned his jeans and jerked down the zipper. Then her fingers were closing around him, stroking him…

He groaned as his control snapped. Then he swung her up in his arms and carried her into the bedroom. Just as quickly as she'd undressed him, he undressed her until finally they were skin to skin.

Almost as close as they could be…

But he wanted to be closer. He grabbed a condom packet and tore it open. She pulled out the condom before he could and rolled it down his shaft.

He groaned again and pushed her back onto the bed. But he didn't immediately join their bodies. Instead he made sure she was ready for him—with his fingers, with his mouth…

She squirmed against the mattress and arched against him, crying out as he gave her pleasure. He wanted to give her more. But before he could, she was grabbing his shoulders and pulling him up the bed. Then she shoved him onto his back and straddled him.

Maybe—with all the attempts on her life—she needed to feel in control again—because she controlled the pace, sliding up and down, rocking back and forth…driving him out of his mind.

Tension gripped his body, and sweat beaded on his

brow and upper lip. Then she leaned down and kissed it away, kissing him deeply.

He slid his hands up from her hips to her breasts and teased her nipples into taut points with his fingers. Then he arched up from the bed and closed his mouth around one.

She cried out as she came, her inner muscles gripping and convulsing around his shaft. He thrust up, seeking his release, as he gripped her hips and moved her up and down, and finally the tension inside him broke.

A low, deep groan ripped from his throat as pleasure overwhelmed him.

She moved off him and dropped onto the bed, trying to catch her breath. He was panting, too. He forced himself up, though, and into the bathroom to clean up. When he returned to the bed, she was asleep—her breathing slow and even.

Careful not to disturb her, he slid into bed next to her and pulled up the sheets. She rolled over, and it was as if she'd been looking for him because she settled against him. Her head against his shoulder, her arm across his chest.

He settled his arm around her and held her closely. She was safe now. But he knew that once she awoke she would insist on leaving—on putting herself in danger again.

And he was afraid that it was only a matter of time before one of the killer's attempts to get her proved successful. It was only a matter of time before Pandora lost her mother and Blake lost...

Everything.

That was what Juliette was beginning to mean to him: everything.

Chapter 18

"Is she okay?" Juliette anxiously asked as Patience Colton brought Sasha out of the kennel the next morning.

The beagle wagged her tail and greeted Juliette, who had dropped to her knees, with wet kisses. Her entire brown-and-white body moved with excitement at seeing her. And not even a whimper slipped out.

"She's fine," Patience assured her. "I gave her a sedative to calm her down last night, so she would sleep. And she's raring to go this morning."

Juliette breathed a sigh of relief. "I'm so glad."

"Like I told you last night, she still needs to take it easy for a couple of days, though," Patience advised her. "Just until the swelling goes down."

"Will that be long enough?" Juliette asked. A couple of days wasn't too long—not after she'd worried that she'd lost her last night when she'd heard the whimpering in the dark.

"Yes," Patience said.

"Thank you," Juliette said. "I need her."

"What about my brother?" Patience asked.

Juliette glanced uneasily around the training center. The vet was not alone in the long brick building. Hayley Patton worked as a trainer there, but she must have been late because Juliette didn't see the blonde woman when she looked around. Of course she'd heard that Hayley was using her fiancé's death as her excuse for everything—for calling in sick to work, for being late...for not paying her bills.

"What do you mean?" Juliette asked Patience, even though she was pretty certain she knew. Blake's sister was asking her what her intentions were for her younger brother.

"Do you need him?" Patience asked.

Juliette was afraid that she did—especially after last night. She'd felt so safe and secure in his arms that she'd slept more deeply than she had in a long time. But she shouldn't have felt safe with him because she had a feeling that he could hurt her badly if she let herself fall for him.

"I don't need him," Juliette said. "I can take care of myself. I've been doing it for years."

"And your daughter," Patience added. "You've taken care of Pandora for years on your own, too. Why did you tell Blake now?"

"He saw her," Juliette admitted. "And he figured it out."

"And if he hadn't?" his sister asked.

Juliette tensed. She'd known he was back in town because everybody in Red Ridge had been talking about his return. She'd even known where to find him. But she hadn't sought him out—hadn't gone to tell him that he was a father despite Elle urging her to do it.

Patience waited and watched, then nodded. "If you really don't need my brother, then you should let him go now," she said.

"I don't have him," Juliette said. While she'd admitted to being afraid that he might break her heart along with Pandora's, he had expressed no such fear. His heart was safe from her. While he wanted her physically, he wasn't as emotionally invested as she was.

"It certainly looked like you had him last night," Patience said.

Juliette's face flushed with embarrassment. But the vet couldn't know what they'd done in Blake's suite. She must have been talking about the way Blake had acted when they were in her office.

"And he's been following you, trying to protect you," Patience said as she glanced around the kennels. "I'm surprised he's not here now."

Juliette had snuck out again before he'd awakened. But she wasn't about to share that with his sister. Her face heated even more with embarrassment, though.

And Patience nodded again, as if she'd figured it out anyway.

"I don't want Blake following me," Juliette said. Maybe his sister could talk some sense into him, but she didn't think it was likely since she and the chief had already failed. "I don't want him putting himself in danger."

"Then cut him loose," Patience said. "Before he gets

hurt. Make it clear you want nothing to do with him. Or he might wind up the next victim of the Groom Killer."

Juliette gasped. "We're not getting married. I don't even think he's going to stay in Red Ridge." And if that was the case, she and Pandora were the ones who would wind up getting hurt. Not Blake.

But his sister was right—for all their sakes. She had to cut him loose.

Damn it!

She'd done it again. She'd slipped away while Blake had been sleeping. Fortunately the bodyguards had stayed on her. They'd assured him a patrol car had been following her, as well. So she was safe…

Was he?

After last night, he knew he was beginning to fall for her. He shouldn't. He still couldn't trust her. She hadn't told him about his daughter. Even now, she admonished him for not seeing Pandora enough while pushing him away when he had. Did she want him to be part of their lives?

Her indecisiveness left him wary—so wary that he was meeting with a lawyer who had called him at his father's urging, and Blake had agreed to talk with him.

"I want to make sure my daughter is taken care of," Blake said.

Unlike his father, Blake made that his first priority. He wanted to make sure Pandora always had what she needed. That was why he wanted to keep Juliette safe—because she needed her mother more than anything else.

He really should have skipped this meeting until after the killer was caught. He couldn't really focus on this—or the business he'd tried conducting earlier—

with thoughts of Juliette in his head. He remembered that flash of gunfire behind her picture window before the glass had exploded.

Her falling in the parking lot the day before...

Yes, it was only a matter of time before the killer tried again. He had to be caught.

"You can draw up some trust papers for her," Blake said, "and set up another meeting with me to sign those." He also wanted to give Juliette a lump sum amount of cash for back child support. She'd been caring for their daughter alone for much too long.

The lawyer was obviously a friend of his father's because he looked at Blake the same way his father did—like he was an idiot. He shook his head and patted back his slicked down comb-over to make sure a hair hadn't fallen out of place. Maybe the guy should have followed Fenwick's example and just gotten a toupee.

"Before you do anything," the lawyer said, "you need a paternity test to confirm the child is yours."

Blake shook his head.

"You need that test to see whether or not she's yours—not just because of the money but for custody reasons."

"What do you mean?" He had no intention of taking the child away from her mother. He was doing everything within his power to make sure they weren't separated.

"If she is yours, this woman denied you years of your daughter's life."

Blake flinched at the reminder. He'd been trying to let that resentment go. He didn't need to rehash it now. "That's the past. I can't change that," he said.

"You can take those years back," the lawyer insisted. "You can take the kid away from her."

Blake snorted. "How?" Juliette was not an unfit mother. The lawyer was insane. This meeting had been a mistake. He'd known it from the moment he'd opened the door to him.

"Why?" another voice asked.

The lawyer whirled around, and Blake saw Juliette standing behind him. She must have slipped silently into the suite while they'd been talking. How much had she heard?

Obviously enough that she looked furious.

"Why would you try to take my daughter away from me?" She wasn't asking the lawyer, though. She was asking Blake.

"I wouldn't," Blake assured her. "I can't."

But she was too angry to listen. He could see that now.

"I will fight you!" she said. And she turned toward the lawyer now. "You won't take my child away."

"If you didn't want to risk losing her, you shouldn't have tried to pass her off as a Colton," the man replied.

And Blake saw what Juliette always did—the snobbishness that made her think she was not in his league. He hoped like hell he had never acted that way—the way his father and his father's friend acted.

Superior.

Arrogant.

Juliette must have been too angry to speak. She just shook her head, turned and ran from the suite—slamming the door behind herself.

"Get the hell out of here!" Blake told the lawyer. But he was already heading to the door and opening it for himself. "I wouldn't have you represent me if you were the last lawyer in Red Ridge!"

Leaving the slime bag attorney to show himself out, Blake hurried out into the hall, but he caught no sight of Juliette or the bodyguards.

She was gone.

She's gone.

Not just her little kid who'd disappeared after going to the police station after the park that day. But now the K9 cop had disappeared, as well.

Where the hell had she gone?

Into hiding with her daughter?

He'd thought she was too proud and stubborn to do that. He'd been counting on her being too proud and stubborn to go into hiding. But a couple of days had passed with no sign of her.

She hadn't gone back to her house. The front windows were boarded up like it had been abandoned after the shooting. Too bad that damn mutt had alerted her to his presence that night. He might have been able to hit her if she hadn't ducked down so quickly. Then she'd returned fire, which had made him duck and miss again.

That dog was a pain in the ass. Literally. It had bit him when he'd been running away.

He should have done more than kick it after he'd shaken it loose. He should have shot the damn thing. But maybe he'd kicked it hard enough that it had been seriously injured.

Maybe that was why he hadn't seen her working.

But that still didn't explain where she'd gone.

She wasn't staying at the Colton Plaza Hotel, either. The suite on the twenty-first floor had only had one occupant the past couple of nights.

Blake Colton, billionaire businessman.

He was the guy who'd hired those damn security guards to protect her. But as if that wasn't bad enough, he kept getting in his way himself.

What the hell was some billionaire trying to play bodyguard for?

The K9 cop must be important to him.

Blake Colton must not mean much to her, though, since Juliette Walsh hadn't been to the hotel.

But he hadn't seen her anywhere around Red Ridge. Maybe she'd taken her daughter and left town.

Since he'd taken care of their last problem, his bosses were trying again to get him to leave town—before he got caught. They did not appreciate how good he was.

Nobody had ever caught him, and nobody would—because he didn't leave witnesses alive.

He had to find the woman and her daughter. He had to get rid of them for good.

Chapter 19

Finn stood at the podium at the front of the briefing room, staring out at his officers. They all looked as frustrated as he felt. Too much time had passed with too few leads. On the Groom Killer and on the killer after Juliette and her daughter. Maybe the killers had both left town.

The thought didn't give him any relief, though. He didn't want them gone from Red Ridge. He wanted them gone—permanently. Locked up behind bars for the rest of their miserable lives—for the lives they'd taken.

Until the Groom Killer was caught, nobody in Red Ridge would feel safe getting married. Including Darby...

She was too worried about him to marry him. She loved him too much. And he loved her too much to go long before making her his bride.

They had to catch that killer and soon.

The same for the park killer. The thought of a child being in danger was keeping Finn awake at night even more than his late-night visits and calls.

At least Red Ridge PD had some additional manpower now. "Let me introduce the newest member of our team, West Brand. He's on loan from our neighboring Wexton County's K9 unit while Dean Landon continues to recover from his gunshot wound."

The dark-haired man raised his hand in a slight wave at his new coworkers. Red Ridge PD was a close-knit group. They didn't readily welcome outsiders. So they didn't greet him any more warmly than he had them.

"His dog, Tam Lin—" Finn continued, gesturing to the Labrador sitting next to the new officer "—specializes in explosives detection."

Like Dean's dog did. Hopefully West could help fill the void in the department since Dean had been shot.

"Now let's get out there," Finn said. "And be careful…" He didn't want to lose anyone else. Before Juliette could leave the room, he called out, "Walsh…"

She stopped, Sasha at her side. "Yes, Chief?"

He waited until everyone else filed out of the briefing room. Then he asked, "Are you sure you're ready to go back out there?"

"I was never not ready," she said. "Dr. Colton wanted Sasha to take it easy for a couple of days."

Finn should have had his cousin, the vet, suggest the dog take longer to recover. Even though he'd been shorthanded the past couple of days, he preferred that to having to worry about Juliette.

And Blake…

Something must have happened between them, because she had insisted he not join her and Pandora at the safe house, where she'd spent the past two days.

"I'm not sure it's a good idea to put you back out there," he said. "We have Brand now—"

"You still need me and Sasha," she said. "She's the best drug-sniffing dog on the force."

He couldn't deny that. And he couldn't deny that there were too many drugs in the city. While they managed to apprehend some of the users and small-time dealers, they hadn't been able to get the suppliers at the top. Even though he had a pretty good idea who they were...

"Why don't you want me back at work?" she asked, her blue eyes narrowed with suspicion. "Did Blake get to you?"

He shook his head, though he couldn't deny that his cousin had tried. "No. It's been quiet the past two days— no more shootings. Everybody's better off with you in the safe house."

She flinched. "I can't stay hidden forever," she said. "I have a job, a life..." Her throat moved as if she was choking on emotion. But she fought it back to continue, "...a daughter. I want to know she'll always be safe. And the only way to do that is to catch that killer."

He nodded but cautioned, "There's no way to always keep her safe, though. There are other dangers than this killer out there."

"I know," she agreed with a heavy sigh as if she was already aware of another danger. "Can Sasha and I leave now? We need to check the airport."

He nodded in reluctant agreement. He'd put an extra car on her. But not Brand. Not yet...

He wanted the team he knew and trusted. He wasn't

sure yet what to make of the new guy. He was going to
have to look into him a little bit more…

Juliette had spent the past two days trying to keep her
daughter safe. That was why she'd refused to let Blake
visit. Let him sue her for custody if he wanted.

As he'd pointed out to her, the Coltons' reputation
wasn't the greatest. She could beat him in court…if she
could afford a lawyer.

Damn him…

He was following her, too—along with another patrol car and those bodyguards. She didn't see the bodyguards, but she knew they were there because she hadn't
tried to lose anyone this time.

She glanced at Sasha. The beagle was bright-eyed
and bursting with energy. She couldn't wait to get back
to work. The rest had done her good.

Juliette hadn't been able to rest. She hadn't slept well
without Blake's arm around her. Hadn't slept well with
worrying that she might lose her daughter…

Would Blake try to take her?

He'd claimed that he wouldn't. But she hadn't let him
say any more after his lawyer had insulted her. What
a sleaze…

She pulled her car into the parking lot at the airport
and drew in a deep breath. She couldn't be distracted
now. She had to stay focused on her job. Her life and
Sasha's depended on it. The airport was small with limited flights, just commuter planes going to bigger air-
ports in the vicinity. Because of that, the security was
minimal, which made it a great place for dealers to try
to run drugs.

"Come on, Sasha," Juliette said as she unclipped the

dog from her harness. The beagle was so eager to do her job that she immediately started toward the building.

The tightness in Juliette's chest eased somewhat, too. At least with this, she knew what she was doing.

With Blake, she had no idea. His sister wanted her to cut him loose for his safety. What about hers? She was the one in danger from him—of losing everything. Her daughter and her heart...

She shook her head, forcing herself to focus. If she didn't, she might lose her life, too. Because she had no doubt the killer was probably out there—waiting for another chance to try for her.

Dante and Flash backed her up, walking through the airport in tandem with her and Sasha. She knew her fellow officer wasn't looking for someone running drugs, but for the killer. The murderer never got close, though—except for that night in her house and in the stairwell at the hotel. He'd been close then, and at the park when she'd seen him after Pandora had witnessed the murder.

She shivered as she remembered the cold look in his eyes. That look was so different than the one in the eyes of the people she busted for drugs. They looked desperate. Scared. He had been frighteningly calm. And determined...

As she and Sasha moved through the crowd, she noticed one of those desperate-looking people. The teenager carried a duffel bag. When she and Sasha drew closer, he shifted it to his other hand—as if that small distance would make Sasha unable to sniff the contents of it.

Juliette quickened her pace to close the distance between them, and Sasha tensed, starting to react. The beagle knew what was in that bag.

The teenager began to walk faster. But the terminal was small. With her on one side and Dante on the other, he really had nowhere to go.

"Stop!" she called out to him.

He hurried up instead—heading toward the men's room. As if that would keep her out...

He probably intended to flush his drugs.

"Stop!" she yelled again.

Dante and Flash had stepped between him and the bathroom. So he stopped and turned back toward her.

And in addition to that look of desperation in his eyes, there was one of fear. He looked so damn scared.

But Juliette wanted to scare him more; she wanted to scare him into telling her what every other drug dealer and user in this town was reluctant to do.

Who the hell was the shooter?

"What do you have in that bag?" she asked.

"I don't know." He dropped it to the floor. And Sasha was immediately on it, her nose pressed to the ratty canvas. "It's not mine," he said. "I was holding it for a friend."

"Let's go down to the police department and talk about your friends," she said. Turning him back around, she snapped cuffs over his bony wrists. He was young, yet old enough to talk without a parent present. Maybe he was even in his mid-twenties. Up close he looked older than she'd originally thought, so she didn't feel too bad about making him even more scared than he already was.

"You know," she mused as she led him toward the

exit while Mancuso picked up the bag, "The last time I was trying to arrest someone, they got shot."

The kid arched his head around to look at her. "You shot 'im?"

She shook her head. "Nope, someone else did. Someone who didn't want that person to talk."

She stopped before pushing open the door to the parking lot. "Maybe we should talk now…before we go out there."

His throat moved, his Adam's apple bobbing up and down as he choked on his fear. "I—I have nothing to say…without my lawyer."

He was definitely older than she'd thought. Old and experienced enough to want a lawyer.

She pressed her hand against the glass of the door. "If you're sure…"

"Nobody wants *me* dead," he said.

She wished she could say the same about herself. And it was almost as if he knew that she couldn't—that he knew who she was and that she'd been targeted.

"Are you sure about that?" she asked. "You sure you don't want to talk to me?"

"I got nothing to say about nothing…"

She doubted that. This killer had taken out two dealers in Red Ridge. So other dealers and even some of their users had to know something about him.

"Okay…" But she hesitated a moment before stepping out into the lot.

There were hangars for private planes close to the airport. Roofs where the killer could go for the vantage point he liked to take his shots from.

She pushed open the door and advised him, "Keep low…"

But she was worried—even as Dante came up beside her. He nodded at her to go. She drew in a deep breath before stepping outside.

She didn't want the kid to get shot, or Dante. And she sure as hell didn't want to get shot. Then she made the mistake of glancing into the parking lot. And she saw Blake standing there—out of his car, watching her.

His sister was right. She needed to cut him loose—needed to make sure that he stopped following her around and putting his life in danger. She didn't want him to try to take Pandora from her.

But she didn't want him dead or injured, either.

Blake was so damn glad to see her again. He'd missed her the past couple of days. But she'd refused to see him at the safe house.

He could have just shown up since the bodyguards working for him knew where it was. But he hadn't wanted to cause a scene that might upset her and Pandora. With the killer's threats hanging over their heads, they were upset enough.

And the last thing he wanted was to upset his daughter. So there was no way he would ever try to take her from her mother. Juliette should know that. But she wouldn't let him explain that meeting with the lawyer.

She had refused to talk to him as well as see him. And he couldn't talk to her now. She was busy, bringing in another suspect.

And he remembered what had happened last time—at the bus terminal. It wasn't safe for her to be out here. Surely she knew that.

Why did she keep putting herself in danger?

It was about more than just doing her job, though. It

was about Pandora, too. About taking the killer off the streets to protect the little girl.

But the killer did not share Blake's reluctance to separate mother and daughter. He had no such qualms about taking away the little girl's mother.

And just as Blake had feared, shots rang out again.

And just like at the bus terminal, Juliette dropped to the asphalt. Unlike that day, though, she was on top of the teenager she'd had in handcuffs. She was using her body to shield his.

She would have had to take a bullet for him.

Chapter 20

The shots hadn't been close at all. But Juliette hadn't told the crying teenager that. She'd let him believe she'd saved his life back at the airport. And since bringing him to RRPD, she hadn't bothered to assuage his fears yet.

Blake's bodyguards had covered all the rooftops close to the airport, so the killer hadn't been able to get within range for a bullet to actually hit her or her suspect this time. No matter how angry she was with him, she couldn't deny that Blake had saved her life many times—personally and with that security agency he'd hired to protect her and their daughter.

While she appreciated that—or maybe because she appreciated that—she needed to talk to him. He'd been so worried at the airport, so scared that she'd been hit.

Juliette needed to make him back off, to keep him away from the danger and herself. Just as she'd known five years ago, they were too different. They had no future together—besides coparenting their daughter. And she wasn't sure he really even wanted to do that.

But she couldn't think about him now. She couldn't think about anything but getting this kid to talk. Fortunately, because he thought she'd saved his life, he'd agreed to speak to her without a lawyer now.

"He tried to kill you," she told him as she settled onto the chair across the table from him.

The room was small and stark with just plain concrete block walls. There was a solid steel door behind the kid, and a mirror on the wall behind Juliette's head. She knew the chief stood behind that mirror, probably with Carson Gage. The detective and the boss knew she was the right one to question the kid, though.

Getting shot at together, her seemingly saving his life, had forged a bond between them. One she intended to exploit. "He's no friend of yours…"

"I don't know who *he* is," the young man said. His hands were cuffed to the table, so he had to lean forward to wipe away the tears that had leaked from his eyes. A strand of greasy black hair flopped over into his face. He blew it away and said, "I don't know who you're talking about."

"He's a hired assassin, right? Hired to take out the dealers who've been skimming from your boss or bosses." Everyone thought the Larson twins were behind the drug problem in Red Ridge. But the RRPD hadn't been able to prove it—despite having them under surveillance.

Was that why the killer had looked familiar to her even though he'd never been arrested? Had she seen him one of the times she'd been doing surveillance on the Larson twins?

"I work at a fast food place, lady," the young man replied. "I don't know what you're talking about..."

She shook her head. "The drugs in your duffel bag—there was too much for your personal use." He was likely a dealer working for the Larson twins. But Red Ridge PD hadn't been able to get any evidence against them because they probably hired people to clean up after them. People like the man from the park...

She rose from the chair. "It's fine if you don't want to help yourself. We've got enough to put you away for a long time..."

The room was small, so she was already at the door, reaching for the knob, when he called her back. "Wait, wait, wait!"

She paused, hesitated for a long moment before turning back toward him. "What?"

"What if I give you something?" he asked. "Could you make that stuff go away?"

"Are you bribing me?" The kid really was an idiot.

He shook his head. "No, no...not that. If I give you some information..."

"About him?"

"I told you I don't know who you're talking about..."

And she was beginning to believe him. She uttered a weary sigh before asking, "What have you got?"

"Do we have a deal?"

"I need to know what you're offering," she said.

"A big shipment," he said. "It's coming in on Friday at midnight..."

She lifted her shoulders in a shrug. "We'll have to see how big. Where's it coming in?"

He paused for a long moment, as if trying to determine if he could trust her. "Train station…"

On the midnight train…

It made sense—more sense than this kid trying to move drugs through the airport during the day.

She turned for the door again.

"Where are you going?" he asked. "Do we have a deal or not?"

"I'm not the one who makes deals," she said. "That'll be up to the district attorney's office." She'd already booked the kid on possession with suspicion of distributing. Someone would be picking him up soon to bring him to jail. She stepped out and closed the door behind herself.

And found the chief and Carson waiting for her in the hall. "Good work," Finn Colton praised her.

Carson nodded in agreement.

She felt no pride, though. She'd gotten some information out of him. But it wasn't the information she wanted. She was no closer to finding the man who was trying to kill her and her daughter.

"You'll be working that midnight shift," Finn told her.

She nodded, knowing he needed her and Sasha to find the shipment. Maybe whoever was bringing it in was high enough in the drug organization to know who the killer was. It wasn't a direct lead to him. But it might bring her closer to finally ending this nightmare.

First, she had to end something else, though.

Blake was shocked to open the hotel door to Juliette. After she'd overheard the conversation with the lawyer a few days before, he'd thought she might never come back.

She held out one of the room key cards to him. "I took this that morning…"

She'd snuck out of his arms, out of his bed…

His arms ached to hold her again, and his body ached for hers. She looked beautiful—as always. Tonight she wore some kind of loose dress. It was short and showed off her toned legs. He wanted to pick her up and carry her off to the bedroom. They never argued there.

But he knew they were about to argue. She'd been too furious that day she'd stormed out of here—too furious to give him a chance to explain before now. Not wanting to lose that chance, he rushed into his explanation. "That was not my lawyer," he said. "That was my father's lawyer."

But Blake never should have agreed to take the meeting with him.

"It doesn't matter," she said.

"Yes, it does," he replied. "The guy's an ass."

"He's right about the paternity test," she said. "You will need one—especially if you have any intention of fighting me for custody."

"I don't!" he assured her.

"That's good," she said, "because you'd lose. And I know you hate to lose."

He did. That was why he didn't want to lose her.

"I would never try to take you from your daughter," he said. "That's why I've been following you around, making sure nothing happens to you."

"For her sake?" she asked, and her body was tense, as if she was bracing herself for a blow.

"Yours too," he said. "I don't want anything to happen to you. That's why I think you should quit your job."

Her blue eyes widened with shock. "What?"

"I'm rich," he said. "I can support you and Pandora. You don't need to work. I can take the two of you out of the country—back to one of my places in Singapore or London or Hong Kong."

The color had drained from Juliette's face, leaving her pale but for the dark circles beneath her eyes. "You don't know me at all," she murmured.

"Of course I know you," he said. "I know that you're a good mother who wants what's best for her daughter. This is what's best. You quitting the Red Ridge PD."

She gasped. "I've worked my whole life. And you just expect me to stop?"

"You don't have to work so hard anymore," he said. "I will take care of you and our daughter."

She shook her head. "I won't be your mistress."

He chuckled. "You won't be my mistress. I'm not married." But maybe he should be…then he wouldn't have to worry so much about her and Pandora. He could always be with them.

He waited for the panic he'd felt that day he'd carried Juliette over the threshold to this suite. But it didn't come. Yet…

"I won't be a kept woman," she said with a shudder. "Then your father and his sleazy lawyer will be right to think I'm some kind of opportunist."

He snorted. "If you were an opportunist, you would have told me when you found out you were pregnant. You would have wanted me to financially support you." Instead of fighting him over it…

"You just made this a whole hell of a lot easier," she murmured.

And he tensed now. "What?"

"I came here to tell you it's over…" She shrugged. "Whatever it was…whatever we were doing…it's over… I don't want to see you anymore."

She'd made that pretty clear the past couple of days. But he'd thought she'd just needed to calm down after that horrible conversation she'd overheard.

"If you're still mad about the lawyer, I told you he's not working for me," Blake assured her. "I'm not going after custody…"

"Just leave us alone," she implored him. "You told me five years ago that you had no intention of ever being a husband or a father. So stick with that. Don't make the mistakes your father made."

He flinched as she struck that nerve he'd exposed to her so long ago. "Now you don't want me in her life?"

"Not if you're going to hurt and disappoint her," she said. "And you will when you leave Red Ridge and focus on your business again. So just go now—before she gets any more attached."

"What about you?" he asked. "Are you attached?"

Color rushed back into her face. But she shook her head. "No. No, I'm not…"

"You don't want me?" he asked. He stepped closer, hoping to call her bluff. But what if she wasn't bluffing?

What if she really didn't care about him?

He pressed his lips to hers. But she didn't move. She didn't kiss him back as he brushed his mouth over hers. Then finally she gasped, and her lips parted on a moan.

She was bluffing.

But why?

"So you met her?" Fenwick asked Patience the minute she stepped into his den at home.

"She's a K9 cop, so I already know her," his daughter replied.

"Did you know she had your brother's kid?" His

hand trembled on his liquor glass when he thought of it, thought of being a grandfather.

No. It wasn't possible.

"Of course not," she said. "I just found out myself."

"How could she have kept this secret for so long?" Fenwick wondered. Especially if she was after the Colton money. Had she just been waiting for Blake to be as successful as he was now? Until he'd become a billionaire?

Patience shrugged. "She didn't think he wanted to be a father."

Fenwick flinched. He knew why. Blake didn't want to be like him. But in staying away from his kid, he was acting more like him than not. Fenwick knew he'd never paid enough attention to his children—especially Blake.

He'd been busy. He'd provided for them, though.

Until now…

Now his livelihood was being threatened. Hell, his entire life was being threatened—if he lost his business. But for some reason he wasn't as worried about the business as he was Blake.

"You don't think he's going to do something stupid like propose to her?" he asked, speaking his greatest fear aloud.

He knew how grooms wound up in Red Ridge. Shot through the heart with a cummerbund stuffed down their throats. He grimaced as the image of his handsome son as the Groom Killer's next victim flashed through his head.

"Even if he does…" Patience began.

And Fenwick's heart stopped beating for a moment. His sister—who'd admitted to seeing them together—must have considered it a possibility.

"I don't think she'd accept," Patience continued.

Fenwick shook his head. "She'd be a fool to turn down a proposal from a billionaire."

"She would be in love with him," Patience said. "And I think she might be. She doesn't want Blake getting hurt any more than we do."

Fenwick should have been relieved, but he knew his son too well. Blake was a billionaire because he worked hard and stopped at nothing to get what he wanted.

If he wanted Juliette Walsh, there was no way she would turn him down. The only reason they probably wouldn't wind up married was if Blake got killed.

And that was just too great a possibility.

Chapter 21

Juliette was supposed to be cutting him loose—not clutching him closer. But once Blake had kissed her, she'd lost all control. The passion between them burned too brightly, too hot to be denied. She had tried to keep her lips still beneath his—had tried to resist.

But her pulse had quickened, her skin had tingled, and her heart had begun to pound so fiercely—that she couldn't fight it anymore. She cared too much about him.

So she would make him leave her alone.

Just not yet.

She gripped his shoulders as he lifted and carried her. He didn't carry her to the bedroom, though—just to the couch. He sat down with her straddling his lap, and he tugged her dress up and over her head. It dropped to the floor behind her. Then her bra quickly followed. It wasn't as if anyone else could see them on the twenty-first floor. No other building in Red Ridge was as tall as the Colton Plaza Hotel.

He held her breasts, cupping and massaging them while brushing his palms over the taut nipples. She moaned again at the sensations racing through her. She needed him. Now.

So she dragged off his shirt and tossed it aside before reaching for the button of his jeans. He caught her hand, though. Then he lifted her and stood. He undid his jeans and kicked them off. But he leaned over and pulled a condom from the pocket. He must have been as desperate to be with her as she was to be with him, because he sheathed himself quickly.

Then he sat back down.

Before she straddled his lap again, she pulled off her panties. His hand moved between her legs, stroking over her mound as he made sure she was ready for him.

She was more than ready. She was about to go out of her mind with the tension winding so tightly inside her. It had been only a couple of days since they'd made love. But it felt like it had been years again.

How was she going to give him up forever?

She had to be selfless—for his sake.

To keep him safe...

He pulled her down onto his lap, carefully guiding his shaft inside her. She adjusted and arched, taking him deeper. He felt so damn good—filled her so perfectly.

They moved perfectly together, too, in absolute unison. They were in sync like soul mates.

But Blake was not her soul mate. While he understood how to please her physically, he had no idea how to please her emotionally. It was probably because he'd never been given love that he didn't know how to give it—to her or to their daughter. So she would take only what he could give her now—the physical pleasure.

His hands moved over her breasts again, stroking, caressing…

And his mouth mated with hers, their kisses hungry and intense. Their lips clung, their tongues tangled— their kisses alone brought her to the first peak of pleasure.

Then he thrust harder and moved faster, and another orgasm overcame her, making her body shudder with the intensity of it.

He moved her then, so that he was on top, she lying on the cushions. He made love to her all over again, lifting her legs high as he thrust inside her. And she came again…

Then he tensed and groaned as he joined her in ecstasy. "That was incredible," he murmured.

It was goodbye. But before she could tell him that, he slipped away from her, and she heard water running in the bathroom.

She needed to get dressed and get out of there. But she felt too boneless, too satiated, to move. She forced some strength into her limbs, though, and rose from the couch. She'd just pulled her dress back over her head when he reappeared. All he wore were his jeans, low on his lean hips.

She wanted him all over again.

Then he spoke. "See how good this could be for us? You don't need to work. You and Pandora can live with me."

And suddenly she felt sick rather than satiated. He had just cheapened what they'd done, making it sound like an arrangement rather than a relationship. She shook her head. "I told you I won't be your mistress."

"That's not what I'm saying," he said. "I want to take care of you and Pandora."

"You want to take us away from Red Ridge," she said. "This is our home. We're not going anywhere—especially not with you."

He reached out. "Juliette, you're blowing this out of proportion—"

"I was already trying to tell you that this isn't working," she reminded him. "That we have no future—"

"We have a daughter."

"You need to get your paternity test to prove that." Maybe she could tie him up in court or bluff him into walking away from them.

But the last time she'd tried bluffing—about her attraction to him—he'd called her on it. He'd proved that he affected her.

Too much. But not anymore. All he'd offered her was money and sex. Not his heart.

She wanted his heart. But even if he'd offered it, she might have refused—for his safety. Because she cared more about him than herself. He had her heart. He'd probably had it since that night nearly five years ago.

"What's going on, Juliette?" he asked, his brow furrowed with confusion.

He probably wasn't used to not getting what he wanted. But she had yet to stop working no matter how many times he'd asked her to go into hiding with Pandora. So he should have been accustomed to her not giving him what he asked for.

"If you want to see Pandora again, you better get that lawyer back," she said, "because I'm not going to let you see her."

"What? Why not?"

"Just go back to London or Milan or wherever you call home," she said. "I don't want you here. Pandora and I don't need you."

He flinched as if she'd hurt him. But then he shook his head, stubbornly unwilling to believe her. "Liar," he said.

She didn't argue with him. She just hurried out of the suite. For the last time…

She was not coming back. She had to let whatever was between her and Blake Colton go. She had to let him go.

She was lying. Wasn't she?

Blake had been asking himself that question for the past couple of days. But she had not come to his suite again. She had also stuck by her decision to not let him see Pandora anymore. Was it to protect the little girl, though?

Or to protect him?

"She what?" he asked Finn. The police chief had called him to this meeting in his office at the Red Ridge Police Department.

"She threatened to take out a restraining order against you," the chief said. "She wants you to stop following her around."

He shook his head. "I'm not going to stop."

"She agreed to keep the bodyguards," Finn divulged. "She just doesn't want you."

He was getting that message loud and clear. But what was her motivation?

Was she still furious with him over what the lawyer had said and over what he'd said? He'd denied wanting her to be his mistress. But maybe he did want her to be a kept woman. He wanted to keep her.

But could he trust her?

She had already kept his daughter from him for nearly five years. And now she was trying to do that again. But he wouldn't let her get away with it this time. He was going to have to hire a lawyer and get that paternity test. He would fight her for visitation.

He would fight her on this, too.

"Why not?"

"You're not a bodyguard," Finn said. "You're not a cop. I never should have allowed you to follow her around in the first place."

Blake bristled like Sasha when she caught the scent of drugs. "You didn't allow me to do anything. I can follow her around. I'm not threatening her. I'm trying to keep her safe. No judge in Red Ridge is going to grant her a restraining order."

Finn snorted. "Because you're Fenwick Colton's kid."

Blake bristled some more. It was as if Finn was deliberately trying to piss him off. "I don't know what you're trying to do," he told his cousin, "but you're not going to be able to keep me away."

"Damn it, Blake," Finn said. "You're going to get yourself killed if you keep intervening in police business."

"I haven't gotten hurt yet," he said.

Finn pointed toward his face. But his argument was weak. The scratch had faded and all but disappeared.

He shook his head. "What's the deal? What's really going on?"

With Finn and with Juliette. She'd acted so strangely that night in his suite.

"She flipped that kid from the airport and got him to inform on a shipment coming into the train station on Friday," Finn said. "It's big. She can't be distracted. You can't get in her way."

Panic pressed down on Blake's lungs, stealing his breath away. He had a bad feeling—a very bad feeling about this.

"You need to bring in someone else," he said. He'd heard there was a new K9 cop on loan from some other county. "Use the new guy."

Finn shook his head. "His specialty is explosives. Juliette's is narcotics. She and Sasha are the best," her boss said with pride.

Blake felt a flash of pride, too, and he understood a little bit why Juliette had been so reluctant to quit her job. She didn't just enjoy it; she was damn good at it.

Finn continued, "So no matter what you say, I'm not taking her off this assignment. I need her."

So did Blake. And he had a feeling that if she went to make that bust, he would lose her forever.

But then, he'd never really had her to begin with. They'd had only that magical night so long ago and a few stolen moments since he'd returned to Red Ridge. But if this assignment was as dangerous as Blake felt it was, he might never get the chance for any more moments with her.

She'd taken the bait—just as he'd planned. He'd had no intention of shooting that kid—even if he had been able to get close enough.

But those damn bodyguards had been in his way.

As usual...

If they hadn't been covering all the buildings close enough to the airport for him to get an accurate shot, he might have taken a chance.

Maybe he could have ended this—and her—already. He was getting sick of Red Ridge. It was long past time that he ended this.

Once she was dead, there would be a funeral. Her kid would have to attend. And then she would join her mother—in death.

Just as he'd promised them that day in park. They were going to die.

Juliette Walsh was going to get one hell of a surprise when she showed up at the train station to make her big bust. She was going to get a bullet in her brain. And whoever else got in his way—the bodyguards, the other cops or that rich guy who'd been following her around like her damn dog—was going to wind up dead, too.

Chapter 22

Juliette was in plain clothes for the morning briefing. She wasn't staying. Her shift wouldn't start until later, so that she and Sasha would be fresh for the midnight train coming into Red Ridge station.

Would there really be a shipment of drugs on it? Or had the kid just been trying to get out of trouble?

Juliette wasn't sure if she should have believed him. But he'd been so upset at nearly getting shot that he'd seemed sincere. Hopefully whoever was bringing in those drugs knew about the man from the park. She had to find him. Had to stop him…

Pandora was so sick of the safe house. She wanted to go home. And so did Juliette.

The little girl also wanted Blake.

And so did Juliette…

But this was for the best—for all of them. While he

wanted to protect Juliette, he didn't love her. It didn't sound like his father had ever been able to show love—at least not to his kids.

Was that how Blake was going to be?

If he couldn't show love to Pandora, Juliette would rather not have him around the little girl. Or around her...

And it was better for him this way, too. He wouldn't be in danger anymore.

But when the chief stepped up to the podium to begin the morning briefing, he met her gaze and shook his head. And she knew...

He hadn't been able to threaten or coerce Blake to stop following her around. That was not good. She didn't want him at the drug bust tonight.

She just had an odd feeling about it all, like something wasn't quite right. Like maybe it had been too easy...

"As some of you know, Officer Walsh got a tip that there will be a big shipment of drugs coming into Red Ridge tonight on the midnight train. We're going to be careful to stay out of sight until the train pulls in. Walsh will be there with Sasha. Detective Gage will be backing her up along with Officer West Brand."

Brand. She glanced over at the officer on loan from Wexton County. She had an odd feeling about him, as well. Since he'd started, he'd kept to himself—even when working with everybody else. He didn't volunteer any information about himself, and he gave only vague answers to the questions people asked. He seemed secretive, like he had something to hide.

Yet who was she to talk? She'd kept her child's paternity a secret for over four years. But her secret hadn't affected anyone else.

Except Blake...

After she'd kept that secret from him—his daughter from him—she was surprised that he wanted to protect her at all. But she wasn't naive enough to believe he'd forgiven her or that he would ever trust her. That might have been why all he had offered her was his protection.

Not his heart.

He didn't trust her with it. And she couldn't blame him after her betrayal. Now she was keeping her daughter from him all over again—threatening that he'd have to call a lawyer and go to court to demand the rights she should have given him when Pandora was born.

Lost in her own thoughts, she hadn't realized that everyone else had left until the chief stopped next to her chair.

"Are you sure you're up for this?" he asked.

She uttered a weary sigh. Except for that night she'd slept in Blake's arms, she hadn't had much sleep since that day in the park. Heck, she hadn't had much sleep when she'd heard he was back in town. She'd been scared to see him again. "I'd feel better if you had managed to get Blake to back off. The threat of the restraining order didn't work?"

He shook his head. "How would it? He knows no judge would give it to you. He hasn't threatened you. Instead he's been trying to protect you."

Frustration gripped Juliette. Why was he so damn stubborn? Must have been the Colton in him. But she couldn't say that in front of her boss, who was also a Colton. "I don't need his protection."

"I know," Finn said. "We've got this. Gage and Brand will have your back. And I'm sure those bodyguards will be close, too."

"Are you sure about Brand?" she asked.

Finn's usually open face shuttered, and he looked

away from her. "Of course. Why wouldn't I be sure about him?"

"What do you know about him?"

"He's an explosives specialist," the chief said. "He's good."

That told her what he did. Not who he was. Not anything about his character. "But is he trustworthy?" she asked.

"Beyond reproach," Finn insisted.

And that strange feeling she'd had about the temporary team member intensified. She'd thought he was keeping secrets. Now she suspected that the chief was, too, but that secret was about Brand.

Who the hell was he?

"So he'll have my back tonight?" she asked, needing assurances.

The chief nodded.

But she didn't feel reassured. She understood now how Blake must have felt when he'd learned the momentous secret she'd kept from him. She certainly didn't like being kept in the dark.

She just hoped that she wouldn't wind up there permanently.

Blake waited in the hall outside the briefing room. The receptionist had not wanted to let him past her. But when he'd turned on the charm, she'd relented and pointed him to a chair in the hall. She kept looking at him over the top of silver-framed glasses, though.

He'd watched everyone else file out of the briefing room—but for Juliette and the chief. Maybe Finn was talking her out of going to the bust.

He didn't think so. His cousin had definitely sounded as if he considered Juliette the best officer to follow up on the tip about the drug shipment. But every time she'd gone to the airport or the bus terminal, something had happened. She'd nearly been shot.

Blake didn't like her chances for surviving the train station.

The minute she stepped out of the room with Finn, he jumped up from his chair. She groaned when she saw him and just shook her head.

"Don't harass her," Finn warned him. "Or she might be able to get that restraining order yet."

"I would testify," the receptionist warned him, her dark brows arching into her bangs.

He didn't know if she was kidding or not. No one could seriously think he meant Juliette any harm. Could they?

Juliette walked away from him, toward the front doors of the police department. She stopped before she stepped out, though, and turned back to him. "I don't understand why you won't leave me alone."

"I told you that I'm doing this for Pandora," he said. "I don't want her to lose her mother."

She flinched as if the thought filled her with dread. Then why risk it?

"You hired the bodyguards," she said. "Let them do their job. Let me do my job. Stay out of my way. Stay out of my life, Blake."

A pang struck his heart, and he felt like she'd stabbed him. It was clear that she meant it now.

She continued, "You won't help out your dad with his financial problems because you're worried about your business. How can you leave it this long? Don't you need to go back to your offices?"

He could work anywhere. But that wasn't her point. And he knew it. "You really want to get rid of me," he mused. "Is that why you didn't let me know about Pandora? You don't want to share her?"

Her lips pressed together in a tight line, as if she was forcing herself to hold back some words. She glanced around them and shook her head. Then she murmured, "Not here…"

"Then where?" he asked. "You said you're not going back to my suite."

"I'm not."

She wasn't going to sleep with him again. Had he offended her that much when he'd offered to support her? He knew other women who would have been thrilled with that offer. But Juliette was fiercely independent. She'd been taking care of herself and everyone else in her life for a long time.

But he didn't know what else to offer her. Marriage? He doubted she wanted that; she'd been pointing out to him over and over again that they had nothing in common.

But they had something very important in common. Someone, actually.

Their daughter.

"Let me come see Pandora," he said.

"I told you—"

"I know—get a lawyer," he said. "I can—if you want me to…"

She pursed her lips again as to hold back some more words. And he wanted to kiss them. He wanted to kiss her so badly.

But she was right. Not here…

He wasn't giving up, though—on their daughter or on her. "Someone else can handle Sasha tonight," he said. "You don't have to go."

Her blue eyes widened with surprise that he knew

about the shipment. Then she sighed. "Sasha is my partner. I'm going with her tonight."

Just as she didn't want her daughter getting hurt, she didn't want her dog getting hurt. Was that why she'd threatened him with the restraining order? Did she not want him to get hurt, either?

Was that why she kept pushing him away? For his own protection?

Before he could ask, she pushed open the doors and walked out of the department. He tensed, like he did every time she was out in the open. He expected bullets to fly, expected that psycho to shoot at her.

But nothing happened. She made it to her vehicle without incident. And he released a breath of relief. She was safe for now.

But she wouldn't be tonight—not during that drug bust. She would be in danger then. That was why he had to be there. He had to try to save her from herself.

But who would save him from her?

Patience watched her brother as he paced her office. He'd always had more energy than she and their sisters did. That was why his mother had given full custody to their father. She hadn't wanted to deal with a hyperactive little boy.

But Blake hadn't exactly been hyperactive. He'd been hyperfocused. Once something had caught his interest, he'd focused all his attention on mastering it. Like football and basketball and golf and lacrosse…

Whatever sport he'd played in school he'd practiced incessantly. And when he'd gotten interested in business, it hadn't been enough for him to work for someone else—especially not their father. He'd had to build his own.

He wasn't the kind of person who delegated or hired people to carry out his orders. He had to be personally involved. He had to get his hands dirty.

Maybe that was why he persisted in following Juliette around. He didn't trust that she would be safe unless he was the one protecting her.

But Patience wondered and worried that there was more to it than that. "You love her," she said.

He abruptly stopped pacing. But he didn't turn to her. It was as if he didn't want her to see his face—probably because his feelings were written all over it.

She should have been happy that he could feel—that he could care about someone else. That meant that he wasn't as much like their father as Patience had worried that he was. But she wasn't happy about that—because she was afraid that caring about Juliette Walsh might get him killed.

"You love her," she repeated.

He shook his head. "I don't know what love is," he remarked. "I've never seen my mom or dad in love. Lust, maybe, but not love…"

And maybe lust was all he'd thought he'd felt for Juliette. But Patience could tell his feelings went much deeper than attraction.

"We're not our parents," she said.

"I sure as hell hope not," he said.

And she could tell that it worried him, that he didn't want to be like their father.

"But what if I am?" he asked her. "Would it be better if I just walked away from her?"

"Juliette?"

"She hasn't given me a choice," he replied. "She wants nothing to do with me."

So she had cut him loose like Patience had suggested. She should have been relieved. But seeing the look on his face, the pain, she felt a horrible heaviness pressing on her heart. Guilt.

She probably should have kept her mouth shut.

"I'm talking about Pandora," he said. "Should I walk away from her? Is she better off without me in her life?"

Patience sighed. "Oh, Blake…"

What had she done?

She'd only wanted to keep her brother safe. She'd been so worried about his life, though, that she'd gotten his heart broken with her meddling. Maybe she was the one who was like their dad.

"I'm sorry," she murmured.

"It's not your fault," he said.

But he didn't know what she'd done. She'd opened her mouth to tell him when his cell rang.

He pulled it from his pocket and accepted the call without so much as a glance at her. It reminded her of how their father had always taken calls no matter what was going on—her recital, one of Blake's games…

If he'd bothered to show up at all, he'd been on his phone the entire time.

"Yes," he answered his caller. "I'll be there. Thanks…"

The call disconnected before he could say anything else.

"Business?" she asked.

He shook his head. "Juliette. She's letting me see Pandora tonight. Now I just have to figure out what's the right thing to do. If this should be the last time I see my daughter…"

Patience hoped it wouldn't be. But she was more worried about him losing his life than leaving the country.

Chapter 23

She had been wrong—about so many things. Juliette realized that now as she watched Blake play with Pandora. Even though his father might not have been able to show him love, Blake could show fatherly love.

He obviously loved their daughter.

She had been a fool to keep them apart. Instead of being selfless, she'd been being selfish. Sure, she wanted him out of danger. Hell, with everything going on in Red Ridge right now, she would prefer he left the country.

But she should have never kept him apart from Pandora—not those first four years of her life and definitely not now that they'd met. They hadn't just met. They'd connected in a way that had Juliette experiencing feelings she wasn't proud of: jealousy, possessiveness.

She had always been her little girl's favorite person. But already Blake had come to mean so much to her.

And it was obvious from the way he looked at her, the way he touched her hair and kissed her forehead, that she meant so much to him, too.

Juliette's heart ached just from watching them. Then it warmed and swelled as love replaced the jealousy. She loved them both so much. All she wanted was for them both to be happy. But she wasn't sure how she could make that happen or even if she could.

She couldn't do what Blake had asked; she couldn't give up her job and move away from Red Ridge with him—not even if he was offering more than a sexual relationship. She loved her job, her friends—this city. Red Ridge held the memories of her parents, and memories were all she had left of them now.

But he wasn't offering her more than a sexual relationship except for his protection. She didn't need that, either.

"Mommy! Mommy!" Pandora called out to her.

And she realized she'd been lost in her thoughts. She forced a smile. "What, sweetheart?"

"Sing me the song, sing me the song!" Pandora implored her. She was tucked into bed already.

Blake had supervised teeth brushing and had pulled up the covers while Juliette had just followed them around, watching them and yearning. If only Blake could love her like he loved their daughter, maybe they could have this life together—maybe they could become the family Pandora so obviously wanted them to be.

"Mommy has a special bedtime song she sings when I can't get to sleep."

Her face heated with embarrassment. Pandora must have been tone-deaf to appreciate her singing.

Blake's lips curved into a grin. "Really? Mommy sings?"

"I'm surprised it doesn't give her nightmares," she admitted.

When he chuckled, her heart flipped. She had fallen for him—so hard. That must have been the reason for her jealousy. Not that she envied his love for their daughter but that she wanted some of it for herself, too.

"Sing, Mommy," Pandora demanded.

She was such an imp.

Juliette could deny her nothing. That was why she'd called Blake. Her daughter had wanted to see her daddy. She'd asked the past couple of nights as well, but Juliette had used the excuse that he was busy. But when she'd tried that tonight, Pandora had asked if he was too busy for her.

And Juliette's heart had cracked with her daughter's pain and her own guilt. That might be the case, someday, when Blake had to return to his businesses. But it wasn't now. She was the one who'd kept them apart.

Knowing that she deserved more than some embarrassment for what she'd done, Juliette began to sing. Her voice rose and fell, missing notes and cracking, as she sang "Twinkle, Twinkle, Little Star." It was so bad that Blake winced for her or maybe because she'd hurt his ears. But Pandora applauded.

Her daughter wasn't hard to please. Maybe she would be okay with whatever time Blake could make for her around his business trips. Maybe they could figure something out to make Pandora happy.

But Juliette knew Blake couldn't make her happy—unless he was willing to give her his heart instead of just his protection.

"Now you, Daddy," Pandora urged him. "You sing now!"

"I'm not sure I know that one," he said, obviously stalling.

"Everybody knows 'Twinkle, Twinkle,'" Pandora said, as if he was an idiot. She was already a master manipulator at four years old.

Beneath his breath, he murmured, "You are my father's granddaughter...persistent..."

So he'd recognized the manipulation, as well. But he caved for it, probably so that he wouldn't feel like an idiot, and began to sing. Of course his voice was perfect, just like everything else about him.

Instead of clapping, though, Pandora began to snore. Blake had managed to make the song sound like the lullaby it was intended to be.

"She's not going to ask for me to sing that again," she remarked as she pulled the light blanket to the little girl's chin and kissed her forehead.

Blake leaned over the child to do the same, and he pressed his mouth to the exact same spot Juliette had kissed. Even though they didn't touch, she felt her lips begin to tingle.

She wanted him to kiss her.

She wanted him. But she wanted more than sex. She wanted this—this evening. Love. Family.

But he hadn't offered her that. And even if he had, she was in no position to accept it now. Not with a killer determined to get rid of her and their daughter. And if Blake were to propose, then a killer would try to get rid of him. A different killer—the Groom Killer—but one probably even more dangerous than the one after her.

She hurried out into the hall. She needed to dress in her uniform, needed to get Sasha and head to the train station soon. But she'd only made it outside Pandora's bedroom door when Blake grabbed her arm.

He whirled her around and pulled her close to him. And then he was kissing her.

Her hands slipped up to the nape of his neck, and she held him there for a long moment, kissing him back. But then she moved her hands to his shoulders and pushed him away. Panting for breath, she said, "I didn't call you here for that."

"I know. You called me here to talk me out of following you tonight," he said.

Heat rushed to her face. That had been one of her reasons. But Pandora was the biggest reason. She was always the biggest reason for everything Juliette did.

"Can I talk you out of it?" she asked.

"Only way I won't be there is if you're not," he said.

"Blake, this is a bad idea…"

"I agree," he said. "That's why I think you should stay here—with her—with us…" And he lowered his head and kissed her again.

She wanted to stay—so badly. But his coercion reminded her of that last night in his hotel suite. And she jerked away from him. "I will never be your kept woman," she said. "I have a job that I love. I'm not giving it up for you—to follow you around the world."

Not even if he loved her. But of course, he didn't. If he loved her, he would understand her—and how much her job meant to her. But he didn't even know her.

His voice a gruff whisper, he said, "Your job is dangerous enough when there isn't a killer after you. But there is one. You need to be extra careful now."

"I need to not be distracted," she said. "If something

happens tonight, it'll be because of you—because you're in my way. You're the one who should stay here—with her."

"In case you don't come back?" he asked. "See, even you have a bad feeling about this."

She did. But she wasn't sure why. Maybe it was because she didn't entirely trust that the young dealer had been telling the truth. Or that she didn't entirely trust the new guy on loan from Wexton County.

The last thing she needed tonight was to worry about Blake, too. Most of her worry was about him, like maybe he was the one who was going to wind up getting hurt, and this time it would be more serious than a scratch on his handsome face.

She'd wanted to push him into going away—leaving the country. She knew she didn't really want to lose him. She loved him. But she couldn't tell him—not now— probably not even after the Groom Killer was caught.

Because if she confessed her love and he didn't return her feelings, she would be more embarrassed than she'd been singing in front of him. No. She would be worse than embarrassed; she would be crushed.

Maybe Blake should have listened to her. Maybe he shouldn't have shown up. If something happened because he'd distracted her, he would never forgive himself. And if Pandora ever learned he was to blame, she would never forgive him, either.

But he was being careful. From the bodyguards, he'd learned how to keep more to the shadows—how to make himself invisible. He wore a hat, the bill pulled low over his face, so that he wasn't recognizable.

Juliette knew he was there, though. She kept glancing at where he sat in the chairs. Had he made a huge mistake in following in her here?

It seemed as if he just kept making mistake after mistake with her. He kept offending her when he didn't mean to. All he wanted was to take care of her.

But to a woman like Juliette, one as fiercely independent and strong, he should have realized that was an insult. She didn't need taking care of.

What did she need?

Her daughter. Her job. The killer caught…

What about him? Did she need him?

She'd pushed him away easily enough tonight. But then she'd known she had to leave—that she'd had to come here—because of that tip.

Would she have pushed him away if she hadn't had to leave? Would she have pushed him away if he'd told her he was starting to fall for her?

His heart lurched as he realized that he already had. Hell, he'd fallen for her nearly five years ago during that incredible evening they'd spent together. He'd never connected with anyone the way he had with her, and not just physically or sexually but emotionally, as well. He'd told her things he'd never shared with anyone else.

Somehow, something about her had compelled him to trust her with his innermost thoughts and feelings. But then, when he'd learned she wasn't who he'd thought she was that night and that she hadn't told him about his daughter, he'd lost that trust. And with that trust had gone his feelings for her.

But watching her with their daughter, watching her do her job…

He'd fallen for her all over again. And loving her was

why he was so determined to keep her safe. Maybe if he'd told her that, she wouldn't have come here tonight.

But he doubted it. He doubted even his love could stop Juliette from doing her job. She loved it too much. And because he loved her, he never should have tried to get her to quit it. He should have supported her. Instead of trying to take her and Pandora away from Red Ridge, he should have told her he'd come back here—permanently.

Would any of that had made a difference to her? Would she have accepted his proposal?

What the hell had he done? He hadn't proposed. He hadn't asked her to marry him just to be available to him. No wonder she'd been insulted.

He'd made a mess of everything.

He needed to fix this. He glanced at his watch. It was too close to midnight to bother her now. He didn't want her distracted. He wanted her totally focused on her job, especially tonight.

He had such a bad feeling about this potential bust. The informant's tip was highly suspicious to him—that a user or some low-level dealer would know about a big shipment. Why would anyone have told him about it? It seemed like his boss would have worried that he'd either spill his guts or try to hijack the shipment.

But Blake knew nothing about drugs or police work. He did know about business, though, and that would have been like his telling the mailroom clerk about some electronics invention. He wouldn't have done it because he would have worried that the kid would blab.

It almost felt like someone had wanted this kid to blab. Why? To make sure that Juliette would be here? To set her up? Was this an ambush?

He looked around the train station. Nobody looked

like him—like he was trying to disguise himself. And the killer would have had to be wearing a very good disguise, or Juliette would have already recognized him. She kept looking uneasily around the station. But maybe the guy was waiting for her outside like he had at the bus terminal and the airport.

The bodyguards had the surrounding buildings covered, though. They were also watching the parking lot for anyone driving up. The knot of apprehension in Blake's stomach eased somewhat. Nobody could get close enough to her for a bullet to strike her out there.

A distant whistle alerted him to the arrival of the train. Red Ridge was old-fashioned enough that their trains still had whistles. He glanced at his watch. A minute before midnight. There was the squeaking of brakes as the train began to slow down to stop at the terminal.

Juliette and Sasha stood near the doors through which everyone would enter the station. And that was when it struck him...

The only place he, the bodyguards and Juliette's fellow officers didn't have covered...

The train.

And with absolute certainty, Blake knew that it didn't carry any shipment of drugs. It carried the killer. He was going to get off the train.

Blake jumped up from his seat and leaped over travelers' bags to race across the station toward Juliette.

Her eyes widened with alarm as she saw him approaching. She'd told him to keep his distance. But he didn't care. He couldn't let her get shot.

"He's on the train!" Blake shouted.

And just as he did, the doors slid open and a man stepped through them. He hadn't seen him before. But he instinctively knew who he was. So did Sasha, because the beagle began to bark and snarl.

Blake jumped forward, diving toward Juliette. He needed to knock her down—needed to get her out of the line of fire. But in doing that, he put himself there—right before the shots rang out.

Chapter 24

It all happened so quickly. Juliette had had no idea why Blake suddenly charged toward her. He was shouting but she'd only heard the last word of what he was saying, "Train!"

Then she'd realized what he already had. The killer was on the train.

She'd drawn her weapon, but before she could fire at the man who'd stepped through the doors, Blake had knocked her down. Shots rang out. People screamed and ran for their lives.

She pushed Blake off her and returned fire. The man darted back through the open doors and onto the platform. Sasha's leash had slipped from Juliette's hands, so the beagle tore out after him.

Juliette turned toward Blake, who lay on his side next to her. "Are you okay?" she asked.

His head jerked in a sharp nod. "Yeah, yeah! Are you?"

She nodded.

Then he urged her, "Go! Do your job. Get that son of a bitch!"

Love swelled her heart. He couldn't have said anything sweeter to her unless he'd professed his love. His confidence in her—in her abilities—was nearly as important to her as his loving her.

She rolled to her feet and rushed off after Sasha, letting her barking lead her past the train. He hadn't jumped back inside, but Brand was moving through the cars as if he had. He was wasting his time.

She signaled at him as she ran. But she didn't wait to see if he got off the train and followed her. She had to catch up to Sasha before the killer hurt the beagle again.

Or worse.

She hurried along the edge of the platform, past the train cars—beyond the circle of light from the station. Only a sliver of moon shone overheard now, casting a faint glow on her. She glanced down and noticed something on her arm.

Blood?

Was that blood?

If so, it had to be Blake's. Had he been hurt?

He'd assured her that he was okay. Had he been lying? Or hadn't he realized he'd been hit?

Her pace slowed as she considered turning back. But then a shot rang out, the bullet whizzing through the air near Juliette's head. If she turned away now, the killer would shoot her in the back. And she wouldn't be able to help Blake then—if he even needed help.

He'd told her to do her job. And she needed to focus

on that now. She needed to stop the killer before he hurt anyone else.

Past the stopped train, she leaped off the train platform to the tracks below. The trainyard was pure dark down there—beyond even the glow of that sliver of moon. She couldn't see anything, but she knew he was down here—somewhere.

As if understanding she needed guidance, Sasha barked again. Juliette let the sound of the beagle's barking lead her farther from the station. She ducked low and peered into the shadows, looking for movement.

Where the hell had they gone? He hadn't had that much of a head start on her. Finally she glimpsed a flash of white and brown as Sasha jumped up and down near a dark train car that sat beside several others on the trainyard. Maybe there had been a stash of drugs somewhere and Sasha had found it.

Or maybe she'd found the killer.

Juliette gripped her weapon tightly as she approached that train car just as Sasha managed to leap up and get inside it. She nearly called her back, but she didn't want to alert the man to her presence yet—if he was inside it.

She wanted to get closer, but she didn't get much nearer before flashes of light emanated from inside the car and gunfire rang out.

Blake pressed his hands against the floor of the train station and tried to push himself up. But his muscles felt strangely weak, and he couldn't summon the strength to push up. So he tried drawing up his knees, too, but pain gripped his side with such intensity that his vision blurred, turning everything black.

He dropped to the ground again, into something wet and sticky. And he realized he was bleeding.

Badly. So badly that there was a pool of blood beneath him. He'd been shot. He hadn't realized it right away. He'd thought just knocking her down had knocked the breath from his lungs. He hadn't realized that the burning feeling inside him was a bullet.

Juliette was going to be so pissed at him. But then he heard more gunfire ringing out—outside the station. And he flinched.

The killer had not given up. He was still trying to take Juliette out. Blake closed his eyes and prayed that Juliette survived—for Pandora's sake.

He didn't want the child to be all alone, and he wasn't sure that he was going to make it. He could feel his blood pumping out—along with his life.

Then consciousness slipped away from him entirely.

Fenwick's heart lurched with dread when he saw the flashing lights on the roof of the vehicle that careened through his gates. He was already opening the front door when Finn rushed up to him.

"What's wrong? What is it?" But he knew: Blake. Blake had been hurt.

"Come with me," Finn told him. Usually the police chief sounded irritated with him. Now he sounded almost gentle as if Fenwick was a child.

He felt like a child as he obediently walked toward the car. A female officer stood next to the open back door.

Was this the woman? The one his son had been following around? As he drew closer, he recognized her as a Gage instead. No. This wasn't Juliette Walsh.

"Mr. Colton," she greeted him, and her brown eyes were warm with sympathy. "I'm sorry..."

His stomach lurched now. *I'm sorry* was what people told you as a condolence.

Was Blake dead?

"Get in," Finn told him. "I'll bring you to the hospital."

Hospital didn't reassure Fenwick any. The morgue was in the basement of the hospital. Blake could have been in it, and maybe Finn was bringing him to identify the body.

But if that was the case, he couldn't ask. The words stuck in his throat along with all the raw emotion. He'd been such a fool where his son was concerned—so stubborn and proud. But then, Blake had acted the same way.

They were two of a kind.

Or they had been...

Fenwick ducked his head inside the car and crawled into the back seat. It wasn't empty. A little girl sat buckled into a booster chair. She blinked sleepy eyes at him.

Green eyes. Like his son's.

Would he see his son again?

Finn slid into the driver's seat while the woman went around the car to squeeze in on the other side of the booster chair.

Fenwick wanted to ask what was going on, what had happened. But all he could do was stare at the child. She smiled shyly at him, and a deep dimple creased her left cheek.

Blake was right.

There was no need for a paternity test. The child was clearly his. She was beautiful.

"Hi, sweetheart," he murmured. He was a grandfather. He had a granddaughter.

The thought humbled and terrified him at the same time. He'd failed miserably as a father. Could he do a better job now? As a grandparent?

Some of his friends claimed that their grandkids had given them a second chance to do it right now. Others just enjoyed spoiling them.

"Are you going to see my mommy and daddy too?" she asked him.

He glanced across her at the Gage woman. Was it safe for the girl to be out? Wasn't the child supposed to be in some kind of protective custody?

"Yes," he replied. "I am."

"My name is Pandora," she introduced herself.

She looked to be barely more than a toddler, but she acted so old for her age, so mature. Apparently her mother had done a respectable job as a single parent. Maybe he'd misjudged the young policewoman.

"What's your name?" she asked him.

His heart warmed his chest, chasing away some of the chill over worrying about Blake. "Grandfather," he replied, his voice gruff with emotion. The word was nearly too big for him, so it was certainly too big for her. He amended, "Grandpa. I'm your grandpa."

"Mommy said Grandpa died a long time ago," she replied, her green eyes narrowed with suspicion.

"She must have been talking about her daddy," he said. "I'm your daddy's daddy."

She nodded. "Daddy got hurt." She glanced at the woman next to her. "That's what Elle said."

He stared over her head at Officer Gage, wondering what the hell she'd been thinking to tell her that. Despite how mature she acted, the little girl was still just a child. A child who'd witnessed a murder already, though.

Maybe the policewoman had thought it better to prepare than to shield her.

"He got hurt saving Mommy."

"So Mommy's all right?" he asked. He couldn't imagine if the child were to lose both her parents. Would he be responsible for her then?

She nodded. "She caught the bad guy. He can't hurt nobody else no more."

But before Officer Walsh had caught him, he had hurt somebody. He'd hurt Blake.

How badly?

Finn kept the lights flashing and the sirens blaring the entire way to the hospital—as if he was worried that they might not get there in time.

How badly had Blake been hurt?

Fenwick couldn't ask. And not just because of the little girl being present. He couldn't ask because he wasn't sure he wanted to know yet.

But they arrived at the hospital within minutes of leaving his estate. Finn opened his door for him. When Fenwick stepped out, his legs shook beneath him, and the younger man had to grab his arm to steady him. Fenwick wasn't sure he would be able to handle it if Blake was gone—if he never had the chance to repair their relationship.

Elle Gage had taken the little girl from her booster chair and carried her. But Pandora wriggled free of the policewoman. Then she reached out and grasped Fenwick's hand with her small one. It was surprisingly strong, though. She held on to him tightly as they walked into the hospital.

For her sake and his, he hoped Blake was all right.

Chapter 25

Juliette heard the automatic doors swish open to the hospital lobby. It was a small hospital, but it still could have been anyone arriving. She was looking for Pandora, though. She'd asked Elle to bring her down because she hadn't wanted to spend another minute apart from her.

And it was safe now. The killer was in one of the operating rooms. Juliette had put another bullet in his shoulder while Sasha had put quite a gash in his arm. If her partner hadn't latched onto him, the guy might have shot Juliette like he had Blake.

Thanks to Sasha and Blake, she was uninjured, though, while Blake was having surgery in another one of the operating rooms. She'd had Elle warn Pandora that her daddy was hurt because she didn't want the little girl to be surprised when she saw him. And she had to see him...just like Juliette had to see him.

She had to tell him she loved him—that she would go with him anywhere if he really didn't think he could stay in Red Ridge. She had been crazy to turn down his offer. She knew now that she would take whatever he could give her—even if that wasn't his love.

When she'd returned to the train station and had found him lying on the floor in that pool of blood...

She shuddered at the memory. One of the bodyguards had been on the ground next to him, staunching the blood with a shirt pressed to the wound. Hopefully Blake hadn't lost too much blood. Hopefully he would be fine...

He had to be fine.

"Mommy!" a little voice called out.

She turned to see Pandora walking into the waiting room. But she was not alone. She held the hand of a familiar, older man. Blake's father.

"This is my grandpa," Pandora told her as if making introductions at one of her tea parties.

Juliette nodded. She had no idea what to say to the man. *Sorry I got your son shot* didn't seem appropriate—at least not in front of her daughter—even though it was an accurate account of what had happened.

Pandora saved her from having to say anything when she tugged on Fenwick Colton's hand until he looked down at her. "Mommy says Daddy is a prince," she told him. "So that makes you a king."

A chuckle slipped out of him. "I'm hardly a king, sweetheart."

Since he was the mayor, some people referred to him as the king of Red Ridge. But that was probably because he tried to rule it like a dictator.

He squeezed the little girl's hand and told her, "But yes, your daddy is a prince—a prince among men."

"A hero," Juliette told him. "He saved my life."

"How is he?" Fenwick asked her.

"The doctor should be out here soon," she said. "He'll tell you." He wouldn't talk to her. She wasn't next of kin. She was nothing to Blake but his baby mama.

The waiting room doors swished opened again, and four women rushed inside—Blake's sisters. They hurried over to their father but stopped short when they saw Pandora holding on to his hand. He picked up the child and told her, "These are your aunties."

"Auntie Layla." He pointed toward the blonde whose hair was cut in a face-framing bob.

"Auntie Bea." This blonde's hair was longer and wavy. She was clearly stunned at her new title, though, her mouth falling open in shock.

"Auntie Patience," Fenwick continued.

The dark-haired vet smiled at the little girl.

"And Auntie Gemma," he said.

The chestnut-haired woman stared at Pandora, her dark eyes wide and filled with horror. She was clearly not a fan of children.

But Pandora was a fan of beauty. She stared at the woman in awe and almost reverently whispered, "You are so pretty. You must be a princess."

Layla and Patience laughed. And Patience said, "She guessed that right."

Gemma smiled back at the little girl. "Well, aren't you a sweetie?"

Fenwick tightened his arm around the child. "Isn't she? She's amazing."

Patience walked over to Juliette and whispered, "Guess he doesn't need that paternity test after all."

So that really had been his father pushing for that, not Blake. Blake had never questioned Pandora's paternity—except the first moment he'd seen her.

He'd known before he'd ever asked, though. He'd known the minute he saw her.

"Mommy, we got a big family now for tea parties," Pandora said. "It's not just you and me anymore."

Her face flushed with embarrassment. While Fenwick Colton had accepted his granddaughter, she doubted he would accept Juliette—especially since it was her fault that his son had gotten shot.

Patience squeezed her arm. "She's right…"

But Juliette shook her head. "She's young." And too naive to understand how the real world worked. Cinderella never wound up with Prince Charming in Juliette's world—in Red Ridge.

The waiting room doors opened again, but these were the ones from the employee part of the hospital. A surgeon stepped through them. Was this Blake's doctor Or the killer's?

Juliette didn't care how the man she'd shot was doing. She cared only about Blake.

"Family of Blake Colton?" he called out.

Juliette gasped. And the color drained from the face of every one of Blake's family members—even his dad. It didn't sound good—not for the doctor to call out like that, like he was making a notification.

Juliette had had to do that a couple of times when she and Sasha had found some teenagers who died of a drug overdose. She'd felt so horribly for them. It had been the worst feeling of her life until her daughter had been threatened and then Blake had been shot.

His dad turned and handed Pandora to Juliette before heading toward the doctor. But Patience took the child from her arms and handed her to Elle. Then she grabbed Juliette's hand and tugged her along behind her father.

"You're family now," Patience said.

But she wasn't.

Fenwick's throat visibly moved as if he was choking down fear. "How—how is he, Doctor?" he asked.

"He lost quite a bit of blood from the wound, but all his organs were missed. Except for some tissue damage, which should heal quickly because he's young and healthy, he's going to be just fine."

There was a sudden expulsion of air, as if everyone had released the breath he or she had been holding.

Fenwick reached out a shaky hand and grabbed the doctor's. He pumped it in a hearty handshake. "Thank you. Thank you! When can I see him?"

"He's in recovery now. I can take you."

Fenwick started after the doctor, but Patience called him back. "Dad. You should let Juliette go."

She shook her head. "No. No. I wouldn't...his father should go."

Pandora must have wriggled down from Elle's arms because she was pulling on Juliette's hand. "Is Daddy okay? Is Daddy okay?"

Juliette nodded and smiled. "He's just fine."

And with the killer caught, he would stay that way. He wouldn't have to put himself in danger to protect her anymore. She watched Fenwick walk off with the doctor, and she longed to go with him.

While she believed the doctor that Blake would be

fine, she wanted to see for herself that he was. Hell, she just wanted to see him. That wasn't all she wanted to do, though. She wanted to touch him and hold him and kiss him and tell him that she loved him.

That she had always loved him.

And she didn't care if she made a fool of herself.

Finn had not gone inside the hospital with the others. He'd stopped to talk to the officers who'd arrived from the crime scene at the train station.

"Did you find out who he is?" he asked Carson Gage.

The detective shook his head. "Still haven't ID'd him. We took prints from the train car he was in when Walsh shot him, but Katie didn't get a hit yet."

Their tech was the best. If his prints were in the system, Katie would find them. But if he was as good as he seemed to be, maybe he'd never been caught before.

"I saw him," Dante Mancuso said as he joined them.

Finn had sent him in at the last moment—when he'd started thinking about how easily that kid had given up the information to Juliette. Too easily...

But by the time reinforcements had shown up, it would have been too late—had Blake not jumped in front of that bullet and taken it for Juliette.

"You saw him at the scene?" Finn asked, not understanding what Mancuso meant.

"I saw him before going in and out of the Larson twins' real estate office," Mancuso said.

"Really?" he asked, as excitement coursed through him. Maybe this was it—the break he needed to finally bring down the twins.

Dante nodded. "Sure of it."

Carson sighed and cautioned them, "That alone

doesn't prove a thing. He could have been buying or renting property through them."

Finn could guess what kind of property. He'd arrived at the hospital worried only about one man surviving his gunshot wound. Now he wanted the killer to survive, as well—so they could get him to talk. He was facing so many charges, including murder, that he might be convinced to turn over evidence against the Larsons in exchange for a deal.

Finn would call the district attorney—right after he'd checked on his cousin.

Blake must have still been unconscious. That was the only excuse for what he was seeing—his father weeping beside his bed. Tears streaked down the man's suddenly old-looking face while his shoulders shook with sobs.

He reached out and tried to pat his head. "It's okay..." he murmured weakly. "I'm alive..."

His father pressed a hand to his face, as if trying to hide his tears now. But it was too late. Blake had seen them. There was a time that he wouldn't have believed his father cared if he was alive or dead. Fenwick had certainly never called and checked on him after Blake had left Red Ridge.

His dad drew in a deep, shuddering breath and straightened his shoulders. "I—I know that..." His shoulders slumped again, and his voice cracked when he continued, "I just came so close to losing you forever."

"I'm fine," Blake assured him. At least, he hoped he was. He still felt so damn weak like he had when he hadn't been able to get up from the floor of the train station. But at least his side wasn't burning like it had been. It was mercifully numb now.

"That's what the doctor says," his father confirmed. "But I can't get over how close a call you had…"

Blake didn't care about himself right now, though. He remembered the gunshots he'd heard right before he'd lost consciousness. "Juliette," he said. "Is she okay?"

"Pandora's mother?" His father nodded. "Yes, she's fine. She and my granddaughter are in the waiting room."

"And Sasha?" he asked—knowing that like him, the beagle would probably have taken a bullet for Juliette gladly.

His father's brow furrowed. "Sasha? Who's that? Is Pandora a twin?"

Blake chuckled. "Sasha is Juliette's partner. She helped me warn her. She started growling and barking. She saw him before Juliette did."

"Sasha's a dog?"

Blake nodded. "She's very protective of Juliette."

"Patience didn't have to go in to work on her, so I assume she's fine."

If the dog had been hurt, Patience would have been taking care of her.

He sighed. "Good. That's good…" He focused on his dad again. "Pandora is here?"

"Yes." His father smiled. "She's yours."

Blake smiled with pride in his little girl. But he couldn't resist reminding his father, "I told you I didn't need a test to prove it."

"I didn't know if you could trust that woman," Fenwick said.

Blake hadn't known, either. But now he'd realized that he could. That night, nearly five years ago, he'd given her every reason to think he wouldn't want to know he had a child. He'd been so adamant about never being a father or a husband. Now he'd changed his mind about both.

"I can trust her," Blake said. "That's why I'm going to marry her."

Fenwick shook his head. "No way! No way in hell will you propose to her!"

"Damn it, Dad!" Blake yelled as his strength suddenly surged back with his fury. "Don't you dare say she's not good enough for a Colton. She's too good for a Colton. She's too good for me. After her dad died, she took care of her sick mother. When I met her, she was working two jobs to pay off the medical bills and put herself through school. She's proud and smart and brave..."

And incredibly independent. Would he ever convince her to marry him?

"You fool," his father said. "I'm not denying any of that. She must be pretty amazing to have raised that child alone like she has and done such a damn good job."

"Then what's the problem?" Blake asked. And his head began to pound with confusion. Maybe he'd lost too much blood. While there was an IV pumping something into his arm, he didn't feel like himself yet. That spate of anger had zapped what little strength he'd rallied.

"You can't propose because proposing gets a guy killed in this damn town!" his father exclaimed. "I've nearly lost you too many times to let you risk your life again."

"He's right," Juliette said as she stepped into the room with his father.

Fenwick smiled with approval at her.

"You can't propose to me," she said.

But was she saying that because of the Groom Killer or because she didn't love him?

Chapter 26

Fear coursed through Juliette when Blake slumped over and passed out cold. She rushed toward the bed and felt his neck for a pulse. It was there beneath her fingertips—weak but steady. None of the machines attached to him were going off, so his vitals must have been fine. She breathed a sigh of relief.

"Is he okay?" Fenwick asked, his voice cracking with his fear.

She nodded. "I think he just overdid it."

"*I* overdid it," Fenwick said. "I never know how to talk to him. We always wind up fighting instead."

Juliette had thought he was the last person for whom she would have ever felt sorry—until now. She could feel his pain and frustration. She squeezed his arm.

"You love him," she said. "That's all that matters to him."

Tears glistened in the older man's eyes. "I haven't always shown it, have I?"

She shook her head.

"To any of my kids," Fenwick continued with his self-recrimination.

"It's not too late," Juliette said.

He stared down at his son lying so still in the hospital bed. "It almost was."

"He's going to be fine," she assured him. But she was trying to convince herself of that, too. He was so pale.

"He won't be if he tries to marry you."

She nodded. "I know."

"That's the only reason I said what I did," he continued. "He's right. You're probably too good for a Colton."

She glanced down at Blake again. "Not this Colton…"

Blake was such a good man. A prince. A hero.

His lashes fluttered, and his lids began to flicker as if he was trying to open his eyes.

"I'm going to leave before he wakes up," Fenwick said. "I don't want to upset him again."

"I'll go, too," she said.

But Fenwick squeezed her shoulder. "Stay. He wants to see you."

He wanted to marry her. Had he really said that? Had he said all those wonderful things about her that she'd overheard? Or had her ears been playing tricks on her?

They were ringing a little yet from all the gunfire. It had echoed inside that empty train car where Sasha had tracked the killer.

"His sisters should come see him," Juliette said. When a nurse had told them that he could have two visitors, all of Fenwick's daughters had urged her to go back to join their father.

She wasn't certain if that was because they'd seen how upset she was or because they hadn't wanted to be in the same room with their father and Blake.

"His daughter should come visit him," Fenwick said. "I'll go get her." He rushed off as if eager to see the little girl again.

"He's going to spoil her," Blake murmured.

Juliette turned back to the bed to find that his eyes were open now, and he was staring at her.

"Are you okay?" she asked.

He sighed. "No…"

"I'll get a doctor," she said, but when she turned to leave, he grabbed her hand. His grasp was surprisingly strong. He was already getting better.

The tightness that had been in her chest since she'd realized he'd been shot eased somewhat. He was really going to be all right.

"The only reason I'm not fine is because you turned down my proposal," he said.

"I didn't turn it down," she said. "I just told you that you couldn't propose."

His green eyes narrowed with irritation. "Same thing…"

"No," she corrected him. "And I'm not saying no. I'm saying not yet. Not until the Groom Killer is caught."

His eyes brightened, and a smile curved his lips. "So you will marry me?"

"I love you," she replied. "I should have told you sooner, but I was trying to protect you."

"You got mad at me for trying to protect you," he reminded her.

"Are you mad at me?" she asked.

He shook his head. "I was at first—for keeping Pandora a secret. But I couldn't stay mad."

"You should have," she said. "You should be furious with me over that. I don't know how you will ever forgive me." She wasn't sure that she could ever forgive herself for the years together that she'd stolen from the people she loved the most in the world.

He reached out with his other hand and slid his fingertips along her jaw. "I gave you every reason to think that I wouldn't ever want to be a father. So I understand."

She released a deep and ragged sigh. She'd worried for so long that he would never forgive her. But he already had.

"You are amazing," she murmured. "Thank you for saving my life."

"Told you that you needed me," he said. But he chuckled self-deprecatingly. "Did you get him?"

She nodded.

And his breath shuddered out in a ragged sigh of relief. "Thank God. Thank you. You really are a wonderful officer. I won't ever suggest you leave your job again."

She smiled teasingly and asked, "Until I'm in a danger again?"

His skin paled again as if that thought hadn't occurred to him. But then he drew in a deep breath and shook his head. "Not even then. I understand how much it means to you."

"You mean more," she told him. "You and Pandora. Now that she's safe, I could leave Red Ridge…" She would feel bad leaving before the Groom Killer was caught. But Blake was more important than anything but their daughter.

He shook his head again. "No. Neither of us is leaving. I'm going to move my headquarters to Red Ridge. I'm staying here. I'm staying—" he swallowed as if choking on emotion before continuing "—home."

"You didn't consider it that five years ago," she reminded him. As well as making love that whole night, they'd talked, too; he'd shared so much of himself with her.

"It wasn't then. But when I came back and found you and Pandora…" He swallowed hard again.

She reached for the cup of ice chips a nurse must have left next to his bed. But when she held out the spoon, he waved it off.

"You and Pandora made Red Ridge home for me," he said. "And I do want you to marry me."

"Why?" she asked. While she'd professed her love, he'd made no declarations of his own.

"Because I love you," he said. "I think I've loved you since that night when we conceived Pandora."

"That was a magical night," she agreed. "I felt like Cinderella. And you were my Prince Charming."

"Prince Charming gets Cinderella in the end," he reminded her.

"This is no fairy tale," she said. She'd stopped believing in happily-ever-afters long ago—when she'd lost her mom. But then she remembered her saying that everything had happened for a reason.

That reason wasn't just Pandora now. Blake was that reason, too.

"We don't have to make it official," he said. "I just need to know that you will marry me. I love you so much…"

She loved him too much to tell him yes. She loved him too much to risk losing him again.

* * *

Blake held his breath, waiting for her answer. She just shook her head. And his heart broke.

But she looked like hers was breaking, too, as tears filled her eyes. "I can't," she said. "I can't put you in danger ever again."

"You can protect me," he said. "It's your turn, after all."

Her lips curved into a smile. "Really?"

"I've spent the past few weeks protecting you from this park killer guy..." He sighed wearily. "So it's your turn. You can protect me from this Groom Killer. You're a damn good cop, Juliette. I trust you to keep me safe."

"Yes," she said.

"Yes, you'll protect me? Or yes, you'll marry me?" he eagerly asked.

"Daddy's gonna marry Mommy!" a high voice exclaimed.

"Shh..." Grandpa cautioned his granddaughter as he carried the little girl into the room. "We're going to keep that a secret for a while—just between all of us."

Juliette nodded in agreement. "That's the only way I will say yes, if we keep it a secret."

Blake really didn't want any more secrets between them. But since this was one they were agreeing to keep together, he was fine with it. Hell, he was fine with anything as long as Juliette would agree to marry him.

"I would get down on one knee," he said. "But I wouldn't be sure I could get back up again. So I'm just going to ask you..." He trailed off, waiting for someone to interrupt him.

But she didn't stop him this time, and surprisingly enough, neither did his father.

So he continued, "Juliette Walsh, will you be my Cinderella bride? My wife? My partner? My soul mate?"

She nodded and nodded and nodded. "Yes, yes, I will."

Pandora clapped her hands together in glee. "Yay. Now Daddy needs to give Mommy a ring." And she jerked the candy ring pop from her finger and held it out to him.

Blake exchanged a glance with Juliette. "I told you he was going to spoil her." His father must have been the one who'd bought her the candy. And she must have been the reason that his father had not tried to stop him from proposing—because he didn't want to disappoint her.

And if his father could change that much just since meeting his granddaughter, Blake had no concerns about the kind of father he would be. He would do everything within his power to never disappoint her, either.

He took the ring pop from his daughter's sticky fingers and held out his other hand for Juliette's. She placed it in his palm and he slid the plastic ring over her knuckle. The *diamond* was a half-licked glob of blue candy. But she stared down at it like it was real, her blue eyes welling with tears.

"Isn't it pretty, Mommy?" the little girl mused. "It matches your eyes."

Blake grinned. That it did...

As soon as he was out of the hospital, he would get her something better—something that would last forever—just like their love.

Fenwick Colton had never been as determined as he was now to make sure a wedding took place as soon as possible in Red Ridge. And it wasn't Layla's wedding that he was anxious to have happen.

He wanted his son to marry the woman he loved; he wanted to watch that adorable little girl of Blake's walk down the aisle swinging a basket of flowers. Just the thought of it—of how pretty she would be as flower girl in one of the pretty dresses from Bea's bridal shop— had him blinking back the tears stinging his eyes and burning in his nose.

He had never been as damn emotional as he was now—except maybe when he'd lost his first wife. But he'd nearly lost his son. Again. He'd lost him five years ago when Blake had left the country.

But tonight he'd nearly lost him for good—for dead. And if word got out of Blake's recent engagement, Fenwick could still lose his son—to that psychotic Groom Killer.

Police chief Finn Colton couldn't let that happen.

"What the hell are you doing to find Demi Colton?" he demanded when he cornered the chief in the waiting room. He wanted that crazy daughter of his trashy cousin's behind bars with the killer who'd tried to hurt his granddaughter and her mother.

"Like I told you before, I'm not sure that Demi is actually the killer," Finn said, and he sounded tired. With the dark circles around his eyes, he looked tired, too.

The guy needed to get more sleep.

But Fenwick hadn't been sleeping himself—not since these killings started and Hamlin Harrington ended his engagement to Layla. Fenwick had been worried about losing his business. But now he knew that was the least of his concerns.

He was worried about his family, and with Pandora

and Juliette, that family had just gotten bigger. So he had more to worry about.

"You don't know where she is, so you can't know that she's not in Red Ridge. You need to assign some officers the sole responsibility of finding her."

Finn grimaced.

Fenwick knew that he was telling the man how to do his job. But apparently someone had to, or this damn Groom Killer would never get caught. And since he was mayor, Finn pretty much worked for him, anyway.

"I already assigned two officers to find her," Finn said begrudgingly.

"What? Coltons or Gages?" he asked with a derisive snort. He wouldn't trust either of them to bring her back. The Coltons might let her go and the Gages might make sure she was never found.

"Michaela Clarke and Liam McTiernan," Finn replied. "They're checking all the motels and short-term leasing places across Black Hills County."

Fenwick nodded. "Good. That's good."

They would find her. They had to. Fenwick was pretty sure his son's wasn't the only secret engagement in Red Ridge. There were a lot of other couples who wanted to get married.

After seeing the love between Blake and Juliette, he felt a little uneasy about Layla marrying Hamlin. She obviously didn't feel about him the way that Blake felt about Juliette. But that was just because she was even more like Fenwick than Blake was. She was all business.

Blake was a family man now.

And Fenwick couldn't be happier or prouder of his son. He just wanted to make sure he stayed alive to marry the woman he loved. But he and Juliette had kept each other alive while one killer was after them and their daughter. He believed they would do it now, as well, because they had too much to live for—they had their family.

* * * * *

SPECIAL EXCERPT FROM

LOVE INSPIRED SUSPENSE
INSPIRATIONAL ROMANCE

A K-9 officer and a forensics specialist must work together to solve a murder and stay alive.

Read on for a sneak preview of
Scene of the Crime *by Sharon Dunn,*
the next book in the True Blue K-9 Unit: Brooklyn *series*
available September 2020 from Love Inspired Suspense.

Brooklyn K-9 Unit Officer Jackson Davison caught movement out of the corner of his eye: a face in the trees fading out of view. His heart beat a little faster. Was someone watching him? The hairs on the back of Jackson's neck stood at attention as a light breeze brushed his face. Even as he studied the foliage, he felt the weight of a gaze on him. The sound of Smokey's barking brought his mission back into focus.

When he caught up with his partner, the dog was sitting. The signal that he'd found something. "Good boy." Jackson tossed out the toy he carried on his belt for Smokey to play with, his reward for doing his job. The dog whipped the toy back and forth in his mouth.

"Drop," Jackson said. He picked up the toy and patted Smokey on the head. "Sit. Stay."

The body, partially covered by branches, was clothed in neutral colors and would not be easy to spot unless you were looking for it.

He keyed his radio. "Officer Davison here. I've got a body in Prospect Park. Male Caucasian under the age of forty, about two hundred yards in, just southwest of the Brooklyn Botanic Garden."

Dispatch responded, "Ten-four. Help is on the way."

He studied the trees just in time to catch the face again, barely visible, like a fading mist. He was being watched. "Did you see something?" Jackson shouted. "Did you call this in?"

The person turned and ran, disappearing into the thick brush.

Jackson took off in the direction the runner had gone. As his feet pounded the hard earth, another thought occurred to him. Was this the person who had shot the man in the chest? Sometimes criminals hung around to witness the police response to their handiwork.

His attention was drawn to a garbage can just as an object hit the back of his head with intense force. Pain radiated from the base of his skull. He crumpled to the ground and his world went black.

Don't miss
Scene of the Crime *by Sharon Dunn,*
available wherever Love Inspired Suspense books
and ebooks are sold.

LoveInspired.com

LISEXP0820

HARLEQUIN

*Heartfelt or suspenseful,
inspiring or passionate, Harlequin
has your happily-ever-after.*

With new books published
every month, you are sure to find the
satisfying escape you know you deserve.

SIGN UP FOR THE
HARLEQUIN NEWSLETTER

Be the first to hear about great new
reads and exciting offers!

Harlequin.com/newsletters

HNEWS2020